Lady's Pursuit

Lady's Pursuit

A **Knight** AND **Rogue** NOVEL

HILARI BELL

HilariBell.com

Wild Writers Books
thewildwriters.com

DEDICATION

To Ginger—who convinced me that Fisk needed his own dog.

Lady's Pursuit

Chapter 1

Michael

A damsel in distress—
or at least, a damsel mysteriously vanished and quite
possibly in distress—is a most fitting task for a knight
errant. But this damsel had gone missing from the High
Liege's court, and peril lurked there. Not for me, which
I would have shrugged off, but for those I held most
dear. Which is probably why I made the mistake of saying, "She's only been gone for about twelve hours—that
could be accounted for by a lame horse or a broken
wheel. Surely she's returned by now. I say we send this
fellow back, and wait for word that all's well."

The messenger, who'd ridden all night to deliver the
letter my sister held, looked indignantly at me, but he
spoke to my sister. "The Heir's fair worried, Mistress.
He bid me get this letter to you as fast as I could ride."

Fisk, Kathy and I stood on the landing of my brother's lodging, which he'd begun to hint he'd like us to
vacate eventually—a request that seemed reasonable,

given that the knocking of the messenger had roused us shortly after dawn. Kathy was clad in a well-worn dressing gown, her mouse-brown hair in a tousled braid down her back, and the rosy light reflected in her spectacles as she read. There was no reason for Fisk to look at her as if she was the source of the sunrise...which increased my apprehension about going to court.

"Meg didn't take a coach," Kathy told me, still reading. "'Tis a bit incoherent—he must be really worried—but Rupert says she left on foot. She might have rented... Why does he think she'd rent a carriage to come to me? Or come to me at all, for that matter."

This was addressed to the messenger, who shrugged. "I'm to bring back your reply, if you don't return yourself, Mistress Katherine. And escort you if you need it."

"She doesn't need an escort," said Fisk. "We'll take her."

"I don't think..." I didn't think that was a good idea, but I couldn't reveal my reasons in front of the messenger.

"I do think," said Fisk. "And so does Kathy. You're out-voted. Partner."

They held to that, despite all the sensible arguments I raised after the messenger had departed—I even went so far as to remind Fisk what had happened the first time we rescued a damsel in distress. This memory made him pale, and I might have won the day. But Katherine was set on learning what had happened to her friend, and Fisk couldn't bear to appear cowardly before her, so right or wrong, I lost. We departed from the university town where my brother lived before breakfast.

I may have sulked a bit over my failure to dissuade them, for when he was my squire, Fisk never overruled me. That was why he had ceased to be my squire, and if this was what he'd felt like in the past, when I over-ruled him, I could hardly blame him.

I still thought we would arrive at Crown City and find the lady safe returned, with a tale of some minor mishap to entertain us. But there is little I like more than riding my good horse on a fair day, with a fine hound frisking at our heels, and the two people who—despite their stubbornness—I loved best in all the world riding beside me. They loved each other too, and watching them together yet another problem came to my attention.

We had stopped to water the horses and they sucked greedily from the stream, with our hound True lapping at their side. 'Twas the hottest part of the long summer day and we were all coated with road dust, but instead of taking this brief respite to wash, stretch their legs, snatch a bite to eat, or even help me with the horses, Fisk and my sister sat on the bridge's low railing hold-ing hands.

'Twas charming, and I was tempted to annoy Fisk by saying so. But a more important matter was at stake.

"You two agreed to conceal your arrangement from the court, but if you go on acting like this..."

"He's right." We were still several hours ride from Crown City, but Kathy let go of Fisk's hand as if it had grown thorns. "Everyone at court knows Father. And the people who hate him will be even quicker to rat us out than his friends would."

The phrase "rat us out" sounded odd coming from my sister—Fisk's influence, no doubt. But it seemed this kind of transmutation traveled in both directions.

"We agreed because Michael refused to come if we didn't," Fisk pointed out. "We'll have to tell your father anyway, sooner or later. It's going to take a while for me to put together enough money to ask for your hand."

"Or," said Kathy, "we could get married, let him disown me, and then work out the rest of it."

Fisk, the cynical, practical ex-con man, who claimed to think all laws and most principles nonsense, simply shook his head.

I found it nothing short of miraculous that love had made my erstwhile squire determined to court my sister properly and honestly...but in truth, this reformation couldn't have overtaken Fisk at a worse time.

"You'd better keep lying," I advised him. "If Father hears about this he'll do everything in his power to separate you."

And when my father did everything in his power, he succeeded.

Fisk, who all but lived by lies, grimaced in distaste. "Then you're right—we'll have to put up an act. Can you pretend to dislike me, love?"

"With ease," said Kathy dryly.

But her eyes softened and her hand crept toward his. Fisk's hand was already opening to receive it.

I tried to think of some way to prevent my father from clapping his underage daughter up in a tower, and having Fisk cudgel-crewed off to the northern timber camps. Or somewhere even worse.

Nothing came to me.

We reached Crown City in the late afternoon. Here in the Realm's capital the street hawkers were selling everything from sausages to news-sheets to an offer to carve your face onto a cameo brooch. I kept True close to the horse's heels as we rode through the bustling streets.

Most dwellings in the central plains are made of plastered mud brick, strengthened with great beams. The farther into the city we went, the larger the buildings became, and the more stone appeared in their construction. I saw gray granite, creamy marble, and a lovely rose-colored stone that judging by its rarity had been shipped from some distant quarry at considerable expense.

The palace rested at the top of a low hill, loosely cupped in a bend in the Erran River, which ran through the city, crossed by a score of bridges. In these peaceful times, 'twas unusual to see patrolling guards on top of the high wall that had once been part of the old fortifications—though their braid and button encrusted tunics were more designed to impress than to defend anything. And those guards may have been more functional than they looked, for as we soon learned, someone had informed the Heir of our approach.

After we passed through the gate, Kathy, who had lived in this palace for some time, guided us off the carriage drive and across a well-cut lawn toward stables that she claimed lurked behind one of the sprawling wings. The palace had clearly begun as an old-fashioned keep, surrounded by numerous outbuildings and enough room for a good-sized village to take shelter behind its wall. But when the need for such defenses vanished with the ascension of the first High Liege, the outbuilding had given way to graveled paths, flower-beds and fountains, and the keep had sprouted additions in a number of architectural styles, like branches of peach, pear and cherry grafted onto a gnarled old apple tree.

'Twas from a wing that sparkled with white marble and diamond-paned windows that a young man emerged, vaulting over the terrace railing in his hurry to reach us. Lace frothed at his throat and wrists, and his collar and cuffs were crusted with gold embroidery...but once you got past his clothing, his rather ordinary face was tight with concern.

"She's not with you?" he demanded, as soon as Kathy was within earshot. "She didn't go to you?"

I had genuinely believed the lady would have returned by now, and my concern deepened—this task might require a knight errant after all.

"She's not back yet?" Kathy had shared my hopes. "That means she's been gone a night and two days. Rupert, something's wrong."

"You think I don't know that?" The young man's mouth twisted with worry. "I'd be frantic by now, except that if anyone kidnapped her it was probably Father. And he wouldn't hurt her, no matter how crazy this is."

At twenty-four, Rupert Roger Yvain Justin Ware was only a few years older than Fisk and me. But I knew his age, and all those names, because he was the oldest son of the High Liege, declared heir to the throne of the United Realm, and upon his father's death he would become Liege and Ruler to us all.

"Why would your father do that?" My sister dismounted, and tossed her hired horse's reins to the Liege Heir as if he were an under-groom. "I know he's a bit miffed about Meg, but he has no reason to kidnap her. I mean, it's not like you're going to fall out of love if she's gone for a while."

Rupert Roger Yvain etc. led her horse toward the stables, and Fisk and I dismounted to tag along.

"And why do you think that anyone kidnapped her?" Kathy added. "At this point, I have to admit she might have met with an accident, but it might not be too bad."

"Then why hasn't she sent a message, to me or her family?" Rupert asked. "It must be that she can't, either because someone's stopping her, or because...because she can't. And besides, there's the note. Someone sent that and she went to meet them. If whoever it was didn't kidnap her then why haven't they come for—"

"You do realize," I said gently, "that none of us knows what you're talking about. Slow down, Your Highness, and tell us about this note."

It checked him, as I'd hoped it might, and he drew a deep breath.

"She got a note. Delivered by a paid messenger, shortly after breakfast yesterday. According to her maid, she took it into her room to read and then came out wearing a light cape—it's still cool in the morning sometimes. Then she rushed off in a great hurry. I was hoping she'd gone to you, since you're the closest friend she has. But she didn't, and she hasn't been seen since. So either the person she met took her, or something worse has happened. If I wasn't so furious, I'd be *relieved* to think that Father has her."

"But that's crazy," said Kathy. "There's no reason for anyone to kidnap Meg."

Rupert's mouth tightened mulishly. "Someone sent that note, and then she vanished. And there's something you don't know, Kathy. Meg recently found out... I mean, she realized..."

"She got pregnant," said Fisk. "That's...unfortunate."

"You say that like she was the only one involved," Kathy said critically. "You could just as well say that *he* got her pregnant. Rupert, this is my brother Michael and his rude friend Fisk."

Despite their repeated failures to pretend indifference while we traveled, Kathy sounded convincingly annoyed and Fisk looked nettled.

"I'm sure they participated equally," I said soothingly. "And I see that having a child would bind them even more tightly, which might distress the Liege. But at this point there's no purpose to be served by separating you from your mistress. The damage is done."

"You're forgetting," said Fisk, "about the project."

"What proj— Oh. How...unfortunate."

We'd first learned of the Heir's desire to wed his mistress in the course of what I claim as our last adventure, and Fisk refers to as "our most recent fiasco." And one part of that adventure, which had entailed bribery, blackmail, scholarly sabotage and attempted murder, centered around an alchemical study designed to create Gifts in the Heir's Giftless mistress—or at least, to make her bear Gifted children.

There are a host of lesser talents that seem to accompany the Gift for sensing magic, but the magic sensing Gift is the one that matters. Danger and disaster haunt those who harvest or destroy magica plants and animals, so 'tis easy to see why the people who could use that Gift to protect their fellows became barons and lords in the first place. 'Tis less necessary for human survival now...but had he not disowned me, my father would have been displeased to see even his fourth son marry a Giftless woman. If my oldest brother had wanted to do so, the unlucky girl would have found herself shipped off to those far north timber camps before you could blink.

I was impressed that the Liege Heir's Giftless lover had managed to remain by his side long enough to become pregnant, and that might speak well of the High Liege's common sense. As Kathy had pointed out, kidnapping someone's lover didn't make them fall out of love. But if this Meg was pregnant...

"'Tis too late," I pointed out. "When 'tis born, your first child will be Giftless. And unless you marry your lady before the birth, it won't inherit, anyway."

Which might actually give the High Liege a motive.

We rounded the end of the wing as I spoke, and the long low buildings of the stable came in view. The grooms saw Rupert as well, and a small swarm started toward us.

"Then why hasn't she sent a message?" Rupert asked once more. "Or a note, or a..."

The grooms reached us, taking not only Kathy's horse, but also Chant and Tipple. However my attention was distracted by the shouts of several gardeners, who had failed to keep True from chasing a rabbit into a flowerbed.

"...so I think whoever sent that note must have taken her," the Heir concluded.

In truth, 'twas more likely she had met with an accident so severe that she couldn't reveal her identity or send for help—which made it painfully clear why he clung to the theory that his father had his lover safely tucked away.

Not wanting to convey this depressing fact I called my dog, who came loping up with his tongue hanging out in a big, canine grin. Hounds are bred for tracking instead of speed, but he likes chasing rabbits even though he never catches them. I ordered True to go to the stable with the grooms and he obeyed me as well as he usually does, frisking around them and emitting his rasping non-bark. True is mute, but that doesn't stop him from trying.

Rupert watched this show in some bemusement. "I wasn't worried at first. Meg's free to come and go as she pleases."

One of the grooms produced a rope and captured True, and the others were leading the horses away—though they weren't moving briskly. If Rupert didn't mind them overhearing I saw no reason I should care.

"I started to wonder when she didn't show up by afternoon. When she wasn't back by dinnertime I sent to her family, to see if she was there. Her brother came back with my messenger, and he said they hadn't seen her for several days."

He'd turned toward the palace, seemingly without thinking about it. Neither Fisk nor I was dressed for court—indeed, neither of us owned clothes fit for court—but we weren't there to attend upon the Liege.

"That's when I checked with her maid, and then I went to Father and asked for a troop to search for her in town, see if she'd met with some accident..." The distress in Rupert's face melted into anger. "He said she probably got the vapors, as pregnant women do, and ran off to a friend somewhere. That she'd come back when her nerves settled. Meg isn't some flighty ninny, but... Once her pregnancy became known, all the people we had working on ways to make her children Gifted... Did Kathy tell you about that?"

"We came across one of those projects," Fisk said. "And from what I saw, if your father kidnapped her to keep her out of the scholar's hands, he did her a favor."

"Their solutions aren't safe to try yet," Rupert agreed. "They acknowledge that themselves. But some of them are getting close, and all their solutions work while the child is forming in the womb. The moment Meg said she was pregnant they practically swarmed out of the woodwork. And some of their 'promising results' were pretty horrible. I'd never put Meg or our child at risk, and she knows that. But she was upset, and I thought she might have gone to you, Kathy."

'Twas now nearly evening. A night and the better part of two days was a long time for someone in Mistress Margaret's state to go missing. It seemed that something must have happened to the poor woman, and 'twas clearly our duty to discover what it was. And yet...

"Pregnant women can be taken by odd fancies," I said. "We've an aunt who refused to leave the ground floor of any building the last few months before her child was born."

"That's right," Kathy said. "And it wasn't that she couldn't climb the stairs. She said the child didn't like being surrounded by air. By the time she was ten, Lucinda had climbed every tall tree on the estate. But even if some odd fancy took her, why wouldn't Meg have sent a message?"

"You're forgetting the note," said Fisk. "It does sound like someone sent for her. Of course, she might be staying with the person who summoned her, and it's her message that she was going to be gone for a few days that went missing."

That was more likely than kidnapping and more hopeful than some horrible accident. Both Rupert and Kathy's faces brightened.

"'Twould be nice to know what this note said," Kathy added. "Did Meg take it with her?"

"From what her maid told us, I assume she did," Rupert said. "If she left it behind, Griswold would have given it to us."

"Not necessarily." Kathy abruptly changed course, away from the palace and stables, toward a small grove in a far corner of the palace grounds. "Griswold's in the pay of half the court. Meg never lets her see anything if she can help it. She might have burned the letter, or taken it, but if it's not completely ordinary she wouldn't leave it out for Gris to find."

Rupert's expression proclaimed that his lover had confided none of this to him. We all followed my sister like a string of ducklings, down a neat, graveled path through the trees to a cottage so quaint, so ornately carved, that it looked like something out of a child's fable.

'Twas clearly built to allow the liege to house some unwanted guest out of sight of the palace. Despite cheerful red shutters and artfully sculpted statues, 'twas too near the outer wall and too surrounded by trees for flowers to grow. Luxury, yes, but I started to wonder if the woman who lived here might not have chosen to flee after all.

Kathy didn't bother to knock, but flung open the door calling, "Griswold? Where are you?"

There was a lengthy pause before a woman's voice replied, "Here, Mistress Katherine."

The sound came from a room to one side of the entry, and Kathy opened that door too, in time for us to see the maid folding a half-written sheet of paper that she then tucked into the bosom of her gown. 'Twas clearly not the note that had summoned Mistress Merkle out of the palace yesterday, for the ink was so wet it left a smudge on her skin as she slipped it out of sight. And there was a lot of skin to smudge.

The sound of Mistress Griswold's name had conjured up visions of an elderly hag, or at least a middle-aged matron, but Mistress Griswold was a well-formed woman in her twenties. The face under her starched cap would have been attractive if her expression hadn't been so sly. She rose from the desk politely, and there was no reason a lady's maid should not use the desk in a deserted study to write her own missives...but there was a subtle insolence in her stance that set my nerves aprickle.

"We're going to search Meg's room for clues to where she might have gone." The Heir had noted her attitude as well, and there was a steely note in his voice I hadn't heard before. "You may go back to the palace and take the rest of the day off, unless your mistress returns."

Griswold could see something was afoot, and she didn't want to miss it.

"I'd best stay, Highness. In case you need tea, or a message carried or summat."

"That wasn't a suggestion." Rupert's voice was quiet, but I wasn't at all surprised when Mistress Griswold dropped a curtsy and scurried from the room.

"I had no idea." The Heir's voice was still soft, but the sternness had vanished. "Why didn't Meg tell me her maid was spying on her?"

Kathy cast him an enigmatic look. "Ask her that, when you see her. The bedroom's upstairs."

The study and front room had been furnished with subdued good taste, lots of polished wood and brocaded cushions, which had probably been there when Mistress Meg took up residence. I expected to see some feminine frippery in the bedroom, but if anything the décor there was more spare—the only feminine touch was a bowl of violets on the dressing table, now half-wilted. Shelves that had been designed for china figurines were crammed with books. Fisk was already drifting toward them. I wondered if this was Mistress Meg's own taste, or if she'd created a room where her lover would be comfortable, but my impression of this house had changed from the first time I saw it—this was a home, not a cage for a pretty bird.

Rupert's eyes, as he looked around this room, which his lover had made her own, were filled with such terror that I looked away.

"Where do we start?" he asked.

With a sigh, Fisk turned away from the bookshelves. "Anywhere she might have hidden a letter—more likely letters, because if someone's going to hide one they don't stop there. At least it's probably in this room, because the maid said Margaret read it and rushed straight out."

"Unless she took it with her," I said. "She didn't burn it. The hearth is clean." And in high summer, the servants wouldn't have come to clear it.

"Unless Griswold's lying." Rupert's voice was tight with angry chagrin. He had hired this spying maid, probably without giving her a second thought. Most nobles think little about the people who serve them. I hadn't myself, when I was young.

Kathy started opening drawers in the large bureau, and went to the bookshelves, opening books and riffling through the pages. 'Twould be a good place to hide papers from most servants. Fisk went to the hearth and began twisting and tapping things in search of a secret compartment—though if such a thing existed, surely Rupert would know of it.

'Twas I who found the note. And 'twas not in any obvious place, nor some secret vault, but in a travel bag tucked into the cupboard beneath the window bench. My respect for Mistress Meg rose another notch, for 'twas a hiding place that worked simply by being an expected object in an expected place. She'd even left the flap unbuckled, a subtle signal that there was nothing within, but there were a number of papers in the satchel with the note we sought on top of the stack.

"I think I've figured out how to get Papa to accept your situation," Kathy read aloud. *"Meet me at the Pig at ten and we'll have tea and talk. Agnes"*

"Who's—"

"Agnes is her older, married sister," Kathy told Fisk.

"And the Pig is the Pig in a Basket Inn," Rupert added. "Meg's brothers and sisters meet people there when they don't want to bring them home."

Did he know that because Mistress Meg had met him there? But... "Why not meet at Mistress Agnes' home?" I asked. "If they didn't want Griswold eavesdropping."

"Good question," Fisk said. "And unless it was nearly ten when this note was delivered, why fling on a cloak and rush out?"

"It wasn't long after breakfast when she went through the gates," Rupert put in. "Around nine, as nearly as the guards could remember."

"Griswold's been known to exaggerate," Kathy said. "She gets paid more for dramatic mysteries than for ordinary meetings with a sister. Meg might just have gone to meet Agnes."

"Then why hasn't she come back?" Rupert repeated for mayhap the dozenth time.

Fisk was sifting through the papers. He found another letter and compared the two.

"Is it forged?" Kathy asked.

"How should I know? It looks like the same hand, but that's not that hard to do."

Mayhap 'twas not hard for Fisk, who numbers forgery among his many unfortunate yet useful skills. But I had another idea, and I took the mysterious missive from him.

Alone in the world, as far as I know, I can see magic as a soft glow around things that possess it. Ironically, this ability of mine might also be said to be the result of a scholarly project, much like the ones they planned for Mistress Merkle and her child. Remembering the agony and nausea as those potions had burned through my body, I didn't envy her if she chose to attempt them. Lady Ceciel's experiments had been perpetrated upon me without my consent, but now, years after the fact, I was finding the results...well, interesting, at least.

First I simply looked at the note with my magic sensing Gift open. In truth, this Gift is always open, and I had already noted a soft glow coming from the magica phosphor lamp at the head of the bed. Phosphor moss is the easiest magica plant to harvest and care for safely, but few can afford it for reading in bed.

The note had no magic, but once my Gift was centered on it I reached within and found the heavy lid that was how I envisioned the thing that kept my magic from welling forth. I could all but see it in my mind, a great stone slab covering a well of roiling light. I imagined my hands closing on the stone and shoved...and nothing whatsoever happened. I then imagined myself trying to tip the stone up, or even swinging my clenched fist down to break it.

However, the thing that blocked my magic was not a stone slab, but a rational thinking mind, and it seemed that Fisk's latest notion, that visualization and imaginary symbols might allow me to sneak around that block, had worked as well as his last few ideas—which was to say, they'd all failed.

I opened my eyes to scowl at him, but he was speaking to Rupert and Kathy.

"If you really think this might be forged, there's an easy way to find out. Just ask Mistress Agnes if she wrote it."

"Her husband's an apothecary," Kathy said. "But I don't know where his shop is."

"I do." Rupert cast another glance around the room and sighed. "'Tis near enough it would take more time to saddle horses than to walk."

He seemed reluctant despite his concern, and for the first time I wondered what Mistress Margaret's family thought of her becoming mistress to the Heir.

Had she been my sister, Father would be threatening the Liege and his son with everything from lawsuits to armed rebellion if he didn't marry her. But my sister was Gifted, so such a marriage was possible, and my father was a baron who wielded more wealth and power than many lords.

It seemed we were about to learn how an ordinary merchant would feel about such a thing, for Rupert turned and led us out. I followed, and Fisk started after us, but Kathy seized his arm, dragged him back into the room and shut the door.

So much for pretending indifference. Living with the two them over these last weeks I'd become accustomed to these little interludes, so I distracted Rupert with a question about Mistress Meg's usual routine. In a few moments the door would open again—and if the light in Kathy's eyes and the deep contentment in Fisk's expression gave away their secret, I found I couldn't regret it too much.

CHAPTER 2

Fisk

When Kathy pulled me back into the room and closed the door, my first thought was that she planned to steal a few kisses. I wasn't at all unhappy about that, though it seemed an odd time for it. But one look at her expression told me romance was the last thing on her mind.

"What if Meg ran off?" She spoke in the low voice that's actually less audible than a hissing whisper. "What if pregnancy, the thought of what might happen to her child, just made her decide to cut and run."

"Rupert doesn't seem like someone who'd force her into risky treatments," I said. "If she simply refuses, her child's in no danger."

"I'm not talking about treatments," said Kathy. "At least, not entirely."

"But...oh." I knew almost nothing about this court, but I'd read enough history to know that even an illegitimate child's life could get dicey if a handful of powerful nobles decided he'd make a better liege than the one they had. Or if the Liege thought someone might think that.

"But wouldn't the child being Giftless put a damper on that kind of thing? It could even be a girl."

"It could be a girl," said Kathy. "And being Giftless might keep people from thinking of it as a potential heir. But it also might not, and Meg may have decided not to take that risk. She was willing to put up with a lot to stay with Rupert, but a child could change that calculation."

"That's why you asked if the note was forged. You think she might have written it herself, as an excuse to leave the palace."

"And to keep the search focused on the city, while she runs into hiding," Kathy said. "If that's what happened—and it makes more sense than thinking she met with an accident, and no one found her or reported it. But if that's true, *should* we be trying to find her?"

Why had I thought I wanted a woman with a quick mind, who could pose hard questions?

"I don't know," I admitted. "But the best way to find out is to track her down and ask her. Is Rupert the sort who'd keep her against her will? Or take the child from her?"

"No," said Kathy. "Even if he didn't love her, he's not an idiot."

"Then find her and ask her," I said.

"But Fisk, Meg *knows* Rupert's not that kind of idiot."

Which made the worse alternative more likely. I hated seeing fear in those clear gray eyes, but I couldn't deny it.

"Then it's even more important to find her. And if we keep this door shut much longer, Rupert's going to guess about our...arrangement."

I had wanted to call it an engagement, but it seemed that in noble families you need your parents' consent to be engaged. Kathy had already agreed to marry me without her family's consent, and I was the one who said we ought to try to get it, so maybe it was unreasonable to feel—

My not-quite-fiancée broke though my spinning thoughts with a kiss that, after a moment, made me stop thinking about anything but how soft her skin was and the warm body in my arms.

I was quite sorry when her quick, logical mind took over, and she pulled away and opened the door to go out and join the others, but you can't have everything. At least, not all at once.

Mistress Agnes wasn't at her husband's shop. The apothecary, with a cold glance at Rupert, said she'd gone to her parents' house to wait for news of her sister.

Rupert and Katherine both knew the way to the wool merchant's manor—they no longer lived in rooms above their warehouse, though the family had started there, and they were still near the warehouse district.

This was sufficiently far away that it would have been quicker to ride, but we were now so far from the palace and our horses that it would take even more time to return for them. Neither Kathy or Rupert were thinking about food, but Michael has been involved in—or created—enough calamities to know you need to eat. We stopped at a cart with a smoking brazier, and purchased paper cones filled with charred meat and roasted vegetables, well-seasoned with salt and fresh herbs. The meat might have been beef, as the seller claimed, though I doubted it.

The long walk also gave me time to watch Rupert, in his fancy coat, parading though the street completely oblivious to the attention he attracted. Many of the people we passed bowed or dropped a curtsey, and he'd nod absently if he noticed them. There were others he greeted by name, mostly asking them if they'd seen Meg in the last two days and asking them to watch for her, with so little self-awareness that he might have been speaking to people his own rank.

I've read silly ballads about noble heirs who assumed a disguise to travel among their people unnoticed. And there have been a handful of battlefield commanders who shed their badges of rank, and visited the troops' campfires on the night before a battle. The stories claimed they were seeing to their troops well-being, but I rather thought they were making sure their men were ready to fight in the morning—which in turn made sure they wouldn't find themselves and their officers alone on the field, with a bunch of people carrying sharp and pointy things marching toward them.

Rupert wasn't in disguise—but while everyone noticed the value of his coat and clothing, a surprising number of ordinary citizens seemed to know him. Personally. His rank was clear—he just didn't make an issue of it. I wondered if it was falling in love with a merchant's daughter that had taught him to see people as people, or if he'd always been like that. It might be why she'd fallen for him.

Either way, the horrible accident theory was looking more likely, and more tragic, with every block we walked. Though someone had written that note. If it was Agnes, then why was she at her parents' house waiting for news instead of telling everyone about their meeting?

The merchant's manor, when we reached it, had windows of the new, thin glass diamonds instead of the old thick rounds, and its sculpted lintels and cornices were in a paler stone than the rest of the building. It had cost as much as most of wealthy nobles' mansions, which meant that this merchant either wanted to join the ranks of the gentry, or to challenge them. The crest above his door hinted at the latter, for the sheep, yarn and cloth it featured defiantly claimed the origin of the fortune that had built this house.

"What's the difference between a weaver and a bandit?" I murmured into Kathy's ear, as Rupert plied the knocker.

"Is this the right time for that?" my true love asked impatiently.

"So you *don't* know. It's that—"

A manservant opened the door, and we learned that Mistress Agnes was at home and he had orders to bring anyone "about this business of Mistress Meg" straight in.

We followed him down a hallway furnished with a mixture of new furniture and antiques that some unfortunate noble had been forced to sell, and I leaned over and whispered, "A weaver gives you his previous victim's fleece, before he fleeces you."

Kathy choked, and hastily straightened her face when the servant looked back at her.

Mistress Agnes was dressing for dinner, but moments after the man told her maid that "these people are here about Mistress Meg," she came into the sitting room, hastily tying the sash of the dressing gown she'd thrown over her petticoats.

"Is she back? Have you heard..."

She saw that Rupert wasn't alone, and hesitated.

"These are Meg's friends," Rupert said. "And we haven't heard anything, but we've found something cursed strange. Did you ask Meg to meet you yesterday morning?"

"Last time I saw Meg was about two weeks ago." Mistress Agnes exchanged nods with Kathy, who she evidently knew. "She'd just broken the news, and we were talking about how Pa had taken it."

He evidently hadn't taken it well, because she glared at Rupert. He looked a bit wilted, but pressed on.

"Then what do you make of this?"

She read the note, her eyes widening. "I didn't write this. It looks like my hand. It looks exactly like my hand. Is this where she was going? But why would—"

The sitting room door opened, interrupting a spate of questions no one could answer.

"I heard someone's come about Meg."

Master Merkle had already dressed for dinner; his coat wasn't crusted with gold, but the weave of the cloth was finer than the Heir's. His wife, crowding in behind him, was plump and pretty, with soft brown hair and a comfortably worn face filled with anxiety. Her silk gown was almost fancy enough to match Rupert's garb.

"There's something odd going on, Pa." Mistress Agnes handed him the note. "This was sent to Meg yesterday, but I didn't write it."

Meg's mother pushed under her husband's arm to read along with him—she evidently didn't read as fast as he did, for she squeaked in protest when the paper crumpled in his clenched fist.

"This is what brought her out of the palace?" The question was aimed at Rupert, and Master Merkle's broad shoulders seemed to swell with anger.

"So we believe. We found it hidden in—"

"Then you'd best find out what kind of court chicanery you got my daughter involved in and fetch her back. Her and her babe, unharmed. And when you do they can come to us, and not mess with crazy dangerous experiments, turning them into—"

His wife had been prying the note out of his fist. Now he broke off, glancing at his hand—probably looking to see if her nails had left marks.

"I'm sure Rupert is doing his best to find her." Mistress Merkle spoke absently, her gaze on the note. "Though this does look like someone plotted to lure her out, and there's no one we know with reason to do such a thing."

Court chicanery. The words hung in the air like smoke, and Rupert shriveled under Master Merkle's furious gaze. But he spoke with surprising dignity.

"Since we've now confirmed that Mistress Agnes didn't write it, I shall try to find out who did. If you'll excuse me."

Master Merkle had to step aside to clear the door, and he loomed as poor Rupert brushed by him. We listened to the Heir's footsteps as he went rapidly down the hall—'twas a wonder he wasn't running. But the farther away his daughter's lover got, the more Master Merkle's shoulders deflated. By the time we heard the front door open and close his anger had drained away, leaving only a worried father.

"You can't keep chasing him off," Mistress Merkle said. "Like it or not, our Meg's fallen for him. I grant that it's a waste of her training, but she'll have the Heir's ear. Someday the Liege's ear, and that's worth something. Besides...he loves her, too."

"He's in love with her now," Master Merkle said. "Who's to say how he'll feel in a year, or five, or twenty. That's what marriage is for, curse it."

I thought that marriage should be more than a shackle to bind people who might fall out of love. If it wasn't for Michael's insistence on secrecy I could have put my arm around Kathy, and told her about the loving partnership my parents had. But she was already speaking to the Merkles, her voice soft with compassion.

"We can't find any reason for someone at court to lure her out either, and I wondered...do you think Meg could have written it herself? If she wanted to hide somewhere, mayhap till after the child is born, where would she go?"

Master Merkle growled under his breath. "Curse the lot of them, thinking to force their magica potions on my daughter. There's plenty of gifts that have nothing to do with magic."

He didn't need to look at the riches with which he'd surrounded his family—his determination, and the business it had created, were as much a part of the people in this room as their bones.

"You must have made some enemies, coming up like you did." I spoke for the first time, and everyone looked as startled as if a chair had asked them to shed a pound or two.

"Not as many as you'd think."

Mistress Merkle nodded agreement as her husband spoke.

"I try to treat folk fairly. It makes for better business, in the long run. There's a few who don't like me, I can't deny, but none of them would try to hurt my family. No, it's from the court this is coming, from the life *he* dragged her into. I didn't even want her to go to university!"

"You know perfectly well," said Agnes, "that nobody drags Meg into anything. You didn't want her to go to university—said it wasn't a proper pursuit for a lady—but you ended up paying for a full four years and a Master of Law degree."

"For all the good it'll do us, wasting her sharp mind as that young...man's leman."

I knew several of the words he'd chosen not to use, and I thought Michael quite courageous when he spoke up.

"Yet if she fled, as Kathy seems to think, she didn't come to you. I understand why you might want to conceal her, but Rupert loves her. To leave him so frightened would be terribly cruel."

"Which is why Meg wouldn't do it," Agnes said. "She might want to run away from court—she did want to! But she'd never leave Rupert, not like this, without a word of explanation."

"And she'd no need to run farther than this house," her father said. "I don't have to conceal my daughter in order to protect her. From anyone."

My father hadn't been strong enough to protect his family—but if he'd been able to, he would have.

Michael looked envious, Kathy looked wistful, and I resolved to become a father who both could and would protect his children from everything.

But as the crest over Master Merkle's door reminded me, that took money, and I hadn't yet figured out how to get it.

Unless, of course, someone was willing to offer a reward for Mistress Margaret's safe return?

Before I floated that idea, it might be a good idea to make sure she was still alive to be returned. If she wasn't, asking for money would make me look like a total cur. And while I didn't mind showing Michael that side of me—he's seen it often enough—it wasn't something I wanted to display to Kathy.

"We should go on to the Pig, and see if Mistress Margaret turned up there," I said.

Polite protestations would have been ridiculous, so no one asked us to stay. We went back out to the street, where we found Rupert pacing as he waited for us.

"That man intimidates me," he said. "Did you learn anything?"

"The Merkles have no enemy who'd seek to harm their daughter," Michael told him.

"So 'tis court chicanery after all." Rupert sighed. "But except for Father, I can't think of anyone at court who'd do this."

"No woman who'd have a chance at you if Margaret was out of the way?" I kept my voice light, but the question was serious. Kathy wasn't the only eligible girl who'd been summoned to court to woo the Heir, once his father realized he was serious about the Giftless girl he'd picked up at the university.

Rupert shook his head. "I made it perfectly clear I was committed to Meg."

I looked at Kathy, who shrugged agreement.

"I like your notion," Michael put in. "Let us go to the Pig in a Basket, and see if Mistress Meg went there yesterday."

So we did, and for once our destination was only a short walk from the Merkles' mansion. The innkeeper, the tapster and the serving maids all knew Meg by sight, and none of them had seen her in the last week.

"She never even made it to the inn." Rupert's voice held a quiet menace that reminded you just who he really was. "At nine in the morning, on busy streets, there's no place between here and the palace that she could have suffered an accident without it being reported to the town guard. Someone... I'm going to have a talk with my father."

He turned and strode off, and I found myself feeling an incongruous sympathy for the High Liege of all the United Realm.

CHAPTER 3

Michael

By the time we reached the palace 'twas near dark. Lighted windows glowed throughout the sprawling pile, but in one wing the whole lower floor was alight, and a carriage was pulling up to the door with a late arrival—clearly some court function was in progress.

Except for Rupert, we still weren't dressed for court. Kathy came closest, but even her well-cut habit was more suitable for a morning ride than palace ballrooms. As for Fisk and me...

The front door opened when Rupert approached—with a party going on, the servants would be alert to admit visitors. But when Fisk and I stepped across the threshold a manservant came from behind one door to block me, and another popped out and seized Fisk's elbow. The master of household was speaking to Rupert, and the footman before me murmured, "You want to go round back, to the stables. Grooms don't—"

"They're with me," Kathy said. "And they're coming in."

Kathy had lived in this palace as a guest of the High Liege for almost a year, and the servants were accustomed to taking her orders. But not orders as odd as this. The man's mouth opened to protest...and then closed.

"Yes, Mistress Katherine."

I was sorry when he stepped aside to let me pass—I'd rather have gone back to the stables than witness what looked to be an ugly family fight. And having that fight here and now was probably a bad idea.

My father once told me that calling the court that surrounded the High Liege a nest of vipers was an insult to snakes. He went on to claim that most of those who populated the place were leeches, only with a ferret's viciousness. He'd capped it by saying that this wasn't really an adequate description, because no animal but man had so much capacity to spy and lie.

So 'twas with a sinking heart that I followed Kathy, who caught up with Rupert just as he reached another set of double doors, beyond which the wailing cry of viols sounded faintly. Two more servants stood ready to open these doors, clad in an elegant blue and silver livery that was doubtless better suited for the event transpiring within than Fisk's and my traveling clothes.

Fisk, standing a pace or so behind Kathy, had assumed a stance of respectful servitude, and his clothing, always neater than mine, might let him pass as her footman, or even a clerk, and thus become almost invisible in that gathering.

There was no excuse for a groom—which I evidently looked like—to follow the Heir into a ballroom. Worrying about being underdressed should be beneath a knight errant, but I was still relieved when Kathy caught Rupert's arm and dragged him aside, planting her heels and pulling with all her slight weight. She may have been aided by the fact that the footmen, after a glance at Fisk and me, had not opened the doors.

"Are you out of your mind?" she demanded. "You can't talk to him about Meg in *there*. Go to his study and have someone send for him."

"Everyone at court already knows about Meg and me." Rupert might have walked off his anger...but what remained was the determination of fear. "And I want the rest of you there as witnesses. We forgot the note, but Father knows you well enough to take your word for it."

"That doesn't mean he'll accept my conclusions," Kathy said. "We should— Curse it!"

The doors swung open and a man and woman, sparkling with gems and flushed with heat or drink, started out of the room. They stopped abruptly when they saw the Heir. The man began to bow, and the woman to curtsey, but Rupert was already brushing past them.

With another oath, one so pungent it made Fisk blink, Kathy shot into the crowd after him. I met my partner's gaze and he shrugged.

"We shouldn't let her go it alone."

I wasn't so sure of that. 'Twas Kathy's choice to involve herself, after all. But I had agreed to let Fisk make some of the decisions, so he could also lead the way. I gestured for him to proceed, and he cast me an irked look, but he squared his shoulders valiantly and plunged after Katherine.

I could see why he might be intimidated. Silken skirts swayed like flowers in a stiff breeze, and some of the younger men wore dress swords with jeweled hilts, suspended from bright sashes. The whole room gleamed, candlelight and phosperlight reflecting from crystal chandeliers, mirrors on the walls, and gold and silver frogging on the gentlemen's coats. In this crowd, Rupert might be modestly dressed. A tall chair stood, empty, on a dais at the far end of the vast parquet floor, and we worked our way toward it through a mass of sweating, perfumed bodies.

The High Liege stood in a cooler corner, near the open terrace doors. He wasn't dressed any more richly than his son, but there was no mistaking him: the attention of everyone nearby was centered on him.

He broke off his quiet conversation, and all but one of the men he'd been speaking with moved aside as Rupert strode up to him. The man who remained was middle-aged and portly, with the flat calculating eyes of a hungry lizard. He nodded courteously to the Heir, his bland expression unchanging.

The Liege's gaze flickered past his son to Kathy. He started to smile, but then his gaze moved on to Fisk and me and his brows shot up instead.

"They're helping me look for Meg," Rupert said. "And we've discovered that she was lured out of the palace by a note, forged in her sister's hand. She's been *taken*."

He'd sense enough, barely, not to accuse his father outright of having done the deed. But the thought was in his face, his voice. The eyes of the courtiers around us glittered with interest, even as they politely turned their backs, to give the Liege some privacy. They didn't move very far away.

"Your Highnesses," the man who had stayed said precisely, "this probably isn't the best place to discuss—"

I thought he had a point, but the Liege didn't seem to care about the listening courtiers any more than Rupert did.

"If this note was in the sister's hand," he said reasonably, "then mayhap the sister wrote..." Kathy was already shaking her head. "Indeed. Well, if this note—conveniently left behind by Mistress Margaret, I take it? If this note was forged, have you considered that Margaret herself might have written it?"

Rupert was fathoms deep in love. This thought had never so much as crossed his mind, and he stared at his father in astonishment. "Why would she do that?"

"Oh for pity's sake! If half the alchemists in the Realm were about to start testing magica potions on me, I'd run for the hills. I know one of your professors said that Gifts could be triggered if the forming child received the right stimulus at the right time, but that sounds cracked to me. And you were supposed to be studying history and law, not taking classes in biology and this new-fangled chemistry."

'Twas clearly an old argument, and Rupert brushed it aside. "Meg didn't have to lie if she wanted to leave me, and she knew it. *Someone* took her."

Once more the accusation was clear. A slender man, sporting fewer jewels than most, stood not far off staring at a painting. Another couple faced each other as if in conversion, but neither of them said a word. It looked like my father was right about the court.

"Your Highness." The portly man's voice was firmer now. "This *really* isn't the place for a personal discussion. Mayhap the Liege could retire to his study, when the late supper is served, and you can deal with this matter then?"

The Liege looked around, as if noticing his audience for the first time. "Arnold's right," he said. "I can get away in a few hours, and we'll—"

"A few *hours?*" Rupert's voice was now loud enough that the ears around us no longer had to strain. "I just told you Meg's been kidnapped! Every hour we waste, she gets farther away and the trail gets colder. But that's fine with you, isn't it? You never wanted me to marry her, and now she's pregnant you've done something about it!"

The individual gasps were so soft I couldn't say that any one person had done it—but because everyone did it at the same moment the sound was perfectly clear. The slim man left the painting and hurried off toward a knot of well-dressed women.

Arnold, who I thought must be one of the Liege's advisors, winced.

The ruler of the United Realm rolled his eyes, and gave up any hope of keeping his family quarrels private.

"Why under two moons would I kidnap the girl? You're not the first Heir to take a mistress, or get children on her either. Please, credit me with a little sense. If I wanted you to lose interest in her—which I do—kidnapping her is the worst way to accomplish it. You're going to be obsessed with this until the chit turns up, probably hale and hearty, having taken a notion to visit the seaside or some such thing."

"You took her." Rupert's voice was low only because he was speaking through clenched teeth. He drew breath and unlocked his jaw before going on. "You took her to keep her from me, to make me forget her, but I never will. Father, I beg you. Where is she?"

"I didn't take her." The Liege's voice was almost gentle, despite the exasperation in it. "And I've no idea where she is."

"You're lying."

The Liege's face hardened, but he made a visible effort and held onto his temper. "Why does love make ordinarily sensible people into idiots? You can run your personal life however you see fit, but your child—at least, your first legitimate child—*must* be born Gifted. So if the girl has run off, for her own sake you should let her—"

"My dear, keep your voice down." A dark-haired woman rustled up and put a gentle hand on the Liege's arm. Judging by the richness of her dress and the concern on her face, this was probably the Liege Lady. I had heard she was beautiful...but that didn't do her justice. She was so stunning, I almost forgot to pay attention as she went on. "You know you don't mean that. No matter what the future holds, she's carrying his child. She must be—"

"I do mean it," said the High Liege. "If he married the wench, I'd have to find some way to dissolve it. That, or disinherit him for Liam, who probably wouldn't give me half this much—"

"Fine," said Rupert. "Do whatever you have to. You always do. But I'm going to find Meg. And then, you and I will have a reckoning!"

"You don't mean that, either," the Liege Lady said.

But Rupert had already turned away, moving toward the open terrace doors. A hum of conversation started up behind him.

Advisor Arnold's mouth looked like he'd bitten into a lemon, but the damage had been done.

Kathy dropped the Liege a hasty curtsey and went after Rupert, and Fisk and I bowed and followed. The Heir was walking swiftly toward his lover's cottage, likely by instinct, because he clearly wasn't thinking.

"He took her," Rupert told Kathy when we caught up to him. "But I'll find her. I'll find her if it's the last thing I do. And marry her, Gifted or not!"

"For the most part, that sounds fine," said Kathy soothingly. "Except I'm not so sure your father was lying."

Neither Kathy nor I have our father's Gift for reading people—and even Father can be fooled, for aside from magic sensing, Gifts are often erratic. But the Liege's exasperation, anger and pity had rung true to me.

"Fisk, don't you think he was telling the truth?" my sister asked.

Fisk shrugged. "It sounded like it. But a man in his position has to be a *very* good liar."

And watching the court, I'd started to wonder...

"Rupert, could someone want to drive a wedge between you and your father? And know that Mistress Margaret's disappearance might do just that?"

'Twas evidently not impossible, for Rupert's steps slowed as his mind engaged.

"I can't think why anyone would. I'm the declared Heir, and my little brother's only two. After Liam there's a number of cousins Father could choose from, most of whom don't even want the job. And Caro's young enough that she and my father could have more children. So even if he disowned me—and if he was going to do that, he'd probably have done it by now—it's not like there aren't other heirs. But if Father didn't take her, and I still think you're wrong about that, then who did?"

He clung to this theory, because if his father held her then Mistress Merkle and the child would be safe. Even the most obdurate father—like mine—would baulk at committing murder to keep his son from a bad marriage. If someone else had taken her, for some unknown reason, his lover and his child might already be dead. My heart went out to him...but my heart would do him no good, and Fisk's wits might.

"You're the expert on crime," I said to Fisk. "What now?"

There were benefits to exchanging a squire for a partner—I just hoped he had an answer.

"I've never kidnapped anyone," Fisk told Kathy hastily. "But if you want to pursue this, now comes the tedious part."

"Of course we're going to pursue it." Rupert shot Kathy a grateful look as she spoke. "What do we do?"

"We know when Mistress Meg left the palace," said Fisk. "And we know where she was going. We follow the route she probably took, asking every street vendor, shopkeeper and beggar we can find if they saw her. When we locate a street where people saw her at one end and didn't see her at the other...well, that's where whatever happened took place. Then we go on asking people till we find someone who noticed something suspicious, and proceed from there. Because Rupert was right when he said that she can't have vanished off a busy street in mid-morning without someone seeing something. We just have to find them."

"That could take months!" Rupert protested.

"Not really," said Fisk. "We only have to cover a few miles. If we leave at the same time of day she did, between us we can talk to the people most likely to have seen her in...oh, two or three days at most."

"That does us no good," Kathy said. "'Tis past ten, and she left at nine in the morning."

"Which means we should get some sleep," said Fisk. "This isn't going to be fast, unless we're incredibly lucky."

"You can stay in the cottage," Rupert said. "I think Meg stocked the cupboards, and Kathy can send for anything you might need. But I...ah... If you'll excuse me?"

He hurried off toward the gate, and Fisk sighed. "It really would be smarter to wait till morning."

"He can't," Kathy said. "I couldn't, if you were missing."

Fisk put his arm around her. "I would wait," he said soberly. "Even if it was you. There's no point being stupid about this, and the people who were out in the morning won't be there at night. He won't find anything."

"'Tis no use trying to stop him," I said. "He does what he must. We'll do what's wise."

So we went to Mistress Margaret's cottage, and Kathy insisted that Fisk and I take the big bed while she slept on Griswold's cot in the dressing room.

She ordered breakfast from the palace kitchen early next morning, and when the servants brought it we learned that for once Fisk was wrong. Several hours after midnight, the Heir had rushed into the stables. He didn't wake the grooms, but he made so much noise saddling his own horse that they roused and went to help him anyway.

He'd then gone galloping out the palace gate, and he hadn't been seen since.

Chapter 4

Fisk

"So, Rupert found a clue." I hadn't said it was impossible. Just unlikely.

"But now the people *he* talked to will be gone. Should we be asking about Meg, now that it's morning? Or Rupert?"

Kathy was only picking at the delectable fruit salad. There was also a basket of muffins, and a platter of two kinds of sausage, sliced ham, and several cheeses. Kathy had lived here for almost a year. I couldn't imagine how she'd kept that willowy slenderness, because I'd seen her eat and she never picked at her food.

Which meant that now she was really worried.

"We'll ask about both of them," I said. "Which will double our chance of finding someone. But *after* we've finished breakfast. Rupert may have succeeded on his first try, but we might not be that lucky."

Kathy's fork dropped to her plate with a musical chime—the china was very fine too. Clearly, my husbandly advice didn't carry much weight.

"We know how Rupert was dressed. Shouldn't we ask Griswold what Meg was wearing?"

She'd clearly been giving the matter some thought.

"We should," I said. "But Rupert will have been a lot more visible. All we need to do is find out where he stopped asking, and that should narrow the search considerably."

It wasn't that easy, of course, but we tackled it sensibly. Mistress Margaret had been wearing a pale green walking skirt with a dark brown bodice on the morning she vanished, and she'd taken a dark green cloak—I wished she'd been more inclined to finery, but Rupert's court coat would more than make up for that.

And it seemed we were going to have some competition in our search—inquiring after Rupert, near the palace gate, we learned that one Captain Varner, and a half a troop of palace guardsmen, had been asking those same questions, not an hour ago. Finding no one who'd seen where Rupert went once he left the palace, the Captain had sent his men into the city to track down Rupert's friends, but we knew where he'd gone last night.

Too bad the captain hadn't thought to ask us.

At my suggestion, we walked down the quickest route to the Pig in a Basket. About six blocks from the palace we started flashing coin and asking questions, till we found someone who'd seen Rupert.

"I was fastening up the shutters," a tapster told us. "He was done up all fancy in that coat, like he'd just come from the palace. Well, likely he had. He asked if I'd seen that wench of his, morning before last. This is an early morning for me—usually I'm just getting out of bed, the time she went by. But he went right on down the street, asking everyone who was out. Wasn't many, at that hour," he added. "So he was moving quicker than you'd think."

Instead of following Rupert's example, talking to everyone as he moved on down the street, we then skipped several blocks and started our inquiries with an apothecary, whose sign told customers to go round to the back and knock if there was an emergency after hours. They hadn't had any late customers last night, but the baker next door said that the man who brought wood for his ovens told him that the Heir himself was out in the street, asking everyone he saw about his girl, who'd gone missing. Fallen in love with a city merchant's daughter, the Heir had, which was maybe good for the city but hard on the girl. Giftless, poor lass...

No one had seen Mistress Margaret, but I made a mental note about how much the common folk knew about Rupert's love life.

We skipped several more blocks and pestered strangers till we found an elderly woman who'd woken up remembering she hadn't watered her window boxes. She hadn't been able to go back to sleep so she got up to do it...and had spoken to the Heir himself!

We went on to the next location, now about two-thirds of the way to the Pig, and found no one who'd seen Rupert.

"It means little," Michael pointed out. It wasn't yet noon but the day was already getting hot, and we stood in the shadow of a cutler's shop. A grinding wheel whined faintly in the work yard behind the store. "There might have been no one about when he passed by here. Or those he spoke to are now elsewhere."

"And no one saw Meg either," Kathy fretted. "Suppose she took a different route. This is the shortest way to the Pig, but she might not have gone the shortest way. If Rupert found a place she turned aside, he might have been asking for her just a block away, and we'd never know."

"I told you this would be tedious," I reminded them.

We went back two blocks, and after only ten minutes found someone Rupert had talked to. We came forward a block, and after almost half an hour were about to conclude that we needed to go back when a fishmonger's wife told us she'd heard a noise in the street last night, and looked out to see a man in a fancy court coat talking to the rat catcher.

Rat catchers are nocturnal creatures, like their prey. We left a message that we'd pay, if he could tell us where the man in the fancy coat had gone, went to the end of the next block...and found no one who'd seen either Margaret or Rupert, even though we asked everyone we could find.

"Mayhap 'tis somewhere in this block that Rupert found his clue." Kathy was grubby and tired—and you have to be in love when strands of hair stuck to a sweaty brow makes you want to kiss a girl.

"Not for certain," I warned her. "But it's possible. We can check out this street, and if we don't find out what happened to Rupert, we'll go back to the cottage, get some luncheon, and come back late tonight, when the people he saw are more likely to be around."

I was tired enough to half hope this would be the case...so of course, that was when we finally got lucky.

It was Kathy who found the old beggar woman, sitting on the steps of a ramshackle house. I was talking to a saddler's apprentice, and paid little attention when

Kathy approached the woman and dropped a few fracts into the bowl that touched the tattered skirt. But while my conversation with the boy ended quickly—he'd been sleeping the sleep of a teenager when Rupert came by—Kathy's conversation grew more intense. I'd already dismissed the apprentice and started toward her when she looked around and gestured urgently for Michael and me to join her.

Unlike Michael, I didn't start to run when the old woman pulled a knife from her skirt and brandished it, for I'd already seen the stumps peeping under that ragged hem.

Many beggars fake an injury to bring in a bit more, but there's no faking the absence of your feet.

Kathy didn't even step back. "They're my friends, Mistress. You don't need that."

"Being your friends won't stop 'em from stealing my coin."

She reached out with her truncated calves to pull the bowl toward her and her free hand twitched fabric over it. Michael's headlong pace slowed.

"We've no need of your coin, good woman." He stopped several yards short of her to prove it, dropping to his haunches so she didn't have to look up at him. "Indeed, if you possess the information we seek, I'll add to your take."

At least he hadn't promised some extravagant amount. For once my purse wasn't lean—unlike Michael, I'd kept my half of the reward we got for bringing down Atherton Roseman. But I was saving that money, and I wasn't about to pay more than we had to. Just these few hours of paying for people's time had put a dent in it.

"She saw it." Kathy's eyes were brilliant with excitement, and I strolled up and put an arm around her.

"She's the one Rupert found. Tell them what you told him, Mistress. What you told the fancy-dressed man you met last night."

The old woman eyed us appraisingly. I didn't drop down to the dirty pavement, as Michael had, but I smiled encouragingly.

She looked at the three of us, and either decided that we were friendly or that if we wanted to rob her she couldn't stop us, because the knife went back to its hiding place.

"So, he's worth money, that fancy man. Maybe more'n you'd pay, if I find the right buyer."

Old and crippled, but not a fool. A whole copper roundel was probably a small fortune to her...so it didn't surprise me to see Michael scramble forward, pulling out a silver ha'. He started to drop it into the half concealed bowl, and I said quickly, "You get this only when you've told us everything. Do you really think someone else would pay more? Assuming you could find them, that is."

Michael gave me an irritated look, but the hand that had started toward her bowl pulled back.

"Seems to me they'll come looking," the beggar said. "Just like you did, asking everyone on the street. So I won't have to go finding 'em, will I? There wasn't no one but me around when that young man came up, all worried like. None but old Sal, who can tell you about him."

"Maybe," I said. "But I'll bet there were plenty of people in the street to see what happened to the young woman he was asking about. And once we know that, we don't need you."

It had been a fairly obvious guess, but Kathy cast me an admiring glance that pleased me almost as much as Mistress Sal's defeated sigh.

"There were some around then. I'm not sure any of the others saw, but they might have. They might have."

"Tell us everything," said Michael. "Answer all our questions fair and true, and I'll make it a silver roundel."

"Oh for..." I rolled my eyes in exasperation, and Kathy gave a lovely little laugh.

"All right," Sal said. "I was out that morning, as well as last night, and I noticed your young miss right off, for she often gives me a fract. I knew she was pregnant, too. She wasn't showing, not yet, but there's a look... And I'm always here on my doorstep."

She patted the step she sat on, and for the first time I looked at the house behind it. It had once been a small, but tidy house, tucked between two taller buildings. Now only a memory of paint clung to it, and the stoop sagged away from the front wall. I'd have bet another silver roundel that the roof leaked. Still...

"You own this place? That's why the beggars' guild hasn't run you off."

All guilds enforce standards on their own trade, but the beggars' guild does it more firmly than most. Towns have been known to evict all beggars, if a few become aggressive or obnoxious. They'd never tolerate the way Sal had drawn that knife.

"That's right. This is my own front step, on my own property. So I can do as I like, and they can't say me nay. I'm out here a lot, though most ignore me. Just like those men ignored me. I saw the coach coming down the street. Started moving real slow, when it came up on her, but I didn't pay it much heed. I was watching her, hoping she'd have some fracts to spare like she usually does."

She was drawing out the tale, not because she wanted more money, but because the attention pleased her.

She clearly had no family—and if her friends had any money, she'd not be in this state. Assuming she had friends.

"Then the coach pulled up beside her," Sal went on. "The door opened and a man jumped out and threw his arm around her. I didn't see it, but he might have had a knife to her ribs, 'cause she didn't move or do anything. He picked her up and handed her to another man, inside the carriage, and they shut the door and drove off, quick like."

"And you didn't report that?" Kathy asked indignantly. "You saw Meg kidnapped, right in front of you, and you didn't scream, or send for the guard, or call out to passersby—"

"I didn't see a knife." Sal sounded a bit defensive. "She didn't scream nor struggle. How's I to know it's not some friend, lifting her up to the coach 'cause she was carrying?" She'd lowered her gaze to the pavement, and her face held the bitter brooding of remorse. "To tell the truth, I didn't think she had been snatched till I saw that man."

"What man?" Michael asked.

"Slight fellow," Sal said promptly. "Wearing clothes supposed to look like a groom or a journeyman, but they was too clean, too... Like a nobleman, trying to dress like he thinks someone on this street should look. I might not have noticed him, either, except that he was holding a kerchief up to his nose, like the gentry do when they smell something bad. Had pulled his hat down, and he was looking around all sharp, to see if anyone had noticed. Scared me some," Sal admitted. "When he looked my way, I stared at the middle of the street and shook my bowl like I was blind. And I kept doing it till after he'd gone, too. Was that made me wonder if...if maybe she hadn't wanted to go off in that coach. But if I'd told the guard that, they'd have laughed in my face. A woman got lifted into a coach—no sign of a weapon, no struggle, no screaming. And then a man looked at the street and walked off. That was all."

But it had frightened her, and I didn't think Sal was easily frightened.

"What did the coach look like?" Michael demanded. "And where did it go?"

"That's just what he asked," Sal told us. "Your fancy gent. Coach was fine, not with gold paint and whatnot, but good wood, real shiny under the mud. I wondered about that too, cause it was pretty dirty and we haven't had rain for a while. Used to be a crest on its door," she continued. "But someone had scratched it off. They varnished over the scratches, but you could tell. You might keep a coach muddy to hide a crest...but the crest was gone, so why bother?"

"Where did it go?" Michael was keeping to the point.

"Down to Halverham road." She gestured to the intersection behind us. "And then turned north."

"That makes sense," Kathy said soberly. "Halverham's the nearest fiefdom border, and the baron's not happy with the Liege right now. If they wanted to slow pursuit..."

"That's something we hadn't thought of," I said, rather grimly. "She could have been taken as bait."

"But Baron Halverham wouldn't kidnap Rupert," Kathy said. "Even if he wanted to, no one would dare. Besides, how could they know that Rupert would find out where she'd gone?"

"Rupert did find out, in just a few hours," I pointed out. "We found it in half a day."

But from what Sal said, it sounded like they'd tried to conceal the snatch. We still had no idea who'd taken Mistress Margaret. Or why.

"Court chicanery." Michael let out a long breath. "One more question, Mistress Sal. Can you sew?"

She looked more startled than I was—knowing Michael, I wasn't surprised at all—but he held up the two silver ha's.

"I can, but it's not fine-lady embroidery."

She spread her skirt for our inspection; it was even more patched than I'd thought, but the stitches that tacked those patches down were small and even.

"If you're thinking I could take in mending, well, it's a kindly notion. But who'd send their clothes to this dirty place?"

She gestured to the shack behind her and some of her defiance fell away, revealing the weary hopelessness behind it.

"Then you'd best spend some of that silver having the place cleaned," said Michael. "Get yourself a bath, and keep everything clean for several days."

He dropped the silver into her bowl, adding a few more bits from the sound of it, then rose stiffly.

"It is a kind thought," Kathy murmured as we started back toward the palace. "But I don't know any court lady who'd send her mending there. I'd hesitate myself. You don't want a torn skirt coming back mended and full of fleas. And her stitches weren't that fine."

"Then 'tis a good thing others aren't so picky," said Michael, striding briskly along. "And if she has the money for cleaning, there'll be no fleas."

"You're thinking the High Liege will send her the servant's mending, in thanks for information about his son?" I asked dubiously. "I'm not looking forward to telling him what we found at all—much less demanding favors in exchange."

Michael's steps slowed. "We must tell him. I'd sooner simply follow them myself, but by Sal's account there were four men involved in that kidnapping, two in the coach, one driving, and the mysterious watcher. And there might be more. 'Twould be irresponsible to go after them without telling someone what we've learned."

"*We're* going after them?" It was more a protest than a question—this was Michael, so of course we were. And I might have used my new-fledged partnership to argue that decision...except Michael wasn't alone.

"Of course we're going," said my dutiful future spouse. "At least, I am. The two of you can do as you like. But as for telling the High Liege... It's this Captain Varner's job to find Rupert, and he can send a score of men after them. Why don't we tell him instead?"

CHAPTER 5

Michael

We had feared we might have to track Captain Varner down in town, but his man told us that the captain was sitting down to luncheon. Would Mistress Katherine care to leave a message...? It appeared that Fisk and I weren't welcome at all, but Kathy changed that by telling him to tell the captain we knew where the Heir had gone.

Once he'd heard that, Captain Varner came out to the hallway to escort Kathy in. His brows shot up at the sight of us, but he made no protest when Fisk and I followed along, even telling his man to send to the kitchen for three more plates.

This suited me, for as he ushered Kathy into the dining room, the pork roast was emitting a most wonderful smell, and the peas and applesauce that accompanied it looked good too. Breakfast had been a long time ago.

"You say you've news of his highness?" The captain pushed Kathy's chair in, and seated himself. "Where did you find him? None of my men have had any luck."

"That's because they're still looking in the city," Kathy said. "But he was right after all, Meg *was* kidnapped. I should let my brother and his friend tell you about it, for 'twas they who figured it out."

"Your brother?" The captain's gaze went from me to Fisk, and he evidently found the family resemblance between us, for it settled upon me. "You've discovered some information, Master...Sevenson, is it? What have you...? Wait. Sevenson. Michael Sevenson? *The* Michael Sevenson?"

I had his full attention now, alas. Being unredeemed—an unfortunate consequence of my first adventure with Fisk—had put me outside the protection of the law, my wrists tattooed with the broken circles of a broken trust, so that any who chose to look could see my status and disgrace. I'd found this embarrassing, awkward, inconvenient, and sometimes even deadly.

But I swear, 'twas worse in all these ways to be known to every guardsman in the Realm as the man who brought down Atherton Roseman. Though I suppose 'twas not deadly. At least, not yet.

"I'm Michael Sevenson," I admitted. "This is my partner, Fisk. We..."

"Ah, the man who lived in Roseman's own household to spy on him. You've quite a nerve, sir."

His admiring gaze turned to Fisk, who is more accustomed to running from guardsmen than being admired by them. He looked so disconcerted that Kathy giggled.

"I'd like very much to hear that tale, from both of you," the captain went on. "I should have expected *Michael Sevenson* to track down the Heir."

"We haven't tracked him down," I said. "Only found a clue as to where he's gone—and 'twas my partner who knew how to find it, not I. But before I reveal our information, Captain, one small request?"

"If it's in my power, sir. What do you need?"

"Do you know who does the palace guards' mending?"

Captain Varner didn't, but he promised that as much work as she could manage would be sent to Mistress Sal, and she'd be paid a good wage for it.

The servants brought in our plates as he spoke, but I was so busy recounting what we'd learned that I'd little time to eat. As my story continued, the Captain's own appetite seemed to fade.

"She really was kidnapped? I thought that was craz— That is, I thought Lord Rupert's fondness had led him to exaggerate."

"It does seem he was right," I admitted. "About her being kidnapped, at least."

If he was right about *who'd* taken her, that would present a captain of the High Liege's guard with a most unpleasant predicament.

"Hmm. His Highness has a ten hour start, and Halverham's only a five hour ride away, so unless your kidnappers stopped short of the border, we'll have to cross into Baron Halverham's fief to pursue them."

He didn't look happy about this.

"So get a Liege writ to cross the border," said Fisk. "I can't imagine any landholder who'd deny you access to track down the Heir."

"Um," said Kathy.

"Um?" I asked.

"Well the thing is, Baron Halverham and the Liege are in the middle of a tax dispute. And if Baron Halverham grants the Liege the favor of letting Liege troops into his fief..."

"The baron will want a favor in return." Captain Varner sighed. "And we have no reason to think anyone means Heir Rupert any harm. I suppose I could just ride up and see if they'll let us in, but that's up to the Liege. I'd better report what you've told me, and get my instructions."

He bolted a final mouthful of pork, clearly preparing to go to the Liege at once—which might give me a chance to eat something.

"When will you be ready to set out?" I asked. "Fisk and I can pack quickly, but we'll need to gather up some gear if we're taking Kathy."

"What? Your pardon, but I'm not taking you along."

"I'm a good rider," Kathy assured him. "As my brother will attest. I won't slow you down."

Captain Varner was shaking his head. "I'm sure you are, Mistress Katherine, but I'm not taking any of you. This is Crown business, and you've already done your part. Be assured, I'll give you full credit for the discovery, Master Sevenson and Master Fisk. But we'll take it from here."

If this turned into the political mess it sounded like, the credit he so generously offered might well turn into blame. But credit or blame, 'twas rightfully ours, so I couldn't complain. However...

"We found the trail your men couldn't," I said. "We might be useful to you again. And if Rupert has caught up to Mistress Margaret, she may be in need of female companionship."

Kathy pounced on this argument, and worried it till the Captain had risen from the table and was ready to depart. I also mentioned that Fisk had skills that might be useful in tracking down a fugitive—though I stopped short of reminding him that I was *the* Michael Sevenson, and I kicked Fisk under the table when he started to.

But despite reputation, feminine pleas, and genuinely logical arguments, the captain's attitude remained the same—this was a professional matter, and the professionals would handle it.

I thought that the professionals hadn't done so very well, thus far...but it wasn't up to me.

"It's not up to us," Fisk told Kathy. "It's up to Varner and the High Liege now."

"If we'd left it up to them this morning, no one would have any idea where Rupert went," Kathy said. "I still think we should go after them."

"Varner and his troop can move faster than we can," I pointed out. "And if there is trouble, with a Liege writ, he can get any assistance he might need from the local authorities."

"But we can still pursue them on our own," she said. "We could follow Varner—or even get ahead of them!"

Fisk understood the difficulties in my meddling with authorities, even if Kathy didn't.

"How about this for a compromise," he said. "It's going to take us a while to assemble gear for you anyway. If Varner manages to catch up with Rupert and Mistress Margaret inside the Liege's land, he'll probably have them back here by tomorrow morning. If he hasn't come back by a reasonable time tomorrow, we'll set off after them."

Kathy scowled. "But all he cares about is bringing Rupert back—Meg's the one I'm worried about! What if she's in trouble?"

"Then Rupert will reach her long before we could," I pointed out. "Most probably before Varner catches up

with him. And when they do, he'll have Varner's troop
to assist him."

"And he's the Heir," Fisk added. "Even if Varner never finds him, he can go straight to any sheriff, baron or
lord in the Realm and get all the help he needs."

Which I, as an unredeemed man, could not.

"Be sensible, Kath," I said. "He's so far ahead of us,
the matter is bound to be settled by the time we catch
up."

"All right." Katherine gave in. "I suppose we can give
them a day."

There was a determined glint in her eye that told
me that one day—half a day, really—was all they'd get.
But she really did need some gear. My sister's riding
habit was well enough for a morning's hunt, but for a
trip that might last much longer she should wear something with fewer petticoats. And sturdier boots, a real
bedroll, something to cover her if it rained, and...

After some argument, we left True in the cottage and
spent the rest of the day in the city trying to find travel
equipment suitable for a lady. We spent much of our
time in the great market where they sold not only tack
and leather goods, but also foodstuffs carted in from
the countryside, furs from the far north, gemstones
from the mountain mines, and silk from the dry lands
of the south. Fisk looked at the gem shops longingly,
and I eyed him askance—but it turned out that he was
only repining his inability to purchase trinkets for his
beloved. Kathy, sensibly, was just as pleased with a pair
of sturdy riding boots, and a small basket of strawber-
ries shared between the three of us.

The market also held lots of narrow alleys, and
stands with hanging rugs or bolts of cloth into which
she and Fisk vanished for longer and longer stretches

of time. But most of her conversation was taken up with thoughts like, "Maybe he found her and they're eloping" or "What if she *was* taken as bait, and now they've got Rupert and a ransom demand is on the way?"

It was late in the evening when we returned to Margaret's cottage, snagging a passing maidservant and asking her to tell the kitchen to send dinner.

True, released to pee, was still romping on the grass when a manservant appeared with a covered basket. After a bit of friendly chatter from Kathy, he told us that although Captain Varner and his troop had set off early that afternoon, neither the troop nor the Heir had yet returned.

It was Fisk who reminded us that there was one more thing we'd need—money. I almost pointed out that Fisk's share of the reward for Roseman was still sewed into the lining of Tipple's saddle pad, and secreted in various other places, some of which even I didn't know about. But he hoards those coins like a miser, and I thought it might be wise for someone outside the palace to know what we'd learned from Mistress Sal. So after we'd eaten, Kathy ordered up a carriage from the stables and we set out to for the Merkles' home.

It may have been wise to share that knowledge, but 'twas not pleasant. Mistress Merkle started to cry when she heard Sal's tale. Master Merkle, white-faced, went into his study and came out with a purse fat enough to see us from the southern dry lands to the northern snowfields.

I resolved to take no more than we needed for our expenses on the journey, and Kathy promised to bring back their daughter, no matter what it took.

Fisk winced, for he knew that she meant every word...and that I would support her.

Despite the carriage, we were all weary when we returned to the cottage—and we had no reason to fear for ourselves. But so many strange things had happened, that when I saw the door I'd closed behind us standing open, a rush of excitement prickled through my nerves. Even though... "Most probably, the servant who removed our dinner dishes didn't latch it."

"A servant would have used the kitchen door."

Fisk shared my qualms. He tried to push Kathy back, as she moved forward to investigate. They were still scuffling when an amused, female voice said, "I thought I'd come inside to wait for you. I hope you don't mind."

"Not at all, Your Highness." I went through the door, and made my bow to the Liege Lady. She'd chosen to await us on a comfortably cushioned chair near the front room's cold hearth. And while she wasn't as richly dressed as she'd been last night, that only served to draw my gaze to the dark hair that swirled in wild curls at the crown of her head. The white skin of her throat and bosom glowed in the fading sunlight, and I added. "You should have had the servants kindle a light for you."

Which was the politest way I could think of to ask why there were no servants present.

"My husband doesn't know I'm here." It was an answer, of sorts, and her lovely eyes studied me. "But I'm concerned about Rupert, and even little Mistress Margaret. Oh, not that anything will happen to them. Wherever she is, I'm sure he'll find her and they'll both be back in a few days. But then what?"

"You expect us to answer that?" Fisk's voice was dry, and that intense gaze switched to him.

"You must be Master Fisk," she said. "The squire."

I think the way her lips twitched annoyed me more than it did Fisk.

"My partner, now," I said. "How can we assist you, my Lady?"

"By finding a way to get Rupert out of this tangle," she said. "'Tis troubling my husband, stirring up the court, and if it goes on much longer it could even be bad for the Realm."

"That's all true," said Kathy. "But what do you think we can do? We can't make Meg Gifted, or make Rupert fall out of love. In fact, barring a miracle from one of those university scholars, which I don't think is going to happen, there *is* no way to fix it. Rupert and Meg—and your husband, and the Realm—are all going to have to work it out as they see fit."

I thought that was a remarkably sensible statement, but the Liege Lady barely glanced at her.

"But you're going to try, aren't you?" she said. "You'll all try."

"Of course we will," I said. "But I don't see there's much we *can* do."

Her gaze moved from me to Fisk, and back again. Then she nodded. "There probably isn't. Good evening to you, Sir Michael. Master Fisk. Mistress Katherine."

She rose abruptly, and swept out of the cottage before I had time to finish bowing.

"What was that about?" said Fisk.

I don't think he expected an answer, but Kathy replied. "Her Gift is reading people, like Father. Though I think she's even better at it. The High Liege often asks her to sit in on conferences and negotiations, not to comment on the subject, but to tell him about the people he's dealing with."

"You think the Liege sent her?" I asked. "She said he didn't know she was here."

"Well, I suppose she might be concerned about Rupert and Meg." But Kathy sounded doubtful.

"Or she might be lying about her husband knowing where she was," Fisk added. "Though since there *isn't* anything we can do, I don't know why he'd bother."

We discussed the matter for some time, but we could make no more of it. And Fisk was right; there was nothing we could do.

So of course, the High Liege sent for us the very next morning.

CHAPTER 6

Fisk

Michael and I scrambled into our best clothes, such as they were. My coat and britches were of sensible broadcloth, and Michael's of worn brown velvet. But despite the fact that his hair hung to his shoulders in a nobleman's long cut, he still looked like a bandit wearing something he'd stolen off a coach. The man simply didn't know how to *look* the part. On the other hand, maybe the High Liege wanted a bandit. And Michael's accent confirmed the rank his hair implied, so I could let him do the talking.

It wasn't that I was nervous about meeting the High Liege—although I was—it just seemed like the wrong moment to announce that I was now a full partner in Michael's enterprises.

Kathy, who'd had a maid bring some of her rougher clothing over to the cottage yesterday—a modest two trunks full—put on a simple morning dress that was probably her attempt not to make the two of us look bad. It failed, but that didn't matter, since the clerk who'd delivered the Liege's summons took one look at her and said, "I'm sorry, Mistress Katherine. My orders are to bring only Masters Sevenson and Fisk."

"But..." She looked deeply disappointed, and if I'd been a mad knight errant I'd have defied the High Liege and refused to go without her.

But I'm not crazy.

"We'll come straight back here," I promised. "And tell you all about it."

"You'd better." She started to give me a wifely kiss on the cheek, a delightful habit she'd begun to form lately, but Michael hastily stepped forward.

"You may take us to his Highness, good sir."

Trying to remember to conceal our arrangement was even more annoying than I'd expected, but my mind was distracted from that by the need to keep bits of grass and leaves from sticking to my shoes as we walked across the dew-damp lawn. We passed down several long hallways, and one was lined with half a dozen mirrors, so I was able to make sure I still looked reasonably tidy.

This was just as well, for when the clerk led us into the High Liege's study, the ruler of the whole United Realm looked us both over for a long moment. And he was looking at me as much as at Michael.

"Masters Sevenson and Fisk. Come in and be seated. And let me start by saying that I owe you something for that business with Roseman."

Michael and I bowed, the clerk took up his station beside the door, and the Liege rose from his desk and came to join us. He was said to have been something of an athlete in his youth. Now, in his late fifties, his body had thickened and his hair begun to gray and thin, but there was still muscle under the fine linen shirt and brocaded dressing gown.

I heard a soft scraping sound from behind the desk after he left it, though not as much noise as a dog would make. Papers settling? A cat, perhaps?

"You owe us nothing, Liege." My idiot partner seated himself on a padded settee and I joined him there. The Liege came and sat in a big chair on the opposite side of a low table. "'Twas our duty to do all we could for you, and for the Realm. How may we assist you now?"

We'd already been rewarded once, but saving the Realm from armed rebellion was a pretty big debt, and I'd have liked to see what figure the Realm's ruler put on it. The Liege, however, was done with the past.

"You can track down my son, wherever he may be, and bring him back."

The Liege sounded rather grim about that simple sounding task, and I felt a flash of sympathy for Rupert.

"Captain Varner couldn't find him?" Michael asked. Though if the captain had found him, the Liege would hardly be asking us.

"He never had the chance. Baron Halverham refuses to let my troops into his fief without a writ explaining why they're there, and I'm not going to write one. Having my named Heir chasing his mistress across the Realm embarrasses my house," Rupert's father went on. "Mind you, a reign that can't endure some embarrassment is too weak to survive...but even a strong reign can't ignore too much embarrassment, before it starts to *make* you weak."

This was more candor than I'd expected from the most powerful man in the Realm, and it made me

extremely nervous. Had he been anticipating this outcome, and that was why he'd sent his wife to check us
out last night? But if so, why had she told us he didn't
send her?

Another noise from the desk distracted me from that
line of thought. It sounded like clothing rustling as
something moved...and cats are notorious for refusing
to wear clothes.

"I can see why you might hesitate to send a troop after him," Michael said. "But since you seem to know of
our dealings with Master Roseman, you may also know
that I am unredeemed."

He said it so calmly the Liege probably couldn't tell
how much that admission cost him. But I knew.

"We have no authority over Rupert," Michael went
on. "If he doesn't want to return, I couldn't even go to
the local sheriff or town guard for assistance. And Fisk
is less likely to get their aid simply because he travels
with me! Frankly, it seems to me 'twould be best to let
Rupert rescue his lady and bring her back himself. If
he asks the local authorities for assistance, any debt accrued will be owed by him, not you. And he can surely
get whatever help he needs."

"Not necessarily." The High Liege sighed. "Not
from—"

The door opened, and the Liege Lady came in.

"Stephen, have you seen... Oh, beg pardon. I thought
you'd be alone at this hour. But I'm hunting, you see."

A slight smile proclaimed some private joke, and as
Michael and I rose hastily to offer our bows, she showed
no sign that she'd ever set eyes on us.

The High Liege's first wife had died two decades ago,
and while I may have been alive at the time, I'd doubt-

less been more interested in toys and sweetmeats than court politics. I had been aware of his marriage, which took place during the year or so after I'd left Jack and before I'd been...legally obliged to become Michael's squire. The Liege's marriage had been written up in all the broadsheets, and discussed quite a lot—when an older man marries a much younger woman, that can be a sign of political weakness too. I couldn't think of any way to make money from it, so I still hadn't paid the matter much attention.

Now, looking at the exquisite, black-haired woman, I completely understood both why he'd married her and the political worries that had followed. Her pretense of never having met us was so perfect that Jack couldn't have done it better.

"Hunting...indoors, Mistress? That's hardly a proper pursuit for a lady." The Liege's voice took whatever joke she'd made and gave it a bawdy edge. She grinned at him.

"It's perfectly proper, this time. I'm trying to get Liam dressed." Silk rustled as she gestured with one hand, and for the first time I noticed that she held a very small pair of shoes. "Have you seen him?"

"Of course not," said the High Liege, in the overly hearty tones of someone telling an obvious lie. "If I had, I'd have to tell you where he was hiding. Right away."

He didn't need to shift his eyes in the direction of the desk, for a stifled giggle came from behind it.

"I wonder where he could be." The Lady edged casually in the direction of the desk. "He's so good at hiding. I may never ever be able—"

"Here! I'm here, Momma!"

The little boy who leapt out and clutched her skirt had his father's pale brown hair and his mother's deep brown eyes. The hair was rumpled, and both his face and the hands that crumpled that expensive silk appeared to be coated with something sticky, but she didn't seem to mind.

"Oh my goodness! You gave me such a fright!"

He was still giggling over that when she boosted him onto the desk chair and started getting him into his shoes, displaying a better grasp of maternal strategy than I'd expected.

The High Liege's eyes were still soft when he turned back to us, but his smile soon faded.

"I already knew about your unfortunate legal status, Master Sevenson. But you being unredeemed shouldn't be relevant, for I don't want you to go to the authorities either. Embarrassment to the throne aside, I can't afford to owe Halverham a favor right now. Or Baron Lorrell or Lord Fillaran, either. In fact, I don't want word of this to reach any landholder north of the Pottage River."

"All the more reason," said Michael, "to let your son rescue his lady on his own."

I noticed that Michael wasn't telling him that we were already packed to set out after Rupert and Mistress Margaret, and I wondered why. Michael certainly wasn't angling for a reward.

"From what Captain Varner told me," the High Liege said, "Mistress Merkle really may have been kidnapped. Rupert isn't... It's not that he's a fool, by any means, except about that girl of his. But to put it bluntly, Sir Michael, my son's a scholarly dreamer. He may or may not be liege material..."

I made an effort, and kept the sudden shock out of my expression. Was the Liege thinking of claiming another heir? It had happened, once or twice, but it was unusual to say the least.

"...but I don't want him following his leman into something he can't handle," the Liege finished. "In fact, the only reason I can think of for someone to have taken the wench is to lure Rupert after her. And that makes me *very* uneasy."

His wife picked up his second son, and quietly carried him out as the Liege went on.

"Surely the men who brought down the Rose conspiracy can track down and return one wayward nobleman?"

Michael didn't look happy about this fatherly request—even though we'd intended to go after Rupert anyway. And while *he* might be above angling for a reward...

"We're not rich men, Your Highness," I put in smoothly. "If we can't go to the local authorities for help we'll need to spread some bribes around, and there's lodging on the road to pay for, and probably other things."

"I can give you eighty gold roundels now, for your expenses," the High Liege said.

I was somewhat disappointed—it was plenty for us to go after Rupert, but it wasn't much more than Master Merkle had handed over.

"And," the Liege went on, "if you bring back my son, without involving anyone else or embarrassing me further, I'll give you a thousand gold roundels. Each."

"We don't—" Michael broke off when I kicked his ankle. The table wasn't high enough to hide this entirely, but I didn't care.

"Thank you, Your Highness. That's most generous."

Generous enough that, assuming Michael would give Kathy his share for a dowry, and combined with the reward we'd been given for Roseman, I'd be able to make the first payment on a very small estate! And with an estate, no matter how small and debt ridden, I could ask her father for Kathy's hand...not to mention the rest of her.

Michael started to rub his ankle, and then thought better of doing it in front of the High Liege.

"I'm supposed to *consult with my partner* before I make these decisions, Your Highness."

"In this case, there's no need for that," I told him graciously. "We'll do it. Or at least, we'll do our best."

Even with that reward in the offing, promising this man something you might not be able to deliver was a bad idea.

"That's settled then," the High Liege said, and Michael suppressed a scowl. "I'll have the purse sent to the cottage where you're staying, and you can requisition anything you need, including horses from my stable. See to it, Gregory."

The clerk who'd brought us here nodded, and we stood, bowed, and left. At least Michael waited till Gregory showed us out the door, leaving us to go back to the cottage on our own, before he spoke.

"I thought we had agreed to consult one another, before making such decisions."

"I knew you wouldn't like being paid for this," I said. "But we were going after Rupert anyway. And it's not as if getting paid for doing the right thing makes the thing we're doing less right. And we will need money for bribes, particularly if we can't approach the authorities. And he's the one who brought up the reward. It's not as if we said, 'Give us money or we won't bring back your son.' So I don't see what your objection...well, maybe I do, but think you're crazy. We were planning to go after Rupert this morning! So it's not as if...ah..."

I'd expected Michael to interrupt me long before this, but he waited till my nervous babbling ran out. Which was curst unnerving, because Michael hardly ever bothers to control himself with me—he must be genuinely angry.

"'Tis not about the money. I don't approve, and you knew I wouldn't, but I know why you want it. As soon as the High Liege told us what he needed, I knew you'd be fishing for a reward. But our agreement, partner, was that we'd consult with each other before making these decisions."

He was right. And when we made that agreement, I had smugly wondered how long it would be before *Michael* broke it.

"I'm sorry," I said. "I was afraid you'd turn down the reward, and that's the only way I've found that I could even begin to get enough money to approach your father... But you're right. I should have consulted you."

"I suppose I can forgive you." That unnerving sternness melted out of Michael's expression. "'Tis not as if we weren't planning to go after Rupert anyway."

"We'll be getting a late start—but that much money is worth waiting for!" I found my steps quickening at the thought. "I can't wait to tell Kathy."

"....so the reward, when we get it, and since Michael says he'll give you his half for a dowry, will be almost enough for me to make first payment on a small estate. Which means I can approach your father!"

Returning to the cottage, we found that my sensible darling had realized we wouldn't be leaving at dawn and ordered breakfast—though I'd been too busy telling her what the High Liege had offered us to eat. I picked up a cold roll, that had been hot when I buttered it, and waited for her to express some of the delight I felt. It's not often you come across a chance to make that much money. At least, not honestly.

"I'm more worried about Meg," my beloved said. "I've no problem with helping Rupert out, or even sending him home. But Meg's the one who was kidnapped, and no one but Rupert and her family seems to be thinking about her at all."

"It's not that I'm not thinking about her." Although I hadn't been. "But I'm wondering if the High Liege wasn't behind that snatch after all. I know what he said about the political cost, but all he has to do is scribble up a writ and warrant and send it out to the local sheriffs. And they'd track down the kidnappers and rescue her, without it costing him two thousand gold roundels."

I saw Michael opening his mouth to object and added swiftly, "He's hiring us to appease Rupert, and maybe throw the rest of his court off the scent. But if he's the one holding her, she shouldn't be in any danger."

The man we'd met might be ruthless if he had to, but he wasn't stupid enough to harm the girl. That kind of thing always comes out, sooner or later, and it wouldn't just be Rupert's reaction he'd have to worry about. It takes a lot to rouse a city to rebellion, and murdering an innocent merchant's daughter would provoke rioting in the streets. Tucking her out of the way for a while would be considered regrettable, but since he couldn't let his son marry a Giftless girl...

"I wish I believed that," Kathy said. "And I suppose he might be stupid enough to think that if Meg's not around, eventually Rupert will fall out of love. But you're wrong about what that warrant would cost him, Fisk. I've been living in court long enough to see how much power some of the lords and barons wield—how much juggling the Liege has to do to balance their needs and desires. And egos! The Realm may look all tightly wrapped from the outside...well, I suppose it is. But the High Liege does a lot of work to keep it that way, and he *has* to maintain his own supremacy."

"And you've only to look at Roseman's plot to see how easily those wrappings can loosen," Michael added.

Since Roseman had almost succeeded in raising half the river plain in rebellion and creating his own little realm, I couldn't argue that point. But...

"How can it damage him to send a warrant asking sheriffs to arrest a criminal who's come into their fief? That's how the system is *supposed* to work."

Although Jack had taught me that if you escaped across a fiefdom border you could rely on at least two weeks, and sometimes as much as two months, before the local liege made up his mind about sending his own men to chase after some other fief's criminals. If the relationship between neighboring fiefs was strained, you might be able to stay there in perfect safety for years. That's how bounty hunters made their living. A pretty good living, in fact.

"If 'twas a crime that didn't involve him, the Liege would probably do just that," said Michael, interrupting my consideration of whether a bounty hunter could make enough money to marry Kathy. "But this is a crime that touches his own house. Any warrant he sends out will be seen by those who receive it as a personal request from the Liege, for a personal favor. And that..."

"...could cause him a lot of trouble in the future," Kathy finished. "So much trouble that if he'd taken Meg, I'm pretty sure they'd never have left the Liege's fief. And since we know they went into Halverham..."

"All right," I said. "If the Liege doesn't have her, we'll go on and rescue Mistress Margaret. After we've caught up with Rupert."

I had too much sense of self-preservation to say, 'after we've taken Rupert home,' but Kathy caught the subtext anyway. I hadn't realized those soft gray eyes could look so steely.

"You can take Rupert home if you want. *I'm* going on after Meg. Who, unlike Rupert, might be in real danger."

"If they wanted to kill her," I pointed out, "they'd have done it already. Killing's easier to bring off than kidnapping, and no one goes to the considerable risk and trouble of hauling a live prisoner around the countryside unless they have a really good reason to keep them alive."

"You don't know who took Meg, or why, so you can't possibly know what might change their minds about that," Kathy shot back. "It could be they want Rupert to follow her, and if you haul him home they'll kill Meg on the spot! But I seem to be the only person thinking about that."

"*I* was thinking about ways to get us married. But since that seems to be pretty low on your agenda, we—"

"Children," said Michael mildly, "you don't have to fight. Or at least, not yet. Rupert is following Mistress Meg. Even if he hasn't caught up with her—rescued her, mayhap—by the time we reach him, 'tis the same trail. Let's go after them both, and make up our minds what to do once we've found them."

This seemed to be Michael's day for being right. My anger was already fading, and Kathy cast me a contrite look.

"By the time we reach them, we might even have enough information to make a sensible decision," Michael went on. "Kathy's right that if Mistress Merkle is in danger, we must protect her. But Fisk is also right about needing that money for you to get married."

"Not really," my beloved said, and my heart skipped a beat before she went on. "All I need to marry Fisk is a willing noble or judicar and 'consent of my blood-kin.' I know that's supposed to be Father, but for legal purposes, Michael's consent would do."

Michael, no doubt thinking of his father's reaction to that scenario, cringed visibly. And the reason I knew what he was thinking was because I cringed too. Though I hope I hid it better. Or he may have cringed because, being unredeemed, he probably *couldn't* give legal consent, even for a marriage.

If I could get my hands on the reward, we'd never need to raise that hurtful question.

"Michael's right," I said firmly. "We can protect your Meg *and* get married."

But I must admit, I did wish Kathy had her priorities better arranged.

That seemed to settle the matter, and we were finishing our breakfast when the High Liege made good on his promise and our purse arrived...though I doubted he'd told Advisor Arnold to deliver it in person.

The advisor, neatly dressed and freshly shaven, had the disgruntled look of a man awakened early by his boss to attend to business he didn't even approve of.

"I want to make it very clear," he said, "that the main reason your services are being retained is to keep this from becoming a bigger scandal than it already is. We don't want the Heir's...impetuosity to become known, much less to be the subject of common gossip."

I thought that ship had already sailed, but he was clutching the clinking purse in a way that told me he wouldn't give it up till we agreed.

"We understand," I said. "We'll be discreet."

"My understanding," said my partner, without any consultation at all, "is that his Highness' first priority is to get his son back."

"That, of course," said Arnold. "But discretion is key. No matter who else you may be working for—"

"I work for no one." Michael sounded somewhat nettled. "I'm a knight errant, in search of adventure and good deeds. To assist the Heir in the safe return of his lady is a deed most worthy of our effort."

Master Arnold snorted, as sane people tend to when Michael claims a profession that's several centuries out of date. It's a reaction we're both accustomed to, and Michael simply folded his arms and waited till the advisor's scornful smirk vanished.

"By the two moons. You're serious, aren't you?"

"He is," I said. "Kathy and I are just along for the ride."

"Well...then you'll be even more willing to be discreet. There's little use in returning Mistress Margaret to her place if scandal erupts around the Heir. You *do* understand that?"

"We do." I rose and held out my hand.

He didn't want to give us the money, but he didn't have another option. He sniffed disparagingly, dropped the purse into my hand, and departed.

It was pleasantly heavy, and if we found Rupert quickly and brought him home quietly, we might be able to keep most of it. And Mistress Margaret, of course.

"Master Arnold doesn't seem particularly worried about the Heir," Michael said. "Much less poor Mistress Meg."

"In fairness, Rupert doesn't much like him," Kathy said. "And Meg, with her education, is kind of an unofficial apprentice for his job. I don't like him either, but I don't think he'd kidnap her just to get her out of his way. The High Liege might well rule for another twenty years, and even if Meg wasn't there, Rupert would probably retire Master Arnold when he takes the throne."

"Besides," I said, "my impression is that the last thing Master Arnold wants is to create a big scandal around Mistress Merkle—which is what her kidnapping has done, whether he likes it or not."

Still, he was the first person we'd met who had any reason to dislike Margaret or Rupert. And where there was one, there would be more. We just had to find them.

CHAPTER 7

Michael

We set off only two hours later than we'd planned, and under the circumstances I thought that was doing well. Kathy wore a split skirt, with matching bodice and a plain linen shirt—a modest effect that was spoiled by a straw hat, bright with flowing ribbons, which she swore was the plainest hat she had. She still looked like a well-off lady, but at least she didn't look like she'd just ridden away from a court hunting party, and she wouldn't be tripping over petticoats if she had to make a dash for it.

Since we had the Liege's support, we went to the royal stables to borrow a horse for her. The head groom said that Po...ah, Traveler, had good stamina and an easy gait, perfect for long journeys. He was a leggy chestnut gelding, and he was also good with dogs, which mattered, because I refused to leave True behind on a trip that might go on for weeks.

Seeing the attention these men paid our horses sparked my wits, and I turned to the groom who'd brought them from the stables and pulled out the tip he'd been awaiting...but I doubled it.

"One question, good sir. What horse did his Highness take when he left the palace? Do you know?"

This caught Kathy's attention, as well as the groom's, and she broke off a conversation with Fisk to listen.

"I didn't saddle him myself, but those who did say he took Champion."

"What does Champion look like?" I pressed on. "Is he a horse people might notice for some reason, like Tipple here?"

The groom grinned, but it was Kathy who answered. "Champion is Rupert's favorite mount—and he's a snow white stallion, who turns heads everywhere he goes. He'll be a lot more memorable than Rupert, or Meg, or that coach."

The chestnut's other name, which Kathy told us was Posy, was explained not half an hour out of the city when we came across a patch of small white flowers. Neither Chant nor Tipple gave them a glance, but Posy shied and baulked, snorting nervously at the innocent blossoms. After Fisk and I had ridden past, Kathy convinced him to follow, but he pranced and rolled his eyes as if the road was lined with hissing snakes.

"No one knows why he does it," my sister told us. "He's palace raised, and he's been like this about flowers since he was a foal. Not all flowers, just these white ones. The best guess is that he may have been stung when he was grazing near them. Or he may just have a phobia."

"I've known men who have issues with flowers." Fisk wasn't quite laughing, though his face was bright with amusement. "But usually not till they've forgotten some significant occasion, and been forced to apologize too often. I trust you wouldn't need a bouquet every night for two weeks, would you dear?"

"I trust *you're* not going to forget important occasions."

'Twas good to see Fisk and Kathy over their spat—and it hadn't lasted long, for they both wanted to marry even if they might quarrel about the means. But a touch of constraint had lingered as we finished packing, and since neither of them was wont to hold a grudge that left me wondering what it was that lay unresolved between them.

But I defy anyone to remain angry or glum while setting off on an adventure on a bright summer morning. Birds chirped and chattered in the bushes and True loped through the fields in his own great quest for the elusive and wondrous rabbit.

We drew near the border in the early afternoon. I thought that once they'd turned back Captain Varner's troop, Halverham's men might well have gone home, but when we reached the border, half a dozen men in green and brown livery were lounging on the grass beside the road.

"Your aunt's a widow," Fisk told Kathy as we approached. "Your mother wants you to stay with her, to be sure—"

"I can make up details as well as you can," said Kathy. "Stop fidgeting."

One of the guardsmen rose and strolled into the road, asking about our business in Halverham. But before Kathy got out more than a handful of words, he'd stopped listening and stepped aside. He wished her a good journey as she passed.

"I don't know why you're so surprised," Fisk said as we rode on. "They were told to stop the High Liege's troops, not random travelers. Though that raises the question of how they knew the High Liege was going to send a troop in the first place."

'Twas a question that hadn't occurred to me, but 'twas not hard to account for.

"If Baron Halverham's people, a sheriff mayhap, reported Rupert's presence in his fief, 'twould be easy for him to guess that a troop might follow."

"Or someone at court might have sent a message and tipped him off," Kathy added. "This tax thing has been going on for months, and a lot of people are taking sides."

"Maybe," said Fisk.

But none of us were really satisfied with these explanations.

We stopped to make inquires in the first village the road passed through, and since Rupert had passed through only two days ago, the offer of a few copper roundels soon produced several people who'd "never seen the like of that white stud, sir. A destrier, like your big fellow here, perfect conformation, and his mane and tail flowing almost to the ground. Fair glowed he did..."

Rupert was still on the main road when he left the village, so we went on to the next town where we got much the same result, and so on all the way through Halverham. We even found the inn where he'd finally stopped to sleep.

"But he left at first light," the groom who'd saddled his horse told us, in exchange for a generous tip. "Looking fair worried, and saying he was losing too much time. He asked me about that coach he was tracking, but I hadn't seen it."

There were several hours of daylight left, and Kathy swore she wasn't too tired, so we went on to the next town before we stopped at an inn. We were still some distance from the Duram border, which we passed at some point next morning without even knowing it, for there were no guards. Duram was a larger fief than Halverham, and since we were delayed by having to find someone who'd seen Rupert in every town, it took us the better part of two days to cross it and go into Medding.

By close questioning, Fisk found that we were gaining on Rupert, who was now a bit more than a day and a half ahead of us. We couldn't tell if he was gaining or losing ground on the coach he followed, but we did find enough people who'd told him about that coach to learn that it carried a "poor sick lady" and her brother, with a driver and two men riding escort.

"So they must be carrying more than just a lady," one man remarked. "You don't need a cashbox escort to drive safely in Baron Medding's fief."

Kathy was rather quiet, even after Fisk pointed out that the only reason to drag a coach across the countryside is because there's someone in it, and I knew she fretted for her friend. Which made it all the more worrisome when she started turning to gaze back down the road behind us.

"I know that look," Fisk said, after the fourth time she'd twisted in the saddle. "You've got the warning Gift, don't you? I don't suppose yours works more reliably than Michael's?"

The warning Gift can tell you that someone is following you. Or that an aunt is thinking about marrying you off to her best friend's daughter. It can tell you there's a letter carrier trying to track you down, but not warn you about assassins on your trail.

Some folk perceive it as an itch on the back of the neck, but for me 'tis a tightness in the back of the mind, a sense that something predatory has you in its sights... which come to think of it, is a very fair description of my aunt Gwendolyn.

"I'm not sure," Kathy said now. "I do feel like there's something behind us, but 'tis not like I can tell you how far or who or why. It could even be the Merkles, thinking about us tracking Meg."

"It's probably that," Fisk agreed. But the next time we stopped to water the horses, he found the sword I keep wrapped in my bedroll on Chant's rump, and pulled the hilt out of the blankets so I could draw it swiftly.

The next fief after Medding was another small one, and the only thing of note as we passed through it was that the plastered-over brick of the plains was interspersed with buildings made in part, or even completely out of wood. From there Rupert turned west into Lander, and Kathy told us Lord Lander was also involved in this tax dispute with the Liege.

The Rippon River flowed out of the western mountains, and Rippon Town was the biggest city we'd seen since we set out, trading timber and ore from the mountains for furs from the north and foodstuffs from the south and east. 'Twas not as big as Tallowsport, which Fisk and I had come to know all too well, but 'twas larger than Crown City, and it might be time consuming to track Rupert through it.

We found the place he'd ridden into town, which was where we rode in, but a few blocks after that we lost his trail.

"I bet he stopped asking about the coach," Fisk said. "This town's too big, and there's too much traffic on this road, for anyone to remember it."

"Then what would he do?" Kathy asked. "He won't give up. Not on Meg."

"What I'd do," said Fisk. "He'd go to all the coaching inns, and see if they changed horses here."

We'd already found one town where they'd done so, roughly a day's journey back, so the timing would be about right, but checking every inn would take a lot of time...

Once this kind of decision had been up to me—Fisk might have argued. In fact, he nagged for days when he disagreed with me, and carped thereafter. But the decisions had been mine. However, Fisk was now my partner, not my squire. And besides, if I acceded to his decision now, some time in the future, when it might matter more, 'twould be his turn to yield to me.

The matter was clinched when Kathy pointed out that if we split up, each asking at inns in different areas, we could cover the town more quickly than Rupert, and might gain some time.

After so many days in the saddle we were ready to walk, and in town a horse is usually more trouble than it's worth. We found an inn and stabled our horses, leaving the dog there as well. True is a great companion riding through the countryside, but in a town his company is less desirable.

Then, over a very late luncheon and with many questions to our waiter, we divided up the town. Kathy was assigned to visit the expensive coaching inns in the respectable part of town, by Fisk and my unanimous consent. We wrangled a bit over who should take the inns on the river road, and who would go to the cheaper inns on the outskirts of the slums, but Fisk won the point by claiming that he knew how to talk to criminals and I didn't. I consoled myself with the knowledge that river docks could also be a rough neighborhood...but they really weren't.

In fact, once I reached the river, I lost some time watching the trade that was the lifeblood of this town. The river was large enough, but while barges departed from its far end to go downstream, there were no boats on the upstream side. This was because every few minutes a raft of logs, bound together with ropes, drifted down on the current. As soon as the men in the lookout towers perched along the bank spotted one, slender skiffs rowed out and their handlers latched long lines onto the ropes that bound the raft together. Then an ox-turned winch towed the huge dripping mass to shore, whereupon a swarm of men pulled the raft apart, and loaded the logs onto drays to be taken to the saw pits.

I now understood why all the buildings in this town were made of wood. In the area Kathy was searching, where shutters and window boxes would be painted in bright colors, the effect might be pretty. Down by the docks, everything was gray with weathering or dark with pitch. 'Twould have looked most drab, were it not for the sunlight sparking on the water, and the chaos and energy of a town at work.

Inns along the river were fewer than on the main roads. Once a few coins had loosened folks' tongues, and they'd told me they'd seen no sign of Rupert or a coach with a crest scratched off its door, I took to asking them where the next inn might be and how to get there swiftly.

'Twas that "swiftly" bit that led me into trouble, for I took the wrong alley between two warehouses and found myself at a dead end. When I turned to make my way back to the street, a man was walking toward me.

My first thought was that he didn't look like a sawyer, or any of the men working at the docks. He wore riding boots and a broad brimmed hat, though it had no plumes or other adornment. His gaze fixed on me in a way that made the back of my neck prickle in primitive warning, but he addressed me politely.

"Master Sevenson? Master Michael Sevenson?"

"I am," I said. "May I ask how you know my name?"

"Forgive me, sir," he said, ignoring my question. "But I have to be certain. May I see one of your wrists?"

If this was a messenger sent after us by the High Liege, 'twould account for the riding clothes, his weathered skin and the fine lines around his eyes—though he wasn't much older than I. He was slim, but he had the broad shoulders and muscular wrists of a man who spent time in the saddle. And if the Liege's message was private or sensitive, then making certain of my identity made sense.

So I suppressed my desire to refuse, pulling up my left sleeve and using my right hand and my teeth to untie one of the leather bands I use to cover the tattoos that mark me unredeemed.

At first I had disdained to conceal them, for despite the sentence the judicars laid on me when I refused to pay my debt to the law, I had done right.

But that tale took the better part of ten minutes to tell, and no one believed it anyway. Under the Realm's law, if a man wrongs another, he makes the wrong right, and there's an end to the matter. But men who bear this mark, two linked circles, cracked on their outer edges like links broken out of a chain, are men whose debts have not or cannot be paid. Usually it means they've killed someone, and bribed their way off the gallows—for debts short of death can be otherwise repaid.

The reasoning behind those marks is that since you owe the law an unpayable debt, the law doesn't owe you anything. If any man wrongs you, hurts you, even kills you, the law will do nothing about it, for you are outside its bounds.

The rumor is that unredeemed men starve to death or kill themselves. But I've found that people are kinder, and more reasonable than the law. I've sometimes worked for a day or two and been denied my pay. And many will refuse to hire a man so marked, which I can understand. But 'tis the look on folks' faces when they first see my wrists that led me to finally take Fisk's advice and hide them—and I found their fear worse than their contempt.

There was contempt in this man's eyes, as he waited, but his expression was civil enough. I slipped the leather cuff up my arm and extended it.

Whatever message he carried must have been important, for he took a moment to study the mark and make certain of it. Those tattoos are made with magica ink, which cannot be removed even by burning, but only by more magic. To my sight it glowed faintly, but to normal eyes, in the dim alley, even black circles on white skin might be hard to make out.

After a long moment the man nodded confirmation and stepped back as if satisfied—then, with no warning at all, he drew a dagger and plunged it toward my belly.

I jerked away, but only the training my father's arms master pounded into me, not so many years ago, brought my arm sweeping in to knock the strike aside and save my life. I leapt back, and back again as he came after me, trying to grab his knife wrist with my left hand as he struck once more. My right hand fumbled for the knife hilt at my belt and finally found it.

My knife was four inches shorter than his, intended for slicing meat at table and cutting tangled string, or brambles out of a horse's tail. His was a weapon, both edges honed for slashing and with an extremely sharp point.

But reach matters less than speed in a knife fight, and my blade would cut his skin no less readily than his would...had cut mine. As we circled I realized that my side stung, and something wet and warm soaked my shirt and vest.

I shouted for help, but knew 'twas of no use even before he smiled. He'd chosen this place well, the warehouses that surrounded us held timber, not people, and the clamor of the saw pits would drown out any sound that might reach the distant street.

Most of my mind was occupied with watching his knife weave before my belly, his left hand hovering over it to guard and grab if my own blade struck. I was also trying to remember every bit of the debris I'd had no reason to notice, to keep him from backing me into something that might trip me. The cobbles were smooth and rounded underfoot—fine for cart wheels, but awkward even to walk on, much less fight.

However, the tiny part of my mind that wasn't engaged in survival was screaming, and I drew a breath and said the words aloud.

"Why are you doing this?"

Another of those empty smiles tugged the corners of his mouth, but that was all. 'Twas as if I was already dead to him, and no question I asked could matter. Real fear arose, cold, under the controlled exuberant panic of the fight. For the first time, it occurred to me that I should try magic.

I had once controlled a drunken bully by pushing magic though my animal handling Gift, and that oft-used ability to calm and persuade came to my mind as the grip of a well-used tool comes to the palm. I wrapped my will around this Gift, which isn't supposed to work on humans even if they're drunk, and shoved at the heavy lid that covers my magic...and yet again, nothing happened.

I had used magic once before, to protect myself in a fight, but here there was no deep swift river to—

He must have noticed my momentary distraction, for he lunged again.

I leapt back, grabbing for his knife wrist with my free hand. He used his free hand to grab mine, and only a swift swipe of my blade kept me from being gutted. I followed up my block with a slash that opened the back of the hand that gripped mine, jerking free and away as his blade flicked toward my face.

We resumed our wary circling, but I was panting now. Blood dripped from his left hand onto the cobbles, but I could still see that sharp blade flashing past my eyes.

He was trying to kill me, and unless something happened to prevent him, he might succeed. A heartfelt wish for someone to find us, a stumble, a bird to distract him, surfaced in me...and without my even willing it, I felt the slab of thought and intention that blocked my magic slip aside.

Light and power welled from the center of my being, rising and flowing—to my considerable surprise—down though my legs and out the soles of my feet.

I didn't dare look down, but 'twas not my imagination. At the edge of my vision, I saw a soft glow running over the cobbles, like a flooding stream that has come out of its banks... And then I slipped on those glowing stones, scrabbled for footing, and fell.

I had enough control to fall backward instead of toward him, and I began to roll as soon as my butt hit the stones, trying desperately to get out of reach before his knife descended...

The splattering thump of his fall was the sweetest sound I'd ever heard. I stopped rolling, and looked up to see my would-be assassin lying in the midst of a huge puddle of glowing stone.

"What under..." He tried to stand, but his feet flew from beneath him before he'd taken a step, and an understandable confusion slowed his reactions.

I rolled to my hands and knees, and crawled as fast as I could toward the nearest place where no magical glow illuminated the cobbles—cobbles that were as slick under my hands as greased glass. They were so slippery that even crawling my knees kept sliding back or to the side, and I thrust my fingers into the space between the stones to keep my hands upon them.

I heard another fall behind me, and incredulous cursing, but I didn't look back. Indeed, when I reached the stones that didn't feel as if they slithered beneath my hands, I scrambled to my feet and ran all out for the open end of the alley, where sunlight glowed and people moved on the street.

'Twould not take him long to start crawling, as I had, and even if he couldn't see his destination, he'd find the edge of that magical slipperiness soon enough.

I intended to be long gone by the time he did. As soon as I came across a passage, between a rope weaver's yard and a paint maker's, I cast a glance over my shoulder to be sure he wasn't in sight and dashed down it.

On the next street I felt I might slow to a brisk walk— which I much preferred, for my knees were bruised from crawling rapidly over stone, and the stitch in my side from running was almost as painful as the cut.

I pulled the cuff that covered my tattoos back down, and tightened the laces I couldn't knot with one hand, wondering at what my magic had done—for *I'd* had little to do with it.

I had no idea how long the magic that had flowed over those stones would last. It could have vanished minutes after I departed, or it might remain for days. If it lingered there for weeks, would other folk find it? Would some scholar come to study the ordinary patch of cobblestones that had suddenly acquired a most peculiar form of magic?

A professor who studied the human mind and Gifts once told me that the reason man has no magic, and animals and plants do, is because our thinking brains block our access to it. This seemed to me a reasonable explanation for why my magic only surfaced, uncontrollably, in times of great danger or stress—and since that day I'd tried to find some way to bring it forth at will and shape it as I wished. This was the third time it had appeared more or less when I wanted it to, though it had only once taken the form I desired. And what was the point of having such a terrifying and freakish

Gift if I couldn't control it? How could I practice, experiment with it as Fisk suggested, when the only time it seemed to work was when my life was in danger?

I zigged and zagged through several blocks, changing my route at random until I was certain I'd lost him, then made my way back to the inn.

The cut on my ribs had stopped bleeding shortly after I'd stopped running, but it had made a mess of my shirt, drawers, britches and vest.

"Not to mention mending them, once they're clean," said Fisk, mopping dried blood off my back. "Stop twisting around; you'll open it up again."

"'Tis not so deep," I said, ignoring his orders and craning my neck to look at the cut. "It stings more than anything."

"Maybe." Fisk reached for the bandages. "But that knife went through two layers of cloth before it reached you. Whoever he was, he wasn't playing around. Which seems odd, in broad daylight, with a mark who's dressed as if he hadn't two fracts to rub together."

"I don't think he sought to rob me." I'd been thinking about this as I walked home. "He never asked me for my purse, which most robbers do. He only asked my name...no, he already *knew* my name! He asked to see my wrists, to confirm my identity before he struck. He followed me down that alley because he wanted to kill me, and for no other reason."

'Twas a thought I found chilling, and Fisk's expression was sober.

"There must have been some reason. Oh, I agree he was stalking you. But why would he want to kill you? We haven't left that many enemies in our...hmm."

I'd already compiled the list. "Lady Ceciel. She didn't seem to bear much of a grudge—indeed, she should have been grateful we didn't haul her back to face trial—but we did put a stop to her experiments. Master Worthington lost everything because we exposed his scheme. That miller in Mickelson, who was cheating his customers. Master Humphreys, whose poor wife we helped to escape him."

"Several others." Fisk's hands, wrapping bandages around my body, slowed. "Any number of wreckers, some of whom must have escaped. And a lot of Roseman's men were loyal to him... All right, there are quite a few people who might hold a grudge. But I think most of them would want to do it themselves, instead of hiring an assassin. You're sure—"

"Positive." I had already answered this question twice. "I've never seen him before today."

"That you remember." Fisk tied off the bandage, and picked up the bloody rags he'd used to mop me up. "You didn't meet some of Roseman's men, who stayed at his town house, and neither of us even set eyes on most of those wreckers. And there's another possibility, too. Thank goodness I'll be able to get all this blood out of sight before Kathy gets—"

The door flew open as if on cue, and my sister burst into the room.

"They didn't change horses, but I found... What happened? Fisk, are you hurt? You're covered with blood!"

In fact, he'd kept himself remarkably neat as he cleaned me up, and I hadn't yet put on a shirt to conceal my bandages. The cloths Fisk held looked gruesome I grant you, but still... It must be love.

Fisk reached the same conclusion, and the soft look he kept only for Kathy came over his face.

"I'm fine, and Michael's only got a clean cut, so he'll be fine too. But remember that sense you had, that someone was following us? It looks like you were right. We'll tell you the whole tale over dinner."

"If Michael can ride," said my loving sister, "you can tell me on the road. I didn't find an inn where they changed horses, I found where Rupert spent the night. He left there just this morning, heading west. We're less than a day behind him!"

CHAPTER 8

Fisk

Michael told Kathy his story as we rode westward. She couldn't think of any reason someone would kill to keep us from finding Rupert, but she didn't seem too surprised.

"'Tis Michael," she told me. "You can send him off to the safest place you can think of, and he'll still get into trouble."

"I'm right here," Michael pointed out. "And 'twas not my fault those bees had built a nest in Uncle Rory's garden shed. And that time with the millstream, I hardly..."

I'd have found this argument amusing, if not for the fact that anyone who wanted to kill Michael was probably...unhappy with me, as well.

I also knew that, just because over the next few days Kathy no longer sensed anyone tracking us, that didn't mean no one was tracking us.

❖

We rode toward the mountains until sunset forced us to make camp, and according to the people in the last village, we'd narrowed Rupert's lead by another hour. Kathy wanted to press onward, but with the larger moon waning toward a Darkling Night, Michael refused to risk the horses' legs. I was more concerned for our necks, but it was because of the horses that Kathy agreed.

My noble not-quite-fiancée made no fuss about sleeping in a bedroll on the ground, which I found remarkable...until Michael told me that as a girl she'd tagged along with her brothers on hunting expeditions, sleeping rougher than we were now. She giggled at my shocked expression.

Michael woke us before dawn, and it was cool enough we were glad of our coats. We watched sunrise from the saddle, the light first painting the mountains' highest peaks with peach-colored light, which brightened as it rolled down their sides.

The next village we passed through was small enough that we found Rupert's trail swiftly, and he was now only three hours ahead of us. Further, he was only a day behind the carriage, which in a small town this far from Crown City was almost as remarkable as Rupert's horse.

The connection that occurred to me was so tenuous that I hesitated to mention it. Unfortunately, Kathy was getting to know me pretty well.

"Out with it, love. What's bothering you?"

We were riding away from the village, and it wasn't too hot yet...so why did she look so kissable? But she also looked like a woman who wanted an answer. I sighed.

"It may be nothing, but we've been talking so much about that coach, it got me thinking. Michael, do you remember what Quicken's brother-in-law told us about the nobleman who bribed him to report on the project?"

He had to think a moment, calling it back to mind, though it was less than a month ago we'd been desperately trying to discover who was sabotaging the Heir's project—and framing Michael's brother Benton for murder in the process.

"He said the man who paid him, and took Quicken's reports, was a slender man with a noble's accent. His coach was fine, though the crest had been... No, surely that's too great a coincidence. It can't be the same coach. Why should it be?"

"Since we have no idea who they are, or why anyone would bribe Quicken to spy, or why someone's evidently kidnapped Mistress Merkle, I can't say. But note the common thread?"

"That the goal of the project was to discover some way for Margaret to bear a Gifted child. But—"

"And reports on that project were paid for by a man who traveled in a coach that once had a crest on the door," The connections grew tighter as I thought them through. "A slender man presided over Mistress Margaret's kidnapping...in a coach with a scratched-off crest."

"I said I see it." Michael sounded a bit testy. "But there must be scores, hundreds of coaches and carriages sold by their owners when they acquire a newer vehicle. Once the first owner sells them, the new owner would be bound to remove the crest. Indeed, the seller would probably remove it before he let the coach go."

"I know that. I said it might be nothing."

But people were more likely to paint over a crest than scratch it off, and since the project had been about Mistress Margaret...maybe it wasn't so tenuous after all.

The last village was even smaller, only a few dozen cottages and a smithy where the forge hadn't even been fired since there was no work today. The idle smith, who was happy to trade his time for a few coins, remembered Rupert, and also the coach that had passed through just yesterday. It was dusty, and moving too fast for the horses to keep up that pace much longer, but they likely hadn't had to. Jane Scarson had been cutting lettuce in her garden and she'd seen it turn onto the track that led to the old keep, with four men riding beside it like it carried a payroll or some such thing.

"Four men riding escort?" Michael asked intently. "'Twas only two the last we heard of them."

"Well they must have picked up two more, 'cause there was four when they came through here, looking around all sharp like."

"Does the road they took go anywhere beside this old keep?" Kathy asked. "Tell us about it."

"Not much to tell. Baron Tatterman's grandfather was the one who moved out, and they say it's still sound, though no one's lived there for nigh fifty years. And no reason for anyone to go there now, far as I can see," he added.

For the most part he was probably right, but it sounded like an ideal place to hold someone prisoner for weeks, or even months. Kathy, Michael and I exchanged a glance that acknowledged this.

He gave us directions that were full of local land-marks like, "then take the track that runs through that field where Mack Dunn planted that fancy squash three years ago," but Michael, raised in the country-side, thought he could find it.

The road that left the village wasn't bad, for a coun-try road. The lane we turned off on, to go in the direc-tion of the keep, consisted of two ruts free of grass and weeds. The track that led to the keep itself was only a slightly wider break in the bushes, and I'd have ridden past it if Michael hadn't stopped us.

He was proven right a few hundred yards later, when a damp patch of earth showed the clear lines made by carriage wheels and a number of hoof prints. One set looked fresher than the others, even to my city eyes.

"We're about to catch up to them!" Kathy's face glowed with triumph, and I was pretty pleased myself.

If we could free Mistress Margaret and take her and Rupert home, I could claim the reward. If we couldn't free her, I could convince the others, Rupert included, that we needed to get help from the Liege...and still claim the reward. If we took the straightest route back to the palace, not needing to stop and figure out where our quarry had gone next, we could probably reach Crown City in less than three days.

"Let's go get your friend," I said.

But Michael pulled Chant to a stop. "Listen."

The sound he'd heard was a faint, but persistent se-ries of bangs. Then they stopped, and I had just con-cluded that whatever it was had finished when they started again.

"Come on." Michael kicked Chant to a canter.

Kathy followed immediately, but I took a moment to curse before sending Tipple after them. I don't like running horses over rough ground, but I liked the thought of Kathy learning about my fears even less.

Michael had been thrown onto a saddle before he could walk, and judging by Kathy's horsemanship, their father must have treated his girl children the same way.

Fortunately, we didn't have to go far. The sound of banging, soon interspersed by shouts, grew louder. The woods thinned and the old keep came into view.

This close to the mountains, rolling foothills had begun pushing their way out onto the river plain, and this keep had been built on one of them. It must have a well inside because there was no stream in sight, and this had prevented them from building a moat—but every other defensive measure of the day was visible. The tall stone walls sported towers at the corners, and there would be a walkway behind the rampart, where bowmen could hide and swordsmen could fight. There were even spouts for them to pour hot oil and pitch down on invaders, and it was just as well there was no one on the ramparts now because the place was being assaulted. After a fashion.

Rupert stood in front of two great wooden gates, secured with iron hinges, banging on one of them with a rock. As we slowed to a trot, he dropped it and ran back a dozen paces to shout, "I know she's in there. I saw her at the window! And if she's hurt in any way, I'll devote my whole life and all the Liege's power to tracking you down. Meg! Meg, can you hear me? I'm coming!"

It didn't look to me like he was coming anytime soon. When Michael and Kathy dismounted I took all the horses and tethered them, including Rupert's weary, once white stallion. He seemed grateful for the attention.

I was happy to leave the distraught Heir to Michael and Kathy—if he'd been waving his arms and babbling at me, I'd have been tempted to slap some sense into him. Though as I drew near enough to see him better, my exasperation lessened. The fancy gold-embroidered coat had been traded somewhere along the line for one of plain cloth, which went badly with his silk vest. His britches were so dusty they almost matched the coat, and several days of stubble bristled on his chin. He looked so bedraggled that it occurred to me to wonder what it had been like to travel across the countryside for five days without escort or servants, for what was probably the first time in his life.

And he hadn't quit. All things considered, the kid had earned some slack, even if this was nonsense.

"I saw her at the window." His voice was hoarse with shouting, emotion, or both. "She was looking out, almost as if she was waiting for me. She screamed when she saw me, and they came and dragged her away. But she's in there!"

"So that's when you started pounding on the gates with a rock?" I asked pleasantly.

It cut through his hysteria as Michael and Kathy's sympathy hadn't, and he glared at me.

"I *knocked* and demanded admittance. But no one answered."

"And then you started pounding a rock on gates designed to withstand a battering ram?"

"Then I walked around the walls," Rupert said with some dignity. "Looking for a postern door or some other way in. But this is the only entrance."

"So then...?" I asked.

Color rose in his stubbled cheeks. "I started pounding on the gates with a rock. And you're right, 'tis stupid, but after all this time... She's *in* there!"

He looked like he was about to pick up the rock again, and Michael spoke hastily. "So now what?" His voice was low, having clearly realized that just because we couldn't see them, that didn't mean they couldn't hear us. "Fisk, can you burgle us in?"

"Are you mad?" My voice was quite a bit louder than his, and Kathy cast me a questioning look. "This place was designed to keep an army out, and the gates are latched on the inside. Unless you can fly, there's no way in short of siege ladders and catapults. We'll have to go back to the High Liege and get a writ. And a troop to enforce it."

"Go back?" Rupert's voice didn't just rise in volume, it shot up half an octave. "I'm not leaving this spot till I've got Meg with me!"

"And how do you propose to get her out of there?"

I let the silence draw out long enough to make it clear he didn't have an answer, and then went on.

"We can't be sure that... Whose fief is this? Baron Tatterman? We can't be sure he's the one holding her, even if it is his keep. But now that we know where she is, the Liege can write up a writ and warrant demanding that Tatterman either release her, or aid the Liege's troops in getting her out. It's not even noon yet. If we rented fresh horses and made really good time, we might be back here with a troop in three days."

We probably couldn't, but it wasn't so ridiculous that anyone who might be listening could discount the possibility.

"But what if—" Rupert began.

My clever darling laid a hand on his arm, and only Michael and I were close enough to see her nails dig in.

"Fisk is right, Rupert. We can't assault a keep with just the four of us. The faster we leave, the sooner we can return. Call up to Meg, and tell her we'll be back soon, and set her free."

Rupert had broken out of his funk enough to realize we were up to something, so he did as he was told, and even mounted his horse and rode off with us. The way he kept turning to look back added verisimilitude, so I didn't try to stop him.

He even waited till we were out of sight of the keep before he reined his horse to a stop.

"What do you think you're doing? It would take at least five days to go to the city, gather a troop and get back here. And that's assuming Father would give us even a writ, much less soldiers. I think those are his own men in there!"

"Baron Tatterman's not particularly political," said Kathy. "I don't know if he's involved in the tax thing, but he doesn't come to court much. Why not ask him for help?"

Asking anyone for help was exactly what the source of the reward *didn't* want us to do. But I saw no need to mention that.

"We're about to find out who holds her," I said. "They think we're going back to Crown City to get a writ and an army, so—"

"They may think that," Michael put in. "Or they may start wondering why we were discussing our plans so publicly, and think again."

"It wasn't my most subtle performance," I conceded. "But they've got to believe there's at least a chance we're going to the Liege for assistance. And if they're working *for* the Liege..."

"They'll know he won't give it to us." Kathy's eyes were bright with admiration, which I found quite pleasant. "So they'll just sit there, because they know they're safe."

"And if they pack up their coach and run," I went on. "We'll know they're *not* working for the Liege. In which case, we really should go back and get a warrant."

The glow in my beloved's face chilled abruptly.

"Rupert, you should know your father has offered Fisk and Michael a reward to bring you back. Though I don't think *Michael* cares about that."

"The reason I care about it is because *I* want to get married." I tried not to let my exasperation show, but I may have failed. "I thought you wanted that too, but if I'm mistaken, I'd appreciate it if you'd let me know."

"I don't want to marry anyone at the cost of my best friend's life." Kathy didn't even try to hide her anger. "I thought *you* understood that."

"I don't give a rat's ass if either of you gets married," Rupert said. "I want Meg safely out of there, and I don't know..."

His voice cracked, but his determination never wavered.

Michael sighed. "There's no point in this, for Fisk has the right of it. If 'tis the Liege who holds her, they'll stay where they are. And she'll be safe enough while you return to Crown City to deal with your father. For I see no way to pry her out of that keep with just the four of us."

It was clear that Rupert didn't like this, but he was thinking now and he nodded reluctantly.

"And if 'tis not my father who holds her? What then?"

"Then, even if they suspect we're bluffing, they won't dare to call it," I said. "They'll have to move her."

"And in that case... Assume there's one man in the coach with Mistress Margaret, the driver, and four men

riding escort, that makes it six against the three of us."
Michael's voice was serious, but the joy of "adventure"
brightened his eyes. "Even so, they'll still be more vulnerable to whatever we can contrive on the road than
they are behind those walls."

"Six to four," said Katherine, who'd never been in a
fight in her life. "And don't count Meg out, either."

Michael and I were tactfully silent. Unfortunately,
Kathy isn't a fool. At least now she was glaring at both
of us.

"Don't worry about that," Rupert said. "'Tis not likely
to arise, because I still think those men are working for
my father."

"Then let us find a place to make camp," said Michael. "Somewhere we can watch the gates and remain
unseen. In a day or two, we shall know one way or the
other."

Michael's proposal was so sensible that none of us
could argue—though there was plenty of aggravation to
go around. Rupert alternately fretted and sulked. Kathy
scowled at me, and tried to do things around the camp
that would prove she could fight as well as any man—
but after years of traveling together Michael and I had
that process down pat, and she mostly got in the way.

There was no place to camp where we could see
the gates and they couldn't see us, which wasn't surprising once you thought about it. But we did find a
place where one or two people could hide and watch
the gates. If any happened, they could call back to the
small gulley where we'd spread our bedrolls.

I don't know if Michael was more worried we'd start kissing or that we'd quarrel, but he chose to watch with Kathy himself, leaving me to take the next watch with Rupert. That wasn't as bad as I'd expected, because no one can stand on an emotional peak forever. After we'd both grown thoroughly bored staring at blank stone walls, I asked about his stint at the university where he'd met Margaret. We got into an interesting discussion of Magolis' theory that history wasn't based on individual actions, but on larger needs and forces. I thought Magolis' ideas had some merit when it came to the great drought that started the warring period. If your people are starving, even a village mayor will take up arms, much less a baron with a troop at his disposal. If one of them hadn't gone first, another would have. I was less sure about Margolis' assertion that sooner or later someone would have united the Realm—the first High Liege had needed to be insanely ambitious and incredibly capable to bring that off.

Rupert not only thought the whole theory was nonsense, he argued his point cogently enough to prove Kathy's claim that he had more brains than he'd showed so far.

Not that Kathy or I had been showing a lot of intelligence lately.

By late evening, we decided they were unlikely to set off tonight, the horses were thirsty and our water flasks were running low. We left Michael to keep watch, while Kathy, Rupert and I took the horses in search of a stream. When we found it, I loaned Rupert some clothes from Michael's and my packs, and washed his dirty coat and britches while he gave himself a cold shave. Kathy took the time for a rough wash as well, splashing the cool water over her face and up her arms. She looked so lovely with the orange light of sunset gleaming in the droplets that ran down her throat and fell from the dripping strands of her hair...

I told her I'd never ask her to abandon Mistress Merkle to her fate, Kathy said she did want to marry me, and we went back to camp much happier than when we'd left it.

Michael must have figured that more making up would be good for us, because next morning he put us on gate-watch together—though crouching on hard ground behind a screen of bracken is not my idea of a romantic setting, and we were both half asleep.

We were just beginning to wake up enough for conversation when the gates opened and a coach rolled out, escorted by four riders.

Kathy warbled like a bird, which was the signal we'd agreed on. I noted that while the driver didn't appear to be armed, all four riders wore swords on their belts. I only saw one crossbow, hanging off a saddle, but that didn't mean there weren't more.

We were too far from the road to see inside the coach, but the driver and escort outnumbered us five to three...and to my considerable sorrow, it looked like that might matter.

I'd *really* been hoping that Rupert would be right.

He and Michael crawled up beside us as the coach rolled past, and it did match the description Quicken's brother-in-law had given us; darkish wood, well-varnished but with very little gilt. I'd pictured the place where the crest had been scratched off as a circle or an oval, but it had four symmetrical branches coming off a central core, like a fleur de lis or a stylized flame.

The Heir was controlled now, but his face was white with the tension of watching his lover pass so near.

"If Father doesn't have her, then who does?" The coach was pulling away, but he kept his voice low. "Who could possibly want to hurt *Meg*?"

"We don't know." Kathy's soft voice reflected his pain and terror, and the fragment of irritation that still lingered from our quarrel left me.

"It might make sense if they were after you, Rupert," she went on. "But if they were, they'd have run out and seized you when you were banging on that gate. So we don't have any idea who's behind this. Or why they're doing it."

"We've got to go." Rupert turned to crawl back to the horses; the coach wasn't quite out of sight. "We've got to go after them, now!"

Michael grabbed his arm. "Not so swiftly. We'll follow at a distance, and wait till we can try something that might succeed. They think we're all riding toward Crown City, so they may become careless."

"I hate to say it," I added, "but we really do need a writ and warrant. Even if we could overcome them—at least five men, likely six, and maybe more—what then? We can't hold that many people prisoner. We'll have to get help from the authorities, and without a writ..."

And as we all knew, Rupert was the best person to convince the High Liege to write one.

Then my sweetheart spoke up.

"You can forge a writ. Can't you, Fisk? I know you've done forgeries in the past. You've bragged...ah, you've said so."

"Thank you, darling," I said dryly. "You do know that forging a Liege writ is a hanging offence? Treason is one of the few crimes besides murder that carries that sentence."

"I'll get you off," Rupert said.

"You can't even get your father to give you a writ!"

"Fisk," said Michael. "We don't know who holds this girl, or what they intend by her."

They were all staring at me, curse it. And Katherine's heart was in her eyes.

"Oh, all right. We'll go after her. And I'll see if I can pick up what I need in the next large town. Forging a Liege writ isn't simple. They use special paper, and..."

It may have been crazy. I knew it was crazy. But when Kathy kissed me, it all seemed worthwhile.

CHAPTER 9

Michael

Since I first took up knight errantry, I've done many odd things. I must confess, I never thought highroad robbery would be one of them, but the undeniable fact remained—we needed to hold up a coach.

And as the day went on, I found my respect for bandits rising; 'tis not as easy as you might think.

The first problem, as we shortly determined, is that 'tis difficult to set up an ambush for a coach you're *following*.

Had we been ordinary bandits we could have chosen some lonely place, set up a roadblock, and robbed the first person who came into our snare.

We needed to rob one particular coach, whose destination and route we didn't know. We might have simply followed them to a deserted stretch of road and ridden down on them...had they not outnumbered us two to one, which made a straightforward assault sheer folly.

No, we had to ambush them. And if possible, we needed to whittle down their numbers as well.

No possibility of that arose till they stopped for luncheon the next day, in a town where the main road ran through, instead of crossing another road they might have taken. We'd been able to draw nearer in the busy streets, and when they pulled into an inn yard we simply rode past, and then turned down a side street to discuss the matter.

"I think they're heading north," Kathy said. "This is Littledean, which means we're only about six miles from the Pottage River. Beyond that all the landholders are angry with the Liege about mineral rights. We'll get no help from them, and it's the last place the Liege wants to send a troop. From the gossip I've heard, what Roseman tried is giving some of them ideas."

"Roseman failed," I pointed out. "But if we can assume the coach will continue in that direction, let us ride ahead and see if we can find a place to block the road."

"Even if we block the road," said Fisk, "there's still six of them and three of us."

The barest thread of a plan was rising in my mind. "Mayhap not, if we can block the way so well that someone has to go get help to clear it. And no, Rupert, we can't go back and assault them in an inn full of innocent bystanders."

Rupert, who'd been waiting for an opening in the conversation, didn't look convinced.

Fisk added, "Not to mention grooms and waiters, who'd fight to protect their customers. From people who look more like criminals than the guys in the coach do."

"Unless the sheriff would help us," Kathy said slowly. "Surely if Rupert presented himself, and told the sheriff a kidnapping was taking place in his town..."

There was a long silence. Fisk didn't want to go to the law because the Liege and Master Arnold had told him not to, and he didn't want to imperil his reward. I didn't want to, because as an unredeemed man, my mere presence would make the authorities reluctant to aid anyone I was with. Though if Rupert thought he could pull it off, I was willing to try.

"No," said Rupert finally. "If I had my proper entourage, had some clean clothes and that kind of thing, I would. As it is, 'twould take me so long to convince them I'm the Heir the coach would be long gone."

"So 'tis up to us, and we must press on ahead of them and see what we can arrange." I would have kicked Chant to a gallop then and there, had the street not been filled with shopping housewives, apprentices on errands, and a collier's cart that took up half the lane.

Once we were free of the town we set off at a canter, but soon slowed to alternating between a walk and a trot, which is the best pace a horse can maintain—and we rode for several hours before we found what we were looking for.

The good part was, 'twas a perfect place to block the road. Indeed, 'twas the only place we found where we could set an obstruction and they couldn't simply drive off the road and around it.

The bad part was, 'twas the bridge that spanned the Pottage River. If they crossed despite our efforts, we'd be unlikely to get any help from the authorities even if we had days to convince them.

The other bad part was that open fields surrounded the bridge, the nearest cover being a copse of pines almost a quarter mile back down the road.

"They'll see us coming," was the first thing Rupert said.

"So they will," Fisk agreed. "But we might be able to use that to our advantage. If their attention was fixed on someone riding toward them, people hidden down below the riverbank might be able to get pretty close before they were seen."

Trust Fisk to know how to run a highroad robbery.

"First we'll need to block their entrance to the bridge," I said. "Thank goodness there's not much traffic." In all the way from the town we'd passed just one farm cart, and I prayed that luck would hold.

"How can you block the bridge?" Kathy asked. "There's no gate, no big rocks, and anything you could move into their way, they could just move out of it. They won't be that far behind us, either."

"I've an idea for that," I said. "'Tis simple."

Well, 'twas simple in concept. In reality, dragging one of the logs I'd seen embedded in the river's mud up onto the road, even with a rope and four horses, was one of the trickiest things I've done in some time.

'Twas easy, if muddy, to clamber down the steep, six-foot bank and select a log large enough that 'twould be impossible for men to move, but small enough for our horses to drag. I had already resigned myself to losing my good, long rope... A long rope is something most don't bother to pack, for 'tis bulky and one seldom needs it. Fisk's and my roving life was sufficiently un-predictable that I did carry rope. We used it seldom... but when we needed it we needed it badly, and 'twas there.

Even with the rope, cut into four pieces and tied off to each saddle, the great muddy log, with spikes of root and branch protruding, twisted and rolled as we hauled it forward. Rupert had to climb down to help me wrestle it into a position where it could be towed over the lip of the bank, while Fisk and Kathy handled the uneasy horses.

Once we got it out of the riverbed, 'twas much easier to drag it over the flat ground. As Fisk and Kathy supervised its placement across the entrance to the bridge, Rupert and I splashed into the river's shallows to wash off some of the mud, for we were coated with the stuff from brow to heels.

By the time we hauled our dripping selves up the bank, Fisk had cut the ropes free of the log and coiled them, and we all mounted and cantered down the road to the copse, to wait and plot.

"Why can't they use their horses to pull the log aside?" Rupert asked.

"They can," I said. "Both the carriage horses and the ones they ride...if they have some way to tether the log to saddle or harness. They'd need a rope that's both long enough and strong enough, and I'm betting they won't have one."

"I'm more worried..." But Fisk fell silent before he finished, for the coach had come into view.

'Twas still accompanied by four outriders, and Fisk had told me during our morning ride that one of them carried a crossbow. What surprised me was not that they had only one, but that they had one at all. They're fearsome weapons, but their short heavy bolts veer off course long before an arrow will, and they're expensive as well, so few favor them for hunting. The only reason I'd gotten the chance to shoot one was because my great great grandfather's guardsmen had taken it from an assassin after he'd put the bolt through great great's shoulder, leaving him unable to raise that arm above his head for the rest of his life.

Crossbow bolts might not be as accurate over long distance, but they destroy what they hit. I'd no desire to encounter one from the sharp side.

We'd tethered our horses and True on the far side of the small glade, and there were other horses pastured nearby so even if one of them neighed 'twould not give us away. True, being mute, could make no sound even if he wished, but our good horses were silent too as we watched the carriage roll past. The outriders didn't look as if they thought we might be following. They rode two before the coach, and two far enough behind it that the dust wouldn't trouble them. Both pairs chatted casually, as men will on a long ride.

Rupert's fists were clenched so tight his knuckles whitened, but they were still six to our three.

"What worries me," Fisk murmured, after the last rider was out of earshot, "is how many men they'll leave behind. If they send one man for help to clear the road, that leaves still five to three. And for all we know there might be two or three men in that coach with Mistress Margaret. And they'll all be on the alert, once they've seen the log."

"Five to four," Kathy said stubbornly. She and Fisk and been arguing about her part in this affray since we left town—and so far as I could tell, neither was winning.

"If they send just one man for aid, we can ride from the other side of the copse and ambush him before he reaches town," I said. "Once they realize he's not coming back, they'll send more men, mayhap two more, which would bring their number even to ours."

"Leaving three to five of us at the coach, if they sent off two more men," Kathy said. "Assuming Meg's in a position to fight."

The riders out in front had seen the log. They cantered forward and dismounted to inspect it, one going so far as to grasp the protruding roots and try to roll it. The only thing he accomplished was to muddy his waistcoat and britches, and he was rubbing them with a kerchief when the coach came up and stopped.

At this distance we couldn't tell who was in command or what he said, but the riders abruptly turned to gaze outward, looking for the ambush that log all but proclaimed.

"What if they're smart enough to send two men for help, right from the start?" Fisk's voice was low, though the kidnappers wouldn't hear anything short of a shout. "Or even three, to keep us from taking them out on the road."

"I think the four of us could probably take two," I said, and Kathy gave me an approving nod. "But if they split their number and send three, we simply wait till the riders have passed and then attack the coach."

"Well, waiting while they ride past will be simple," Fisk said.

I didn't bother to reply, for the drama at the bridge commanded my attention.

No ambush having occurred, the outriders turned their attention to the log—though I noticed the coach driver kept his gaze on the countryside, and his high perch gave him a fine view.

The outriders all dismounted and tried to move the log, which resulted in naught but more muddy clothing. One of them then went to the back of the coach, where he opened the luggage compartment and searched through it for some time before pulling out two long leather straps.

"Spare reins for the coach horses," Rupert said, as they tied the log to two saddles and prepared to lead their horses forward. "We should have known they'd have those."

"I did," I said. "But I doubt they're strong enough."

Two horses might have been able to drag the log over the hard-packed earth of the roadway, but I was proved right when one of the taught straps snapped, recoiling so hard it struck the horse who'd pulled it. He bucked and kicked, and his fellow, still fastened to the log, shied violently.

And the fact that they'd used those flimsy reins in the first place meant...

"No one carries rope," I murmured.

"Yes, you told me so," said Fisk—rather unfairly, as I'd said nothing of the kind. Though remembering years of his complaints when we'd unpacked and re-packed the unwieldy coil... I must confess, I'd thought about saying it.

Considerable discussion ensued at the bridge, but the end of it was that three wary-looking men mounted their horses and trotted back toward town. To my considerable satisfaction, one of them was the man with the crossbow strapped to his saddle.

"We'd best get moving," I told Rupert. "Fisk, you should be able to see when we reach the river, but be sure to give us time to get to the bridge before you and Kathy approach."

"I'm in no hurry," Fisk assured me. "None at all."

"I am," said Kathy. "But we'll wait."

The final plan was a combination of Fisk's idea and mine. He and Kathy would ride slowly toward the coach, drawing the villains' attention and mayhap even pulling the remaining outrider away from our target. Rupert and I were already wet and muddy, but there were other reasons we should be the ones to creep down the riverbed under cover of that high bank. One of those reasons was Fisk's passionate insistence that once the distraction had done its work, Kathy should turn the horse and gallop out of range of the fighting. But since he had no way to force Kathy to fall in with that plan... At all events, while everyone was watching Fisk and Kathy (who I thought would be quarrelling robustly at that point) Rupert and I could creep up and get the drop on them.

'Twas not the best plan, I admit. But given even numbers and the lack of cover around that coach, I defy anyone to come up with better.

We hadn't time to scout the dry gulley that ran from behind the copse down to the river, and the bottom was overgrown with weeds and low bushes, so it took some trouble to traverse.

The end of the gulley was far enough from the bridge that I risked standing up to wave at the place where we'd left our allies. I couldn't see them, concealed in the trees, but when we departed Kathy had been whittling the branches off of a stout "walking stick." Fisk, in no way deceived by this euphuism, said he'd come up with a way to make them look less like the people these men had probably seen all too clearly from the old keep's ramparts. He would be trying to contrive some way to keep Kathy from using that stick as a weapon, too, and since the only horse we had that wasn't remarkable in some way was Posy, I thought this was asking a lot, even of Fisk...but my ex-squire and new partner is most inventive about such things.

Rupert took my orders without question, and he made less noise in the log-choked shallows than I'd expected. With the task at hand, and so much riding on it, his nerves seemed to settle and his face showed a cool resolve I found quite heartening.

As we drew near the bridge I spotted a log that had been thrust up against the bank by some long past flood, providing...not a ramp, mayhap, but at least a mounting block to climb out of the riverbed.

Even better, some of those small bushes were growing on the flat ground above it. I signaled for Rupert to hide under the bridge while I climbed up to wait for our diversion to appear.

It took them long enough that my wet clothing grew cold. My muscles might have stiffened, but for the exuberant energy of action that sang through me. And as it turned out, 'twas worth the wait.

Fisk and Kathy came trotting down the road. The first thing I noticed was that Kathy, now wearing an ordinary skirt that showed her legs to her knee as it slid up, was mounted on Tipple, while Fisk bestrode Posy. He had also stripped the ribbons from Kathy's straw hat and wore it himself. Her hair, which had been braided round her head when these men saw her last, now flowed free. Fisk had also given her one of my more voluminous shirts, which hung loose over a huge mound of something-or-other that had been bound to her stomach.

Given the anxiety with which Fisk leaned over her, it didn't need the way she clutched her girth, or the groans I'm sure she was emitting even though I couldn't hear them, to tell everyone who watched that a new babe was about to enter the world.

I shook so hard with laughter, I almost slipped from my perch. That fake pregnancy was not only a fabulous distraction, 'twas awkward enough it might actually keep her out of the fight. And if it didn't, 'twould serve almost as well as light armor to protect her vulnerable belly.

One should *never* underestimate Fisk.

"What do we do?" I heard one of the kidnappers ask. "What do we do if she pops it *here*?"

"Warn them away." This voice held authority, its accent much finer than the first speaker's. "Tell them the bridge is blocked."

"But they can ride around the log," the third man said. "Wouldn't that be the best way to get rid of 'em?" I heard the first faint groan from Kathy, and he added. "Get rid of 'em *quick*!"

They'd never be more distracted than they were now. I signaled to Rupert that 'twas time, and drew my sword, slowly enough to keep the steel from rasping as it came free. I was still well below the top of the bank, but I leapt up high enough to land my belly on solid ground and crawled as quickly as I could to the bushes—which proved too short. I might have been partly screened from the rider and the coach's passengers, but the driver could look right down upon me.

Fortunately, he was staring up the road with the consternation any man would feel at the sight of a woman who was apparently about to give birth right then and there.

I stood as quietly as I could and began walking toward the remaining outrider. Fisk covered my approach with a shout for help, was there a woman with them, could he borrow the coach...?

The man was still mounted, which was a pity. Had he been on his feet I might have been able to strike his head with my sword hilt and thus take him out of the fight. But his head, clad in a broad-brimmed felt hat much like the one I often wore, was beyond my reach.

It would have been possible to run my blade through his unprotected back, but even though I knew him for a villain I couldn't slay him in cold blood—indeed, no man who wasn't a monster could.

His horse was aware of me, one ear flicking back, but it offered no other warning of my presence. I patted its rump reassuringly, before reaching up to grab its rider's belt and drag him, with a startled squawk, from the saddle.

This brought his head into range and had it not been for his hat, and his quick lurch to one side, I might have ended my fight with him right there. But startled as he was he started moving instantly, and what should have been a solid thump behind one ear glanced off.

He drew his sword as he turned, shouting a warning, and I slashed his wrist in yet another blow that could have ended our fight...only to discover that, like me, he wore a stiffened leather cuff beneath his sleeve.

Blood welled from his wrist but 'twas not enough. As he came fully to his feet he lunged at me, with a low and expert stroke I should have expected but did not. I barely managed to parry as I scrambled out of his reach.

The first lesson my father's arms master had taught me—by dint of several painful bruises—was to keep my gaze on my opponent. I parried several quick thrusts, but he seemed to be more interested in testing my guard than running me through. Even as I noted that this man knew what he was about, I saw Fisk, with

Kathy's long stick in his hand, dash behind my opponent's back...and keep right on running toward the coach.

But my surge of exasperation subsided when I heard the clack of wood striking wood and the thrum of a bowstring. I never saw the arrow, but whoever 'twas aimed at, Fisk had kept it from finding its mark—and that stick was long enough for him to keep the man from getting off another shot, which mattered more than ending my small affray.

My opponent lunged once more, a stroke that started low but changed course and swept up as I moved to block. Had I been trying to strike at him I might not have managed to parry, but I was simply blocking his blows. This was another of the arms master's lessons, for 'tis easier to defend yourself than defend and attack...and, he said, if you just wait long enough your chance will come. This gave me time to observe my opponent as well. He was some years older than I— as most men are—with a bravo's bold mustache and rough, serviceable garb. But the body beneath those drab clothes was hard, lean, and quick enough to keep me jumping.

Our circling brought the carriage into view. I didn't dare take my gaze from my attacker, but I heard Fisk trying to persuade the driver to put down his bow and give it up, and caught a glimpse of Kathy, big belly and all, standing on the narrow iron step and reaching through the window in the coach's door—probably trying to unlock it. As I watched, she shrieked and pulled back, clutching her hand. But even when she fell away from it, the still coach rocked. Rupert must have gone around to the other side of it, for guttural grunts and gasps revealed some battle—

Seeing my distraction, my opponent tried another swift low strike. I managed a partial block, but it still sliced into the skin above my knee like a hot wire. My leg held when I leapt back, so it couldn't be deep, but 'twas clearly time to end this.

"Fisk," I shouted. "No, *Kathy*. Grab a rock and bash this fellow. You can break into the coach later."

We had circled so I faced the carriage once more. My attacker twitched, but he didn't make the mistake of turning round. If Kathy came to my aid he'd have to turn and face her—and then, either way, he'd be done for.

He knew it too. He stepped to one side, away from the river, then took another step, his blade beginning to fall.

"You can leave," I told him. "Get on your horse and just ride away. Whatever they pay you, 'twill not be worth—"

A clangor of warning rang though my body, as if all the alarm bells in the Realm pealed suddenly in my ears. I was already down, rolling away, before I realized that 'twas my warning Gift that had spoken, though I'd never felt it near this strongly.

Yet, quickly as I moved, the crossbow bolt tore a long scratch across my ribs before it flew through the space where my body had been...and then punched through my opponent's side. He dropped his sword and shrieked as his blood splattered.

I caught a flashing glimpse of a man clambering out of the riverbed, hampered by the crossbow he carried... and even in bright sunlight, I could see the glow of magica around it.

I shouted a warning, and launched myself in a scrabbling, diving roll under the carriage—the only thing in sight that might stop a crossbow bolt.

I came to my feet on the other side, and was almost kicked in the face. Rupert had somehow wedged his whole upper body though the window in the carriage door. 'Twas the largest of the three windows, but 'twas still not large, and he seemed to be firmly stuck there as he struggled with someone inside.

Since the driver was the only opponent I could reach, I resolved to take at least one villain out of the fight, and started to climb up to his bench...only to drop back in a hurry, as he turned and aimed a kick at me.

I had just time to realize that Fisk was no longer holding his attention on the coach's other side, when my partner came dashing around the coach's rear wheels.

"There's a man over there with a crossbow!"

"I know. That's why—"

The carriage abruptly stopped rocking, and the sounds of combat ceased. Rupert slithered out, his face flushed with exertion where it wasn't darkening with bruises, but his movements were slow and controlled.

I looked within, since the window was no longer full of Rupert. Even in the shadowed interior I could make out the flash of a knife, held to the throat of a plump woman with wildly tumbled hair.

But that was all I had time to note, for the driver saw his opportunity, dropped his bow and seized the reins. The man the crossbowman shot had dragged himself into the saddle and was galloping back toward town, but the driver had to pull off the road to turn the carriage, and it lurched wildly over clumps of grass and bracken. I heard a squeak from within, and hoped that Mistress Meg had only been nicked. But most of my attention was taken up by the fact that the coach's departure left nothing between me and the man with the crossbow.

And now that I saw him, standing still and calmly spanning his bow, I recognized my would-be assassin from the alley in Rippon.

His clothes were streaked with river mud, revealing how he'd come upon us without being noticed, and he clearly knew what he was doing with that glowing bow. Not because he showed any special expertise in spanning it, which is not hard to do, but because he'd gotten the distance right. He was too far off for any of us to rush him before he was ready to shoot—which should have been far enough to affect his accuracy, but that didn't seem to trouble him. Indeed, if we rushed him he could wait till we drew so near he was certain to hit his target...and that didn't take into account that ominous, golden glow. He might be able to kill whoever he chose, at any range, but I knew 'twas me he wanted. And that meant 'twas time to employ the final lesson I'd learned from my father's master of arms—to run.

"Down the bank!" I yelled at my companions.

But instead of joining them I was already racing, not for the dubious shelter of the riverbank, but toward the bridge. I ran mayhap a dozen yards before my warning sense sounded the alarm once more, and without a backward glance hurled myself over the nearest railing.

I heard the snap of the bow, and something hot and hurtful ripped across my hip. Then I was falling, snatching in a breath as cool water rushed up and swallowed me.

I felt the tug of the current immediately. I wanted to drift far downstream before I surfaced for air, but I'd been running and fighting before I dove in and my lungs began to burn. I'm a good swimmer, and I exhaled before I surfaced, took two quick deep breaths, and pulled myself down just as something sliced into the water where I'd been.

A man on shore may run as fast as a river flows—if he runs on a smooth dry road. But unless the current is very slow, a man moving over clumps of grass, full of hidden branches, rocks and sinkholes, over gullies and around bushes, will not keep up the river's pace for long.

The weight of my boots, and mayhap my purse and the knife at my belt, helped to check my tendency to float back to the surface. And except for rising into the sunlight and air to snatch a quick breath every now and then, I was able to relax and let the river carry me.

'Twas not safe, of course. I might have been pulled into a tangle of logs, or thrown against a rock lurking beneath the placid surface...but all those risks struck me as being far less than the danger posed by an assassin with a magica crossbow. I stayed in my silent watery sanctuary till I was near certain my assassin could no longer be with me, and then surfaced and looked around for several long moments before swimming to the shore.

Drifting with the current should have been restful, but by the time I reached water shallow enough to stand my legs wobbled, and I was breathing hard.

Water streamed from my hair and clothing as I emerged from the river, and I took a moment to pour out my boots and wring my socks before I climbed the steep bank. I checked the small cuts I'd gotten during the fight and they'd already stopped bleeding—the place the crossbow bolt had skimmed my side was little more than a long scratch, and the cut on my hip not much deeper. It could have been far worse, and I began the walk back to the copse where we'd tethered the horses and True, soberly acknowledging how lucky I'd been. That walk took longer than it might have, for I took the time to stop and watch for assassins at the edge of any open space I had to cross.

I saw no sign of the man with the crossbow—a magica crossbow, no less!—or of any other threat, but it did give me time to think. None of my conclusions were pleasant.

Eventually I neared the road. I might have had some trouble finding the copse, approaching it from this side, was it not for the sound of furious argument in three gloriously familiar voices—two male, one female. For a moment relief made everything, even my still sodden clothing feel light.

I had been nearly certain I was the assassin's target—but only nearly, and that small shred of doubt had grown heavier with every moment of the long walk back.

"We can't go anywhere till Michael returns." Fisk sounded like he'd said this more than once, and there was more patience in his voice than I'd have expected.

"But their lead is getting bigger every minute we sit here!" Rupert sounded as if he'd made this point before, as well.

"That doesn't matter much," Kathy said soberly. I noted that her skirt and my shirt were now daubed with mud, though she'd lost that ridiculous belly. Even Fisk's neat garments showed a few muddy spots.

"They'll be watching for us now," my sister went on. "Even if we could stop the coach again, they won't send anyone off. If we put up another barricade they'd just turn and take another route, and we can't—"

'Twas True who saw me first, for he's a fine watchdog whatever Fisk might say. He came loping out of the trees, all wagging tail and rasping, soundless barks, and I had to stop and reassure him. But I'd not even finished stroking his silky ears when Kathy ran up and threw her arms around me—I suppose I wasn't much more muddy than she was, though wetter.

Fisk didn't hug me, but his smile was the rare, warm one that held no trace of sarcasm.

I'd seen those smiles more often since he and Kathy had plighted themselves to each other, and I made a mental note to please my sister by telling her that.

"Excellent." Even Rupert sounded as if he meant it, though not for the same reason. "He's back. Can we go after Meg now?"

"We can follow them," I told him. "But Kathy's right, we don't dare try another such attack. The man I fought may be injured, but there will be six of them again, as soon as they rejoin their fellows." And I wasn't the one who'd injured him, though that was another problem. "We shall have to come up with a different plan before we approach them once more," I finished firmly.

And that was something of a lie. We would need a different plan, but I'd likely play no part in its making.

We ignored Rupert's complaints and took our time saddling up, and we let the horses walk. Even Rupert admitted that the last thing we needed was to come across that coach while they were still on the alert.

I told them about my escape down the river, which took little time as 'twas a simple affair. They told me what had happened ashore, after my departure.

"We ran for the bank, as you said." Fisk sounded un-wontedly serious. "I was standing right there, lowering

Kathy down, when he got that second bolt loaded. He looked right at me—could easily have taken the shot—but he turned and waited for you to surface. So it is you he's after, not any of us."

I had been fairly sure of that, but 'twas reassuring to have it confirmed. Or at least, it clarified things.

Of more interest was the others' account of the fight at the coach. While I had engaged the outrider, and Fisk kept the driver from shooting anyone, Rupert and Kathy had sought to extract Mistress Meg from the carriage.

"'Twas hard," Kathy said, "because the man guarding Meg could move freely within, and we had to go through the windows."

"Meg's wrists were chained to one of the hand straps." Rupert made an upward grasping gesture to demonstrate. "The chains were long enough that she could lower her hands to her lap, and not much more, but she fought like a wildcat, kicking... She bit his jaw when he leaned across to smack Kathy's hand off the latch. I only hope..."

"They may hobble her ankles together if she was kicking," Fisk said briskly, "but they're not likely to do worse. Why should they? Their goal seems to be to keep her prisoner, and they acted like professionals. It's the enthusiastic amateurs you have to worry about," he added. "So that should reassure you."

Rupert's gloomy expression lightened a bit, until Kathy spoke.

"Professional what? Kidnappers? Why should that reassure us?"

"Professional bully boys," I said. "Men who've some training in arms, and don't much care where they sell their skills. Roseman had a number of such men in his employ, and it should reassure you because they're no more brutal than they must be in order to get the job done. They regard unnecessary violence as a waste of time and energy, and they know the punishment if they get caught will be more severe. Professionals know there's always a chance they'll be caught, so they don't take useless risks. Of any kind."

Kathy looked as if she wanted to go on arguing, until Fisk caught her eyes and glanced at Rupert, and she subsided.

But this led me to consider my would-be assassin, because for all his skill with a crossbow, and for that matter a knife, he didn't strike me as belonging to the same class as the professional thugs who guarded Mistress Meg. Indeed, as he calmly reloaded his bow, his deliberate style had been that of a craftsman engaged on some complex task...or one of those amateur enthusiasts, of whom Fisk spoke with such deep reservation.

I mentioned this, and then went on, "Whatever compels him to keep after me must be important—he appears to be quite fanatical about it."

"He might just have been helping his partners escape from us," Kathy suggested.

"If they're working together, why doesn't he travel with them?" Fisk asked critically. "And why is he just trying to kill Michael, and not the rest of us?"

"Why would anyone try to kill Michael?" Kathy asked. "He's the most harmless person I know."

Fisk and I exchanged glances, and decided not to tell my little sister about the list of enemies we'd accrued over these last few years. I suppose my assassin could have been one of them, though it felt like the wrong answer. And he'd given up a clear shot at Rupert, which was the only answer that did make sense.

We stayed at an inn that night, in a town where folk said the coach had only a three-hour lead on us. Indeed, we stopped earlier than we had to, to keep from catching them.

Rupert had finally been brought to realize that no good could come of following right on their heels, and he'd also had the sense to fill his own purse before he went galloping out of the palace. He leased separate rooms for Kathy and himself, while Fisk and I shared another—though watching Fisk's eyes narrow as I agreed to this arrangement, I know he suspected it might not come to that. Thereafter he watched me, with a casual closeness that fooled even Kathy.

I must confess, I had thought of simply slipping off, leaving them a letter to explain. But Fisk was my partner, and he'd earned the right to be involved in such decisions. Besides which, given the choice between letting me ride into danger without him, or seeing Kathy do the same, I knew what his decision would be.

And if knowing this made my heart ache a bit, my joy for them was greater than any small pain on my own behalf.

I made no effort to conceal my departure from the taproom "to seek my bed," and Fisk followed me into our room before I'd even had time to sort part of our common purse into my own.

"Did I succeed in fooling them?" I asked, before he could speak. It stopped him for a full beat, because he'd been about to accuse me of trying to befool him.

"Yes. In fact, Kathy went up to her room soon after you left. Rupert's still drinking," he added. "But he probably needs it, if he's going to get any sleep. Michael, this is crazy. Which shouldn't surprise me, but I thought you were getting more sensible lately."

"What other choice is there?" I heard the calm in my own voice with some gratification, for in truth I wasn't at all happy about this. "That man is hunting me. As long as I travel with you, he endangers you all, and Mistress Meg as well! We might have won her free today, had he not intervened. Suppose next time he decides that my companions are too much in his way, and he should remove you? Or suppose 'tis Katherine standing behind me when he misses his next shot?"

I saw Fisk flinch at this idea, and went on to clinch the matter.

"I place my trust in you, partner, to keep everyone safe and see this matter through, while I deal with... this other matter."

A familiar sarcasm swept some of the concern from Fisk's expression.

"Do you really think I'm going to fall for that 'I trust you' line? I'll do whatever I think best, whether I live up to your crazy trust or not!"

"Which is *why* I can trust you." I couldn't help but smile at his puzzled scowl. "Because you'll do what you think best, and you have no more desire to see Kathy hurt than I do. She and Rupert would go on without us if they had to. You know that."

"We could rent our own coach," Fisk said. "And chain them up inside it. The Liege didn't say his son had to return voluntarily. In fact, I think he'd like it better that way."

"But if you did that to Kathy, there'd be no point in getting the reward." Having no plan to stay I'd not unpacked, and I now picked up my saddlebags. "'Tis too dangerous for this man to be stalking me while we're engaged on another perilous quest. I'll return as soon as I've dealt with him."

"Dealt with him how?" Trust Fisk to put his finger on the one question to which I had no answer. He must have known it, for he went on, "You know, I could rent a carriage and chain *you* up inside. And when your stalker turns up, Rupert, Kathy and I take care of him."

"Rupert and Kathy? You might as well recruit the bunnies in the field—or True! They've no more experience dealing with assassins."

"You're not exactly noted for the size of your body count," Fisk pointed out.

"Neither are you. I don't know what I'm going to do," I admitted. "I shall have to learn what he wants and why he's doing this. I'm taking True as well as Chant," I added. "Mayhap he'll be of some use."

"Oh, you're definitely taking the dog," Fisk said. "Though when it comes to being useful..."

There was no more to be said so I departed, leaving Fisk in a state of even more worry than usual. I was sorry for that but we had no choice, and I trusted him to see to Mistress Meg's affair until I could rejoin them.

With that happy thought in mind, I rode to another inn in the same town and got myself a room. The full Creature Moon was trying to make up for the waning Green Moon, but Chant has a weak leg and I don't risk riding him at night unless I have to.

The next morning I made my way back to the bridge where we'd ambushed the coach. Someone had dragged our log aside, opening the road once more. I had some notion of setting True on the assassin's trail. He can track a sausage for several hundred yards, but sausages proved to be more important in his scheme of things than assassins.

I had once, in a moment of desperate need, sent Chant a surge of magical energy that had let him over-leap an impossible gap.

I now tried to give True a magical Gift of tracking, but to no avail. I also tried, somewhat vaguely, to use magic to find the trail myself—but since there's no Gift I know of to let a man follow another's trail, 'twas no surprise that the lid over the seething well of my magic stayed firmly shut.

I wasn't unduly dismayed, for I'd expected both these results. I'd come here mostly to distance myself from the others, and because I'd nowhere else to go, but I expected no difficulty in finding my assassin.

I had only to wait, and he'd find me.

Chapter 10

Fisk

My beloved faced a hard dilemma the next morning—she wanted to yell at me, she wanted never to speak to me again, and she couldn't do both. I felt for her. Really. (Well, no, not really.)

"You should have waked me! And Rupert, too!"

"You couldn't have stopped him," I said reasonably. "*I* couldn't stop him."

"That's not the point! The point is that the two of you made the decision without even consulting... I'm not speaking to you!"

Rupert was too busy wincing and trying to shield his eyes from the light to join in. But at least the argument, combined with the results of his indulgence, kept him from trying to hurry us off before breakfast.

And I admit, there was an odd emptiness in the place where Chant and Michael should have been riding.

On the other hand, I did not miss the dog.

We'd already guessed that the kidnappers were traveling east to Potford, where there was another river crossing, but we had no idea where they might go after that. And according to Rupert, the bridge at Potford was in the midst of town, and too wide for us to block, anyway.

"Have you been there?" I'd never heard of anything in that sleepy river town that would attract the Heir to the Realm. "I thought it was nothing but a stop on the road to Borrowston."

"My father and I went through it on the way to Borrowston," said Rupert, and my brows rose.

Borrowston was the largest city in the northern Realm. The residents called it "the Sword of the North," but everyone else who'd been there called it "that ghastly frozen swamp." It was a sea of mud in summer, a sea of frozen mud in winter, and the fumes from its smelters poison everyone year round.

"Why did you go to Borrowston?" I asked. "Why would anyone go there? Even kidnappers surely have better choices than that."

If they didn't I might have to go there, and Borrowston's mosquitoes were said to carry off...well, not horses, but rabbits and small dogs.

"I've been to all the major cities in the Realm," Rupert said. "Father's always trotting off to one fief or another—either to argue with someone, or just parade around with a troop and make his presence felt. Until I went to university, he took me with him. Borrowston's not as bad as they say." He smiled suddenly, though the bruises that darkened one side of his jaw must have twinged. "They do more than smelt the ore—and there's copper and tin too, not just iron. They have mills that beat iron into steel, and they make brass. There are sculptors who've set up shop there, for access to the metals. But they ship the gold, silver and gems down-river to Carralan, to the stone cutters."

The education of the Heir of the United Realm was more extensive than I'd thought.

"What about the mosquitoes?" I asked.

He grinned. "'Tis not that they're bigger...but there are a lot of them."

It made sense for the High Liege to make sure his Heir knew all about the Realm he'd govern, just as Michael's father would make sure his heir knew every corner of his own fief. Just as I might someday show my son...what, pastures full of cows and sheep?

I had a hard time picturing it. I looked at Kathy, riding pointedly on Rupert's other side; the thought of her holding our child in her arms was enough to resign me even to sheep and cows.

So the quicker we got Rupert back to his father, the better.

"Since you know so much about what's going on in the Realm," I told him, "maybe you can deduce where they might be taking Mistress Merkle."

Rupert shook his head. "Not without some idea of who's behind it, or what they want. If they do cross the Pottage, we can assume they're trying to avoid Father's authority...but Baron Tatterman, who owns the keep where they first stopped, isn't at all political, as far as I know."

It turned out he knew a lot about the fiefs we passed through over the next two days, and not just about the barons' politics. He talked about the dangers of coal mining, the unusual prevalence in magica herbs in the marshes around Kerrigen, and as we rode past a large flock of sheep, he even treated us to a lecture on hoof-rot and how it could be prevented.

Kathy, country-raised, appeared to be interested in this. I shuddered.

Tracking the coach through small villages was so easy that we had some trouble keeping behind it, and we didn't dare overtake it till we had a plan. When we hit Potford, where they'd already crossed the Pottage, I suggested that Rupert take the time to purchase clothes that made him look less like a runaway nobleman. He also picked up some ordinary tack for his horse, and Kathy borrowed some tools at a livery stable and cut that flowing mane and tail down to a more normal length. Champion was still outstanding, but at least he was no longer a walking signpost—and Rupert's bruised face made him look a bit less noble as well.

The High Liege, not to mention advisor Arnold, had specifically told us not to give any landholders on the other side of the river material to embarrass the throne, and upsetting the men who held the purse strings was no part of my plan.

But while Rupert was trading a magnificent saddle for a cheaper one, I took the opportunity to slip into a stationers shop and purchase a roll of their finest paper, and some better ink than the stuff I carried.

Not embarrassing the High Liege was important...but so was getting out of this with a whole skin. And I don't care how furiously your liege is feuding over mineral rights, no local sheriff or judicar could completely ignore a High Liege writ.

All of this took us the better part of the afternoon, and we decided to spend the night there, letting the coach draw a bit farther ahead of us. After we crossed the river the next morning, I let Rupert hurry us along almost as fast as he wanted, with the result that we rode into Alton at dusk. And while a number of people had seen the coach drive into town, no matter how many coins we flashed, no one at the other end of town had seen it depart.

Alton was a market center, almost a small city, but someone should have noticed the coach we were looking for driving out...unless it hadn't driven out.

"They must have stopped here for the night." Rupert's voice was tense with hope. "Maybe this is the chance we've been looking for."

"How could they take Meg into an inn?" Kathy asked. "I can see stopping for luncheon—they could say she preferred to eat in the coach. But they can't leave her in the coach overnight, and they can hardly haul her through the taproom in chains. She could start screaming, or tell a chambermaid she was being held against her will, beg some groom to go to the sheriff... They can't have stopped at an inn."

"They might," I said. "Particularly if your friend is smart enough to pretend to be too frightened to try anything."

Particularly if she *was* too frightened to try anything. There are plenty of ways to cow a prisoner into submission, but I wasn't about to say that to either Kathy or Rupert, who both assured me that Mistress Merkle was indeed that smart.

Without Michael here to lure all the assassins in the Realm, we decided it was still smart to split up the search. Though I sent Rupert and Kathy off together, to check out the expensive coaching inns while I took the rougher part of town by the stockyards. And we all agreed to return to the stable where we'd lodged our horses by nightfall at the latest.

If anyone found the right inn before nightfall, we agreed to immediately return and get the others. To clinch the matter, I pointed out that any rescue attempted before everyone was asleep was almost certain to fail—and that would result in yet another plan we couldn't use again.

Kathy saw the logic in this, and nodded immediately. Rupert thought it through and nodded reluctantly. I hoped I could count on one or the other of them to remember their promises, on the off chance they came across the inn where our villains were staying.

Because I knew villains, and those men would avoid a respectable upper-class inn like the plague.

So I went about my own search with some hope of success, a hope that intensified as I approached my sixth inn.

The Addled Cock had once been a thriving inn and tavern. It loomed over the smaller shops and houses around it, three full stories of sagging beams with cracked plaster between them. The sun was getting low, but even that cheerful light couldn't make the Cock look good. The tavern was still thriving, judging by the noise that came through the taproom window and the number of people going in for dinner...but thriving was relative, in this neighborhood of broken shutters and peeling paint. The whole street wore an air of, *You don't bother us, we won't bother you.* And the big sprawling inn that lorded over it added, *And if you do bother us, we'll knock out your teeth.*

At first glance, you'd have thought that the fence around the inn's yard would fall over if you sneezed at it, but there were no missing planks, even in the narrow passage that separated it from the bakeshop next door. The alley behind the yard was bigger, and the stink from the inn's midden—they threw their garbage over the fence, instead of into a composting bin—explained why no one else was there. There was a gate into the alley, and my knife slipped easily into the crack between gate and fence post...only to discover that this was the kind of latch that slid aside instead of lifting.

I stepped onto the fence's central beam and swung myself up to look over it. The compost bin had long since overflowed, which explained the pile in the alley. A surprisingly sturdy stable occupied one side of the yard. In the remaining weedy ground, the coach with the crest scratched off its door was parked beside three others. I wasn't even surprised—this place practically screamed Den of Thieves. Then the fear hit, and my heart began to pound.

I had found it. I should immediately go back and tell Rupert and Kathy. That was the agreement.

But if I did they'd come up with some crazy scheme to get Mistress Margaret out of there, and we didn't have enough information for scheming.

If this was a burglary, I'd have spent a week scouting the place, figuring out their schedule, trying to spot some weakness. Well, if I'd been planning to burgle *this* place, I'd have waited till I sobered up and then wondered how, even drunk, that could have seemed like a good idea. Den of Thieves, after all.

We didn't have a week. That coach would drive off tomorrow morning, and my beloved would never let a chance like this slip away.

That was the thought that decided me. I didn't want Kathy anywhere near this place, until I'd scouted it as well as I could. I might not let her near it after that, even if I had to leave her bound and gagged while Rupert and I went...adventuring, the old gods help me.

There was no one in the yard now, and no time for caution or finesse. I stepped up to the fence's highest beam, resting one hand on top of the planks before I leapt over. It was a six-foot drop onto packed earth, so I didn't land lightly. But nothing sprained, and I scurried over to duck behind a pile of moldy straw beside the stable. There I knelt for a while, watching the inn and pulling splinters out of my hand.

There was a weedy kitchen garden, and today had been washday, but you can't tell much about what's happening inside a building by looking at its back wall. So I listened instead, and the clamor from the kitchen windows confirmed that they were starting to serve dinner.

My stomach grumbled, but I ignored it. In a place like this, on the downhill slide, dinner meant that most of the inn's employees would be working in the kitchen or the taproom. And most of the guests would be in the taproom eating. Which might give me a chance to check out the other thing I'd noticed. In this neighborhood very few windows held glass, and on this warm summer evening all the shutters had been thrown open to catch the breeze—all but the shutters of one window on the third floor.

I was once a very good burglar. My mind automatically plotted the best route—shinny up the drain pipe to the slanting beam, up that to the cross beam, and if that crack in the plaster wasn't too crumbly... The shutters were latched from the inside, but they were dilapidated enough I could probably slide my knife blade through to lift the bar—and then swing them open to find, what? A fence making a deal for stolen loot? A bunch of footpads divvying up the take?

I had to do it, to keep Kathy from coming here, but I needed more information before I went up that drainpipe—and there was laundry drying on the line, which gave me an idea.

I folded a couple of sheets and hung them over my arm. If I met a customer in the hallway they'd take me for a member of the staff. If I met someone on the staff, I could tell them there'd been an "accident" with the sheets in my room, and that I hadn't wanted to bother anyone. If I looked embarrassed enough they wouldn't ask for details.

It was harder to find another way into the building. The back door opened into a hallway that passed right by the kitchen, and the front door was next to the taproom where dinner was being served now.

I'd hoped for a side door, but there weren't any. I did, however, find a window that opened into an unused parlor toward the back of the house—and like all the other windows, its shutters were open.

Burglars love summer.

I threw the sheets into the room, followed by my boots, for the windowsill was higher than my shoulders and hard soles scrabbling against the side of a building are noisier than bare feet. Inside the room I found a corner where I couldn't be seen and tidied myself, refolded the sheets, and calmed my breathing. Then I walked quietly to the door, peered out to be sure there was no one in the hallway, and strode down the empty corridor as if I'd been working there for years.

It's tricky to walk confidently through a place you've never seen before. You can't look around to see where you want to go, you can't hesitate, and you can't hurry too much either.

This hall led straight to the front entrance, with the stairs coming down on the left. Doors on the right side of the hallway opened into half a dozen parlors, proclaiming that this inn had once served people who could pay to dine in private. They were all empty, now.

A big archway on the other side of the entry hall revealed the tables at the back of the taproom, complete with customers awaiting dinner and a girl serving them. She was taking an order, mostly turned away from me, and I swung around the newel post and walked upstairs with my sheets.

I have no idea if anyone noticed me, because after that first glance I never looked back.

I was prepared to walk past whoever I met with a pleasant nod, and offer either story if they stopped me, but I met no one on the stairs as I climbed to the second floor and then the third. The third floor hallway was empty on this side of the building, but the room I wanted was at the back. I walked (confidently) down the hall, turned the corner...and saw that I'd hit the target. The man who sat on a plain wooden chair, outside the room with the latched shutters, was one of the three who'd ridden past our hiding place to get help to move the log.

The knife in his hands didn't intimidate me; he was using it to entertain himself, carving something on the head of a stick. The shavings made a mess on the floor at his feet.

He might have been watching us from behind the ramparts at the old keep...but he also might not have, and to turn back the moment I'd seen him would look suspicious. I balanced the sheets on my arm, and gave him a pleasant nod as I walked past him and on around the corner at the far end of the hall.

It was so quiet I heard the chair creak as he shifted his weight—he could hardly help but hear my footsteps. So I kept on walking till I came to an open door, which I closed behind me without trying to be either loud or quiet.

This was an inner room, with no windows and four beds that were probably rented to those who couldn't afford a private room. I wanted to sit down and breathe till my heartbeat slowed, but Jack had taught me that verisimilitude was best achieved by the real thing. I stripped one of the beds and remade it, and if my sheets weren't as tightly tucked as the chambermaid had left them, I doubted anyone who rented this bed would complain.

Since our adventure with Roseman, I hadn't thought about Jack and the things he taught me nearly as much as I used to.

With the perfectly clean sheets crumpled up in my arms, I went back around and past the guard once more. This time he didn't even look up as I went by.

Down the stairs, down the corridor to the empty parlor, and out the window to the yard. I was about to throw the sheets in an empty laundry basket when a thought occurred to me.

I now knew all I was likely to learn. The room where Mistress Margaret was imprisoned was on the third floor, behind latched shutters, with a guard outside the door. Maybe one inside with her, as well?

If we came back in the middle of the night the rest of the inn would be asleep...but how many more guards would be in that room?

The sun had dropped beneath the horizon while I was inside, but even in the deepening dusk, anyone who happened to look could see me climbing up that wall to the shuttered window.

On the other hand, there wasn't anyone around to look.

The staff and customers were busy with dinner, and the odds of finding Mistress Merkle alone in that guarded room were better now than they would ever be again.

Besides, Kathy would be with us if we came back later. If I got Rupert's wench away now, there'd be no reason for Kathy to come within a mile of this place...

Love really does make people crazy.

I went back to my blind behind the straw pile to cut the sheets into strips and knot them into a rope. The strips had to be pretty thick before I trusted them to hold my weight, and the knots used up a lot of their length. I had to take several more sheets off the drying line before I had a rope I thought was long enough, and it made an unwieldy bundle wrapped around my chest.

Michael may have had a point about carrying rope with you.

But this was the best I could do, and only one man had come back to visit the jakes while I worked.

Soon dinner would end, a lot more people would take that trip, and then Mistress Margaret's kidnappers would go to the rooms where they planned to spend the night.

If I was going to get her, it had to be now.

I took one more moment to unlatch the back gate and tuck my boots unobtrusively behind the fence, before I walked across the yard to the house. I didn't sprint—it was almost dark now, but someone running through the yard might still draw a cook's gaze. They'd assume someone walking was returning from the privy.

Like the rest of this inn, the drainpipe was sturdier than it looked, and the empty rain barrel beneath it gave me a useful boost.

I may have done crazier things than burgling a busy inn while everyone was still awake, but I couldn't think of any offhand. And Michael wasn't even here.

Climbing the wall was a straightforward job, if you knew what you were doing, and most of the people who might have caught me were in the middle of dinner. The blackened beams that crisscrossed the wall protruded almost three inches, which was enough for bare feet, and the crumbling plaster gave me enough purchase to balance myself, though I didn't dare put any weight on my hands.

So I probably shouldn't have been sweating as hard as I was when I reached those third floor shutters.

I took my time, listening for voices or movement within the room, but heard nothing. Wouldn't it be ironic if they had Mistress Merkle in some other room, with four men guarding her, and had left this one man to watch over their gear? Or they might have decided to eat in shifts, in which case there'd be at least two men in there with her.

But I couldn't stall forever and my feet were beginning to ache, so I drew my knife from its sheath. It slipped neatly through the gap and this was the right kind of latch—I pushed the shutters open, looked in, and met Margaret Merkle's astonished gaze.

She sat on the bed, with one hand clapped over her mouth as if to keep any sound from escaping, and a chain fastened one of her ankles to the bed frame.

But I must confess, the first thought that crossed my mind was, *This* is what all the fuss is about? Her hair was a darker brown than Kathy's mouse, and if I weren't already in love with a girl who was willow slender, her well-padded figure would have been appealing. But the nose above her hand was snub, and her features were, at best, pleasantly ordinary.

However, the second thing I noticed was that she hadn't made a peep, despite her obvious surprise. She didn't even twitch the ankle attached to that noisy chain. And there were bruises on that ordinary face. I began to understand what Kathy and Rupert saw in this girl.

I touched my lips to signal continued silence, and took the time to wedge the room's only remaining chair—very quietly—under the doorknob before I went to her.

"I'm from Rupert." It wasn't completely accurate, but it was the quickest way to gain her trust. "Can you go out that window on a rope?"

I thought of her pregnancy then, for the first time— but she wasn't showing yet, and whatever strain this rescue might place on the child, surely the strain of being held prisoner was worse.

"Whatever I must." She copied my unvoiced murmur so well her reply was almost lost in the whisper of cloth as I pulled out my picks.

I had hoped I might need them.

"There are five men in the gang who kidnapped me," she went on, soft, but urgent. "I don't know who hired them or why. I don't think they know why, but there's another man who gives them orders. He's about five foot seven or eight, slim, with a noble's accent.

He's always wearing a mask when I see him, but his clothes are expensive, well-made. He only came close to me once, and I bit his hand. Hard enough to break the skin, bring blood. So he'll be marked, at least for a while. I knew Rupert would come for me."

Her voice shook then, for the first time. I was concentrating on the lock, but I now had no difficulty understanding why Kathy had befriended this girl, and Rupert had fallen for her.

No need for reassuring chitchat with this sharp brain and cool nerve.

"When you get down go straight to the back wall," I said. "Don't run if you don't have to. Draws the eye. The back gate's unlatched. If there's no alarm, wait for me there. If you need to run, find Rupert at Bottner's Stables, east of the central square. Got it?"

"Gate. Bottner's. East of the central square."

She even waited till I gently removed the cuff before rising from the bed to help unwrap my sheet rope.

If I hadn't been in love with a woman who was just that smart and brave, I swear I'd have tried to cut Rupert out.

The first adventure Michael dragged me into had begun, more or less, with him lowering a woman from a tower on a rope. At the time I'd been critical of his technique, but I now took it all back.

It was fairly easy to fasten a sling for Mistress Meg, and she sat on the windowsill willingly, while I sat on the floor with my feet braced on the wall. She lowered her weight onto the sheets as slowly as she could. But then came the moment when she had to let go of the frame, her weight hit the sheets and therefore my arms...and I almost dropped her.

My butt flew off the floor, pivoting on my braced legs, and it was only because the first knot hung up on the sill that I managed to keep her from falling twenty feet to the hard-packed earth of the yard.

Straining every muscle in my thighs and back, I lowered my body back to the floor and then worked my feet slowly up the wall to brace under the jutting windowsill, which gave me enough leverage to begin to lower her down.

I don't know if the sheets were harder to grip than a rope would have been, and while some knots were dragged over the sill by her weight, others stuck. I had to brace myself with just one foot while the other kicked them free. They also made a soft thump as each knot went over, though the slither of smooth fabric was almost silent.

My arms and shoulders were burning when her weight left the rope, so suddenly that I fell back, one elbow knocking loudly—and painfully—on the floor.

I didn't even take a moment to curse, for as I rose to my knees, yanking the sheet up yards at a time, I heard the guard's chair scrape and the doorknob turn. The chair under the knob skidded half an inch before it stuck.

"Girly? You better not be up to tricks in there."

The threat in that heavy voice was unnerving enough for me—and I wasn't a girl, or his prisoner.

But the sling that had carried Meg down was now in my hands. Thinking with the speed of terror I looped it around the protruding ledge of the windowsill. It wasn't as secure as I'd have liked but it would have to do—the guard was slowly banging the door open, the chair slipping a bit farther with every push.

I grabbed the rope and rolled over the sill as the door flew open, sending the chair skidding across the room. His bellow of rage sent me sliding down as fast as I could get over the knots, the sheet twisting under my hands.

I was just a yard from the ground when he cut the rope, and I was running for the back gate almost before I landed.

It was full dark now, and with no moonlight, in a poor neighborhood, that's very dark.

Meg hadn't been able to find the gate—which looked just like the rest of the fence, except for hinges so rusty they were much the same color as the wood. She was sobbing under her breath when I ran up, but that was all. It took me several long moments to locate the gate, and I knew where it was! But finally my groping fingers found the latch, I shoved it wide and we ran out...into a pitch-black alley full of crates, barrels, and softer—but slippery—debris.

I thought of my bare feet then, but a shout from the back of the inn vanquished any desire to stop and pull my boots on. I gripped Meg's arm and we ran into darkness.

I regretted the boots after the first few strides, for there were a lot of hard sharp things in that alley. But Meg was the first to fall, a staggering stumble that I pulled her out of by dragging her forward till she found her feet again.

I was the one who ran full tilt into a wheelbarrow full of dirt. I know it was full of dirt because I fell on top of it and pushed it over, sending its contents cascading over my hands—though the pain from my kneecap was so intense I hardly noticed. I was limping when Meg hauled me to my feet and I wanted to stop, but orange light welled out behind us. Turning back I saw three men, two of them carrying torches, coming through the inn's back gate.

This was enough to send me, not running, alas, but hobbling rapidly down the alley—which was even darker after I'd looked at the bright light.

"Faster!" Meg demanded. "They're gaining."

"They can see where they're going."

I stubbed my toes on what felt like a slab of solid granite and hopped four strides, proving my point, and it occurred to me that *she* wasn't barefoot.

I glanced back again. They weren't just gaining on us, they were doing it rapidly.

It was Meg they wanted, not me. After all my fussing about the reward, a bit of heroism on my part might please Kathy. Once Meg was gone, they had no reason to do me much harm, they certainly wouldn't bother to hold me prisoner, and the risks of killing me should far outweigh any little grudges they might be carrying.

And my toes were killing me. It felt like several might be broken.

"Run!" I told her. "Go get Rupert. I'll hold them as long as I can."

She was too sensible to argue—I was really beginning to like this girl. She dropped my arm and ran into the night with the speed of terror. And of someone wearing shoes.

I drew my knife as I turned back, heroically, to face my oncoming foes...and promptly discovered that heroism is as stupid as I always thought it was. The man in the middle stopped to engage me, but the other two ran around me on either side and right on after Meg. There wasn't a thing I could do to stop them.

The man who'd stayed to fight with me carried one of the torches. I just had time to be glad that he hadn't picked up his sword when he swung the torch instead, and sent me jumping back.

That rapid swipe made the flame flicker. It almost went out, and he tipped it upright and held it still till the flame grew brighter. He passed the torch to his left hand and drew his own knife, moving with a deliberation that told me he believed he could take me down at will.

Unfortunately, I agreed with him.

"We don't have to—" I began, but a woman's scream for help interrupted me.

Meg went on screaming, smart woman that she was, but my opponent only grinned. We both knew that in this neighborhood no one would answer.

He wiggled his blade, more in comment than in challenge, and started to circle to the right.

I limped in the opposite direction, not sure if my toes or my knee hurt more, and Meg's screams were abruptly muffled by what sounded like a hand clamped over her mouth.

They had her. I had lost this round, and the best thing I could do now was to go back and tell Rupert and Kathy what had happened. There was no point in a knife fight.

"Look," I said. "There's no reason for this. If you just step aside, I'll get out of your way."

His lips twitched. Then he chuckled so merrily that for a moment I hoped he might agree...until I realized he was looking over my shoulder, behind me.

I think I started to turn...

The first thing I was aware of, on awakening, was the pain in my head. It seemed to radiate through all my nerves, even my fingernails throbbing in time with my pulse, and my stomach rolled. I'd have thrown up, but I was afraid it would hurt too much.

After a few moments either the headache backed off, or I grew more accustomed to it, because I started to feel pain from my knee and toes. I remembered the chase, the fight, and Meg's capture. I started to grind my teeth, but the motion of my jaw sent a shaft of pain down my back and I stopped.

I was lying on the inn's midden heap, with my face in a mass of wet tea grounds. They were comforting-ly cool, and smelled a lot better than the scents that leaked past them. Trouble sat beside me, his muscular rump warm against my ribs, rumbling a low warning growl...

Trouble couldn't growl.

I took far too long to pursue this thought to its logical conclusion, and realize I'd better open my eyes. Dark-ling Night was almost two weeks off, and the nearly-full Creature Moon had finally risen, shedding enough light to reveal the creature beside me. I suppose it was a dog, though it looked more like someone had crossed a jackal with a rabbit. Its muzzle was long and pointed, its ears pricked, but its haunches were absurdly small for its torso. Its ears were bigger than a dog's should be...but no rabbit had ever possessed those big, jagged teeth.

I might have moved then, but the dog's round eyes were fixed on something beyond me, and that deep growl was such a clear warning that I managed to raise my head and look.

Almost a dozen pair of tiny eyes caught the moon-light, glowing back at me in eerie green. I heard movement in the shadows, behind those watching eyes.

Rats had come to feed on the midden, and I was the freshest morsel in it. That was enough to bring me to... well, not my feet, but my hands and knees. Rats have a wicked bite, and they've been known to kill people who are helpless.

I felt curst helpless, because the moment I moved the dog skittered away. The rats retreated too, though not as far as the dog had. Continuing to move seemed like a very good idea.

I had crawled several yards, dragging my proba-bly-broken toes on the hard ground, before I remembered that I'd left my boots beside the gate. It took a bit of groping to find them, and cramming my swollen toes inside was almost as painful as I'd feared. But once I had my boots on I felt so human I managed to drag myself up the fence to my feet, and walk a dozen yards before I sat down with a jar that made my ears ring.

I don't remember lying down, and when I woke again the moon had hardly moved, my head was clearer, and the dog was by my side. Teeth, growl and all.

"Surely you have something better to do," I said, and it shot away again at the sound of my voice.

But speaking didn't hurt as much as I'd feared, and my brief nap had done me good. I managed to get to my feet without the fence to lean on, and once I was upright I was able to keep walking.

The dog must not have had better things to do, for it followed me down the alley and out into the street. After some painful thinking, I figured out the direction of the stable where we'd agreed to meet. At nightfall, which was now many hours past, so I wasn't amazed when I heard Rupert and Kathy's voices calling my name. I wanted to call back, but shouting would hurt too much. I did walk toward the sound and eventually found them. Even by the light of the smaller moon, I saw Kathy's eyes widen.

"What in the world...?"

"I tried to rescue Meg." I was swaying on my feet. I rather hoped one of them would notice this and support me, but it didn't seem manly to say so. "Failed. Completely, and now they're on alert. We'll have to—"

"I didn't mean you," said my beloved. "Though you're a mess. What's *that*?"

I looked around and found that my new friend was still with me. Or rather, it was twenty feet behind me with its tail between its legs.

"It's a dog," I said. "At least I think it is, and I owe it a meal. It saved me from the rats. You know, if this is going to be a long conversation, I'd like to sit down."

Her attention finally turned to me, and a strong slim arm went around my waist. Despite the fact that I smelled like a midden heap.

I wasn't paying much attention to anything but walking—which needed focus just then—but after a while I became aware of a curt note in Kathy's voice, and a subtle stiffness in the body I leaned on.

"Are you mad about something?"

"Not yet. I'm waiting to hear *why* you didn't come back to the stable after you found Meg. Like we all promised to do. Then I'll see whether I get mad or not."

Something told me that she wouldn't like my real reason...and I wasn't up to coming up with a decent lie.

"Thank you," I said.

It was decided—by Kathy and Rupert, since I wasn't inclined to talk—that we'd take rooms at the next inn we found, and Rupert would return to the stables and fetch our horses. And more important to me, the saddlebags that held the magica willow bark Michael can find so easily, and harvest without getting whoever used it killed since his herb-talker mother had taught him how.

Its ability to relieve pain was, well, magical, and I *really* looked forward to drinking some.

The only snag arose when Rupert got a look at "the next inn."

"Champion? In those stables? Will he be there in the morning?"

It actually looked more respectable than the Addled Cock, and besides...

"Don't you know the difference between a bandit and an innkeeper?"

Talking hurt enough that I stopped there, but Kathy finished for me.

"As long as you're staying with him, an innkeeper won't let anyone *else* rob you. 'Twould be bad for business to have horses vanishing out of his stables, Rupert. Go get them."

It was Kathy who paid for several rooms, and told the innkeeper that the dog was with us and not to chase it off—my head hurt too much to protest this assertion.

She also ordered up plenty of water, hot for washing, and cold for compresses, and cleaned me up before she let me lie down. She even worked up the nerve to push a bowl of scraps and a huge raw bone under my bed, where the ferocious looking mutt had taken refuge.

At some point, Rupert returned, I was finally able to drink the magica tea, and the pain in my head retreated enough that I thought I might survive after all. I even managed a faint protest.

"That beast has to be full of fleas."

"Who cares," said Kathy. "He saved you."

"Not really. How did you know that?"

"You told me. Go to sleep."

The magica willow bark did its job so well that I could—despite the sound of a monster rending flesh and bone under my bed.

CHAPTER 11

Michael

I set my trap that first night. I thought 'twould take him some days to find me again, but I wasn't prepared to bet my life on it. So I made camp as I usually did, except for the absence of Fisk and the others, trying to convince myself I didn't miss them. I failed at that, but admitting that I missed them reminded me how important it was to keep them safe. The thought of them, all happily pursuing Mistress Meg, may have made me somewhat lonely. The thought of anything happening to them was intolerable.

Once camp was in order—with Chant tethered at a distance that would keep him out of any fray—True and I scouted carefully around it, paying particular attention to places from which our camp could be seen. This was a task at which my human senses might easily fail—if he saw me coming, my assassin had only to hide in some dense bushes, or even up a tree, and

I'd likely stroll right past him. 'Twould be much harder to conceal himself from True's nose—so when True frisked past those likely blinds with tail a-wag, I knew no one was there.

After the sun had set, I stepped out of the firelight and cut some leafy boughs, which I rolled up in a blanket, poking and prodding till they formed a reasonable semblance of a man. I laid the bundle in my bedroll and covered it up. I thought it looked quite like my sleeping self.

I had no way to make a convincing dummy of True, but since he'd not been with me when the assassin attacked, the man might not know I traveled with a dog. And that might give me an advantage.

True and I then retired to the place I'd chosen for us to hide. 'Twas well screened by the bushes, but with a reasonable view of the camp—and a passage by which I could exit those bushes without making too much noise, when our quarry was distracted by the task of killing "me."

I'd put several big logs on the fire to burn low and long, giving me some light until the Creature Moon rose—soon after sunset and nearly full. The Green Moon, with its slow orbit, was now rising almost at sunrise. 'Twould be less than two weeks before the night occurred when no moon rose at all.

My father claimed that the superstitions that have arisen around Darkling Night are absurd. He said magic obeys natural laws, like all else, and cannot suddenly run wild and prey on the unwary, no matter the state of the moons. So my family treated the Darkling Nights like any other—though I know the servants did not.

Sitting with my drawn sword beside me, watching the light flare over my "sleeping" form when a log emitted a brief tongue of flame, I wondered if I'd be willing to spend Darkling Night watching thus, or if I'd succumb to superstition and find an inn and human company. The two moons' orbits vary so widely that they almost never go dark on the same night, and 'tis never the same day or season. The last had been, what, five years ago? Before I set out on a life of errantry, and long before I met Fisk. Had I really pursued this mad profession for four years?

I had, and even lurking in the bushes waiting for an assassin to kill me, I found I was absurdly proud of myself.

He didn't come to kill me that night, and True and I emerged from the bushes next morning, stiff and weary, to break camp and set out once more.

Since my purpose was to draw my would-be killer away from the others, I rode back along the way we'd come. I had intended to stop at the towns we passed through, and ask if a stranger had been inquiring for us, as we'd been asking after the kidnapper's coach, but by mid-morning I was falling asleep in the saddle. I stopped at an inn in the next town to take a room, and went to sleep with all the din of the waking world in my ears.

This set the pattern for the next few days. I found that if I slept a part of the day 'twas easy to stay awake at night. And if 'twas dull to sit and watch an empty camp, the thought of my pursuer—who must arrive eventually—kept me to the task. He would not give up, and I refused to be less resolute than he.

'Twas on the fourth night of my journey that he struck, and for all my watchfulness 'twas not I who saw him coming.

I don't know what alerted True. I'd been idly stroking his back as we waited, and I felt him stiffen before he came to his feet in a stiff-legged crouch.

The Gift of animal handling works more easily with beasts you know. I reached out to True, bidding silence and stillness. His obedience was grudging but he stayed, even as his hackles rose under my palm.

The Creature Moon was low in the sky, now only a few hours before dawn, and the dark figure creeping into the camp was hooded and cloaked like some malign fate. But there could be no doubt of his identity—the crossbow he carried glowed in the dark, almost as bright as the distant moon.

True twitched under my hand, and I sent another wave of calm and control toward him.

The assassin had already spanned his bow, but he had either the sense or the training not to walk about with a bolt on the string, for he stopped several feet from my bed to knock the quarrel.

Indeed, there was no reason for absolute silence—had I suddenly awakened, I'd be too fogged by sleep to do anything before he made his shot.

But of course the form in the blankets didn't stir. He took another step to bring himself even closer, aimed, and sent a bolt into the blankets right where my heart should have been.

At that distance, the bolt would have passed though most of my torso, and mayhap out the other side—the branches stopped it not at all.

I started to move as soon as he shot, but True was even faster off the mark. The assassin barely had time to hear that his bolt had not struck flesh before True's teeth clamped on his ankle...and didn't let go.

Sheer astonishment slowed me for several seconds—
True, who loved *everyone*, pulled at the man's ankle,
trying to drag him down for a more lethal bite.

The assassin staggered and drew his knife—which
was enough to shake me free from my frozen surprise—
and that hesitation on my part might have proved fatal
for my good and loyal friend.

But absurdly, having drawn his blade, the assassin
looked down at True, still worrying the thick leather of
his boot, and did not strike.

The distraction True provided gave me a perfect
opening. I tossed my sword to my left hand and struck
with my right fist, a clean blow to the point of the
chin that hurt my fist, but snapped his head back like
a puppet's.

He toppled, stirred a bit, and then subsided. I knelt
and bound his hands behind his back before turning
to True, who finally removed his teeth from the man's
boot and gave me a tentative wag.

"Yes, 'tis over," I told him. "You're a good dog, and a
splendid watchdog, and the next time we see Fisk we'll
tell him all about it."

My assassin began to move as I bound his feet. I took
a moment to put a folded blanket beneath his head before turning to shake the rustling branches out of my
bedroll.

The crossbow bolt had buried itself fletching deep in
the earth, and after wiggling it and finding it stuck fast,
I decide to leave it there. I thought about packing up
my bedroll, but since we wouldn't be leaving till morning and I had no use for it, I laid the blankets out and
rolled him onto them. His eyelids fluttered, but it was
still several minutes before sense returned to his gaze.
He looked around and saw me sitting across the fire.

His expression, as he realized his captivity, was an odd mix of fury and resignation.

"You're going to have a hard time holding me prisoner," he said. "It's not like you can turn me over to the local sheriff. Or even complain."

He knew full well that I was unredeemed, that he could kill me with no consequence to himself. Still...

"Just because you can do so with impunity is a poor reason to kill a man," I said. "Or to stalk him for weeks. Why are you doing this?"

His shoulders twitched in the slightest of shrugs. "You'll have to sleep sometime. And keeping someone tied up isn't as easy as you might think. I've tried."

The thought of anyone as this man's prisoner chilled me. And why would he say this to me, of all folk?

"You're not afraid I'll kill you, to spare myself the bother? You've tried to kill me three times, so I can hardly let you go. And as you said, I can't go to the law."

This time his shrug was visible, but he said nothing.

"What does that mean?" I was a bit nettled by his insouciance, truth be told. "You can't be indifferent to the thought of your own death. No man is."

"Not indifferent," he said. "But sooner or later I'm going to get killed doing this. I accepted that a long time ago."

He seemed quite sincere about this, which I found almost as horrifying as his attempts to kill me.

"Doing this...?" I asked, with genuine curiosity.

But this time he turned away. After some time had passed, he actually went to sleep. On my blankets.

'Twas not as if I was using them, but seeing him so heedless of any threat I might pose was irritating.

However, I had no intention of threatening him, not in the way he was so obviously prepared to fight.

All those long nights watching an empty camp had given me plenty of time to work out a solution to the dilemma of holding a man prisoner...even without assistance from the law.

CHAPTER 12

I awoke with a brilliant idea. And maybe it was because I still had a bit of a headache that I spilled it without thinking first.

"We don't have to go after them anymore."

Kathy had risen from the small table where breakfast was spread when I opened my eyes, and started toward me, but now she stopped. Heedless of this clear warning, I babbled on.

"I don't think I told you last night." My memory of that time was hazy. "But I talked to Meg, and she bit the man who oversaw her kidnapping. Hard enough to draw blood, so he'll bear marks. All we have to do is go back to court and find a slim nobleman with a bitten hand—or figure out who's not there, and should be—and go looking for him. Once we find him we'll know who, and probably why, and can break this thing wide open without...ah..."

Without Katherine ever being in danger. But Katherine now stood halfway across the room, looking at me like I was a cockroach who'd died in her porridge.

I realized that I had made several mistakes.

A worried whine from under my bed confirmed this, even before she spoke.

"Will you ever stop thinking about money?"

"You talked to Meg?" said Rupert. "When? How was she? Is she hurt? Of course she's frightened, but is she... How is she!"

"She is frightened," I admitted, tackling the easier problem first. "But it'd take more than a kidnapping to break that woman's nerve. If I wasn't already..."

I looked from Rupert's frightened eager face to Kathy's stern one, and revised my comment.

"Your Mistress Margaret is pretty impressive. We didn't get away, but that was bad luck, not any failure on her part."

Kathy still looked angry and...disappointed? My heart flinched, even as Rupert said, "Get away? How did you get close enough to talk to her? Is the child all right?"

I sighed and rubbed my head, which really did ache, but even that didn't thaw my beloved. So I told them the whole tale of last night's thwarted escape—or most of the tale. I excused my failure to return by stressing the need to reach Meg's room while most of her guards were still at dinner...and I'd been right about the heroic thing. By the time I finished Kathy was perched on the foot of my bed, the eyes behind her spectacles bright with interest.

"I couldn't tell about the child," I finished. "She's not showing yet, and I'm not a midwife. But aside from a few bruises she seemed fine. She's too smart not to be scared, but it's not stopping her."

"And yet," said Kathy, "you're willing to leave her in their hands, while you go back to the city and claim your reward?"

I was annoyed enough to sit up, ignoring the twinge of pain it cost me.

"It's *our* reward, so *we* can get married. But it might be the smartest way to tackle this thing. He wouldn't be taking such pains to conceal his face, if his identity wouldn't reveal something. Once we know who's behind this, and why, the Liege can bring the hammer down and force them to order their thugs to let Meg go. Which would be safer for her and the child, as well as us!"

It wasn't even a lie, but as I said it my conscience pricked. We also might not be able to find the man Meg had bitten. If I'd been in their hands, I'd have taken more comfort from the knowledge that friends were right behind me, scheming for my escape, than from them going back to Crown City. Even if that was the best way to get to the bottom of this. But it *was* the best way, curse it.

"Rupert has to go back," I finished with husbandly firmness. "Because he's got the best chance of convincing his father. And you should go with him, because you know the court—you might be able to see who *isn't* there. I can follow Meg, keep track of the coach, and keep trying to figure out a way to free her."

"I'm not going anywhere," said Rupert. "It sounds like you came close to succeeding. You might have if we'd been with you, as we agreed. No, I'm not blaming you. There would have been more guards later, and it made sense to try when most of them were eating. But if you came that close alone, together we're bound to find a way!"

"Well said." Kathy rose off the foot of the bed. "I'm going to take the dog out, and then we can go back to that inn and see if they're still there. Though I wish you'd had time to come get us."

So much for husbandly firmness. Maybe I wasn't doing it right—lack of practice, no doubt—but there was a note of reserve in her voice that told me she hadn't entirely bought my excuses.

Once again, I wondered why I'd chosen to fall for a *smart* woman.

"We need help," Rupert said. "Curse it, we need the law! If they're still there I'll go to the sheriff, writ or no writ, no matter what it does to Father's negotiations. When I'm Liege they can *have* their stupid mineral rights!"

I let this pass, because I knew the kidnappers would be long gone. I had no appetite for the simple breakfast of biscuits, sausage and cheese, though I did drink another cup of magica willow-bark tea. Soon after that I managed to rise and dress, without too much pain.

Getting the dog out from under the bed was impossible—or at least, more trouble than it was worth, and he started to growl again. We finally left the door open, and the window as well—there was a covered porch below, and from its roof the strange mutt could probably reach the ground.

I was curious to see the beast by day—darkness and concussion must have warped my vision, because no dog could look like the picture in my memory. But that deep growl trumped curiosity.

"And the Addled Cock is even less friendly," I told Kathy, as she put on her straw hat and plain blouse and skirt—the closest her wardrobe came to slum ware. "Not a proper place for a lady, at all."

"Meg was there." She sounded a bit critical, I thought.

"And I tried to get her away, too," I said. "She'll be long gone by now. So there's no reason for you to—"

"Because it's not proper? I hate to tell you this, love, but marrying *you* is no proper pursuit for a lady. Do you want that to stop me?"

I didn't...and I was pretty sure the kidnappers really had moved on, so I led my friends back to the Addled Cock and into the alley behind it. When we looked over the fence, the coach wasn't there.

Even Rupert could see that following so closely that they became aware of us would result in a tighter guard on Meg, so we returned to our inn to spend a day letting me get over my headache.

When we got back there was nothing but dust under the bed, and since we didn't hear any hysterical maids, the dog must have sneaked away.

Rupert, at loose ends, went out to learn which road the coach had taken out of town, but Kathy stayed behind. Visiting the site of my heroic stand had softened her suspicions so much that she was prepared to take advantage of Rupert's absence, at least for a kiss and a cuddle...

Unfortunately, I really did have a headache.

I was also a bit irritated by her refusal to do the sensible thing and return to court—which really was the best way to resolve this, and I was foolish enough to say so. Again.

After a second quarrel, which made my headache even worse, she said she was going to look for the dog and flounced out.

I paced the floor and argued with the Kathy in my head, who proved much easier to debate than Kathy in person. But eventually my nerves settled enough for my hands to steady, and I began the delicate—and highly illegal—process of forging a High Liege writ, demanding all due assistance from any of his liegemen to the bearer.

Forgery was one of many things Jack didn't have the patience for, but when he saw that I did, he'd hunted up a tutor for me. And old Calfor may or may not have been lying when he said all forgers had their pupils use the Liege's signature as their practice piece. It was a signature you were never supposed to use, because the consequences would be so severe, which he claimed made it perfect. Now that signature came to me as easily as my own—maybe easier, since I seldom signed anything. I could still hear Calfor's voice telling me to put more pressure on the down strokes, and loosen my grip on the quill so the letters wouldn't look so tight. A forger's goal isn't to make a perfect copy of someone's signature, because no one signs their name exactly the same every time. The trick is to make it look like something your mark *might* have produced. I filled a scrap of cheap paper with practice signatures till my writing loosened up, then started drafting the warrant. Thanks to my father I write a fine hand—that was what had drawn Jack's attention—and a writ might have been written by any number of clerks. The problem there was to strike the proper balance between legal formality and menace, and I went through a couple of drafts.

I read my final product to Rupert and Kathy when they returned, together and dogless, though Rupert now knew which direction the coach had gone, and one of the grooms was being laughed at for claiming that a golem had taken up residence under the stable.

They thought I had the tone about right, so I wrote up a clean copy and signed the Liege's name with a relaxed flourish—as if I was completely unaware this could get me hanged. It took several minutes to dry, but there was one more thing I had to practice...

"What'll you do for a seal?" Rupert asked. "Father wears that ring even when he sleeps. And if he does take it off, it's guarded."

"As it should be." I put the red wax stick I'd purchased beside the lit candle, and went over to the saddlebag that held, among other things, Rupert's spare clothing. "The Liege's seal is a legal guarantee, and it signifies a lot of power. But your family crest isn't just on that ring. It's on the sign of a tavern down the road, The Liege's Arms. It's on those little flags people wave when your father rides by in a procession, and someone who wants to flatter him passes them out. It's even..." I pulled it out to show him as I spoke. "...stamped on your fancy coat buttons."

Mind you, the Liege's seal ring was a flat stamp and Rupert's buttons curved at the edges, but a bit of wiggling in the wax helped disguise that. And if I remembered correctly, the seal was a bit bigger... On the other hand, how many sheriffs, or even barons, would have a copy of the Liege's seal around to compare it to?

Forging a writ was treason... But I'd rather take my chances with the Liege than have Kathy take her chances with the thugs in some back alley, so I decided not to bring that up.

We set out next morning on the coach's trail, and we weren't more than a mile from town before we spotted the dog following us. Or rather, Champion spotted the dog and shied so hard he'd have thrown a less skilled rider.

By day the beast looked less like a rabbit, and more like someone had taken a normal dog and eliminated its neck and abdomen, sticking its head directly onto its shoulders and its hindquarters onto its ribcage. Its back legs were shorter than its front legs, so its rump sloped down, giving it the rabbit-shape I'd noticed in the alley.

Aside from that it had a rough-looking coat, black brindled with brown, big pricked ears and a pointed muzzle. And the teeth were every bit as startling as I remembered.

It took us the better part of the morning to catalog these details, because the dog turned tail and ran if we so much as looked at...him, in fact. He spent so much time running away that we could tell.

The dog vanished when we encountered other traffic on the road, but when we stopped at a stream to water the horses and eat luncheon, he emerged from the underbrush like some primitive hunter's nightmare and sat on his haunches watching us. He kept about thirty feet away.

Kathy insisted on giving him the remains of the smoked ham, which should have provided another meal for the three of us, and some bits of bread as well. She also, for reasons known only to the female brain, put the food somewhat closer to us.

At least the horses had accepted the beast—they went right on cropping grass as he ate.

"If you feed it," I said, "it will keep following us."

Rupert and Kathy exchanged a look I couldn't read.

"He's already following us," she said. "What should we call him? Monster comes to mind, but that might make people think he's not friendly."

"He isn't friendly." The beast had already wolfed down his meal and gone back to watching us from a distance. Though his gaze was mostly fixed on me. And it wasn't as if *I* fed him.

"How about Gargoyle?" said Rupert. "That fits too, and it sounds more kindly."

"'Tis too hard to say," my love replied. "*Here Gargoyle, here Gargoyle.* It feels like your mouth is full of pebbles."

"Why would we want to call him?" I asked. But no one listened to me.

Fortunately, the mutt didn't follow us into towns—which might have created a panic. He usually found us shortly after we emerged, no matter what road we chose. I thought he might give up when we took rooms at an inn one night—a possibility Kathy and Rupert found distressing for some reason. But we were rapidly gaining on the coach, and Rupert had to admit that catching them would be a disaster. And following too close might make them come after us, which would be worse.

We'd been on the road for less than two hours the next day when the dog rejoined us, and Katherine insisted we stop to feed him breakfast. Rupert, who was all but twitching to hurry us along, made no objection. Listening as they bandied names for the dog back and forth—Weirdness? Oddity?—I could see why the High Liege thought they'd suit each other.

I wasn't jealous, exactly, of the way they gossiped about mutual acquaintances, or shared some memory of Mistress Meg...but I didn't remember Kathy laughing that much at anything I'd said lately.

My mood grew so surly I was hardly speaking to anyone by the time we went to sleep—camping in the countryside that night. Next morning I woke with the monstrous dog in my bed.

This time I knew it wasn't Trouble, and moved slowly and warily. But it only watched me with gold-brown eyes as I reached out to let it sniff my hand, before gently scratching around its neck and down its spine. Either a good night's sleep or the dog's wary pleasure eased my black mood, and that rough-looking coat was surprisingly soft. But after a few minutes my fingers were coated with greasy dirt. The beast needed a bath, if we were going to find him a home. And how we were going to accomplish that when he wouldn't approach us, I had no idea.

Then I had an idea.

"Any chance you've got a Gift for animal handling?" I asked Rupert.

"Sorry. Not a trace."

He didn't look sorry.

"What can you do, then?" If any of his Gifts would have been useful in finding Meg, he'd have told us long since. But if he had some ability I could put to use with the dog...

"Finding runs in my family," said Rupert. "But it tends to be focused on particular things. Water for me. I can tell you that the nearest freshwater spring is about two

Понравился

hundred yards south of here...but where Meg might be, I have no idea."

He sounded pretty bleak about it, and Kathy hastily moved the conversation onward.

"'Tis too early to try to bathe the dog. He has to trust us for that."

"He doesn't trust us within twenty feet, unless we're asleep," I said. "Maybe a net? And a big tub. We could just lower him in, netted, and let him thrash around and wash himself."

"Or we could be patient," Kathy said. "He's ten feet closer today than he was when we started."

Since I didn't have a net or a tub I had to give up on that idea, at least for now.

The coach headed north and west again the next day, which meant we probably weren't going to Borrowston. But the towns along these back roads were so small they seldom had more than one inn, and the coach never stayed there.

Rupert was alarmed when he realized they must be camping out—though why he thought Meg would be in more danger there than in the Addled Cock, I didn't know. Kathy said, bluntly, that if they wanted to rape Meg they could do it anytime—but if Meg had been raped, she wouldn't have been as composed as I'd said she was. I added, more tactfully, that the kidnappers seemed to be more professional than that.

Rupert was somewhat consoled...but he still wanted to catch up to them, and we still didn't dare get close enough to threaten them. I was pretty sure, at this point, that they'd been ordered not to harm Meg. I doubted they'd been given the same orders about us.

The dog continued to follow his traveling food dish — at least, that's how I'd have thought of us if I'd been him. He slowly came closer, but he still wouldn't get within reach unless we were asleep. Judging by the tracks we found in the morning, he spent most of the night in or near my bed, though he also spent some time near Kathy, and checked on Rupert occasionally.

"How about Rabbit?" I suggested. We were riding along a muddy track that followed a stream. "He still looks a bit rabbity to me, and he's such a coward that it fits him on a spiritual level."

"Rabbit?" Rupert turned in the saddle, probably looking at the dog's teeth. "Really?"

"I like the irony," Kathy said. "And you can call it. *Here Rabbit, here Rabbit.*"

The dog pricked his ears, and for a moment I thought he might come. But then Champion, who had been so well behaved I'd forgotten he was a stallion, snorted and lashed out with his hind legs as if an assassin was sneaking up behind him. He then bolted down the road at a full, mud-splattering gallop.

Rupert was as startled by that first kick as the rest of us, but he kept his butt in the saddle somehow, and I saw that he'd decided to let the horse run off that panicked burst of speed before reining him in.

On a smooth, muddy road, that should have been a good decision. But Kathy and I barely had time to bring our own horses to a trot, when Champion caught a front hoof on something in a puddle and fell hard, throwing his rider.

He might have rolled over Rupert too, but someone had trained the Heir well. Rupert was already curling into a ball when he hit the ground, and he kept on roll-ing, out of the path of those thrashing hooves.

Horror froze me in Tipple's saddle, desire to look away from the catastrophe warring with the desire to race to Rupert's aid. By the time I shook off my pa-ralysis, we'd almost reached them and they were both regaining their feet. Rupert was almost as white as the few mud-free spots on Champion's coat, but he wasn't limping as badly as the horse was.

"Easy, big boy." He grasped the reins just below the bit, though whatever had sent Champion into flight didn't seem to be bothering him now.

"Walk him a bit," said Kathy. "Slow and easy. That's the fastest way to learn if there's any damage."

"Are you all right?" I asked Rupert, since no one else seemed to care. Including Rupert.

The dog was nowhere to be seen.

"Umm. He's favoring the right fore. Looks like 'tis bleeding, but he's so muddy I can't be sure."

I unpacked a cook pan and filled it with water from the stream, and after a bit of rinsing we found a bloody scrape just above Champion's ankle, or whatever that's called on a horse.

"He's putting more weight on it," Kathy said. "I think he'll be all right, but we should take it easy for the rest of the day. We're beginning to get too close to Meg's coach anyway. We can stop here."

But I was wondering what could have made that wound.

Having no desire to get dirtier than I already was, I picked up a stick and began poking it into the mud. I found it almost immediately. Or rather, I found one of several flat slabs of rock that lay just under the surface of the puddle.

"They'd keep wagon wheels from sinking in," I said. "They were probably above the surface at first, and sank down after they'd been driven over a time or two. But whoever did this should have set them tighter, so a horse's hoof can't go into the space between the stones. It's a wonder Posy and Tipple didn't trip."

"We were pulling them in when we reached this stretch," Kathy said. "They could pick their footing. If we'd been moving faster... The wagoner who did this should be fined half his load!"

We resolved to report it at the next village, but Kathy still wanted us to do something about it. I took off most of my clothes—Rupert's were already so muddy that it didn't matter. We wrestled the large flat stones out of the mud and hauled them as far as we could off the road. That wasn't very far, but at least they wouldn't lame any more horses.

The dog still hadn't returned, the afternoon was hot, and Rupert and I were coated with mud, so we all went into the stream for a wash. Kathy, who'd used the time to mix up a poultice for Champion's leg, washed Rupert's clothes upstream, while Rupert and I scrubbed off downstream. I finished before he did, so I was the one who ended up washing Champion...and saw a faint streak of blood trailing down the horse's rump.

Despite the fact that Rupert wore nothing but wet drawers, he and Kathy both crowded close to inspect the small red dot it came from.

"Something stung him," Rupert said. "That's why he bolted."

"Maybe," said Kathy. "Well, I suppose it must have been. Though it's not swelling like a bee sting. Horsefly bites can bleed, but horses don't usually bolt like that for a fly."

"If something left a mark like that on me, I'd run."

I wished Michael were here. He knew everything that would sting a horse, and how both horse and man could defend themselves—though some of his anti-fly potions were so smelly I'd rather have been bitten.

Whatever it was, it didn't seem to be after the horses now. Since it had found us by the stream, we moved a good distance away before making camp, and Kathy and Rupert promptly dismissed the matter.

Given those well-hidden stones, I couldn't quite let it go. But the assassin had clearly been stalking Michael, not the rest of us. And if the men who held Meg wanted to get rid of us they had more direct—and effective—methods at their disposal.

I didn't want Kathy to think I was paranoid, even if I was, so I said nothing.

CHAPTER 13

Michael

My prisoner slept in, somewhat to my annoyance. I could have waked him when the sky began to brighten, but I wanted a good look at him by daylight so I let him sleep a bit longer.

I judged him to be some years older than I, mayhap twenty-six or -seven. He wore his hair cropped short, and his accent, though educated, had not sounded noble the few times I'd heard him speak. His face, stripped of personality by sleep, looked quite pleasant.

Having observed all this, I prodded him awake. The first expression to cross his face was bafflement at finding himself bound. Then he saw me, and memory flooded back. But the expression that flashed over his face before the self-control returned wasn't fear, as I'd expected, but a hatred so intense, so personal, that I was startled out of my silence.

"Do you know me, somehow?"

I would swear I'd never set eyes on him before, but as Fisk pointed out I hadn't met all of Roseman's men.

He might even be kin to someone I'd brought to the attention of the law.

He shook his head, slightly, and proceeded to ignore me, except for the practical aspects of his captivity. And he'd not overstated the difficulty of holding a man prisoner.

I had to help him up from the bedroll, for he couldn't stand with his hands and feet tied. After some thought, I rigged a hobble that at least let him walk without aid. I had to untie his hands to let him relieve himself and eat, and then tie him to a tree so I could do the same myself and pack up the camp. I'd have worried about taking my eyes off him for more than a moment, but True watched him for me, his lips drawn back in a silent snarl. He also emitted his rasping, voiceless bark whenever the man so much as shifted his feet, which seemed a bit unfair in True. My would-be-assassin could have slit the dog's throat before I could have stopped him. He even looked concerned when he observed True's muteness—though he'd not hesitated an instant to slay me!

But I suppose an assassin may also care for animals, so I had some hope of success when I saddled up Chant and went to ask him, "Where did you tether your horse?"

He didn't answer, didn't look at me, but I fancied I saw dismay behind that cool mask.

"'Tis your horse. If you tethered him loose, or your rope is weak, he might be able to break free when the thirst sets in. If you camped near a road, or some farmhouse, he might make enough noise for someone to find him. But if he can't break free and no one finds him, he'll die slowly and most cruelly. I'd spare any beast that, were it up to me, but I can't waste time searching for a hidden camp. And 'tis not my horse."

In truth, if he refused to speak I intended to set some local farmers looking for the place, offering a good reward for his horse and gear—though a good reward would leave my purse thinner than Fisk would approve.

But he looked up and met my gaze, and my bluff must have been convincing for contempt flashed in his eyes.

"It's west of here. I'll guide you."

After some thought about logistics—having him in Chant's saddle, even if I held the lead, could go wrong in so many ways—I bound his wrists to one of the straps on my saddle and removed his hobbles so he could walk, close beside me and under my eye. 'Twas uncomfortable for him, but it didn't last long—the camp was less than a mile distant.

His horse was a leggy roan mare, with a white blaze and good manners. He'd camped by a stream so she didn't need water, but I gave her a handful of oats from the supply I keep for Chant and Tipple while I packed up his gear. This didn't take long, for he'd only paused to pull off his saddle and packs, not even taking the bedroll off his cantle.

'Twas a struggle to get him mounted, even with his cooperation—and that cooperation was motivated more by True's bared teeth than by my knife.

He might care for animals, but my good dog did not return the favor, and I took proper heed of that.

After a bit more thought I unbuckled his stirrups, which would make it harder to keep his seat should he see a chance for escape, and tied a loose loop around his waist and then to the pommel of his saddle. If he tried to gallop off and couldn't keep his seat, he was assured of a short and most uncomfortable ride, which would have made me hesitate to try it. My final precaution was to leave his horse haltered instead of bridled, with the lead rope tied to Chant's pommel. I then threw his cloak over his shoulders, fastening it so his bound hands wouldn't be visible from a distance, though my intention was to avoid being seen.

I did manage to keep anyone from observing us, though riding around the field where a farmer and his sons were harvesting took us miles out of our way, and a party of youngsters out for a picnic forced me to hold a knife to my prisoner's throat for quiet as they passed.

His silence then puzzled me. On horseback he might well have avoided getting his throat cut, at least for long enough to shout, and my silently snarling dog probably couldn't have reached him.

When I thought more on that, it occurred to me that this man had been stalking me for over a week, possibly many weeks. Even if he couldn't immediately kill me, he no longer had to struggle to find me. If I wasn't careful, I might end up helping him to complete his task! I resolved to be *very* careful.

But with all these delays, 'twas early in the evening when we finally reached Baron Tatterman's abandoned keep.

The kidnappers had left the front gate open—indeed, I saw no means by which it could be latched from the outside. Once within, I lowered the bar that secured those great wooden doors, and taking Rupert's word that the walls were intact, I pulled my prisoner from the saddle and left the horses to roam while we explored the keep.

The front doors were locked, and so were the doors at the back and side. But someone had failed to close the pantry shutters, and that window was big enough for me to climb through, and even drag my prisoner though after me—assisted by True, who kept close watch at his heels.

Beyond a few necessary orders, we hadn't spoken all day. As we walked through room after room, some vacant, some with furniture shrouded against dust and time, the silence felt different from that of wood and field: older, emptier.

It took a bit of searching to find the room I knew would be there, for 'twas not some dank cellar storeroom, but what had once been a servant's chamber, on the second floor above the kitchen. I spotted it instantly, for 'twas the only door on the corridor that had a bolt on the outside.

The brass of bolt and fittings shone with newness, in stark contrast to the tough, ancient wood. Inside, the window was high in the wall, mayhap a foot square. There were no shutters, but one un-rusted iron bar had been bolted across it from the outside. 'Twas furnished, after a fashion, with a straw pallet covered by several woolen blankets, and a honey bucket. The blankets and walls were gray, the straw of the pallet tan, and the only note of color in the place was a single blade of straw, cast off in a corner, which for some reason had turned bright red. At least 'twas not the brown of dried blood...but that only made it more curious.

After a few days, you'd go mad from boredom in this room, and my prisoner looked at it in dismay.

I thought of Mistress Margaret, imprisoned here for weeks, or even months, had we not startled them into flight, and my face must have showed my feelings. My would-be-assassin had opened his mouth to protest, but he not only closed it, he took a step back.

This room had been remodeled by professionals, to hold a prisoner, and I had no doubt of their ability.

Indeed, seeing this place made me worry even more for my friends. I had no doubt of Fisk's competence, Kathy's good sense, or Rupert's determination...but there were six kidnappers.

I'd been forced to send my comrades into danger without me, and that was this man's fault. But 'twould be foolish to underestimate him and that odd red straw nagged at me, so I made a quick search of the place.

I found Margaret's note in the only place it could have been hidden, beneath the straw pallet. 'Twas written on the stones of the floor in red wine, using that reddened straw for a pen, and the words were so faint that without the sunlight that streamed through the small window, I wouldn't have seen them.

But she'd still taken the time and trouble to write it— not a brief note, but a scrawl that covered most of the space beneath the pallet. My captive came to stand beside me as I read.

Stephen 28, 3rd Finday of Berryon. I'm Margaret Merkle, daughter of Stanly Merkle, of Merkle and Mace Woolen Goods, and I've been kidnapped. I'm being held by five men, who call each other Wilber, Morry, Angus, Jutt, and Rip. There's also a man who doesn't always travel with us, but seems to be their supervisor or employer. Wilber is just under six feet tall, in his early thirties, with a paunch, ginger hair and a mustache. Morry is...

She went on to describe all her kidnappers, the masked nobleman who had supervised her kidnapping, and the carriage, inside and out. These long, careful, useful descriptions were followed by an appeal for anyone who found this message to convey it to her father, Liege Heir Rupert Ware, or the local authorities.

By the time I'd finished reading that sensible and courageous document I was so full of admiration and

fury I could almost have done my captive some violence.

"This is the woman you're helping to hold prisoner,"
I said. "Those men are the thugs you're serving. Shame
on you, sir. Shame."

His eyes, still on that brave note, did not meet mine.
But his cool mask was in place and he said nothing.

I drew my blade and cut the rope from his wrists. I
had to call True out of the room, for my good dog still
wanted to stand guard over this man.

But with my assassin locked in that terrible room,
I had no qualms about leaving him while I inspected
the keep. Mistress Margaret's kidnappers had evidently
intended to make a long stay; both kitchen and stable
were well stocked, and someone had recently repaired
the kitchen pump and fastened a new bucket at the
stable well.

I drew water for the horses, and coaxed them into
their stalls by the simple expedient of forking down
some hay. Looking at the supplies in the kitchen, I
doubted that the men we'd seen had laid them in—
few professional bullyboys know what to do with a full
shank of smoked ham, much less plain flour and raw
oats. 'Twas the cooked sausage and cheese they'd cut
into, leaving those things that required preparation.
And while I'm a fair camp cook, I hoped my stay would
too short for me to need that skill.

Those supplies, which they probably couldn't use
well, implied accomplices beyond those we knew of—
but even as the need to rejoin my friends pressed on
me, the need to keep this assassin from trailing after
them was the more urgent.

Of course, the quickest way to deal with him would
be to leave him to starve, but I am no murderer.

Which left only the long solution, alas.

In my youth, I had helped my father's master of hounds tame dogs that had been abused or turned savage—the one often following from the other. And though some (such as my erstwhile squire) might have argued with me, I was reasonably certain the hound master's techniques would eventually gentle even the most obdurate man.

They had, after all, worked on Fisk.

CHAPTER 14

Fisk

The dog returned several hours after we'd made camp.

"You were no help," I told him. "I'm going to name you Useless."

He didn't seem to care, sitting on his shrunken butt and regarding me a bit less warily than usual. He was closer than usual too, and the incident—from which he'd run like the coward he was—seemed to have changed his attitude toward us. Next morning, though he didn't let anyone but me touch him, he stayed in camp and then accompanied us down the road.

We stopped in the first village we came to, and complained about the hidden stones in the mud hole. The locals knew nothing about it, but after the town's farrier had removed the poultice Kathy had made and inspected Champion's scraped leg, he took us seriously. In fact, he promised that if he ever came across the man who put them there he'd give him "a talking to."

Since the farrier was also the local smith, with arms like ham hocks, this threat was more formidable than it sounded. But we all agreed that the guilty party was some passing wagoner, and that hoping he wouldn't do it again was probably the most we could do.

The dog was still bypassing villages, but he now walked with us on the road. It was clear that he'd joined our expedition—which I didn't mind—but if I was going to touch him on a regular basis, there was one thing I insisted on. When we made camp that evening, the first thing I did was put a kettle on to heat some water. Katherine produced the mild soap she used on her own hair, and Rupert sacrificed his expensive, embossed belt to make a collar, cutting it down and punching new holes for the buckle.

Getting the collar *on* the dog was up to me, but by dint of shameless bribery—he liked dried meat even better than fresh, maybe because he could chew it for a long time—I got it fastened. He didn't bolt immediately, so I took that as a good sign, and looped a rope through it to tie him to a nearby tree.

"Bathing regularly is a cornerstone of civilization," I told him, adding hot water from the kettle to a pail of cold I'd fetched from a nearby stream. "Which makes you a flea-bitten barbarian. Barbarian. That's not bad name."

"Still too fierce," said Kathy. "He's a kindly soul."

"He's a quivering mouse," I said hopefully, stripping down to an old pair of britches. I've helped Michael bathe Trouble, and I knew just how tricky this was likely to be. I was also aware of Kathy's gaze on my body— so aware that it was a good thing I was both distracted, and in short order drenched with cold, dirty water.

He was better behaved than I expected—by which I mean that he didn't even try to bite—but holding on to that twisting, yelping, soap-slick form, I ended up calling him a lot worse things than "barbarian." However, he calmed down a bit for the final rinse, and seemed to enjoy being dried off with my dirty shirt.

I let him out of his collar when I finished—if he ran off, I didn't want him to get caught on something. But despite the indignant looks he gave me he remained in the camp, possibly encouraged by the scent of cooking stew. And I was proved right about the civilizing influence of a bath, because he let Kathy pet him.

Either that, or his spirit was broken.

"I think someone owned him once." Katherine's slender elegance made a wonderful contrast with the mutt's misshapen oddity, and his tongue hung out in an expression that, on Trouble's face, I'd have taken for a canine grin. With this dog, one's attention focused more on the teeth. "He's been bathed before. He's had a collar on, too. In fact..."

She went over to the stew pot, and fished out a piece of carrot, tossing it from hand to hand to cool it.

It was hardly surprising that the dog followed her—she'd been feeding him, after all. But then she held up the carrot.

"Sit!" she said crisply, and the dog did.

I had to open and close my mouth several times before I found my voice.

"Well...well."

"Good boy!" Kathy gave him the carrot, which he accepted as his due, and she gave me a smug look, accepting my admiration as her due.

Though I still think I was right about the civilizing influence of a bath.

The dog stayed in camp all night. The next morning, by the sacrifice of a few bits of biscuit, we learned that he also knew stay, come, and heel, though he was a bit rusty at that last command.

Thus armed, I put the collar on him before we went into the next village and tied his leash to Tipple's saddle. But the problem wasn't that he'd run off, far from it—it was getting him to stay far enough away that the horses didn't trip over him. At one point he tried to take shelter under Tipple's belly, and she stopped so quickly I almost went over her head.

His tail was tucked so tightly between his legs that several people glared at us for abusing him. But most of the others glared at the odd and ferocious looking beast, and if he'd been on his own they'd have driven him off with sticks and thrown stones.

"Which is an excellent reason to dislike towns," I told him. "I don't blame you in the least. But if you're going to stay with us, you need to get over that."

Toward that end, in the next village I insisted on stopping for luncheon, and we sat on the lip of a fountain in the town square to eat it. And slowly, as passersby stared but did nothing more, his exaggerated wariness relaxed until he was willing to lie at my feet instead of trying to hide behind them.

After luncheon, we asked our usual questions, learning that Meg's abductors were roughly a day ahead of us. Fancy coaches were an unusual sight in these small towns and country villages, so we had no trouble keeping up with it. With a little effort we could have caught it...but then what?

If they'd been stopping for the night at inns, at this point even I would have given up on pleasing the Liege and taken our forged writ to a sheriff, to see what he could do. But the inns in these smaller towns were too respectable for them to risk letting anyone see that they held a helpless girl prisoner. They never did more than order a meal to take with them and change horses, before moving on.

If we could have figured out their destination, we might have gone ahead of them and persuaded a sheriff to arrest them when they came into town. But while they were generally moving north and west, their course was so erratic I wasn't sure they had a destination.

Catching up with them would only have put them even more on guard, so all we could do was follow, and hope they'd decide they'd lost us and go to ground once more.

This was a conclusion Rupert didn't much like...but he didn't have any better ideas, either.

And at least this left us free to use the inns, because by this time the dog wasn't the only one who needed a bath.

The grooms' reaction when I led the dog into the stables convinced me that we'd better keep him with us. We picked up our packs, I took his leash in hand and we went into the inn...where the first serving maid to see him dropped her tray, spilling an empty teapot and half a dozen cups and mugs. Several of the cups broke, but that wasn't the dog's fault. Which I was politely pointing out when the innkeeper appeared to see what the commotion was about.

"Get that...that... What is that?"

"Chicken is my dog," I said. He was proving his right to the name by trying to hide in Kathy's riding skirt, which wasn't nearly big enough to conceal him. "And either he stays, or we go. We want two rooms, and baths for all three of us."

I could see the man inflating his prices as I spoke, but he was also looking at the dog. So were two maids, the barkeeper, and half the patrons from the taproom, with more coming to join them as the word spread.

"And a private parlor to dine in?" the innkeeper asked hopefully.

"Certainly not." Two of the customers from the taproom had hounds beside them, and one lady carried a tiny furball in her arms. "Craven is very well behaved. Sit."

To my delight, he pulled his head out of Kathy's skirt and did so. The innkeeper sighed.

"You'll keep it on a leash? I can't have something that looks like that running loose."

"If your patrons are that timorous, then we will. Come along, Mousey."

"Oh good," Kathy murmured, as we followed a maid up the stairs to our rooms. "We're keeping him."

The maid cast another glance over her shoulder at the slinking beast, clearly demonstrating the problems adopting that dog would entail.

"I'm still working on getting us married," I pointed out. Without a lot of help from her, though I had sufficient sense not to say so. "It's a bit early to be adopting dogs. Do you want him? A lot?"

I really hoped she didn't.

"It doesn't matter what I want," Kathy said. "Although I do. But you've taken him under your wing, and once you adopt someone they're yours. Forever. You then proceed to mother them."

"I do not!"

Motherly wasn't how I wanted Kathy to think of me. If she'd wanted some manly moron, I suppose she wouldn't have chosen me in the first place...but *motherly?*

I didn't like that idea at all, but if Kathy thought I was motherly, did *she* like it?

Women are peculiar. Even the best of them.

We all smelled sweeter when we gathered to go down for dinner, and there was some debate about whether to take the dog with us. But he needed to get over his excessive timidity eventually and there was no better time to start than now, so Kathy gave in. Rupert seemed to have something else on his mind and paid no attention to our discussion. I tied a lead onto the dog's collar and only a few people in the hallway stared at him. Probably because there *were* only a few people in the hallway.

As we approached the taproom the scents from the kitchen wafted out to meet us, setting the dog's nose atwitch. The menu written on the chalkboard by the hearth looked appealing.

We then had to choose between taking a table (more expensive) or seating ourselves at the public board (less private). A small hubbub broke out when I led the dog in, as the people who'd heard stories from people who'd seen him this morning craned their necks to see, and he shrank closer to my boots. He was doing very well, but I decided not to test him with the common bench and we took a table instead.

The chosen Heir to the throne of the United Realm attracted no attention in the taproom—and he wouldn't have protested, or maybe even noticed, if I'd chosen to share the public bench. This was one of the things I liked best about Rupert, and we seated ourselves at the table in amity—the dog darted beneath it like a rabbit with the hawks hovering. A serving maid bustled up to take our order; roast squab for me, roast pork with white beans over cracked wheat for Katherine, and a bone for the dog. Rupert decided on a slice of the beef that turned on a spit in the big hearth, and at least he waited till the maid trotted off before he spoke.

"How long has it been, do you think, since Meg's had a bath?"

Kathy's eyes, which had been bright with the challenge of bringing the dog into a new place, fell guiltily.

"She's not dining in an inn tonight," Rupert went on. "She'll be chained to one of those coach benches, or mayhap sleeping on the ground, surrounded by men she fears. And probably hates."

"You're right," I said. "It's high time we got her out of there, and I'm all in. What's the plan?"

I might not have been so sarcastic if the same thought hadn't crossed my mind when I stepped into the tub. Mistress Meg's situation was bothering all of us, but there was no use dwelling on it—so unlike Rupert, I tried not to.

He glared at me now, with angry color rising in his cheeks.

"All right. We catch up to them, following far enough back that we can keep our eyes on the coach."

"If we can see them, they can see us," I pointed out. "But let's assume we can skulk through the woods, or keep enough distance that they don't connect the three of us with the four people who attacked them at the bridge. Then what?"

"Then we'll be near enough to strike when some opportunity presents itself! Hiding behind them like this, we've no way to seize a sudden chance. We have to be able to see what's happening to her!"

"No, we don't." Kathy spoke up before I could. "Rupert, what chance do you think is going to occur? And one that would let the three of us overcome six professional swordsmen? Men who'll be expecting us, particularly if we follow them as closely as you suggest. I hate not knowing what's happening to Meg, too. But unless we can figure out where they're going, and beat them there in time to get help from the sheriff, we have no choice but to wait till they hole up somewhere like they planned to do in Tatterman's keep. When they do that, we *will* go to the sheriff. But they won't stop if they think we're still behind them."

The maid carried a tray over as Kathy finished, and unloaded our plates. She set the bone, on its own clean plate, on the table and departed.

So when I heard him sniffing, and felt the dog's body vibrate against my leg, I thought he was smelling the bone.

"I wish they'd head a bit more to the west." Rupert picked up his fork and put it down again, probably thinking about what Meg was eating now. "If they'd go into my Uncle Roger's fief, he'd send out—"

The dog shot from under the table and clamped his teeth, not into the bone, but in Rupert's sleeve.

Rupert wasn't hurt—the beast had only cloth between its jaws—but he emitted a startled yelp. Several
women screamed.

I was startled as well, but I knew what to do.

"Bad dog," I said sternly. "Let him go at once."

I may have known what to do, but the dog didn't.
His teeth remained fixed in Rupert's sleeve, though his
gaze slid toward the table.

Rupert showed more courage or more idiocy than I
had, gripping the dog's jaw with this free hand and trying to pull it down. Having seen that the dog wasn't
running through the room savaging people, those ridiculous women stopped shrieking. I grabbed the bone
and offered it to the dog—who completely ignored it,
though he looked a bit wistful.

Kathy came around the table to grab the beast's muzzle, and between them she and Rupert pried his jaws
apart.

"Bad dog," I repeated, as he sank back to his
haunches.

He crouched even lower, and I thought he was
ashamed. But as it turned out, he was pulling back the
bowstring for another shot. This time he leapt under
Rupert's arm and snatched his plate, yanking it off the
table to the floor. The gravy-coated beef landed with a
splat, but some of the fresh peas that had accompanied
it rolled twenty feet before they stopped.

I understood why the dog preferred Rupert's dinner
to his, but his method of expressing that preference
might explain why he was a stray. I grabbed his collar
to keep him from claiming his prize, but he made no
effort to do so, sitting solidly on his haunches and ignoring, not only my scolding, but also the absurd commotion his antics had produced.

Honestly, from the sound of it you'd have thought he'd torn someone's throat out, instead of just dumping a plate—something that happened in taprooms all the time.

I pointed this out to the serving maid, the tapster, assorted diners, the innkeeper's wife, and the innkeeper himself when he arrived on the scene. But in the end, we were banished to our rooms. At least they let us take the food we'd been served, though we had to pay for another meal for Rupert. That second serving, which arrived from the kitchen very quickly, was less well-dressed than the first.

The dog strolled up the stairs behind us, seeming completely unrepentant.

"Well, he's getting over his excessive timidity." Kathy's face was alight with unvoiced laughter.

"I thought dogs were trained not to take food off the table," I said. "Though if one of those hounds had done the same there wouldn't have been half the fuss, and if that woman's little dust mop had done it everyone would have laughed. They're just prejudiced by your appearance," I added, to the dog. "Don't let them upset you."

The dog, who'd retreated to a corner instead of crawling under the bed, didn't seem upset. In fact, he gave us a brief tail-wag—the first we'd seen from him.

In the end, we settled down to finish dinner in a happier state than we'd begun it. We were alert to stop and scold the dog for any move he made on our plates, but he just sat in his corner and watched us eat.

Kathy insisted that this was sufficiently good behavior that he deserved his bone after all. I didn't think so, but I wanted her to keep smiling so I agreed.

Rupert, whose sleeve had several small holes in it, held no grudges.

He was still fretting about Meg, but he really didn't have a plan. Following close behind them would clearly do more harm than good, so he eventually stopped arguing. To reward his good behavior, I agreed that it wouldn't hurt to reduce the coach's lead to half a day, though we'd have to be careful not to overrun them.

Honestly, he was harder to train than the dog.

I regretted my concessions when Rupert woke me before dawn. We'd agreed to get an early start, but that didn't mean I was happy about it. I put a leash on the dog to take him out, and said I'd ask the grooms to saddle our horses while Rupert woke Kathy.

The dog gave me a good excuse not to help the grooms, so I was able to listen to their conversation... and I was groggy from my early rising, so it took me longer to make the connections than it should have.

"I suppose there's plenty in that midden could spoil bad," one of them was saying. "But I never saw the like of it. Maybe twenty dead, and some still twitching. Mistress wanted to rake off all the scraps from last night and bury 'em, but Master just set a boy to keep other animals away—better than the rat catcher, he says, and cheaper too."

My sleepy brain finally woke up.

"Wait, are you saying that something thrown out from last night's dinner is killing rats? I thought rats could eat anything."

In fact, I could think of only a few exceptions—and all of them were labeled "poison."

Kathy and Rupert arrived as I spoke, carrying their own packs, and we all listened to the man's reply, though there wasn't much more to the tale. A cook taking an early scrap bucket out to the midden had seen dozens of rats lying dead around it, and run back to report this gruesome oddity. And to get a manservant to carry out the scraps, because whatever had done *that*, she wasn't going near it. Looked like a plague scene, it did...

Ugly thoughts stirred in my nasty, suspicious mind.

Kathy had no more desire to see dead rats than the cook, but Rupert accompanied me out to the midden where a boy stood guard over the scattered corpses. Dozens of dead rats was an exaggeration, but I counted eight small stiff bodies. And some had probably crawled off to their holes to die.

I picked up a stick and did some poking, and soon turned up a hunk of last night's beef. The rats had consumed enough of it that I couldn't be sure, but it appeared to have been discarded before anything human tried to eat it.

Rupert's face was so pale I could see his freckles, even with the inn blocking the new sun's light.

"I owe your dog a bone," he said. "A lot of bones. And no hard feelings about the sleeve, either."

I clearly wasn't the only one with a suspicious mind, but I had to point out...

"There's no proof it was the beef that did this. And no way to prove it was your dinner, even if we fed it to some other animal and watched it die."

However there were things we could do, even though they weren't proof, either.

We went back to the stable, paid a groom an absurd amount simply to hold our good dog's leash for a while, and then we all went into the kitchen to annoy the busy staff with our questions. The early morning shift wasn't composed of the same people who'd fixed dinner, but eventually we managed to get a description of a slim man, who some had thought was staying at the inn and some thought wasn't. He'd wandered into the kitchen last night and asked a lot of questions about the food, where it came from and how it was prepared.

He'd been annoying, but since he was probably a customer they'd answered, and aside from that pretty much ignored him. They thought was in his twenties, or thirties, or maybe early forties, with brown hair. Or maybe dark blond. Some said he had a noble accent and some didn't think so, but they all agreed he was a bit on the short side, and slim.

None of them could say whether he'd had bite marks on his hand, or not.

"It's him," said Kathy, as we retreated from the kitchen and headed for the stable. "It's the same man who was overseeing Meg's kidnapping. I'm sure of it."

"No, we're not sure," I said. "We may think it's the same man, but we can't even be certain someone tried to poison Rupert, or that the man they're talking about is the one who did it."

"And why would anyone want me dead?" Rupert added. Kathy and I both turned to stare at him, and he grimaced. "I know, I know. But Liam, who'd take my place as Heir is only two, so it's not likely he's plotting to seize the throne."

"What would happen if he died too?" I asked.

"Caro would probably produce another heir. She might anyway, and even if someone managed to kill me, Liam, Caro, and all her future children, there are a host of cousins my father could choose a new Heir from, and no way to know who he'd pick. Not to mention the insanity of anyone thinking they could kill the High Liege's sons and his wife and get away with it."

"Maybe," I said. "Well, almost certainly. But we've already theorized that one reason for kidnapping Mistress Meg could be to get to you. If you were to die of natural causes—food poisoning, say—and your father, stepmother and brother all died in a carriage accident, who'd become High Liege then?"

"My Uncle Roger," said Rupert. "The one whose fief is west of here. But I spent some summers there, after my mother's death, and I know him well. He loves Father, hates court, and is perfectly happy managing his own estate. The last thing he wants is to become Liege, and his son Corbin feels the same way. After that it gets messy, because the judiciary council would have to choose between Roger's daughter's husband or my Aunt Genevieve's son, and there's no saying what they'd do. Trying to kill me just doesn't make sense. Besides, if the kidnappers wanted to kill me, why not do it back when I was banging on the fortress gate?"

"Because they needed to make it look like an accident," Kathy said, with a promptness that told me she'd been thinking about it. "But if they're not trying to kill you because you're the liege heir... Do you have any personal enemies?"

I didn't have to listen to his reply—Rupert wasn't the kind to go around making mortal enemies.

Unlike Michael. But Michael's assassin had not only attacked him twice, he'd ignored a clean shot at Rupert to go after Michael instead. And both his attempts had been...straightforward. Of course Michael was unredeemed, so if someone wanted to kill him they could just do it. But this still felt different.

"How under two moons did we end up with more than one assassin on our trail?" I demanded. "This is crazy! We could try to track him down..."

A slim, brown-haired man somewhere between twenty and forty-five. Right.

"I don't want to waste time," said Rupert promptly. "I want to catch up with Meg. And you said we could get closer."

Kathy's reply came more slowly. "'Twill be a lot harder to track one man, from such a vague description, than a coach with a crest scratched off its door. It *could* have been an insect that stung Champion, and something else in the midden that killed those rats."

Not one of us believed that, but it was possible. And they were right about the difficulty of finding the man, so we set off after Mistress Meg as we'd planned.

But I resolved, in the future, to listen to my dog.

"Rat. How about that for a name? He looks a bit rat-like to me."

"Under no circumstances," said Kathy, "are you naming our dog Rat."

I liked the possessive way she said "our dog" so much, I was happy to let her veto any number of names. And it seemed our luck had turned in other ways, as well— in the next town they told us the coach had departed on a westward road. Three towns and the better part of a day later, it was certain—the coach was headed west, toward Uncle Roger's fief.

CHAPTER 15

Michael

I delivered breakfast to my prisoner the next morning by opening his door, with drawn sword in hand, and pushing the tray inside with my foot. True assisted me with a silent snarl.

Last night I'd shoved in a jug of water and a bit of somewhat stale bread, so he wasn't starving—I'd eaten little more myself, before spreading my bedroll by the kitchen hearth and going to sleep. I'd been awake the previous night, after all. But he should now be ready to appreciate fried sausage links, hot porridge with cream and honey, and a handful of blackberries from the overgrown ruins of the kitchen garden. Plenty of berries, for the thorny bushes had taken over half the plot.

'Twas an excellent breakfast and he should be grateful...mayhap, someday, he would be.

For now, I left him without a word spoken between us and set off to search my temporary home, with True frisking at my heels. Away from my prisoner, he reverted almost instantly to his happy self, a change that was almost miraculous even to someone who knew dogs.

Because I was looking for them, I found a surprising number of useful things that had been left behind when the residents moved out, particularly in the work rooms where the owners may have assumed there was little of value. But the trowel with the chipped edge would serve well for grubbing out the onions and carrots whose tops I'd seen among the weeds, and that bucket only needed a new handle...

The rooms the baron and his family had used were pretty much bare, and some of the ceilings in the older wing leaked. But on the corridor above the kitchen, not far from the cell, I found two bedrooms with blankets, pillows and fresh straw ticks. Three beds in each room, which made me think that the two men who'd joined the coach had awaited it here.

Anxiety for my absent friends pricked, but I couldn't return to them till I'd dealt with my assassin.

Toward that end I went out to the stables, and after giving both horses a pat and a handful of berries—the crop was abundant, and they'd only have gone to the birds—I opened my prisoner's pack and started searching through it.

His magica crossbow was of considerable interest to me, for I'd not had time to examine it. I could tell little of its nature by looking, except that some magic inhabited it—but studying it closely, I saw that the glow seemed to come from the metal-lined trough and wire string, rather than the wood that surrounded it.

Any good herb talker can safely harvest magica herbs for healing, and if someone should cut down a magica tree, or accidentally slay some magica beast, a savant could help them make the proper sacrifice. The wood or hide could then, theoretically, be used safely, though few would want to take that risk.

But the only time I'd seen this glow around a thing that never breathed nor grew was when a few bits of glass were enchanted by a madman, who had wielded magic as easily as a smith used his hammer, or a cook his knife.

I had magic in me...but I must confess, my attempt to use it to learn more about the bow was half-hearted. Calm and curious as I was, I knew nothing would come of it. And there were other ways to get my answers.

I went through the rest of his things, mostly hoping to find something with his name upon it. Instead I came across a notebook, cheaply bound between two squares of stiffened leather. The pages held, not his name, but information about dozens of other men.

The entries were roughly organized, starting with each man's name and a thorough physical description, sometimes even a sketch. They went on to list the date of his hearing and the charge of which he'd been accused...before, every one of them, being marked as unredeemed.

I knew nothing about the little man, surprisingly gentle, who'd pricked those marks into my wrists. The jeering crowd had thrown muddy slush as he worked, and rotten fruit, though he asked the guards to stop them when the stones started to fly. I'd never heard his name...but it was there, in my assassin's notes.

What wasn't there were the details I'd given the judicars that proved Mistress Ceciel's innocence—which had ultimately gotten the charge against her dropped. Only my crime, freeing an accused murderess from gaol, and my failure to redeem myself by returning her to justice had been noted.

What followed, and not only in my case, were a host of other details that would help someone track or identify the man in question, skills they might use to earn their bread, hobbies that might take them to certain shops, and a precise description of any horses in their possession.

True, who hadn't reacted to the scent on the man's clothing, sniffed at this journal and the hair along his spine stiffened—but 'twas the uneasy chill that swept over me he was responding to, not paper and ink. I gave him a pat, trying to settle my own hackles as much as his, and went on to read the other entries.

A few of the men had committed odd, or inexplicable crimes that the judicars could find no way to settle. But most were the sons of wealthy influential men, who'd killed someone in a drunken rage, or even deliberately, and been saved from paying that ultimate debt by "the compassion of the judicars attending."

There were no pages marked with a dramatic X, or even a name crossed out. But I did find places where a page had been ripped out of the book, and I counted up their number with growing dismay.

Was this man some sort of bounty hunter, who specialized in tracking down the unredeemed? There was no record of an offer to pay this or that amount, on any of the entries.

When the notebook could tell me nothing more, I picked up the crossbow and his supply of bolts—he carried a full score—and took them out to a nearby field, to see if I could determine what it did.

I chose a knot in a dead oak as my target, worked the little forked lever that spanned the bow, and loosed. To my astonishment, my first careless shot thudded into its center.

I'm reasonably adept with the short bow I use for hunting, and crossbows are easy to aim and shoot, but I'm not an archer of this caliber.

I aimed again, this time more carefully. My second bolt struck the knot so close to its fellow that it might have taken one of the metal vanes off the other shaft.

I started to aim more carefully still...and realized I was going about my testing the wrong way.

I turned, walked several paces away from the tree, then spun and shot wildly in the direction of my target, hardly bothering to aim...and the bolt landed less than an inch from the others.

I went a bit mad then, shooting in all directions, striking narrow fence posts from an impossible range, or lopping the heads off flowers.

But eventually I settled down—assisted in regaining my calm by the need to hike out and retrieve my bolts, digging several out of the wood where they were embedded with my knife. And True refused to fetch, even the loose ones.

After a number of shots, I'd established that all I had to do was to point the crossbow in the general direction of the target, think of the place I willed the bolt to go... and there it went, even if my eyes were closed when I pulled the trigger.

Once I got over my astonishment—and I shouldn't have been so shocked, for I'd known the thing was magica—I found there were some limits to its power. It would hit any target within its range, but if I aimed at a target too far off the bolt would lose energy in the normal way and plow into the grass and earth...though still along a straight line between me and the target. And once it left the string the bolt's path was set—if I aimed at a bird in flight, the quarrel would sail right through the place the bird had been when it launched. To hit a moving target I would have to lead it, just as I would with an ordinary bow—but if I judged the distance aright, the spot I aimed for was where that bolt would fly.

Quail or duck might make a pleasant change from pork, for I expected to soon grow tired of eating that big haunch.

Sobered, I retrieved my last bolts and went back to fix myself and my prisoner a belated luncheon. After shoving it past his door I went back to the stables, and searched till I found a pair of hobbles—one buckle was broken but the leather was still sound, as was the chain between them. In addition to the tools I had with me, I found a few others in the tack room's workbench.

The fit wasn't bad, for a man's ankles are much the size of a horse's pasterns, but I had to replace the buckles with some more complex fastening. Given that I had neither locks nor keys, I replaced the buckles with a pair of iron rings, which I could fasten together by wrapping a bit of heavy wire around them, and then twisting it into a tight spiral and clipping the loose ends.

With a pair of pliers he'd have them off in minutes, and with more time even a slender nail might have done the trick. But without tools my makeshift lock should hold, and I could check to be sure they were still fastened before I released him from his cell. He might be able to get the drop on me, knock me senseless or kill me, and then go in search of tools...but he was unlikely to get the drop on True.

I went back to the kitchen and put some pork in the kettle to brown, then out to the wild garden to put my trowel to use, plucking a pocketful of herbs while I was there. And while bread might be beyond my rough and ready skills, biscuits are within them.

My prisoner stepped away from the door on my order, and with True keeping watch I bound his hands behind his back. I then attached my makeshift shackles—tight enough to hold him, but loose enough to wear for days without cutting off the blood flow to his feet.

He watched the process with interest but said nothing, even when I freed his hands and swung the door aside.

"Dinner's in the kitchen. You may have to sit down to manage the stairs."

In the end he chose to hop down, clinging to the rail and moving both feet to the next step together. I remembered Kathy doing that as a toddler, but 'twas easy not to smile at the comparison, and True became so agitated at these sudden movements I had to call him sharply to heel. When we went into the kitchen, the dog retreated to a corner where he could see my prisoner and stared fixedly.

The man looked warily back at True, then down at his place setting, which included neither knife nor fork, but only a spoon. A slight crease appeared between his brows.

"You've some question, Master...? What is your name, anyway?"

I ladled stew into his bowl as I spoke and I'd little hope of a reply, so I wasn't disappointed when I got none. However...

"I must call you something, so I suppose 'twill have to be Master Assassin."

I thought he twitched at that, but I wasn't sure.

"Anyway, True here is your real guard. He's fond of me, and would be very aggressive with anyone who tried to kill me. And since he's seen you do that once already, he probably thinks that name suits you well."

I sat down at my own place—on the other side of the table—and began to eat. With honest appetite, as I was reasonably certain that at this distance even the most skilled fighter couldn't kill me with a spoon.

I let him eat several bites before I went on.

"Although, having found your... What do bounty hunters call them? Warrant books? Having read your warrant book, I'm not entirely sure 'assassin' fits. But bounty hunters are generally paid by the authorities, and return the men they hunt to the law's keeping. Do you do that, Master Assassin? Well, I suppose it makes little difference to me. Though I must say, I wonder that even a bounty hunter would kidnap an innocent woman, who has done no one harm."

He still said nothing, but his gaze shifted aside. Whether he was one of the kidnappers or only allied with them, he knew something about them. But 'twould take more time, alas, before he told me what it was.

"I also found your crossbow..."

I chatted amiably through the meal, with him mostly ignoring me. When True and I returned him to his cell I took a moment to swap his honey bucket for an empty one. I thought I saw a flash of gratitude in his eyes at that, but I couldn't be sure.

The next morning I pushed his breakfast into the room and departed, to spend the day trying to find out who had stocked this keep and loaned it to kidnappers.

I started at the nearest village, buying bread, eggs and a chicken. This gave me an excuse to tell the baker and grocer that I was camping in the area, waiting for a friend to join me, and that I'd seen an old keep nearby which seemed to be deserted...

The conversation wandered a bit, but I managed to learn that Baron Tatterman had sold the keep to a

sawmill owner in Kettering, who had wanted "a coun-
try home." But he'd only come out once, to inspect the
place, and had never come back. Looking for another
fool to sell it to, the villagers supposed.

A sawmill owner seemed less likely to have court
connections than the baron, though both probably
knew the place was empty. I asked a few more questions, and discovered that Tatterman's new manor had
been built closer to Rudley. I got directions to it, and to
Kettering for good measure, though that town was a full
day's ride away.

That evening over dinner I reported on my efforts to
Master Assassin, who seemed genuinely indifferent to
my discovery of the keep's true owner. This surprised
me, for surely his attacks on me and Margaret's kidnapping must be connected, the source of both events
originating in the High Liege's court. But his mask was
back in place, and he showed no interest in anything I
said, eating his chicken as if I wasn't even at the table.

He'd probably guessed what I was about—'twas not
complicated, after all. But his knowledge would make
little difference in the end. Like the creatures of pack,
herd and flock, men must be with their own kind. Sooner or later, if I was the only human he had, he would
accept me.

Indeed, I thought he'd respond faster than some of
the dogs my father's hound master had tamed.

The next day I gave him a wrapped sandwich for luncheon along with this breakfast, explaining that I was
going to Rudley and wouldn't be back till dinner.

In Rudley, I asked myself what Fisk would do, and
presented myself as the agent of a man who wished to
buy a country home and had heard that Baron Tatterman had moved out of his ancestral keep. People here

knew little of the distant keep, though a few had heard the Baron had sold it to some merchant. They referred me to Baron Tatterman for more information. Yes, the baron was in residence at the hall. Where else would he be? Court? No, he wasn't one of those lieges who ran off to the city, wasting time and money better spent on his own land.

Visitors from court? Baron Tatterman socialized mostly with the local gentry. Baron Mortenson, Baron Hopley, and their families, were his most frequent guests, and they weren't ones to go haring off to court, either.

I rode back to the keep in a sober mood, and then went out to cast a hook into the nearby stream. I had sometimes thought that the tenants on our estate knew my father better than I did. If people here said Baron Tatterman was indifferent to court, 'twas probably true.

Master Assassin made no comment on the fish, but I filled the silence by telling him how I'd caught each one, and how the smallest had actually given me the hardest fight.

"Do you fish, Master Assassin? You must, traveling about the countryside as I think you do. I travel a lot myself, and I fish whenever I get the chance. What do you like for bait? I got some worms from the garden, but I know a young man who swears by—"

"I'm not an... I'm not that," he said abruptly. "My name's Wheatman."

I knew better than to show the triumph that swelled in my heart.

"Master Wheatman, then," I said. "Thank you. So what do you use for bait? Have you tried cheese, like my young friend?"

I lingered a few more days in the keep, killing my spare time working on the kitchen garden. Man-taming wasn't something that could be rushed, the trip to Kettering would take some time, and I wanted to secure the ground I'd gained before I abandoned my prisoner for so long.

I took pains to keep the conversation trivial, and he'd begun to respond to my questions, though his answers were short. The night before I left for Kettering I told him where I was going and why, and promised to leave him plenty of water and food in case my return was delayed.

His lips pressed tight, though whether in anger or dismay I couldn't tell.

"Would you leave me a book as well?"

His voice was rough with the humiliation of having to ask. And part of my strategy was to keep him bored as well as lonely, so that dinner with another human being would be the greatest pleasure he had. But I still pitied him.

"I would if I had one, but I don't travel with such things any more than you do. And when Tatterman moved out, he took all the small valuable objects, like books, with him."

He passed some of those empty, echoing rooms on his way to the kitchen each night, so he'd know what I said was true.

"And you know why I can't leave you any tools." I made my voice gentler still, and he nodded jerkily, his gaze cast down.

"But I'll probably return by Darkling Night," I added. "'Tis two nights hence, you know. Though my father didn't believe in 'those old superstitions,' and he wasn't

much for reflection either, so we never paid the Darkling Nights much heed. Did your family?"

I didn't expect a reply, but he said, "We were towns-
men. Several neighbors held big parties, and we'd go
to one of their homes. They let the children stay up
as late as we wanted and we'd run around—indoors—
playing fox and hounds, or hide the thimble, then fall
asleep on a mattress in front of the hearth while the
grownups talked into the small hours."

'Twas the most of himself he'd given me, and I had
to honor it.

"Father sent us off to bed at the usual time," I said.
"But Benton and I—he's the brother closest to my age—
we'd slip away and creep down to the kitchen. Father
may not have believed in the old ways, but the servants
were all telling tales of magica monsters, who only
roused on Darkling Nights, and ghastly things that had
happened to folk who went out when both moons were
gone. The victims were always someone their uncle or
aunt or cousin knew, personally, and they swore the
tale was true... 'Twas never anyone *they'd* known, and
when he grew older Benton started to wonder about
that. He's my scholarly brother, so he tracked down
some of those uncles and cousins and found that either
they'd never heard the tale, or that it had happened to
someone their uncles or cousins knew, *personally*..."

I turned over the supplies I'd promised him the next
morning. And I was genuinely sorry I couldn't leave
him a book.

CHAPTER 16

Fisk

The good part about the coach heading toward Uncle Roger's fief was that he'd help us intercept it—and if he didn't, we'd know he was involved with the kidnapping. Rupert swore he wasn't, and that meant we wouldn't even have to present my forged writ to a sheriff, which I particularly appreciated.

The bad part was that we had to reach his fief at least a day before the coach would, which meant two days of very hard riding.

The worst part was that Kathy endured the long days in the saddle better than I did.

Uncle Roger's "house" was a square stone manor that, despite its size and its master's obvious wealth, managed to look more like a big farmhouse than a mansion—an effect that was enhanced by the elderly man in his shirt sleeves who answered the door.

"Good evening, sirs. You got business here at..." Then

his jaw sagged—and he wasn't looking at the dog, who had slipped into the bushes as we rode into the yard. "Master Rupert? Really? I thought those rumors was... Ah, welcome, Your Highness. I'll go tell the master you've come, shall I?"

Rupert's smile was tired but genuine, and I remembered all the common folk of Crown City who'd addressed him so casually.

"It's good to see you too, Mickle. What rumors? I hoped no one had noticed me."

"I can't say as they've noticed you, sir. But we been hearing that you ran off after some...ah, that you left the court, and might be traveling in these parts. Jacky, come and take these horses round to the stable."

He stepped aside, and Kathy and I followed Rupert into an entry hall that might have been imposing except for a clutter of hunting bows and spears, the muddy boots someone had stripped off just inside the door, and a big dog lying on a cushioned window bench that caught the last rays of the lowering sun.

I trusted that City Mutt lurking in the bushes was smart enough to keep out of the farm dog's way. I was also sorry to hear that city rumors had spread to the countryside...but surely even Advisor Arnold, who'd been so adamant that no one find out about the Heir's peccadilloes, couldn't hold it against us.

Rupert's smile had vanished. "They're talking about Meg? Even out here?"

"Well, you're the Heir, young master. Though I thought that bit about her being kidnapped off the street had to be claptrap. 'Least, till you showed up."

He led the way down the hall, and ushered us into the room where the family sat at dinner with a casual, "Look who's here, Master Roger."

"Rupert, my boy! You look terrible. Are you really chasing after that...ah... I thought that was nonsense!"

Uncle Roger was a muscular man, growing stocky with the onset of middle age. He rose from the table as he spoke, and came over to throw an arm around Rupert's shoulders. A young man, who would look a lot like his father in about twenty years, cast Rupert a sympathetic grin.

"I am chasing after her," Rupert admitted. "But Meg's not an 'ah.' I want to marry her. And we think the people who took her may be heading into your fief. We've been riding like mad to get ahead of them."

"Well, well." Uncle Roger had too much sense to comment on that. "Sit down and have some dinner—you and your friends—and we'll think about what's best to do, eh?"

Plates were fetched so we could join them, and Rupert introduced us to Roger and his son, Corbin. He then set about trying to convince the worldly older man that sending a troop of local guards to intercept his kidnapped mistress was "what's best to do." Kathy put in a word every now and then, and I ate my roast pork and left them to it.

Though more and more, as the conversation went on, I watched them at it. It seemed to me that Roger's reluctance to raise troops to go after the Heir's mistress had less to do with Rupert and Meg, and more to do with Corbin's enthusiasm at the prospect. It didn't feel like either of them had a hand in the kidnapping, but something else was playing out here and I didn't understand it.

Kathy did. As the conversation escalated from discussion through debate and into argument, she spoke less and less, but her gaze was keen.

Rupert, with a self-control that was almost unnatural, managed to win his point without ever saying aloud that someday *he* was going to be High Liege, and that getting in his black books would be a really bad idea. But he came close to it. By the time the meal ended, Roger had reluctantly agreed to send word to several nearby sheriffs, who'd have a troop of twenty deputies assembled by tomorrow morning.

This seemed to confirm Rupert's belief that he wasn't part of the plot, because we should be able to intercept the coach soon after they entered Roger's fief—certainly before they left it. We finished dinner with a berry-laden trifle soaked in cream, and a lot more constraint all around than when the meal had started.

As we left the dining room, Corbin snagged Rupert to "come and check on the horses." I'd have gone straight to bed—I didn't want to show it, but I was feeling the effect of all that riding. But as a maidservant escorted us toward the stairs, Kathy took my arm and asked the girl, "Is there someplace around here we can go to... *discuss* something in private?"

A silver oct assured the girl's discretion and she gave us a cheerful grin, along with directions to a grove behind the stable where everyone went "for a bit of a snuggle."

"I hope we don't trip over half a dozen couples," I murmured as Kathy dragged me out the back door. "If it's where 'everyone goes.' Any chance *we're* going there to snuggle?"

"Mayhap later." Kathy's crisp voice made my gloomy doubts a certainty. "But first, we're going to talk politics."

The sun was setting when we reached the grove, and it was perfect for any purpose requiring privacy: far

enough from the stable where the grooms slept that
you wouldn't be overheard unless you were very loud,
with well-leafed trees to conceal you from sight, but
not so thick you couldn't find a nice place to settle in.
We found a fallen log, with a suggestive hollow in the
grass beside it—but my not-quite-fiancée seated herself
on the log, in a position that was only conductive to
discussing politics. Rats.

"What if it's not one person who had Meg taken?
What if it's several, maybe all these mountain barons
who are upset about the mineral rights, and they're lur-
ing Rupert out here to...to..."

"To what?" I asked reasonably. "If they wanted to kill
him, they've had plenty of chances. They can't hold
the Liege Heir hostage unless they're prepared to rise
in open rebellion—and if they're prepared to do that,
they don't need to take hostages. And if they want to
convince him to side with them against his father, kidnapping his lover is the worst possible way to do it."

"I know." Kathy sighed. "I suppose it doesn't make
sense, particularly over a matter of mineral rights. But
they must have brought Meg here for some reason—
and this is the one place in the Realm where almost
everyone is angry with the Liege right now."

"It could be just that, because they knew the Liege
wouldn't want to owe these barons any favors. Could
they have brought her here so Rupert would *have* to ask
the local barons for a favor? To make the Crown indebt-
ed to them, so... What is this thing with the minerals?"

"Oh, that's a longstanding problem—it flares up every few decades, both sides make some concessions
and it subsides again. At least, it usually subsides. This
time it's evidently hot enough that Roger doesn't want

to raise troops—not even to rescue an innocent woman from kidnappers! And I don't think the High Liege knows that."

It seemed to me that Corbin was happy to have an excuse to raise troops, which made me wonder even more.

"So what is this about, anyway?"

"The first High Liege granted fiefs to his followers on the condition that, while they could farm and fish and hunt the surface of the land, anything buried beneath it belonged to the Crown. They can mine it, but twenty percent of whatever they extract goes back to the Liege. It nets the treasury almost as much as the taxes Father complains so much about, so I can understand why the mountain barons, who often get more of their income from mining than they do from—"

She broke off, but I'd heard it too—those leafy boughs didn't just conceal lovers from the manor's windows, they also warned you when someone was coming.

Kathy was my fiancée in all but name...but I was the only one who knew that. Being discovered lurking in the bushes with me would do things to her reputation that her father wouldn't appreciate.

I rolled her off the log, away from that inviting hollow and into the prickly bushes on the other side. I just hoped that the oncoming lovers didn't park themselves there—or that if they did they wouldn't take too long, or embarrass poor Kathy too badly. Then I recognized Rupert and Corbin's voices.

If I hadn't known about Rupert's relationship with Meg, I might have worried that *they* were about to embarrass us. But like Kathy, they'd come out here to talk politics.

"...we're the ones who dig it out of the ground," Corbin was saying heatedly. "The ones whose men die if the mine collapses, whose towns are choked by the smoke of the smelters, who—"

"You can build the smelters away from the towns," Rupert murmured. "If you put a hill between them, very little of the smoke—"

They came to a stop before they reached our log— though not, alas, far enough off that we could escape without being seen.

"You know what I mean. It's *our* land, in our fief! Why shouldn't we own what's under it, as well as... Are you listening to me?"

"Not really," said Rupert. "To be frank, I don't give a tinker's curse about mineral rights just now."

There was a moment of silence while Corbin took this in. "If we help you get your skirt back, will you care then?"

"For pity's sake, Corbin! Meg's not some skirt, she's the woman I want to marry! She's carrying my child. But beyond that, she's an innocent woman who's been kidnapped. Who's being held against her will, alone and terrified. If *mineral rights* are all you can think of in the face of that, I hope you choke on them!"

"Oh." Corbin took this in as well. "Sorry. You want to tell me about it?"

"Not if you don't want to hear it. I had thought we were friends, but I suppose..."

It might have been friendship. More likely, young Corbin had grown up to realize that his childhood play-mate was now the chosen Heir. He made appropriate soothing sounds, and Rupert—who desperately wanted to talk about Meg, whether his audience wanted to hear it or not—poured out the whole story of his romance, her kidnapping, and our pursuit.

This took longer than it would have if they'd made love.

But if Corbin had written off the woman who carried his cousin's child as a "skirt," I didn't want to find out what he'd think of Kathy if she was found hiding in the lovers' grove with me, so I resigned myself to waiting in patience. At least I got to hold her hand.

I already knew the story, so I was barely listening when Rupert reached my failed attempt to rescue Meg from the inn. Corbin was unimpressed by my heroism.

"That was stupid of him," he said. "For all he knew they might have been eating in shifts; two men in the room with her, as well as the one outside the door."

This was true, and he'd thought of it quicker than I had. I revised my estimate of his intelligence upward, and tickled Kathy's palm with my fingers. The story was nearing an end, and we might soon be free to do a bit of snuggling after all.

"Even if they all slept in the same room with her," Corbin went on, "and Lady Katherine wasn't much use, the odds would have been three to six if you went back later. They'd have been asleep, and dazed if they woke up. Better chance all round."

Kathy's hand, which had been wiggling playfully, went still. I abruptly started paying attention.

"I know that," Rupert said. "Fisk knew it too, but I know why he went in. I'd have done the same."

"To rescue the fair damsel?" Corbin said cynically. "No, I can see why you'd do that, but you said he's involved with the Sevenson girl."

So much for Rupert's discretion. I cursed silently, which was all I could do without making the situation even worse.

"Oh, that had nothing to do with Meg," said Rupert, and I stiffened in sudden alarm. "He didn't want to get Kathy involved in a brawl. Part of me wanted to blame him for that...but if our situations had been reversed, I'd have done the same."

Kathy's hand pulled away from mine.

The rest of Rupert's tale was soon told—he skipped the part about Champion bolting and glossed over the possible poison, though he did ask Corbin to make sure none of the servants chased off the dog.

That mutt was the last thing I cared about. I could barely see Kathy, for it was now almost dark in the shadow of the log, but her stiff back radiated anger... and there was still nothing I could do until Rupert and Corbin finally went back to the house.

Kathy waited till the sound of their voices had faded before she stood and shook out her crumpled skirts. She looked as tousled as if we had been making love... but one glimpse of her face was enough to dispel that impression.

I'm a big believer in lying...but sometimes there's just no point.

"All right," I said. "I wanted to keep you safe. Is that such a terrible thing?"

"You broke your word," she said. "We all promised that if we found Meg we'd come back and get the others. So we could all be safe—and have a better chance of getting her out, too! I'd have thought that mess with Michael would have taught you to consult with your *partners*, Fisk."

"But you're not—"

I didn't even finish the sentence, but it was still too late.

"Really? Yet one of the main reasons I wanted to marry you was because I thought *you'd* be willing to treat your wife as a partner. It seems I was wrong."

My heart was hammering sickly, but I recognized the word that mattered most in that whole terrible sentence.

"*Wanted*? Past tense?"

I didn't know whether to be furious or grateful when she walked away, leaving the question unanswered.

Kathy still wasn't speaking to me the next morning, even after the deputies gathered at the manor and we all rode off to intercept the coach when it came into Roger's fief. We took the time to make certain it hadn't already gone through the first town after the border, then rode out to yet another invisible line across the road and waited for it. And waited.

It was almost sunset before Rupert gave up and admitted that the coach must have turned north again. It wasn't coming into Roger's fief, after all.

CHAPTER 17

Michael

Kettering, which I reached in the late afternoon, was another of the lumber towns that seemed to perch on every mountain river big enough to float a log. Most of the townsfolk were preparing for Darkling Night, which would occur tomorrow. I could see my father's point about foolish superstition; the Green Moon had been gone for days now, and last night the tiny sliver of the Creature Moon had been up for just a few hours before it followed the sun over the horizon.

Yet people in the street called out to friends and neighbors, asking where they intended to go and inviting them to join this party or that. Almost every house already had either an O, for open, chalked on its door, or an X to keep out the wild magic in the owners' absence.

Those who had anything worth stealing would leave their servants behind—if not for that, a burglar could claim a rich haul on Darkling Nights. 'Twas a thing I'd never have thought of before I met Fisk. I wondered yet again how my friends went on without me, if all were well, if they'd found some way to free Mistress Margaret.

I hoped to make progress with that quest now, so I made some inquires and then rode to Half Moon street, where the mill owner who'd bought Baron Tatterman's old keep lived.

After some thought about feed and water, I'd taken Wheatman's roan with me as a packhorse and brought True along for the romp. My garb and my companions marked me as a traveler, and I was able to ride down the street and past that tall wooden house without attracting attention. But what next?

If the keep's owner had knowingly loaned it to the kidnappers, any inquiry he learned about would have him sending off a messenger to warn them. That messenger would either find me in residence, which could have unfortunate legal consequences, or if he reached the keep before me he'd find Wheatman there, which would be even worse.

I cast about the mill owner's house in widening circles, till I found an inn that looked less respectable than those around it and went in to rent a room and lodge my friends in the stable.

When the serving maid brought me an early dinner, I pulled out a silver quart and asked her who on the inn's staff might be willing to offer me some information about businesses in the area.

She looked wistfully at the silver and started to shake her head. I added swiftly that this was for her, for giving me just one name.

"Oh! Most anyone would be willing to help you with that, sir. I've lived here all my life, and I know a lot about any local business you'd care to name. If I was properly recompensed for my time."

You could have had it for half that. I could all but hear Fisk's voice in my ears, but I care little for money. I gave her another silver quart, and she was happy to tell me which merchants on Half Moon street would be most willing to gossip about its inhabitants. Properly recompensed, of course.

She said she could tell me anything I wanted to know, but it turned out she knew little about who might have court connections, so she only got paid for the name of a wine merchant who'd be willing to talk about his customers.

I went to the wine shop and bought the owner a cup of his own wares. I was wary about revealing exactly whose court connections I was interested in—if he knew the mill owner, he might go to the man and report our conversation. But by asking about trouble with servants, I managed to get the name of a footman in the mill owner's employ who'd lost three months' pay when a parcel he'd been carrying had fallen into the mud and ruined his mistress' new hat. He said he'd been jostled in the street, that the box had been knocked right out of his hands, and he'd been bitter about his punishment ever since.

'Twas now coming on dark, on a night that would be very dark indeed, but I made my way to the mill owner's back door and extracted the footman by claiming I had information about a gambling debt owed to him.

He was somewhat suspicious, but as I walked him back to my inn I explained that 'twas information I wanted. And I offered him a gold roundel—which he could say he'd won in a wager—for whatever he could tell me about any connection his master had with court, the High Liege, or even another nobleman who was much involved in the court.

He thought about this for a time, but bitterness over that muddy hat won out and he willingly told me all he knew. However, aside from selling lumber to a number of wealthy men, his master had no court connections... except, of course, for his wife. The footman's vengeful mistress had been in service to the Liege Lady before she left to marry the master. She wrote often to the ladies she'd served with, and some came to visit her here. She didn't go to court herself, though, because she was busy raising "that monstrous little...ah, the young master."

This was the most direct connection to the wealth and power that ruled the Realm I'd found. In fact 'twas the only connection, but through two wives it led directly to the High Liege!

But if the kidnappers were working for the High Liege, why had they fled when we threatened to go for a Liege writ?

I let my cheerful informant depart, early enough that he should reach home before the last of the light was gone. But I sat, musing over what he'd revealed for some time before I went to bed.

It might be a coincidence. Mistress Mill-Owner must know many people at court. But I couldn't dismiss the fact that the only connection I could find to the kidnappers led to the High Liege himself.

In the morning I rose early and wandered down Half Moon street, confirming that the wife of the man who owned the old keep had been in service to the Liege

Lady before her marriage, and further, that her two-year-old son was a monster in child form.

Many two-year-olds are monsters, so I paid that little heed. The High Liege, through his wife, could have learned of the old keep and arranged to use it...and if he was behind Mistress Margaret's kidnapping, we might be in more trouble than we could handle. Meg certainly was. He had hired Fisk and me to bring back his son, not to free his son's mistress. Yet I had a hard time thinking that the man I'd seen playing with his youngest son in his study could be so cruel to his first-born. No matter how tangled his love affairs became.

I rode back to the keep with these thoughts keeping me company. After stabling the horses, I knocked on Wheatman's door, to inform him of my return and exchange an empty bucket for his full one.

He seemed glad to see me, though I was sorry to see the transformation his presence wrought in True.

I prepared dinner somewhat absently, though I didn't forget to cut Wheatman's meat into bits he could eat with a spoon. I also bound his hands, so I could safely check his hobbles before I let him out of the cell. He'd not managed to untwist either of the wires, though the tips of his fingers were raw with a multitude of small scratches. He may have assaulted the bar across his window as well, or the hinges on the stout wooden door, but armed with naught but a wooden bucket, bowl and spoon, if he tried he'd not even left a mark.

In a well-built cell, there's little a prisoner can do without tools, and the thought of courageous Mistress Margaret so confined hardened my heart toward any man who allied himself with her captors.

I refused to apologize for leaving him so long...but since ending our enmity was my goal I didn't upbraid him again, and even told him what I'd learned in Kettering. Either his mask was beginning to slip or I was learning to read him better; when I mentioned that the wife of the man who owned this keep had been in service with the Liege Lady, he twitched.

"I saw that," I told him. "So I must be on the right track. But surely the High Liege could find a more direct way to keep us from freeing Mistress Merkle than hiring you to kill me. *After* he hired Fisk and me to bring Rupert back in the first place. It makes no sense!"

Wheatman had started his dinner with good appetite, but it seemed to lessen as I told my tale. Now he simply toyed with a bit of potato.

"You know, it's Darkling Night," he said.

"I do know, though I confess I've not thought much about it."

"I'm like your father."

Wheatman cast me a rueful smile and I blinked in astonishment, for I'd never expected to see such an expression on his face. It made him look almost...nice.

"I'm not much for reflecting on things," he went on. "But these last few days, I've had a lot of time to think."

"And what conclusions have you reached?" My curiosity was genuine.

"That I'd like to go now," he said. "Or at least, tomorrow morning. I may not be superstitious...but it's dark out there, even if you don't fear wild magic."

'Twas a statement so astonishing I didn't know what to say. He knew I couldn't let him go, until I'd convinced him not to kill me. And I didn't think we'd reached that point.

"I'm sorry I had to leave you so long," I said. And then stopped, annoyed with myself for apologizing after all. But he shook his head.

"It's not about that. Though considering the circum-stances, you've been remarkably kind." That flashing smile of his was beginning to worry me, but he went on, "So I owe you an explanation at least. You see, I had a sister."

That explained nothing, but there was a note in his voice when he spoke those simple words that warned me, even more than the past tense, that this story would not end well.

"Aleen. She was..." He stopped, evidently editing what he'd been about to say, but his expression spoke eloquently of love and loss. "She was a year younger than I, and we were the wild ones in our family when we were kids. I hadn't grown out of that yet, gambling, and drinking too much when I played—which meant I lost too much, as well. But all of a sudden Aleen grew up, and my partner in mischief turned into a young lady with suitors. Some of my disreputable friends were among them," he added. "I threatened them with all kinds of mayhem if they did anything more than kiss her hand. And it was mostly a joke, anyway."

A muscle jumped in his jaw, and I could all but see rage pouring though him.

"I have a sister," I said gently. "I love her dearly, though she sometimes drives me mad. I don't know what I'd do if anyone hurt her."

He looked at me then, and some of the tension drained away.

"That obvious? I suppose it is. But it wasn't one of my wild friends. My mother would never have let them es-cort her home from a party. *They* weren't to be trusted. Herbert Ballantine was a perfectly respectable young man, and an excellent match. Ally was *flattered* he was courting her."

He stopped again and I dared not speak, lest I tip some delicate balance into silence.

"I was with my friends that night, in a tavern playing cards." His voice still held an echo of the grief and fury that must once have consumed him. "Though I probably wouldn't have been escorting her, even if I'd been home. But I'd fallen asleep, mostly drunk, with my head on the table."

He drew in a shaky breath, but a note of wonder crept into his voice as he went on.

"I dreamed of her that night. We were on the beach near our house, where we'd played as children, and she ran to me and hugged me. Her clothes were wet, but I felt such a wave of love from her, so deep and warm... I'd never felt anything like it, but I still noticed the damp, and I asked if she'd been swimming.

"She let go of me and stepped back. 'No,' she said. 'I'm going fishing in Darnstable, if you'd like to join me.' Then she turned and walked into the waves, deeper and deeper until the water covered her head. And in the dream I wasn't worried. I thought she intended to go to Darnstable underwater, and was wondering how that would work when I woke up. And I thought what an odd dream it was, and that I'd have to tell her about it...maybe ask, as a joke, if she wanted to go fishing. And I went and found a bed, and that's where I was when my younger brother came to find me. To tell me she was dead."

"Did she drown?" 'Twas all I could think of to say.

"No, she was thrown off a cliff—inland, not even near the water. They wouldn't let any of us see her, which was probably kind. They said...they said she'd have died instantly, but most of her face was gone."

"But if this Ballantine killed her..."

"He was drunk." Wheatman's voice was calmer than mine would have been, had it been Kathy of whom we spoke. "Drunk when he raped her, and drunk when she threatened to report what he'd done—to me, to my father, to the law. I actually believe he was in a drunken panic when he killed her. If he'd been sober, he'd have noticed that even though the path they were on was deserted, there were people on the street below who could see them struggling. There was no question that he'd done it." Wheatman sounded almost resigned. "And he confessed the whole story, anyway."

"But if he killed her, before witnesses, how did he end up unredeemed instead of hanging?"

That was clearly where this tale led, and 'twas a debt that could never be repaid short of life.

"His father all but beggared himself, bribing the judicars. And I told you Herbert was considered a good match? They said his judgment was 'impaired by liquor,' when he raped her in the first place, and also when he killed her. That because he wasn't fully in his wits, he shouldn't be required to pay the ultimate debt. And since even they couldn't claim any lesser payment would suffice..."

He shrugged.

"I see why you killed this Ballantine." Indeed, had it been Katherine, I couldn't swear I'd not have done the same. "But I had nothing to do with your sister's death. Or anyone's. Nor did some of the other men in your warrant book."

"I know. But... Herbert ran, of course. I'd made threats, and the rest of the town... Well, he had no choice but to clear out. His family moved to another town too, some months later. But you know where I went to look for him first?"

"Darnstable," I said. "Did you find him there?"

"No. He'd run in an entirely different direction, and it took almost a year to track him down. But after I killed him... It was almost like losing a job I'd worked at for most of my life. I had no more taste for wine or gambling, and no desire to run Father's shop, either.

"But I'd spoken to a lot of people in Darnstable, when I was looking for Herbert. Months later, some business rivals burned down a man's dye yard there—they killed two workers who were sleeping in the loft above it—and the dyer remembered me. The men who'd hired the arsonist paid off the judicars—they didn't dare let him be convicted, lest he name them. But there was too much public outcry for the law to simply release him, so he was marked as unredeemed. And that letter came from Darnstable... I found my crossbow there as well," he finished. "Father had given me my share of the business when I set out, and it cost every fract I had left to buy it. But it was worth it, for a weapon that would hit only my target and no one else. The fact that I found a magica weapon for sale in Darnstable clinched the matter. I accepted my sister's invitation to go fishing, and I've been doing it ever since."

There was so much here to speak to that I hardly knew where to start.

"You're wrong about that bow—which you should know, for it missed me twice! And it—"

"I've thought about that," he said. "Your sensing Gift warned you, didn't it?"

"Yes, but—"

"So it was your own magic that allowed you to escape the bow's," he said. "I'll know to take that into account when I'm hunting noblemen in the future."

I found the confidence in his voice unnerving.

"I did some experiments with it," I said shortly. "It can miss birds as well. And you're not going to be hunting the unredeemed, or anyone else, in the future."

His smile was almost serene. "But as an unredeemed man, you would say that, wouldn't you."

I considered protesting my honesty...but when a man takes you for a liar in the first place, such protestations are of no use.

"Would you like to know how I came to be unredeemed?" I asked instead.

"No," he said. "It doesn't matter. Some of the other men I've hunted didn't kill anyone, but I killed them just the same. Men who don't pay their debts... By the time I've caught up with some of them, they've killed again. One man added four deaths to his tally, after the judicars let him go."

In the face of such obsession, there was nothing I could say in my own defense...so mayhap 'twas time to stop defending myself.

"Then let me tell you something that might matter more," I said. "Not long ago, I was pursing a villain as bad as any of the men you've stalked, and probably worse. He was a con man by profession, with several deaths I know of on his account, and probably more. But my partner..." Fisk's relationship with Jack was too complex to explain to this man—particularly since I didn't entirely understand it myself. "My partner chose to spare him. I didn't agree with that choice of his. I almost broke up our friendship because of it."

Wheatman snorted. "And now you realize that he was right, and you should always show mercy, no matter what the crime?"

"No," I said. "I still think he was wrong. What I came to realize is that *I'm* not always right, either. And betting a man's life on your own, fallible judgment is pretty arrogant, to say the least."

Indeed, this man who regarded me so coolly—who'd told me that story, and still meant to encompass my death—was the best possible argument that when you worked outside of the law, you had to be even more careful about wielding both mercy and justice.

I have never appreciated the law that abandoned me more than I did then.

"Are you so sure that you're always right? Certain enough to kill?"

Wheatman's mouth tightened. "Someone has to make those choices. Life or death. I trust myself more than some judicar who's been bribed to let a killer live. If I'm wrong, I'll live with the consequences."

But he clearly didn't think he was wrong. Ever. Which made him all the more dangerous.

"You know, all of this makes me *less* likely to let you go."

"Well, the alternative is to kill me," he said. "And I don't think you will."

I was about to reply that I could continue to hold him, but the certainty in his voice caught my attention.

"Why would I let you go? 'Tis the last thing I want to do, now."

"I know," he said. "But protecting the world from men like you is what I do, and I'm not going to stop. My actions are perfectly legal. You're the one who's breaking the law. Though I don't think either of us cares much about that. What you will care about is that it was the Liege Lady who set me on your trail."

"What?" I could hardly have been more astonished if he'd told me 'twas ghosts or goblins.

"She knows about me, and Ally too, because she came from our town. In fact, one of the maids she took to court is a cousin of mine. When she wanted to stop you, she had my cousin write. I was in the area," he added. "So it almost seemed like fate."

"You use that as an excuse too often."

I remembered the beautiful woman who'd come to check us out, so concerned about Rupert. And later, in the Liege's study, she'd been so playful, so warm, so loving to both her small son and her husband. Surely this was impossible.

On the other hand, she had come to check us out without her husband's knowledge.

"Why would the Liege Lady want to keep Rupert from bringing his mistress home? Or did she want to prevent us from bringing Rupert back?"

I could think of no reason for her to kidnap Margaret Merkle, but as for Rupert...

If anything happened to Rupert, that warm, loving woman's own son would one day inherit the throne.

"I didn't ask her intentions," said Wheatman. "And she didn't say. But she did mention, several times, how 'terrible' it would be if anything happened to the Heir while he was in your company. It bothered me," he added. "Because the Liege Heir is innocent. She didn't say anything direct enough that I could claim she threatened him. But before I left, the last thing her henchman did was try to borrow my crossbow."

He'd clearly refused to lend it...but an ordinary crossbow would do the job as well.

"This henchman. Was he a smallish, slender man, with brown hair and a bite mark on his hand?"

"He wore gloves," said Wheatman. "But the rest of it fits."

"I've got to warn them!" I stood so abruptly that the bench I'd sat on toppled to the floor. "If the Liege Lady's trying to assassinate Rupert, I've got to get back there. Why didn't you tell me this sooner?"

'Twas an absurd question, but he answered anyway.

"I wasn't ready to leave then, and I am now. Besides, it took a while to be sure you wouldn't kill me."

So while I'd been gentling him, he'd been evaluating me.

And he'd gotten the better of the match.

"I won't kill you. I'm going to leave you bound, but you'll find a way out of the ropes eventually. I'll go right..."

I couldn't go now. 'Twas Darkling Night—riding fast by starlight was almost sure to sprain Chant's weak leg, and mayhap break my neck as well. And it would take me days, at least, to track them down.

"You're right. I'm the only one who knows who our enemy is. I have to be sensible about this, not go dashing off in all directions. I'm going to return you to your cell so I can pack, but I'll come back at first light to bind you, and I'll leave the door unbolted."

Wheatman lifted his hobbled feet over the bench and rose.

True snarled silently.

"You do realize that I still mean to kill you?"

I knew he did—though he might find it harder than he thought to kill a man he'd eaten with, and spoken with so intimately.

On the other hand, he'd built his life on this mission to mete out justice to the unredeemed. And having built my own life upon knight errantry, an obsession most would consider more mad than his, I could understand that too. Except for the killing part, we weren't so very different. But the killing was a big difference, and either way...

"I don't care. I have to get back to Fisk and the others. As soon as I can."

And I was going to take that crossbow with me.

CHAPTER 18

Fisk

Next morning we made an early start, trying to find where the coach had turned aside. No one in the three towns we reached in our first day's ride had seen it, and Rupert was starting to panic. I pointed out that we were several days' ride from the last town we knew it had passed through, so there were plenty more roads it could have taken. Kathy, more optimistically, added that instead of turning north or south they might have gone to ground again—and in that case, all we had to do was to figure out where they were, and then we could try our luck with the local sheriff.

Katherine was being... I didn't know what she was being. When my sisters used to say they weren't speaking to someone, I thought it was just one of those things girls did. And since they always went right on fighting with whoever they were mad at, it had even seemed funny.

I still didn't see why wanting to keep her safe was such a heinous crime—and even during our quarrel, Kathy never said she wouldn't speak to me. We discussed where the coach might have gone, and whether to stop at an inn or spend the upcoming Darkling Night camping out. There was some light conversation about a particularly ugly manor we passed by... Still, something was missing when we talked, some quality of engagement, or interest, or...I don't know. We exchanged a lot of words, but she wasn't *speaking* to me.

And it wasn't funny at all.

None of us were superstitious about Darkling Nights, but none of us wanted to camp out either. So that night—when magic was supposed to break the few laws it followed and run wild—found us in an inn so old that the rooms opened off a gallery that ran around the taproom's upper story. The ceiling beams were black with smoke that had escaped the fireplace for...it might have been centuries.

They'd built a big fire tonight, and despite the summer warmth, most of the other customers had pulled benches and chairs over to the hearth, preparing to chatter the night away.

Rupert, deeply worried about his love, went up to bed, leaving Kathy and me at our corner table, as alone as if we had camped in the wilderness. I was pleased that Kathy made no move to join the crowd around the fire...but that may have been because of the dog, who was now hiding under the table.

"So," I said, breaking a silence that threatened to last too long. "What did your family do on Darkling Nights? Tell stories of wild magic and party till dawn?"

"Father thought 'wild magic' was superstitious non-sense," she said. "He didn't think much of reflection, either, so we treated it like any other night." She fell silent again for a moment, before asking too politely, "How about your family?"

"Oh, my father was a great believer in reflection," I said. "At any time. He used the Darkling Nights to pose great questions of scholarship...to four children, most of us not even in our teens."

Memory conjured up his voice. *Name five things humans can do but the animals can't. That's good, Anna, but birds build nests, so men aren't the only ones to build homes.* Sometimes the good memories of my father hurt more than the bad ones that came after his death...but I didn't want the silence to return.

"Judith and I got into a huge debate once, about whether using words was conditional on intelligence, or if intelligence was conditional on using words. I think she was twelve then, and I was nine."

"Who won?"

Curiosity brought Kathy's voice alive again, so I pushed aside the memory of the years when my mother and sisters insisted on continuing the tradition—though all I wanted to think about was where we'd get money for the next month's rent, for the next bundle of peats...sometimes the next meal.

"No one won. Though Judith may think she did. They arose in tandem, words and intelligence; you can't come up with new words to describe the world without intelligence, and you can't form a complex thought without words."

Kathy, who didn't like beer, tipped her cup of tea one way and then the other.

"Your father mattered a lot to you, didn't he?"

This wasn't something I wanted to discuss, even to keep her talking. I shrugged.

"And after he died, leaving his family unprotected, you looked after them," she went on.

"Someone had to. Mother did all she could, but..."

"But then she died too. Don't look so shocked—did you think I wouldn't ask Michael about you?"

"You could have asked me," I said.

For the first time since our quarrel, she actually laughed. "Fisk, my dear, you are so oblivious sometimes. But it sounds like your Darkling Nights were more interesting than mine. What would we do, on Darkling Nights, if we had children of our own?"

I noted the "if," but even that concern was overwhelmed by the thought of *having* children, Kathy's children, which arrived on a lightning bolt of terror and awe.

"I don't know. What would you want to do?"

"Something more interesting than just ignore it," Kathy said, with a promptness that told me she'd been thinking about a day when we might have kids. "But I wouldn't want to stuff their heads with nightmares, either. Maybe your father's tradition is a good one. Though I don't know much about the great scholarly questions."

Thanks to Father, I knew them all.

"Jack agreed with your father," I said. "It really is a ridiculous superstition."

"You know, that's the first time you've mentioned Jack to me in...weeks, I think. You used to do it all the time. Even in your letters."

"I did?" I didn't think I'd talked about him that much. Though when some choice arose, the question of what

Jack would do had usually crossed my mind. And lately... "You know, you're right. I haven't thought about Jack as much as I used to."

"Mayhap 'tis because you beat him," Kathy said. "Beat him at his own game, on a board where he had all the advantages. Doesn't that mean that your way of...of dealing with the world is better than his?"

She sounded like my father, proposing some complex theory, and I was reminded that the most important questions have nothing to do with scholarship.

"Jack taught me more than how to steal. He taught me to survive. In those days, I needed that. Badly."

"There are survival choices beyond robbery and poverty," Kathy said. "Look at this place. No one here is worried about starving, and their prices seem pretty reasonable to me."

She gestured to the comfortable room, filled with warmth, light and conversation. There was no reason for a deserted print shop, full of dust and spider webs, to pop into my mind.

"A small estate would solve that problem for us," I said.

"It would. And so would many other things. Your Jack's range of choices seems a bit narrow to me. You don't have to be Jack. And you don't have to struggle so hard not to be your father, either. But that's your decision. I'm going to bed."

She stood, leaving me to watch her climb the stairs and walk down the gallery to her small room, with plenty to reflect on.

Was it because of my father that I wanted to protect Kathy so desperately? I didn't think so, but then, I didn't think I'd talked about Jack *all* the time. I had to admit that when I faced a dilemma, the question that first popped into my mind had always been *What would Jack do?* But I had beaten Jack, and now that thought didn't come to me so quickly.

When it came to the people I loved, was I asking myself what my father would do, and then doing the opposite? My father's death, in scholarly poverty, had left his family unprotected and it cost us dearly. But he'd also taught us to think and choose for ourselves...and that freedom and choice was exactly what I'd denied Kathy.

But what if the alternative was for her to go into danger? Imagining Kathy in that alley behind the Addled Cock made my blood run cold. If that was her choice, I couldn't give her freedom...

...Even if that was what *I'd* just demanded from Michael?

When Michael and I first met, I'd made plenty of dangerous choices—criminal choices. But Michael released me from my legal debt almost immediately, and a few weeks ago he'd given me the right to make decisions for our partnership as well.

Didn't I owe Kathy that right?

It wasn't that I wanted to take Michael for an example. The idea of asking, in a critical situation, what *he* would do was ridiculous to the point of terrifying.

But remembering how angry I'd been when he wouldn't let me choose how to handle Jack...shouldn't Kathy have the right to decide how she'd handle Meg's kidnapping?

Even if it took her into danger?

Every bit of my mind, heart and soul screamed in refusal. But were some of those screams born of my father's failure to care for his family, and what it had done to us?

This was something I wasn't going to settle in one Darkling Night no matter how much reflecting I did, so I took the dog up to bed. It was a long time before I slept.

The day after that dark night dawned bright and fair, we found the coach's trail in the next town, and best of all, Kathy was *speaking* to me again.

I decided that reflection was overrated.

We followed the coach—heading north once more— through several towns. It was now two days ahead of us and people's memories weren't as fresh, but I had no doubt we'd catch up with it...until we left the town of Tottenham, and promptly lost the coach's trail. We found several people who'd seen it pull out of town, but after that we couldn't find anyone who'd seen it in the next three villages on the northbound road. We spent the next two days wandering in wider and wider circles through the countryside, even into the foothills of the mountains. We began to hope they'd finally gone to ground again, but we still had to figure out *where*.

We were riding down the road toward yet another farming village, arguing about whether we should go back to Tottenham and start over, when we rode around a bend and came across a robbery in progress.

It was so clearly a robbery that it could have been set up on a stage, with a narrator telling the audience in rolling tones, "A Robbery is in Progress."

There was a stream on one side of the road, with clumps of willows casting early morning shadows across it. A small rise, whose corner the stream had carved away, loomed over the scene. The carriage was stopped in the middle of the road, its driver lying bound and gagged off to one side. The only passenger, a plump woman in her forties, stood at sword point squawking protests, while two much younger men went through her traveling chests, tossing blouses and petticoats onto the dusty road and pocketing hidden bits of jewelry.

It's an old traveler's trick, hiding jewelry and coin in with your clothing, but because everyone knows to do it, it never works.

The man who held the sword was directing the others. He was older, maybe the same age as his victim, with a scrubby week-old beard and a coat that looked as if it had never seen soap in its life, though it might have been rained on once.

We'd never seen any of these men before, or the woman, either, and we pulled our horses to a stop. The dog whined.

"We should intervene," said Rupert. "There are only three of them, and only one has a sword. The others just have clubs."

"You're the only one of us with a sword," I pointed out. "And they've all got knives. Besides... Maybe it's because we just pulled a stunt like this ourselves, but there aren't many ways you can ambush someone who's traveling. And what better accident could you arrange, than for a brave young Heir to be shot by robbers?"

"None of them has a bow," said Rupert.

"No one we've *seen* has a bow. And despite the jokes, bandits are actually pretty rare. Michael and I have ridden all over the Realm, and we've never been robbed. Well, that's not quite true." I had almost forgotten being cudgel crewed. And then there was the time... "But all those people were attacking us for some other reason. They simply took the chance to empty our pockets before they went on with their plans."

The dog cowered at Tipple's heels, emitting a grumbling whimper I interpreted as, *I want to growl, but I don't dare.*

"Mayhap," said my beloved, "you and Michael always look so impoverished that no thief would bother with you."

"That doesn't matter," Rupert said. "It might be a trap, but we've still got to do something!"

"Why?" I asked. "If they wanted to kill her, or the driver, they'd already have done it. She might even be in on the scam. And if she's not, and we go galloping up shouting, they might get nervous. In my experience, making someone holding a sword nervous is usually a bad idea."

"Then what do you propose?" Rupert asked. "She might not be in on it, and we can't stand here and watch as the poor woman is robbed."

That actually sounded sensible to me, but I didn't want to say so in front of Kathy. She was Michael's sister, after all. On the other hand...

"Let's do something smart, instead."

Rupert was riding the fastest horse, and he was probably the one in whose honor this dance was being held, so I sent him back down the road quite a way to take up his station.

Kathy and I rode forward together for a while before I left her, roughly half way between Rupert and the robbery. Her horse had barely come to a stop before she started rummaging in her pack for notebook and pen.

I told the dog to stay with her, but he followed Tipple and me almost half way to the coach and then declined to go closer. He was growling in earnest now, a deep rumble that would sound downright menacing if you didn't know him. But I appreciated the thought.

Tipple and I walked closer and closer to the robbery. It didn't entirely stop, although all three robbers and their victim were now staring at me.

This seemed odd too, so I stopped Tipple even farther back than I'd intended. I was near enough to get a good look at them.

"The leader is a man in his forties," I shouted back to Kathy. "He's about five foot eight, a bit heavy but not fat, with black hair, the beginnings of a beard, and no scars I can see. His coat's brown, he's wearing a plaid waistcoat and sturdy boots."

I waited till she'd called this information back to Rupert, and jotted it down for good measure.

The robbers had frozen when I first started shouting. And as they realized that Rupert, at least, would be able to carry good descriptions of them back to the law, their startled dismay was downright ludicrous.

"Ready," Kathy called.

"One of the younger ones has brown hair," I shouted. "The other's more ginger and both are clean shaven. The ginger one has lots of freckles, pale eyes, and a gap between his front teeth."

His jaw had dropped so far I could see that gap, but now it snapped shut. He abandoned the chests, dashed over to the leader, and began an intense whispered discussion. The plump woman was listening, with considerable interest.

"Ginger's in his twenties," I went on. "Brown-hair's a bit younger. They're both wearing those same, thick boots, and—"

"Wait!" Ginger started toward me. "We need to talk to you."

"I'm listening," I called. "Don't come any closer."

"But I got to..."

A whisper from the leader made him jump. He tossed his club away and stuck his knife casually into the coach's side.

"Now can I come talk to you?"

He could have half a dozen weapons hidden about his person, but I was beginning to wonder what he wanted to say. And more urgently, who he didn't want to overhear it. Presumably his people knew all about him, and I'd tell my comrades what he said anyway, so that left...?

"All right. But don't come too close. My dog can cover this distance in no time."

My dog was more likely to run off yelping, but his growl sounded sincere.

Ginger-hair walked forward, thin and lithe as a weasel. As soon as he got into whisper range he hissed, "You got to stop this. You're going to get Tizza killed!"

I don't know what I'd expected, but that wasn't it.

"Who's Tizza? No, who's going to kill her? Where are they hiding? Do they plan to shoot Rupert?"

He hesitated, and I said impatiently, "I promise not to turn and look, but if you want cooperation you've got to tell me what's going on. What does he have? A bow? Or is there more than one?"

If this was an ambush, those were the only questions that mattered. Well, I also wanted to know why they were trying so hard to kill Rupert now, when they'd passed up several chances early on. Something must have changed, and it would be nice to talk to someone who knew what it was.

"There's just one." Ginger seemed to make up his mind as he spoke. "He's got a crossbow, though we're not supposed to know that. We're not even supposed to know he's following us, or why he wanted us to rob some coach right in front of you. He's up on that little bluff, other side of the stream," he added. "Going to do the deed himself if we don't oblige, though he thinks we're too stupid to figure that out. And all he told us about the man he wanted us to kill is that he's the one riding that big white stud. But his men got Tizza, so we got no choice. And you've got to bring your friend up here, so's we can—"

"I can't bring him up if he's going to get shot," I said. "Who's—"

"Don't you go thinking we're stupid. Pa says you're to bring him in with you and the girl between him and the stream, close and fast, like you decided to charge us. We can take him down, make it look like we killed him. Particular if he's willing to lie still, after. The man with the bow didn't say anything about killing you, so we can leave you to haul the corpus away while we track *him* back to—"

The sharp thwack of a crossbow interrupted him, and we both jumped. But we weren't anywhere near the target...and neither was the bowman. Rupert, far down the road where I'd so luckily sent him, didn't even hear the shot. His assailant should have known he was out of a crossbow's range.

We couldn't see the bolt, but a line of dust shot up from the road where it skidded to a stop, at least ten yards short of Champion's hooves.

"Amateur," said my new friend.

I could only agree.

Evidently, "Pa" thought so too.

"This is blown, boys." The disgust in his voice was audible, even at this distance. "Since we're not delivering his price, why don't we go see if we can bag us a toff, and trade him for Tizz instead."

The young robbers responded instantly, leaping through the stream like hunting hounds, though the twenty-foot cliff on the other side slowed them down. Pa was more deliberate, like a great, grizzled bear. But he made it up the cliff as well, and his determination made him even more formidable.

I almost felt sorry for their quarry...until I heard a sudden thunder of hoofbeats. Even so, I put the odds about fifty/fifty.

I rode over to the supposed victim. Despite many huffing exclamations of shock and anger, she hadn't hesitated to grab Ginger's abandoned knife and cut her driver free. She then looked at her scattered clothing in dismay, so clearly torn between fleeing the scene and staying to retrieve it that I decided she might not be in on the scam after all.

So I pointed out that the ambusher the robbers were chasing had fled on horseback, which meant the robbers would be back soon, and urged her to go straight to the next town and report everything to the sheriff. Katherine, who rode up then with Rupert at her heels, helped her pick up her garments, and Rupert gallantly assisted her into the coach. The dog contributed not at all by running around the outskirts of some invisible circle, barking.

Or maybe he did contribute—the nervous horses set off at a trot.

Kathy turned to me to demand an explanation I'd have been hard put to deliver, because I didn't know much more than she did. So I was...well, not glad, but not too sorry to see the bandits emerge from the brush beside the stream as soon as the coach was out of sight.

I also noted that they'd returned, and hidden themselves there, without even the dog noticing their presence.

"Figured we'd let her get out of the way before we talk," Pa said. "She's a silly wench, but the Flintruckers got no grudge against her. Right boys?"

In a comedy they'd have replied in chorus, "Right, Pa." In reality, Brown-hair simply nodded...and Ginger cast a calculating look after the coach.

I was glad the Flintruckers seemed to hold no grudge against me, and resolved to keep it that way. But...

"If you don't mind my asking," I said. "Who's Tizz?"

"And who shot at Rupert?" Kathy added. "And why did you chase him?"

Even Kathy had more sense than to ask why they were robbing a coach.

"Tizz is our sister," Brown-hair said. "And since we lost that fellow, we'd best get back and see if Mam picked up the trail."

"I reckon," Pa said.

Without more ado they turned to go. And I'd have let them.

"Wait," said Kathy. "If your sister's in some sort of trouble, mayhap we can help?"

"We don't need help," said Ginger.

Pa looked thoughtful. "I don't know. There was six of them. With these two, if you count Mam in, we'd be six."

"Seven," said Kathy.

"Wait a minute," said Rupert. "Were the men who... I'm guessing they kidnapped your sister? Were they escorting a coach with a woman inside, and a crest scratched off its door?"

"Mam didn't say nothing about a coach," said Pa. "With or without a woman. And we'd best—"

"Was the sixth man, the man in charge, a slim nobleman trying to pass as a commoner?" I asked. "With a bite mark on his hand?"

They all stopped, staring at me.

"So," said Pa. "Seems like you fellers know who your enemy is. You mind telling us?"

"We don't know," I said. "I was hoping you did."

Pa shook his head, but his face was thoughtful.

"The lady has a point, Pa," said Brown. "We know he's their enemy, as well as ours. Why not bring 'em along?"

"We don't need no one's help," said Ginger stubbornly.

"Maybe, maybe not," said Pa. "You need to learn the difference between looking out for yourself and being prideful. Or at least, 'tween being smart and being stupid. We know he wants to kill this one." He gestured to Rupert. "So's I suppose they'll be on our side."

There's nothing like a shared enemy to make you a friend—or at least an ally—and we soon found ourselves riding beside the Flintruckers, as they led us into the wooded foothills. They walked so briskly that the horses weren't slowed up by much. The dog followed behind, keeping his distance, but he didn't whine or growl, which I considered a hopeful sign.

The Flintruckers were trappers, they said. They'd been out setting a line when five men, led by the man whose hand Meg had bitten, had ridden up to their cabin and departed with Tizz, leaving Mam tied to a chair.

The slender nobleman had stayed to wait for them, and the knife he held at Mam's throat convinced them to listen instead of killing him. The first thing he said was that if he didn't return to his men that night, they'd kill Tizzabeth.

"After that, we couldn't do anything to stop him. He didn't even have to hold Mam hostage, anymore. He told us to find you all, near Tottenham," Brown, whose real name was Doug, told us. "We were to trail you till there was a coach or a rider on the road in front of you, then hold 'em up, making it look like a robbery. And when you came to rescue 'em, we was to kill Master Rupert here." He gave Rupert a friendly nod. "But we were supposed to make sure at least one of you survived, along with the person we was robbing, to make sure everyone knew that it was a real robbery and that Master Rupert died trying to stop us. Any chance you've been having some accidents, lately?"

"A few," said Rupert. "And the woman in the coach we asked about, and whom they've kidnapped too, is my fiancée."

He sounded as if he meant it, and Kathy's brows shot up. I was only surprised the decision had taken him so long.

"Are you sure no one saw her?" Rupert added.

"If there'd been a coach, Mam would have told us," said Ginger, whose name was Cal. "And he didn't say anything about your girl, either. But then, no reason he would. He just gave us our orders; rob someone, kill you. We saw him following us shortly after we got to Tottenham."

"Could hardly miss him," said Pa. "He made more noise than a herd of elk. Running. Though dry brush."

"So we figured he meant to make sure the job was done. And since we were doing the robbing we'd get the blame, even if *he* loosed the bolt."

"Well," said Doug, "you can see why Sheriff Willet might think we'd hold up a coach. Even though," he added, "we've been respectable for nigh on a year now."

"Fool girl," Cal muttered.

"That part's family business," said Pa. "But the long and short of it was, when Master Rupert here was dead they'd let Tizza go."

It seemed to me, as we rode happily through the deserted forest at their side, that they could still arrange that. I was pretty sure that thought had occurred to Cal, as well.

"Don't fret yourselves," Pa added. "He had to die in a robbery, before witnesses. Not get found lying on the road with a bolt through his corpus. Had to be a reason for it, and something that didn't look like some mysterious fellow up and made him dead. But once we get Tizz back, I'd start being careful if I was you, young man, and that's a fact."

"I will."

In truth, Rupert looked almost as worried as I felt. It was one thing to suspect someone wanted him dead—having it confirmed was downright depressing.

On the other hand, whoever it was clearly wanted his death to be known, as well as looking like an accident. If the chosen Heir vanished, the investigation would be every bit as intense as it would for a "suspicious" death.

"You say, 'Once we get Tizz back,'" Kathy said. "Do you have some plan for that?"

"Yes," said Cal.

"Well, it's not exactly a plan," said Doug. "We set Mam on their trail."

"Dang fools," said Pa, and even Cal nodded agreement.

"He figured he had all of us out trailing you, under his eye," Doug explained. "So there'd be no one left to go find Tizz. But Mam's the best tracker of the bunch of us. She was going after Tizza as soon as she was sure he'd gone. And she promised to leave a clear trail, so's we can catch up easy."

"If we need to," said Pa calmly. "I didn't marry a city girl. No offense," he added to Kathy.

"None taken," said my beloved. "I like a man who doesn't think women are helpless ninnies."

"I *don't* think that," I said. "But it's not sensible to go running into a fight with well-armed bravos who outnumber you."

"Like you did, back at the Addled Cock?"

At least the argument helped pass the time. We rode for the rest of the morning and into early afternoon before we reached our destination.

The Flintruckers had picked up our trail near Tottenham, they told us, and followed us for several days before we came up on a target they might plausibly have been tempted to rob.

Cal, in fact, went into some detail on the art of choosing a good mark, reminding me that the Flintruckers had only been respectable for a year, and I wondered why they'd changed. The difference between a bandit and a trapper is that a bandit only skins his prey metaphorically...but I was pretty sure that in this case, there really wasn't a difference.

At all events, by the time they'd been able to bring off the job we'd circled so far that we were relatively close to their starting point. This turned out to be a good thing; when we rode up to the cabin we found Mam and Tizz putting up packs, and on the point of setting off to find their men.

They came out to the porch when they heard our horses, Tizz running to hug her father, while her brothers threw their arms around the pair of them, exclaiming in astonishment.

But Pa simply cast his wife, who'd remained on the porch watching her family reunite, a look that held resignation, respect and amusement, in equal parts.

"Figured you'd do it," he said. "Not even five armed men is a match for you."

"Was only two of 'em, time I got there."

Cal had gotten his ginger hair and lanky body from his mother, and Tizz had inherited the same build—but combined with her father's black hair and dark eyes the effect was more that of lean wolf-girl than the weasel Cal resembled.

"Three of 'em sloped off after the first night." Tizz was looking at Champion. "And if you're Rupert..."

The Heir nodded jerkily, hope warring with fear in his pale face.

"...well, if you're Rupert, Meg says to tell you she's all right, and so's the babe. Far as I can tell, that's true," Tizz added kindly. "She told me all about how she'd been kidnapped, and described the coach they're taking her around in, and asked me to go to the law with it, if you didn't happen by first. But we should go to the law anyway, shouldn't we?"

"Fool girl," Cal repeated.

The discussion was moving inside, and I saw that what had started as a simple trapper's cabin had been built into a much larger house, as room after room was added to the original structure. A rather fine porcelain jug, touched with gilt, sat on the table, though the wildflowers in it were wilted. A couple of silver jugs rubbed shoulders with their common wooden fellows on the mantel, and a nice painting of a bowl of fruit hung on one wall, looking out of place between some buck's dropped antlers and a pair of snow shoes that had been retired for the summer.

I could see why they might not want the law to come calling. Nevertheless...

"I think you should go to the sheriff," I said.

If they sent the sheriff to look for the men who'd kidnapped Tizza, we might be able to get some help rescuing Meg as well. And if the kidnappers had already taken Meg out of this fief, we could use Sheriff Willett's real writ to get cooperation from other sheriffs, instead of risking my forged one.

"Now why would we do that?" Cal's voice was amused. "We got Tizz back, didn't we?"

"Your mam got Tizz back," his father said. "But the rest is about right. Why should we go to the law, Master Fisk?"

"Because you're innocent," I said promptly. "You only stopped that coach because your daughter had been kidnapped, and the sooner you report that the better. The lady you were rob...being forced to pretend to rob, I mean, she's going to tell the first sheriff she can find about you. The sooner you take your story to the law, the better."

"And besides," Kathy said. "Your daughter may be free, but Meg's still in their hands—and has been for weeks! If we can get a writ from the sheriff..."

"That's no business of ours," said Cal, followed promptly by "Hey!" as his mother boxed his ear.

"These people were going to help us," she said. "We're beholden to them for the thought, even if they didn't have to do the deed. Though from what Tizz says, your lady was taken away two days ago. She'll likely be in another fief now, so even a sheriff's writ won't do you much good. You can't track a carriage over dry roads, so there's not much we can do for you. Or the law either, really."

"You're probably right," I admitted. "Though you'd think the law would be good for *something*."

The Liege Heir was listening to this conversation with unusual attention...were we doing all future con men and criminals a disservice?

"Well, it isn't," Mam said. "Not across fief borders. But if your girl's still in our woods, we'll be glad to help you out."

Pa and Doug nodded instantly, and after a moment so did Cal.

Unfortunately, I was pretty sure the kidnappers had moved on.

"Our thanks to you, for the thought," I said. "But if they've got a two-day start, we'd better get..."

A torrent of barking erupted from the forest, and I looked out the window just in time to see the mutt run off before half a dozen men rode out of the trees. Their leather armor didn't match and neither did their cloaks, but there was still something about them that proclaimed their calling—at least, to the experienced eye.

The law had arrived.

"That's a good dog you got there," Doug said.

"Ooooh!" said Tizz, though I'd have sworn none of the Flintruckers would ever make such a feminine sound. "It's Davy!" She darted out the door, off the porch, and ran to the youngest of the deputies, calling, "Davy, I got myself kidnapped! But Mam came after me, and she caught one of them on his way to the jakes, and she cut off part of his ear and threatened to do the same with his balls if his friend didn't let me go."

I cast Mam a startled glance. Even having met her, I'd assumed that she crept through a window, untied her daughter, and they'd both sneaked out again.

She smiled. "Never did think that little fatty flap on the bottom was worth much. Only thing it does is hold an earring, and that's a fact. No need for that, Cal." Cal had thrown open a chest, and was pulling out a bow and quiver. "Like Master Fisk here says, we're innocent."

And Tizzabeth had removed any other option. Pa Flintrucker was already heading out to the porch.

"I was just about to come see you, Sheriff Willett. To report my daughter's kidnapping."

"That's interesting," said the sheriff blandly. "Because I'm here in response to a report that three men, who bear a remarkable resemblance to you and your sons, were robbing a coach just this morning."

"But sir." Tizz was clinging to the young deputy's stirrup, so he probably felt he had to say something. "Mistress Abinger told us—"

"I know what she said," his superior told him sharply. "I want to know what the Flintruckers have to say for themselves."

"Well, the first thing," Pa said, "is that if we'd been robbing coaches of our own free will, we'd have tied some cloth over our faces so's you wouldn't have that fine description! And you know...that is, you know we'd never do such a thing, if we'd had a choice. He said his men would kill Tizzabeth if we didn't do it, Willett. And that's the truth."

Willett shot Davy a critical look, but then he sighed.

"Since the conversations Mistress Abinger overheard seem to confirm that, I suppose I have to give you the benefit of the doubt. But why under two moons would someone kidnap your daughter to get you to rob a coach? Which you'd likely be willing to do anyway."

One of the other deputies was staring, not at the confrontation on the porch, but at Champion, who was tied to the railing.

"Sir," he said. "Doesn't that look like the horse the Liege Heir's supposed to be riding?"

The back of my neck prickled in sudden warning.

"Don't be..." Then the sheriff took a good look at Champion. The flowing mane was shorn, the silvery coat dusty, the saddle plain and cheap. But under all that, the horse was magnificent.

"Where'd you come by this horse, Master Flinttrucker?"

"He belongs to the fellow the men who kidnapped Tizza wanted us to kill," Pa said. "Why do you ask?"

"Can't say," the sheriff said. "But I'd like to meet that man."

"Don't say anything," I hissed to Rupert. "Cal, put that bow back. I can handle this."

I stepped out onto the porch myself, with Rupert and Kathy following.

"Sheriff Willett, I presume? My name's Fisk, and this is Mistress Sevenson, and her brother."

Every man in the sheriff's party stared at Rupert, who seemed embarrassed by the attention. After the rigors of these last few weeks he looked almost as ruffianly as Michael usually did, and not at all like a liege heir.

"So, sir." The sheriff was watching Rupert too. "You'd be Master... Wait, Sevenson? Not Master Michael Sevenson?"

So much for any hope of passing him off as Michael— Rupert couldn't answer questions about the Rose conspiracy for even a few minutes, without giving the game away.

"This is Master Benton Sevenson," I said. "He's, ah... He and his sister are traveling with me, in Michael's absence."

The sheriff looked at Champion, then at Rupert again.

"So why does someone want Benton Sevenson dead?"

"That's personal," I said smoothly. "Does it matter? Surely extorting an innocent family into trying to kill someone is enough to merit a warrant."

The sheriff and I traded stares, but then his gaze flicked to Pa Flintrucker, and away again.

"Master Fisk, would you and Master Benton here go for a stroll with me?"

I could feel the Flintruckers' interested eyes following us as we crossed the porch, and the sheriff dismounted. Kathy tagged along, and though the sheriff looked at her critically, he didn't send her back.

"I don't want to say too much in front of the Flintruckers," he told us. "They're... Well, they're actually not good people, though they could be worse. They were worse, before Tizz set her mind on Davy, and I don't want to see that change. If they found out... What under two moons is that?"

His hand came to rest on his sword hilt, which seemed to me to be an overreaction.

"That's my dog," I said. "Ignore him. You were saying...?"

The sheriff eyed the dog warily, but his hand slowly came off the hilt.

"What were we... Oh, the Flintruckers. That's why I pulled you aside. This part's private, mind you? You won't speak of it, to anyone? Because if the

Flintruckers found out how much the High Liege is offering for the Heir's return, I can't think of much they wouldn't do."

"Reward? How much... Wait, the *Heir's* gone missing?"

It was a pretty good performance, if I say so myself. But the sheriff's gaze was on Rupert, not me.

"That's the confidential part, for reasons that should be obvious. Though with every sheriff and deputy in the Realm getting that writ... Why does someone want to kill Master Barton here?"

"It's Benton," I said. "And this is confidential too." Because Benton would kill me if it got out. "He teaches at the university," I said. "And he got one of his female students... Well, let's just say there was a reason the man her parents wanted her to marry called it off. Though trying to have Benton killed, that seems excessive to me."

"I see." The sheriff cast Rupert a disapproving glower...but under that glower was suspicion.

"I mean to marry her!" Rupert's blushing outrage would have been an even better performance than mine...had he been acting. "I *want* to marry her, but Father..."

"Baron Sevenson also had other plans for his son," I said. "Though at least he gave Benton a horse before he kicked him out. But since we're traveling around the countryside, trying to find where the girl's father has hidden her, we might notice...oh, all manner of things. What is the reward for the missing Heir? You already told us he's gone, so there can't be much harm in passing that on."

The sheriff hesitated a final moment, and sighed. "Some deputy's bound to talk, and then the rumors will start... I expect everyone in the Realm will know inside a week. Which the Liege should have known, anyway."

He did know it, and he must be pretty worried to make the news of Rupert's disappearance public.

"So I might as well tell you," the sheriff went on. "The reward for the Heir's safe return is four thousand gold roundels."

My first thought was that this was four times what he'd offered Michael and me. My second thought, following closely on the first, was that even half that sum would buy me a small estate, without help from Michael or anyone else.

So of course, the next thing the sheriff said was...

"I'd be happy to split that reward, fifty/fifty, with someone who could point out the Heir to me. All they'd have to do is assure me I had the right man. Because bringing the wrong man to the Liege, in the mood his messenger says he's in...well, it might prove fatal for more than a man's career."

And we had something to do with why the Liege was so frightened for his son, and so furious. He'd hired us to bring Rupert home, and we'd thrown in with his son instead. In fact, some of that fury was probably *directed* at us.

That meant any chance to claim that reward, and the small estate I needed to support my wife, was now sliding out of my grasp...unless I took the sheriff up on his offer.

He could use his own men to take Rupert in. All I had to do was turn to him and say, *Half the reward? I lied. This is Liege Heir Rupert.*

And I couldn't do it.

It wasn't because of Kathy's bright gray eyes, fixed on me in imperious pleading.

And it wasn't any need to defy Jack—who'd have sold his own child for a sum like that. Nor was it because my kindly father would never have done such a thing, or Michael either.

I didn't want to do it. I liked Rupert, I respected Meg, and I wanted to help them.

Though I felt more than a twinge, at the thought of so much money slipping out of my grasp.

"I'm sorry," I said sincerely. "I'd love to claim even half that reward. But Benton isn't the Liege Heir. Though if I should come across him, and need help to get him home...well, I hope I'm in your fief if that happens."

"I hope so too, sir," the sheriff said. "In fact, I'd *hoped*... Oh well. Can't blame a man for thinking, with all that money at stake."

You couldn't...but a man didn't have to succumb to it.

Kathy's shining eyes were the only reward I needed.

CHAPTER 19

Michael

First I had to return to the town where I'd left my companions. From there I was able to track the coach, as we'd been doing all along. And several of the people I asked about it told me of two men and a "smart-looking" young lady who'd done the same.

I resolved to keep this description to myself; Kathy had been teased about her spectacles as a child. And Fisk found her beautiful, so I saw no reason to mention that most considered my sister perfectly ordinary.

However, the coach seemed to vanish into thin air after Tottenham. Three people on horseback were much less memorable—though between Kathy's spectacles, Tipple's spots, and the fact that even disguised as an ordinary horse Champion was still very fine, I was able to follow their erratic route.

I was a lot less memorable, which would hopefully make it harder for Wheatman to come after me. In addition to leaving him bound, I'd taken his horse and sold it in a town some distance from the keep. And his crossbow that "couldn't miss" was buried deep in my pack, so he'd have to acquire a weapon as well. But while all of this might slow him down, I had no illusion 'twould stop him.

Some have called me both obsessed, and insanely stubborn, but Wheatman was worse than I in both those ways—he would no more quit his grim vocation than I'd have given up on errantry. I couldn't continue my search by day and stay awake all night, but I took care to hide my camps, and trusted my good True to keep watch.

After two days and seven towns, I realized they were searching for the coach by riding outward from where it had disappeared in a slowly widening spiral. I stopped a traveling tinker and paid him to draw me a map of all the towns and villages in the area, figured out their most likely route, jumped out one ring and started traveling it backward.

I rode into Scranton at dusk. It wasn't a timber milling town, but it was the center of a wide agricultural area and big enough to support two inns. No one at the first inn had heard of my friends—though they spent some time telling me how superior their food, beds and even baths were to those of the Blue Crow.

This told me the Blue Crow's prices would be lower. My purse was growing thin by this time, so I whistled True away from trying to make friends with the inn's cat—who, judging by his hissing, was not fond of large playful dogs—and rode on down the street.

At this hour and season, with the day's work done but the sky still bright, many of the townsfolk had come into the street to run a few errands, or simply stand and chat.

Despite the crowd, I recognized my friends from half a block away—all three of them, alive, apparently intact...and as usual, arguing amongst themselves as they approached the inn.

They didn't see me until Chant caught Tipple's scent, and emitted the bellowing neigh for which he'd been named.

Kathy called my name, but 'twas Fisk's face I was watching. The light of the setting sun glowed on the flash of relief that crossed it, followed by a most joyous welcome.

For just a moment, I let myself feel how much I'd miss him when he married my sister and settled down—wherever they settled, for I had a hard time envisioning Fisk running an estate.

But no matter where they ended up, Kathy was Fisk's future and his happiness. I *refused* to begrudge it.

By the time I rode up to them, Fisk had gotten control of his expression, the beaming joy transmuted into sardonic satisfaction.

"Thank goodness!" Kathy leaned out of her saddle to hug me. "I was never going to forgive you for running off without a word like that, but I'm too relieved. Did that dreadful man try to kill you?"

"More to the point," said Fisk, "did you find some way to...discourage him, shall we say?"

"You sound like I buried him in an unmarked grave," I said. "I found him more tragic than dreadful...though I suppose his results merit that description. I'm not certain I managed to discourage him, either, but I had to come and warn you—someone wants Rupert dead!"

I wasn't about to name that someone in the open street, where several people had stopped to smile at our reunion.

To my bemusement, none of my friends looked startled by this news.

"We found that out the hard way," Rupert explained. "But tracking Meg down again—and this time, curse it, we need to get her free! That seemed more important."

"I can see that. But have you figured out why the... why your stepmother had her taken?" I asked. "I've been thinking and thinking, but I still don't..."

They stared at me as if I'd sprouted horns, and I realized my haste hadn't been completely wasted.

"Ah, so you knew someone was after him, but you didn't know who."

"Caro?" Rupert's voice rose in astonishment, and Fisk looked around the crowded street sharply. "Why would *Caro* want to—"

"A private parlor," Fisk interrupted. "Right now, because we clearly have a lot to talk about. Come along," he added.

I thought that command was redundant, till I followed his gaze down the rope tied to his pommel, to... It had to be the ugliest dog I'd ever seen. At least, I assumed 'twas a dog. There was nothing else it could be. But it looked as if some sculptor in clay had tired of working on it, squashing its rump down and its short back legs into its torso before changing his mind and letting it survive.

Looking down from Chant's back I couldn't make out its expression, but True confirmed my guess as to its species by leaping up to it in a series of playful hops and then crouching, shoulders down, butt up, with his tail wagging furiously. He also appeared to be barking, but I couldn't hear the soft rasp. The creature erupted in a panicked howl, and tried to bolt.

When the leash checked it, it tried to join Fisk in the saddle. Tipple is short enough it might have succeeded, if not for those truncated back legs. As it was the dog managed half the distance, clawing at Fisk's leg and Tipple's side, but it would have fallen back to the street had Fisk not grabbed the scruff of its neck and hoisted it into his lap.

"He just started trying to do this," Fisk explained, ignoring the way the crowd scattered and women shrieked. The dog thrust his toothy muzzle under Fisk's unbuttoned coat, and the terrified yelping stopped. "If I don't pick him up, he makes even more noise."

His voice was indifferent, but the calm hands stroking the dog told a different tale. Would he one day handle my nieces and nephews with the same casual assurance?

'Twas a strange thought—Fisk, a father? But a glance at Kathy showed me she didn't find it odd at all.

At all events, we descended on the Blue Crow en masse—and with four people, four horses and two dogs we created a fair amount of chaos. Particularly since True kept trying to join his new friend in Fisk's lap.

I called him to heel, and made sure he obeyed with a touch of my animal handling Gift. I don't usually use that on True, for it feels like cheating, but given the way the inn's staff responded to Fisk's dog—honestly, you'd think he was a grizzly bear—I thought it wise to show them one well-trained beast. And 'twas not as if the dog offered any threat, cowering as he did in Kathy's skirt.

Though I thought naming him Timorous was taking matters a bit too far.

I soon realized the matter of a name was not yet settled, for Kathy called him to heel as Preposterous, adding, "Here Prepee, here Prepee," for good measure.

Fisk winced.

But eventually we settled in a parlor, still so warm from the day that we threw open the shutters, promising that we'd only discuss "Caro" or "Rupert's stepmother," lest our voices carry.

With Peculiar huddling under the table, we gave the serving maid our orders. True had figured out that his new friend was too frightened to play, and lay beside my chair, his tail thumping the floor.

The first question that arose, long before the maid returned with our dinner, was why I thought the Liege Lady had anything to do with it.

So I explained how I'd tried to determine who might have lent their keep to kidnappers, and what Wheatman ultimately told me. Then I had to explain how I came to be chatting with my would-be assassin. This took longer than the first question, and my duck breast was getting cold by the time I finished.

"If he's at all like you," said Fisk, "he won't give up. Not that easily."

"He's *not* like me." I found it disturbing that Fisk, too, had seen a resemblance between us. "But that's not important now. What's important is that, ridiculous as it seems, it appears the Li—that Rupert's stepmother is trying to have him killed."

"Why is that ridiculous?" Kathy asked. "Once you think about it, she has a clear motive. Just because she's got big dark eyes and shows off her bosom, that doesn't mean she can't have ambition and brains. How do you think she got to be...to marry Rupert's father in the first place?"

"Well..." Looking back on it, I had thought that.

"According to the ladies who don't like her—and there are a lot of them," Kathy added, "—she came to court for the sole purpose of marrying Rupert's father, and she didn't let anything stand in her way. The fair ones admit she's been a good wife to him, but I'm starting to wonder if she didn't intend to make her son liege all... hmm. That would be awfully hard. If Rupert married one of the girls he was supposed to, instead of running off to university and meeting Meg there, he could have several sons by now. Any accident she arranged should have happened to him years ago, before she ever married the Liege."

"I think you're making her too villainous," said Fisk. "And it's not because I'm moved by her dark eyes, or her bosom. But you're right about the timing. If she always intended to dispose of Rupert, she'd have done it at the start. I think she was content with being the wife, and one day the widow, of the most powerful man in the Realm...until Rupert came home with Meg on his arm, and volunteered to take himself out of the succession by wedding a Giftless girl."

"I didn't take myself out of the succession," said Rupert. "I wanted Father to accept Meg, and our children, Giftless or not."

"That may be what you wanted." I was thinking of my own father as I spoke. "But what was the likelihood?"

"The most likely outcome," said Fisk, "if you held firm and married Meg, was that Rupert's father would choose his second son as heir instead. Was Caro sympathetic to your romance, by any chance?"

"No," said Rupert. "She sided with Father. So that doesn't..."

"So she was too smart to do anything that suspicious," Kathy put in. "All she had to do was sit back and watch, while the Liege's opposition to Meg made Rupert even more stubborn. Everything was going her way, and she didn't have to lift a finger!"

A memory flashed into my head, and suddenly it all made sense. "I know what changed! Fisk, remember the man who paid Master Quicken for secret reports, on the experiments to find some way Mistress Margaret might bear a Gifted child?"

"I can see why the...someone would be interested in those experiments." Kathy caught herself this time, but we all looked guiltily at the open window, having forgotten to be discreet in our excitement. "But those results were faked."

"*Those* results were," said Fisk. "Others may not have been. I'll bet her henchman, whoever he might be—"

"Gifford Noye," said Kathy and Rupert together.

"He's always hanging around her when he's at court," Rupert went on. "Father jokes about her having an admirer, but of course she'd never..."

He suddenly realized how much else he'd have thought the Liege Lady would never do, and fell silent.

Behind her spectacles, Kathy's eyes were distant, as she tried to remember things she'd not noticed at the time.

"I'm not so sure about that. If they're lovers, they've been discreet...but you can be. Discreet, I mean, even at court."

"And how would you know that?" The teasing in Fisk's voice was warmer than a smile.

Kathy waved him to silence. "They may not be lovers, but he does what she says. He's been absent from court quite a bit lately. He fits the description too; smallish and slight."

"And capable," said Fisk. "If he's been gathering reports on all those experiments, without anyone else finding out about it."

"*That's* why she kidnapped Meg!" For all his innocence, Rupert was no fool. "One of the experiments must have seemed promising. They're all still working with animals, of course, and none of the reports I saw looked like anything either Meg or I wanted to try. But someone might...someone must have had a breakthrough! They may have wanted to make sure they got the same result consistently, or tone down some side effect—some of the side effects were pretty ghastly. But they must have thought they'd have something to offer us pretty soon, because the one thing all of their theories had in common was that they had to be applied while the child was forming—most of them in the first four months of pregnancy."

"So when *she* learned of this promising report..." I was working it out as I spoke. "...her first thought was to tuck Mistress Margaret away, until her pregnancy was too far advanced for anything to make the child Gifted. And then she could...just let Meg go?"

"Why not?" Fisk asked. "The last thing our Caro wants is for Rupert to get over his dead love—which he would, sooner or later—and then marry some noblewoman and produce a litter of Gifted heirs. This dramatic kidnapping had the beneficial side effect of keeping Rupert's attention fixed on Meg, and making him even more determined to marry her. It's a decent bet that she could then persuade her husband to disown him before any more children came along."

"I am going to marry her," said Rupert. "The first chance I get—even if that's exactly what Caro wants, and Father chooses Liam in my place. This is what Meg and I want. Assuming she'll still have me, after I failed her so badly."

"You haven't failed," I said stoutly. "Not yet. But if all this is true, why take the risk of trying to kill Rupert now?"

"I don't know," Fisk admitted. "Maybe his father is changing his mind about disowning him. Though if he were my son, having to shell out four thousand gold roundels would make me even more... Oh, all right. I have no idea why she changed her mind, but she clearly has. She probably sent Wheatman after Michael when her men reported we were helping Rupert, instead of trying to bring him home—which means there must be some messenger riding back and forth. You wouldn't send this kind of information off with a letter carrier. But the timing's about right for that. The last thing she wants is for Meg to return when those formulas might work."

"And if Rupert does meet with an 'accident,'" Kathy added slowly, "she has no reason to keep Meg alive. It sounds like they managed to keep Meg from finding out who hired them, but she's pretty smart. If they didn't need her alive, to keep you from marrying someone else, I doubt they'd take the risk."

"I'd try to avoid getting assassinated, even if Meg's life wasn't hanging on my survival," said Rupert. "Though that does make it worse. We've *got* to get her back. And we don't even know where that accursed coach is!"

"We'd also better find some evidence against the... against Rupert's stepmother," said Kathy. "If she's capable of kidnapping and murder, I'm not sure her husband is safe either. And no offence, Michael, but I don't see him taking the word of an unredeemed man—about what an assassin told him—as enough evidence to charge his own wife with treason and attempted murder."

They were all right, and I had to admit...

"It does seem as if they've gone to ground once more. And if they hide themselves better than they did the first time, it might take months to find them. If Wheatman hadn't used the information to gain his release—and I know that makes his testimony less credible, though I believe he spoke true—we'd still have no idea who was behind this. Mistress Carolyn has been remarkably careful about leaving evidence, but no one could have predicted the man she sent to kill me would end up talking to me instead."

"She doesn't know you," Fisk murmured.

"So," Kathy summed it up, "we have two sets of assassins after us, and we've no idea where Meg is or how to find her."

A depressed silence fell, and 'twas not only Rupert who felt like a failure. As a knight errant, I had failed at both rescuing damsels and returning missing heirs—not to mention getting Fisk and Kathy married. Even my nascent magic, as it came more and more under my control, was useless.

"We have no choice," I said. "We must keep looking for Mistress Margaret, whether it exposes Rupert to assassins or not."

'Twould also expose my friends to any risk that might still be posed by *my* assassin, but with this Noye trying so hard to arrange Rupert's demise, I dared not leave them. I could see no other way, except to—

"No, we don't," Fisk said slowly.

He then fell silent for so long Kathy ran out of patience.

"We don't what? You can't just leave that hanging."

"What...? Oh, sorry. But we don't have to go chasing all over the countryside. In fact, it would be counter-productive. How have we found out everything important we've learned so far?"

I hate it when Fisk turns scholarly, trying to make me work out an answer he's already discovered. Rupert, just out of university himself, wasn't so fussy.

"We've learned the most from their attempts to kill us," he said. "More from Michael's assassin than from the Flintruckers, but even they... Wait, you're not proposing we let them *try* to kill me."

"Why not?" Fisk asked. "We know they want to kill Rupert—they've tried three times, so they're not likely to give up now. If we just sit still, they'll have to come to us. And make their next attempt on ground of our choosing, when we're ready for them. Once they've—hopefully—failed, even if we can't capture one of them, maybe we can track them back to Mistress Meg!"

'Twas the maddest idea I've known Fisk to come up with...but no one had a better plan.

Rupert wanted to take a room under his own name, to make it easier for them to find him, until I reminded him of the reward his father offered for his return. I'd started hearing rumors about that in the last few days, and my friends' encounter with Sheriff Willet

confirmed it. Given the sums that were rumored—and
for once, the rumors fell *short* of reality—if he revealed
his identity to anyone, he'd be dragged back to his father forthwith.

His sulking over that didn't annoy me, as I was too
amused by watching Fisk sulk over the fact that all his
work in forging a Liege writ had been wasted. He didn't
dare use it, now that every sheriff in the Realm would
have a real Liege writ to compare it to.

I suggest he destroy it, if 'twas so dangerous to carry,
but Fisk said, "You never know."

We kept alert for suspicious people around us whenever we went out, and also set a night watch, which
Fisk, Rupert and I divided between us. Though we
were all awakened in the middle of that first night,
when Monster decided to take True up on his offer to
play. The resultant tornado of jostling furry bodies and
pounding feet was so loud it woke not only us, but the
lodgers on both sides and in the room below—at least,
judging by the angry thumps on our walls and floor.

Kathy offered to take a watch shift too, but she'd
snickered so much when we purchased a mere half a
dozen daggers, to be secreted about our persons, that
we didn't think she'd take it seriously. Though mayhap
'twas *us* she wasn't taking seriously. I also took to wearing my sword whenever we left our rooms, which was
as awkward and annoying as it usually was.

We did not, however, leave a guard in our rooms,
which I profoundly regretted when we returned from
an outing and the innkeeper told us, "Your friend was
here, looking for you, sir."

Fisk started asking about a slim nobleman with a
bitten hand, but I was already sprinting up the stairs.

'Twas no great surprise to find my room ransacked, and the crossbow gone.

The dismayed innkeeper said he hadn't let the man into my room—even though he'd known my name and described me perfectly. Indeed, I couldn't blame the man—I blamed myself, for not finding someplace outside of the inn where we were staying to conceal it. Or at least someplace besides our rooms.

Kathy, in a consoling spirit, said that mayhap Wheatman just wanted to reclaim his possession...but even she couldn't summon up much conviction, and I all but knew we'd see the man again.

Hopefully, I'd see him before he spotted me.

But aside from that, three days passed uneventfully. On the morning of the fourth day, one of the maids knocked on our door and delivered a note.

She said someone had given it to the tapster, and asked that it be passed on to us as soon as possible. Rupert took one look at it and became so agitated he barely managed to wait till she'd departed before he snatched it out of my hand.

"'Tis Meg's writing! But...she'd never write twaddle like this. Could she have been forced to write it?"

He turned it over to read the back, which was a bit irritating as I'd not finished reading the first page. But even knowing she'd not written it of her own will, his face went white when he reached the end.

"Cheer up," said Fisk brutally. "No one who really means to kill themselves sends a note more than twelve hours in advance. 'I will throw myself from the abandoned grain mill into the stream, but Only when the Creature Moon is at its height. Two hearts cannot be so cruelly torn asunder...' I'm amazed they didn't give us directions to the place."

"Not to mention the fact that we know she's a prisoner, and not free to slay herself even if she wished to," I added. "Fisk is right—this is insulting."

"Oh!" said Kathy, who'd been ignoring us to study the note. "I know why she wrote such silly stuff. Look at the first letter of every sentence. *Too much trouble has come from our love. Rupert, my dear... Although... Please...* TRAP. And here again, at the end. *Time will heal... Remorse... Always yours. Pray forgive...* She didn't have to tell us twice."

"She didn't have to tell us once," said Fisk. "The content of that note makes it perfectly clear. The question is, how do we turn it back on them?"

CHAPTER 20

Fisk

It was easy to get directions to the abandoned grain mill—it was the local lover's leap, where all the thwarted lovers went to end everything...only to talk themselves out of it on the long journey. The mill had been placed on a waterfall, a full day's ride from the present town.

Even after the villagers had moved themselves downstream to flatter land, the tapster told us, the mill had remained in the deserted village for some time—mostly because making the trip to get your grain milled once a year was less trouble than moving those big stones and building a new one. Then the miller's daughter had been jilted by her lad, and thrown herself from the mill's second story into the churning water below. The description of how badly the rocks in the rushing stream had battered her lovely face was still the stuff of tales.

The miller and his family had sold the place and moved on, and the new owner had recruited every ox team in the village to move the stones down to a new mill. It was built on a big slow bend, where you could jump into the river if you wanted to, but you had no better chance of drowning there than anywhere else.

But it wasn't just its gory history that made this place so appropriate for an ambush—by the time we got our horses saddled and rode out there, it would be so close to the moment the Creature Moon was high that we'd have no opportunity to set up something clever.

Though the exact time hardly mattered. Whenever we arrived, they'd be waiting for us.

The good news was that "they" seemed to have shrunk in number. There was another clue in Meg's note, that Rupert spotted; everywhere the word "only" and the word "two" occurred, they'd been capitalized. And those words occurred a lot, bless Meg's clever little brain.

The bad news was that, as Rupert said, all they had to do was threaten Meg and our advantage in numbers wouldn't do much good. Why their numbers would suddenly decrease so much was a mystery, and I don't like mysteries—particularly going into a situation where people might want to kill me.

But the worst news was that with only two opponents, there was no way I could talk Katherine out of coming with us.

I'd been so caught up in figuring out how to thwart the plot that I'd forgotten, for one fatal instant, that I also needed to come up with a plan that had absolutely no part for Kathy. I did point out that we were assuming that "there's only two people guarding me" was what Meg was trying to say—and it might not have been. But with so many unknown factors, coming up with a way to "turn their plan back on them," as I'd so cleverly blurted out, was going to be tricky enough without leaving a competent and clever adult behind.

Particularly without her knowing I'd done it deliberately. She'd barely forgiven me for the last time I excluded her, without her knowledge or consent, and I didn't want to get caught doing it again.

Even as this passed through my own mind, I could hear how condescending, how insulting it sounded... but this was *Kathy*.

And I failed to come up with any way to keep her from coming with us, so the point was moot.

Not that I hadn't tried. I proposed several other plans, including one in which we swapped Michael and Rupert's clothing, and used the sudden revelation that Rupert wasn't Rupert as a distraction...

But Rupert said that Noye knew him too well to be fooled for more than a moment, that anything that frightened Noye might put Meg at risk, and he flat out refused.

We couldn't even get there early, to scout the place to create our own trap, so the best plan we could think of was to have Michael leave us at the entrance to the valley where the mill resided. Then he'd find a way to the mill through the woods, while we convinced any observers that he hadn't rejoined us by riding down the road without him. *Assuming*, of course, that they hadn't already learned that Michael had rejoined us.

After that...well, we'd have to see what they'd set up. But with luck Michael might be able to get the drop on them, while they were trying to get the drop on us, and then find some way to distract Noye so the rest of us could jump in and rescue Mistress Meg.

I may have beaten Jack, as Kathy said, but I couldn't help but imagine his probable opinion of *this* plan.

I shared it.

"Cheer up," said Katherine, who'd been almost as tense and worried about Mistress Meg as I'd been about her. "If there's only two of them, like Meg says—"

"Like you assume she says," I mentioned. Again.

"—then we've got them outnumbered! Six to two, if you count the dogs...well, maybe not poor Scaredy. Five to two, then."

"Unless Meg meant that there are only two entrances, or only two hours from sunset to moon high."

Dusk was falling now, with the thin sliver of the Green Moon about to follow the sun down. The waxing Creature Moon was already half way to the top of its arc, but we were coming up on the foothills that held the abandoned mill.

"I think she did mean only two men," said Michael. "And not just because of the note. If they outnumber us so badly, would it not have been simpler to ambush us here on the road?"

He had a point. This overgrown track led only to the old village, where no one ever went. We'd passed half a dozen places where a large group of men could have slaughtered us all.

"Then what happened to them?" I asked. "They were all there with Tizza, before Noye and the other three rode off, leaving just two poor saps to face Mam Flintrucker."

"True. But mayhap 'twas facing Mam Flintrucker that convinced the two men guarding Tizzabeth they should find new employment," Michael said. "Look at it from their point of view; we spoiled their plan to take up residence in the old keep, and we've been driving them all over the countryside ever since. And ambushing them. They haven't once succeeded in harming us."

"Except for breaking my head," I said dryly.

"You don't count," said my beloved. "'Tis Rupert they want to kill, and they've failed every time. You're right, Michael, they've had a very bad month. I shouldn't be amazed if some of them...changed their minds."

"In the middle of a contract, which they've been pursuing for weeks?" I asked skeptically. "They can't ambush us on the road, because Rupert's death has to look like an accident. If he's murdered, someone might start looking at the people who had a motive. I expect their plan is for him and Meg to throw themselves into the millrace, and leave her note to prove it was suicide. I told you to burn it," I added.

Rupert, who carried the note in a pocket near his heart, looked mulish.

"The place doesn't matter," Michael said. "They can simply smash Rupert's head in and toss his body into the water. By the time the rocks were done with him, one or two more blows would make no difference. But they haven't attacked us, and that makes me think Meg might be right, that there are only two of them."

"Or that Noye might have fooled her into thinking there are only two," I reminded them. "And they haven't attacked us, because there's an even better setup for an ambush in that empty village, or the old mill."

Not to mention the fact that Wheatman might pop out of the bushes and shoot us at any moment. But there was nothing we could do about that except leave Michael behind, and since Michael's unexpected presence was our best chance to disrupt Noye's plan...

"We'll know soon enough," Michael said. "This is where I leave you."

The tapster had told us about the sign, marking the entrance to the valley where the village had been so neatly tucked away. The mill had belonged to the Scoffels, and the village that arose around it had been Scoffelton. But time, or maybe some clever vandal, had broken off a corner of the old sign, renaming the town, "offelton."

With the light of day giving way to moonlight, the entrance to the valley was plunged in such deep shadow it was like staring into a giant's mouth.

We pulled our horses to a halt, and Michael rode Chant off into the trees, True, as always, silent at his heels.

The talkative tapster had assured us that there would be other ways to approach the village. Almost certainly. Well, probably.

If I was going to leave Kathy behind, in safety, this was my last chance to do it. She knew it, too. Her gaze fixed on me, the challenge clear in her eyes. And if I tried to stop her, tried to make her an unequal partner, would she eventually leave me, as I'd left Michael in Tallowsport?

Even if I could have stopped her, I didn't have the right.

"I want a wife," I told her. "I want a partner, too. I want our children. I want all of it."

The Green Moon had set by now, but the Creature Moon shed enough light for me to see the sheen of tears in her eyes.

The rapidly rising Creature Moon.

"I want a wife too," there was an edge in Rupert's usually mild voice. "How long do we have to wait?"

"We have to give Michael a while to find some way in besides the road." Kathy's voice was a bit husky, but her words were prosaic. If I was going to have a comrade, in adventure as well as life, it was nice to have one who could keep her mind on the matter at hand. "He'll do a nightjar whistle when it's time for us to come."

I had no idea what a nightjar's call sounded like, which might be why Michael never used that signal with me, but it was a childhood tradition among the Sevensons. Kathy claimed she was better at it than any of her brothers.

Sure enough, the Creature Moon had moved only an inch up the sky when a fluting, three note whistle drifted out of the valley.

"He's in," Kathy announced, and kicked Posy forward without more ado.

I'd have preferred to dither for a few more minutes, make some last minute plans...make a last, futile attempt to change Kathy's mind? But Rupert was practically riding her down in his haste to reach his Meg. I looked down into Frightful's worried eyes.

"It's too late to be sensible," I told him. "She's already in."

And I sent Tipple trotting down the giant's gullet, after my love.

An abandoned village is always eerie. A loose shutter will bang, the scurrying of rats sounds like the ghostly echo of a woman's skirt—until you realize what that sound really is, and then it's worse. But even beyond the shutter and the rats, there's an air of wistful melancholy that hangs over such places, like the dust of worn out dreams. And that's by day.

Scoffelton had been built in this narrow valley because the waterfall, and thus the mill, was here. They'd had easy access to the stream, and many of the men who'd lived in the ramshackle cottages clinging to the hillside must have gone out to the flatter land to plow fields and graze their stock. But even on this warm summer night, the waterfall's mist cast a chill over the valley—in winter it would be both damp and freezing—and the constant roar only made it easier for ghosts to sneak up on you.

For all I knew, the people who'd lived here had been perfectly content with their lives. But in Scoffelton, it felt as if the abandoned dreams had been bitter ones.

If I hadn't been showing off for Kathy, I'd have cringed and scuttled like poor Spineless.

The town was bad enough, but as we approached the old mill several lengths of rusty chain, hanging over a beam outside the door, clanked in proper ghostly fashion. I finally gave in and said, "Oh, come on. Did he actually set the scene, like a traveling player's stage?"

Kathy had dismounted, and was striking sparks to light our two candle lanterns, while I tethered the horses. I thought about taking the dog with us...promptly thought better of it, and left him tied to Tipple's saddle. The last thing we needed in there was a panicked dog.

"Don't be absurd. Someone could easily have left them—" The tinder began to catch at that moment, and Kathy stopped speaking to blow the flame to life.

"Left a chain that goes for a silver ha' the foot?" I said. "And what would it have supported? What probably hung there was a grain sack, stuffed with straw and a few rocks to make it look heavy. Not that they needed any kind of sign when they had *that*."

The great water wheel, now missing most of its cross boards and cut loose from its gears, still spun slowly under the stream's assault.

But Kathy had both lanterns lit, and right now Rupert was afraid of only one thing.

"We've got to get in there, and find Meg before moon high." He grabbed one of the lanterns, and shoved the door open. The hinges squealed so loudly we might as well have knocked. And I found the fact that it wasn't locked more unnerving than the rattling chain.

"We've still got some time," I said. "Why don't we all look around, and find..."

Rupert's lover was within reach and his patience had run out. He took a lantern in with him, but a single candle actually conceals more than it reveals. We saw nothing at the edge of the wavering light but a few broken casks, and the looming ghosts of machines that were too big to move or too old to salvage.

It took him a while just to find the stairs—for of course this drama had to play out on the top floor, where it was easiest to fall to your death.

"...find another escape route, or..."

"If Rupert arrives alone, they can kill him without witnesses and claim 'twas an accident!" And before I could even begin to find some last ditch way to stop her, Katherine ran right after him.

"...or a hiding place, in case we might need one. Or maybe a dozen or so thugs, waiting to ambush us."

But being the sole witness to Rupert's demise was probably almost as risky as being Rupert. I didn't want Kathy in that position, so I was crossing the room as I spoke. By the time I finished I was halfway up the creaking, and probably dangerously rotten stairs.

The only good thing was that Wheatman wasn't shooting at us. Yet.

I couldn't see anything on the second floor...except for the light that glowed, ominously, from the third floor.

Master Noye—assuming Rupert and Kathy were right about the identity of the man holding a knife to Meg's throat—evidently shared my feelings about darkness and old wooden floors. Two lanterns, bright with burning oil, had been placed to either side of him and his captive, and a third lantern sat on the floor behind the stairs.

This increased the resemblance to a stage, but I wondered what, or who, or at least how many, lurked in the deeper shadows beyond the light.

Michael had better be one of them.

The drama of the setting was heightened by the huge, open hatch behind the two central figures—it had probably been built to allow workmen access to the great wheel, turning slowly in the lantern's glare.

It was also the place where at least one young woman had taken a hard and final way out of her troubles, and you couldn't help but remember that too.

As Master Noye intended, no doubt. He even, in the best theatrical tradition, wore a mask that covered the top half of his face. It was made of shaped leather, with a long pointed nose that distracted attention from the shape of jaw and mouth. Looking closer, I could see dark stains where glass gems had been pried off it after some fancy dress ball. The rest of his clothing was neat, but nondescript.

The lower half of Meg's face was distorted by the gag in her mouth, her skirt was wrinkled and stained, and

Noye's free hand twisted tightly in her tangled hair. Judging by the wet cloth near her lips she'd been wearing that gag for some time, and probably the hobbles around her ankles and the rope that held her arms behind her back, as well.

But the thing that told me most about her captivity was a plain wooden chair, now pushed off to one side. Noye had been waiting for a long time. No reason he shouldn't make himself comfortable.

There was only one chair.

I'd already been inclined to dislike Master Noye, and this cemented my opinion—not that this mattered to anyone, him least of all.

"Let her go." Rupert's voice was steadier than I'd expected, and firmer too. "Let her go now, and we'll allow you to walk away. But if you hurt her, in any way, when I'm Liege I will set every sheriff and bounty hunter in the Realm on your heels, and never give up till you are dead."

It was usually easy to forget Rupert was the Liege Heir...but he so clearly meant this threat, had I been Noye, I might have taken him up on his offer.

"Set them on whose heels?" Noye was stupid enough to smirk when he said it. "I don't believe we've ever met, Your Highness."

Rupert hesitated, weighing the options. But making a violent man desperate is never a good choice. Katherine was edging backward, out of the light—I was in favor of that, whatever the rest of her plan might be.

At this point we needed plans, no matter who came up with them, and if she was going to be my partner in this adventure it was time to start supporting her.

"We may not know your name," I said, doing my bit to distract Noye's attention. "But we got a good description of you from a beggar who watched you supervise Meg's kidnapping...and from Meg herself. Is the bite she gave you going to leave a scar?"

His hand tightened in Meg's hair so hard she flinched, her eyes glittering with tears of pain. She must have given Noye a hard time in more than just that bite. I was torn between admiration for her grit, and wishing she'd practiced enough meekness to keep him from holding her so securely.

"You're in no position to threaten me, Your Highness," Noye said. "While I... Mistress Katherine, step out from behind that sifter and join your companions. I assure you, you won't be able to sneak around behind us. There's nothing behind us to sneak on!"

Kathy scurried back into the light, and he cut off his nervous giggle before it properly started—but this man was a lot more scared, and less in control of himself, than he pretended. Which would have raised my hopes, except that it made him less predictable, and thus even more dangerous.

"Where was I?" Noye went on. "Oh yes, I was about to point out that you have no idea who I am, and thus can't threaten me. But I'm in a perfect position to cut your lover's throat...if you and your friends don't throw down all your weapons and step away from them. Now."

He didn't have to tighten his hand on the knife, but a thin red line appeared on Meg's throat, anyway.

Rupert's staff clattered to the floor.

"Knives too," Noye said.

"Wait," I said. "Before anyone goes further, where are your men, Master Whoever? This should be their cue to step out of the shadows, swords at ready, to encourage us to obey instead of rushing you."

If we'd read Meg's note correctly, there was at least one other man—and maybe more she didn't know about. If there weren't any more...we were three to one, and the last thing we should do was throw down our weapons.

Rupert, in the act of drawing his knife, hesitated.

"They're standing ready," said Noye. "Waiting for my order to move."

Despite the grip on her hair and the knife at her throat, Meg shook her head furiously and made negative sounds behind the gag. I did like that woman.

Rupert drew his knife and held it low, ready to fight.

"No, they're not. If you had that many men they'd already have moved in, and I'd be dead. We'd all be dead, since you can't afford to leave witnesses that my 'suicide' was faked. I don't think there's anyone here but us. I think you're bluffing."

I was beginning to think that myself—though surely Noye wouldn't have tried this stunt without at least one man to back him up?

But when Rupert stepped forward all Noye did was step back, taking Meg nearer to the drop behind them.

"I'm not bluffing about this," he said. "If you don't lay down your weapons I'll kill her. I have nothing to lose, you see."

The note of defeat in those final words was more convincing than all his bluster. The squeak Meg gave as the knife bit was even more convincing, and Rupert tossed his knife aside.

But Noye had to have some plan for subduing us, so I kept my club in hand. Katherine looked back and forth between Rupert and me, uncertain.

"I mean it," said Noye. "I will kill this woman, now, if you don't surrender."

This time Meg was expecting it and she made no sound, but a trickle of blood ran down the blade and dripped onto the floor.

"He'll do it," Rupert said. "Put your clubs down."

"You know..." I sounded amazingly calm, given that my nerves were quivering like plucked strings. "...if he wants us to disarm, that's the last thing we should do."

The next stroke of the knife drew a splatter of blood—it wasn't the fountain that would have erupted if he'd cut her throat, but I wasn't surprised to hear Kathy's staff clatter to the floor.

"Fisk, he means it! He'll kill her."

One small hand gripped my arm, the other tugging on the club. Her fingers were cold with fear.

Jack would have shoved her off, and never dreamed of giving up his weapons. My father would have disarmed himself long since, and been helpless now. But this had nothing to do with Jack, or my father.

I found that thought quite freeing. And disarming ourselves just wasn't the smart thing to do.

Rupert took a step toward me, and might have reached for my club himself if Kathy hadn't been in his way.

"Let it go," he murmured. "When he lets go of Meg to subdue us we can all jump him together, even without weapons. Michael can jump him!"

"Do you think he doesn't realize that?" I said it loudly enough for Noye to hear, since it was mostly for his benefit. "He's got someone else out there, who'll come out to help him secure us."

Rupert looked at the shadows and back at Meg, clearly unconvinced. Kathy looked back and forth between him and me, then ran to pick up her staff once more.

I found this vote of confidence gratifying, under the circumstances.

"You're sealing this girl's death warrant." There was a convincing note of panic in Noye's voice.

"Nonsense," I said. "If you kill her we'll capture you. And then you'll hang. You don't dare kill her."

"You don't dare move on me," said Noye. "Because if I let her go, we all know I'm a dead man. That's *why* I have nothing to lose. And if I'm going to die, I promise you I'll take her with me!"

That, unfortunately, rang true. I *really* wished Meg hadn't done such a good job of pissing him off.

And at that moment, I heard the stealthy sound of a footfall behind us, almost lost in the waterfall's roar.

It might be Noye's man, but it also might be Michael. It had better be Michael, but either way my best option was to stall...

"So what do you want out of this?" I asked Master Noye, as sincerely as I could manage.

CHAPTER 21

Michael

I found my way through the low hills and into the abandoned village, before the Creature Moon's soft light had completely replaced the sun's. Some horses don't mind traveling after dark, but Chant doesn't care for it. True, on the other hand, was delighted at the prospect of a moonlight romp. We found a trail some way up the hillside that went from house to house, paralleling the old cart road below.

I practiced silently for a bit and then whistled a nightjar's call—I thought I did it pretty well, considering I must have been about fourteen the last time I tried.

As my companions rode up the valley to the mill, Chant, True and I followed above and a bit behind them. I didn't have to open doors to be sure the cottages we passed were empty, for True's good nose would detect a human presence. His cheerful wagging told me only deer and rabbits walked this path, so I knew no one would burst out of the trees or some black-windowed cottage and attack my friends.

The attacker who was most in my thoughts would be more interested in attacking me, and once again I cursed my carelessness in leaving that crossbow unguarded. However, that was one scent True would react to instantly, and he showed no sign of fear or anger all the way through the village to the mill.

I was about to tether Chant behind an abandoned shack, but I hadn't reckoned with Kathy getting the lanterns lit so quickly, or them all plunging into the towering corpse of the old mill before I could even get down the hillside.

I sent Chant plunging down the slope, and reached the mill's door mere moments after Fisk went in...then stopped, abruptly.

Candlelight marked their progress through the vast ground floor, where flour had been bagged and returned to the farmer—there was probably a gate on the other side a wagon could drive through—but they'd given me no time to find it, and were already starting up the stairs.

What better way to find out if someone responded to their presence than to simply wait and see?

I wrapped Chant's reins around a post, pulled off my boots for silence and signaled True to stay with the horses—a command he knows well. Then I slipped through the door. Fisk had left it open, so I didn't need to set the hinges squealing.

The last of the candlelight faded as they climbed on up. I stood perfectly still, my back against the cold damp wall beside the door, not even breathing as I listened.

I could hear their footsteps, on still more stairs, climbing up to the high third floor. The seconds slipped past, counted by the rapid beat of my heart. Then I heard it;

first the whisper of cloth moving on cloth, followed by the soft pad of footfalls.

My eyes had had time to adjust to the near total darkness, and the faintly lighter darkness where light from some source far above picked out the stairs. I waited till a slightly darker shadow crept up to the lowest stair, then hurtled forward, leaping as he started to turn, using the weight of my body to bring him down.

We fell onto the stairs with a reasonably soft thump, and I was grateful he was on the bottom. But he wasn't stunned, as I had hoped. A grunt of pain was followed by an indrawn breath. I pressed my forearm down on his throat, stopping that incipient warning shout, and drew my knife as he started to squirm.

"I cannot let you cry out," I murmured. The feel of my blade on his skin made the rest of the threat clear.

He stopped squirming, and I managed to keep the knife at his throat as I dragged him to his feet and out the door.

After a moment's thought, and with True tagging at our heels, I hauled him into a nearby house, whose stone walls might at least muffle any sounds he made—I could not keep the knife in place while I bound him.

"True, guard," I said crisply. "I'm going to tie you up, sir. And you should know that my dog will attack if you make any sudden movement."

This was probably a lie. I have taught True to watch over my gear, but he isn't trained to guard a man, much less attack.

However, he sat down and stared at my prisoner as if he was a saddlebag full of sausages, and the man must not have wanted to take the risk—he did not shout when I slowly lowered my knife.

"I didn't want to do it," he said. "We didn't sign up to kill no one, much less the Heir."

"Then why are you here?" Binding a man, if you are alone and he is free to resist, presents a number of challenges. I solved the first of them by dragging his rough coat over his shoulders and half way down his arms. 'Twould not hold him long, but that, and True's silent snarl checked him long enough for me to pull a thin leather thong from my pocket and catch it round one of his wrists. He resisted, as I tried to pull his wrists together, but the coat hampered him, and True was doing a really good imitation of a trained guard dog.

"You can let me go," he said. "I promise, I'll slope off. This wasn't in the contract, and even the wage he's offering isn't worth having the Liege after you."

"You should have thought of that before you took the job," I said, briskly shoving him down so I could tie his feet.

"Yes, but how were we to know she was the Liege Heir's wench? She was the one who told us that, and it wasn't till we already had her and were well out of town. So just hanging onto her seemed safer," he said. "We didn't know anyone was to be killed, till after the master had us kidnap the trapper's girl. Then she escaped, and when the master came back he was talking about how 'he' had to die and I swear, I wanted no part of that. None of us did! If you let me go, I'll take off running and you'll never see me again. Honest. You let me go, and I'm gone. Just like the others."

"So your friends had the good sense and decency to run, when they realized Noye was going to commit murder?"

I had his feet bound by then, and I sat down to remove my stockings. I had clean stockings in my pack that would make a decent gag, but going back to get them would leave him free to make noise for too long, so I'd have use the ones I wore. I was sorry for that, but my options were running out...and I had no idea what was happening in that mill!

"It's one thing to hold onto some wench for a few months," he said. "Our original orders were she wasn't to be hurt, anyway. I wanted no part of murder—but he offered me five men's pay if I stayed. And it's not worth it! If you just let—"

"'Tis not worth it," I agreed thrusting one dirty stocking into his mouth and tying another around it. "But you took that contract, and now you'll pay whatever price the judicars mete out. You'd best pray I get there in time to prevent the Heir's murder, or that price is like to be your life. True, guard!"

I had some hope that even if he managed to spit out the gag, that threat would be enough to keep him silent, and it seemed Meg had been right—aside from Noye, there'd be no one to stop us from rescuing her! So now I needed to find a way into the mill and up the stairs to create a diversion—and away from the stairs, the darkness inside the mill was total.

A faint murmur of voices came from above, but there were no shouts or screams—and in fact, it had taken me only minutes to bind the kidnapper...probably because I rushed the job.

So I took the time to strike a spark and light my own candle from the flaming tinder—and if I was faster than Kathy, the time this took still stretched my nerves more tightly. Cupping one hand to protect the flame, I was about to enter the mill when a soft whine stopped me.

Fisk had left his dog tied to Tipple's saddle, mayhap not wanting to expose the beast to the chaotic anger of a fight... But chaos was what we needed, to spring whatever snare Noye had laid for us—and I'd seen folks' reaction to Fisk's dog over the past few days.

If that toothy monster came rushing out of the haunted darkness it would have made me flinch, even if 'twas running the other way.

The dog whined again, his gaze fixed hopefully on me.

"You'll have to be quiet."

The twitch of his tail looked like agreement. I sat the candle down in the shelter of the doorway, and cut the rope that bound him to Tipple's saddle into a convenient length for a hand-held leash.

I then took a moment to brush his excited mind with my animal handling Gift, pushing the need for silence into his thoughts before I led my ally into the old mill. The only sound was the soft clicking of his claws upon the floor.

With a candle in one hand and a leash in the other I couldn't hold a weapon, but the light let me climb swiftly. A good dog is a better weapon than any sword, and this dog had a heart that belied his odd appearance.

Most who possess an animal handling Gift use it only to communicate their will to the beast it touches. But my father's head groom taught me it could be more effective if you used it to learn what was going on within the mind you sought to command—that you could better soothe a frightened horse if you knew it feared the scent of a hunting pack, instead of a branch that was banging in the wind.

The mutt's mind held a dark, eager determination—and Fisk really had to settle on a name for the beast, because this dog had chosen *him* to be his master and companion. He wanted his human with an intensity that overcame even his fear of the strangers' scents.

'Twas his awareness, that told me there'd been several strangers here, though I couldn't tell how many.

Stirred by fear, my magic roiled beneath its lid of thought and reason. I considered using that magic to go more deeply into the dog's mind, to try to read the scent through his senses and learn how many people were waiting for me. But I could see so many possible perils in that—starting with a bark, or even a bite from an understandably startled dog, and ending with me sinking so deep into the beast's mind that I couldn't get out—that I hastily abandoned the idea.

This was no time for experiments, but for reconnaissance, followed by action.

So 'twas frustrating to reach the top of the first stair and see the bright glow of lamplight spilling down the second flight, along with the sound of voices.

Mostly Fisk's voice, as usual.

In so much light, there was no way I could climb that stair and get onto the third floor without everyone up there seeing me, as well as my canine escort. Which would end any chance of taking them by surprise.

But some years ago, when my funds were at low ebb, I'd worked a few months in a flax mill. The experience had taught me that processing flax takes a lot of effort, and also that big mills are complex structures—they needed to move many things from one floor to the next, in different ways and places.

I set my candle under the steps, since I didn't want to have to relight it. Then I told the dog to stay, firmly, for Fisk's dog had pricked up his ears at the sound of his master's voice. He quivered with the need to find his person, but I felt his submission to my will...and even a dim understanding of my fear that rushing in could put his person in danger.

I added some emphasis to this thought, then closed my eyes, turned my back on the light and took several steps away. I counted slowly to twenty before I opened them and looked into the shadows...and up at the ceiling.

As I'd hoped, patches of light glowed faintly in several different places. The biggest was beside the wall that faced the river, where the upper millstone once protruded into the room above. But with those great stones gone, there was no easy way through the gap.

The small square patch on the opposite side of the room was more what I was looking for.

After a moment's thought—the dog's claws had actually been quite loud—I led Fisk's dog over to the hatch in the ceiling. I couldn't tell why the millers had needed to drop something through the floor just there, but there was no ladder below it. I had to carry over an old workbench, too crudely made to haul away and put a cracked cask on top of it. Then I lifted the dog up, set him on the floor above, and levered myself up after him.

The mutt was shorter than True but wider in the chest, and that truncated body was dense with muscle—even a bit of fat, after several weeks of Kathy feeding him everything in sight.

I had plenty of time to note all these details. Now on the third floor, I picked him up and tucked him under my arm so we could draw near the others in silence.

I had no fear of being seen. We started in the dense shadow at the far side of the big room, and the lanterns only illuminated the drama taking place on what I had to call "center stage."

Mayhap that should have warned me, but it didn't.

A man in a mask, presumably Noye, held a bound woman near the edge of an open service door, beyond which the skeleton of the water wheel turned.

All this action had taken mere minutes to perform, and judging by the conversation I heard as I drew near, Noye was trying to persuade my friends to surrender.

Since Fisk would never do anything that stupid, I was able to take my time closing in on them. The man I'd captured might have been lying, so I kept alert for lurking thugs as I crossed the room...and I found no one. By the time I'd drawn near enough to be sure of it, Rupert and Kathy had thrown down their staffs—though Kathy soon picked hers up again.

"You don't dare move on me," Noye was saying. "Because if I let her go, we all know I'm a dead man. That's *why* I have nothing to lose. And if I'm going to die, I promise you I'll take her with me!"

There was a note in his voice that made me think he meant it.

I was close enough now to see blood trickling down Mistress Margaret's throat, staining her bodice, and I understood why Rupert was wavering—but if they surrendered, Noye would only become stronger. I'd better tell them I was here, and a nightjar's call wouldn't do.

I took a deep breath, thumped one bare heel softly on the floor...and saw Fisk stiffen.

"So what do you want out of this?" he asked Noye.

"What?" Noye shook off the distraction. "That doesn't matter. If you don't throw down your—"

"Yes, yes, you'll kill her. But if we do throw down our weapons, you'll kill her *and* Rupert. And Kathy and me as well, though doubtless in a different way. So we'd be crazy to surrender. But surely there's some way that we can all get what we want, with no one getting killed. Not Meg here, or Rupert, or even you. And if I don't know why you're doing this, it's going to be harder to figure something out."

"It doesn't matter why I'm doing it." Noye's voice had grown alarmingly shrill. "I'm going to kill this woman, now, if you don't throw down your weapons."

This wasn't going as he'd planned. I could almost feel sorry for him.

Him, I thought at dog with all the strength my unaided Gift could wield. *He threatens the Person, just as he does the woman with him. Rush at him, bark at him, he—*

But the dog's nose twitched, his head turning, not toward Noye, or even Fisk, but to the darkness behind me. And looking to see what he had scented, I saw the pale familiar glow of a magica crossbow.

It all came together, in a burst of comprehension; the knowledge that 'twas I who was his target, and further that my friends, two of whom I loved as dearly as anyone in the world, lay in a direct line beyond me.

Then knowing ended, and my heart took over.

I dropped the dog and ran into the light, one arm sweeping out to grab Kathy and drag her with me. Because I was listening for it, I even heard the bow's string snap just as I threw my whole body in a flying tackle that knocked Fisk to the floor.

We were so close to Rupert that his blood splattered over my back when the crossbow bolt ripped into his side.

He staggered under the impact, but didn't yet fall. In the moment of perfect silence that followed the shot I observed, almost calmly, that the bolt had been driven so deep the vanes pressed into his coat. The spreading red stain was high on his side—it must have penetrated his lung.

Mayhap Mistress Margaret knew something of anatomy. The sound that broke the silence was a muffled scream, grating and horrible through her gag.

Noye awoke from his startlement, and realized that even if the means wasn't perfect, he'd succeeded in killing the Heir. He let go of his hostage and bolted for the stairs, with Fisk's dog baying at his heels.

I rolled off Fisk and caught Rupert as he sagged to his knees, lowering him gently to the floor.

Fisk sprang up, and ran after Noye and the dog.

Margaret dropped down beside her lover, moaning with urgency and a terrible grief.

Rupert drew a breath and coughed, hard.

"Meg. I'm so sorry."

"No!" Wheatman came out of the shadows to stand at the edge of the light, the bow lowered, almost falling from his hands. "I meant to hit you. It should have hit you. It's magica. It's supposed to—"

"Well, it didn't," I said.

Kathy had pulled a knife from her belt, cutting the rope that bound Margaret's wrists. But the girl's hands, freed, went not to the gag but to her lover's body.

Rupert, eyes closing, coughed again. This time blood came with it.

I had saved the two I loved best—but I hadn't been able to save them all. And if I'd killed Wheatman when I had the chance, Rupert's blood would not now be staining my hands.

"You missed," I snarled at Wheatman. "And you can add this boy to the tally of others, innocent or not, whom you've wrongfully slain. The whole point of the Liege's law, of all those lawyers and judicars, is to make certain the wrong people *don't* get... Ah, go and be hanged. If you still want to kill me you'll get your chance, because I'm going to help this man."

I turned my back on him, easing Rupert's head from my arms to Margaret's lap...but I couldn't help but be aware of Wheatman, who still held that lethal bow. 'Twas as if I could feel his gaze on the skin of my neck, staring, staring...

I heard him take one step, another, and then he turned and ran. And while I felt a fleeting regret, my mind was focused on the body under my hands.

Margaret stroked Rupert's hair, steadying him as he coughed dark blood onto her skirt. She was no longer gagged, but the only sounds she made were tiny gasps of agonized grief.

"How can you help him?" My sister's face was white, but it held a trusting hope I prayed she'd never lose.

"I can't be certain," I said. "But there's something I can try."

I placed my hands on either side of the bloodstained bolt, reached deep within...and shattered the lid over the seething cauldron of my magic.

Freed from restraint, it surged wildly though my torso, down my arms, and even through my hands into Rupert's injured body. If I opened my eyes, I knew that my changed sight would see not only my own arms and hands aglow, but also the part of Rupert's body where my magic had settled...and stopped.

Strangely, I could feel his wound with my magic, the tear in his flesh like a burn across my senses, the blood slowly flooding his lung like a tide of molten lead pouring into a sponge, pushing out the air.

But beyond that perception my magic did nothing, so making it work was clearly up to me. I reached deeper still, and the thought of anything but the task before me dropped away.

First that blood, which did not belong in the lung. I tried to grasp it with my mind, with a hand made of magic, but 'twas too liquid, too deeply lodged in the tiny pockets and chambers that should have held air.

I had a fleeting thought that, if I knew better what I was doing, I could have made a net of magic that would pass harmless through the tissue of the lungs and gather up the blood. But that net would have to sweep up liquid and leave solid flesh behind, and I didn't know how to shape such a thing.

Rupert was failing, even as I sought for answers, his every ragged breath pulling more blood into his lung than air.... If blood was the enemy, could air be my ally?

I put the force of all that swirling magic behind the air he breathed, pushing it deeper into his lungs than his own muscles could...and the blood retreated a bit before it. Another breath pushed more blood out. I found that if I cupped a bowl of magic over the puncture in the lung, holding back the pulsing blood from his heart, the blood in his lung flowed out more freely with each breath.

When the last of it cleared, I tugged gently on the bolt with my real hand, pulling the sharp head out of the lung, while a hand of magic smoothed over the torn membrane that covered the lung's surface, sealing it once more.

I found the ruptured blood vessels as I pulled the bolt past them. A bit of magic softened their severed ends like wax, and I pressed them back together like pop grass, releasing my grip on the mend only when I knew 'twas strong.

Connecting the densely matted fiber of the muscles was more like spinning loose wool into yarn. I couldn't weave together all those tiny fibers, but I knew that Rupert's own body would follow the path my spinning laid down and grow the rest together in time.

A jagged nick in a rib that had almost blocked the bolt was rubbed out by a magical thumb...

I almost healed the last inch of damage beyond the rib, and the skin above it. But I knew Noye, and even Wheatman, had seen Rupert wounded. If no mark marred his skin, eventually folk would wonder.

Engaged in the task, my magic wanted to finish the job, almost as if it had a will of its own. I had to wrestle it back into its well, like... I was going to say, a reluctant horse into its stall, but 'twas more like trying to shove an angry snake into a bottle. When I finally got it in, the cover snapped down, and my normal senses abruptly returned.

I was cold, and sweating with effort as if I'd run for miles and then tried to lift a weight beyond my strength. My stomach was a bit queasy, too.

I pulled the tip of the bolt from Rupert's flesh, and it ticked against the floor when I dropped it.

"We can say it struck a rib," I said. "And that's what kept it from..."

Three sets of eyes were fixed upon me, wide with astonished wonder—and to my relief, no trace of disgust or fear.

Fisk was watching me too, but any wonder he felt was overwhelmed by smugness.

"See," he said. "I told you you could control it, if you just practiced."

I then had to explain how I'd come to *have* magic—though I was so weary from my first experience of deliberately working...my new Gift? that I let Fisk do most of the talking.

Rupert, who had an interest in natural science, was intrigued by Professor Dayless' theory that many humans might possess magic, but that 'twas blocked by our conscious, thinking minds. But he agreed, along with the others, to keep my secret.

'Twas Margaret, now sitting in Rupert's lap, who looked at me with fearless curiosity and terrifying trust and laid her hands over her still-flat belly.

"Could you use this magic to make my child Gifted?"

"I doubt it," I said. "The magic might be able to do so—I have no idea whether it could or not. But a developing child is so fragile... The slightest misplaced brushstroke of power might do unimaginable harm. But even if I knew I could, I wouldn't want to. Gifts aren't that remarkable, you know. Oh, I suppose in the far back times, when they stopped the unwary from harvesting magica, that was important. But nowadays, all Gifts are is another talent, such as your ability to master complex subjects, like law, or Fisk's ability to set fine stitches. I see no reason to prize Gifts so high when they're really just...another talent."

And this magic of mine was only another Gift, when all was said. More versatile, mayhap, but it made up for that by being less reliable and harder to summon. I would no doubt use it in the future. Watching Rupert's breath stir his lover's hair, as she snuggled against his chest, was a marvel and a deep joy.

But the magic that had wrought this was only another tool in my hand—'twas how I used it that would define me.

Peace flowed through my heart, and I felt an almost painful pity for Wheatman. He wouldn't try to kill me again, of that I was certain, for his trust in his own righteousness had been broken. But he'd also turned his back on the harm he'd wrought. He might one day find another moment, another chance to redeem his soul... but he also might not.

Turning away from this chance, as with all the other choices he had made, defined him too.

I was glad I had not killed him, for if I had I'd be no better than he was—and that was a man I hoped never to become.

"Isn't anyone going to ask what *I* was doing?" Fisk demanded plaintively.

"You went chasing after Noye," Kathy said. "Did you get him?"

I was interested in this myself, as my attention returned to matters more mundane than life, death and magic.

"Yes," said Fisk. "But only because Trouble came dashing up and tripped him on the stairs. He was so distracted by Fearless, he didn't even see Trou... Oh, all right, True. He's earned it."

"Fearless?" Kathy's eyes brightened. "Was he?"

"Not in the least," said Fisk. "He never got within ten feet of the man. But it will give him something to aspire to, and he's barking up a storm if Noye so much as twitches. I left Noye tied to a post," Fisk added. "So the dogs don't need to do anything. But they seemed to be enjoying themselves, so I left them there."

"I left True guarding Noye's henchman," I said. "I wonder if my knots...ah, well." If he had fled, I hadn't the energy or the will to chase after him. And really, there was little need. "We can all testify that Noye kidnapped Mistress Margaret," I went on. "And plotted to kill Rupert, so there's an end to him. But what about the Liege Lady? Unless Noye can be brought to testify against her—and he doesn't seem inclined to—the only one who can name her is Wheatman. And I doubt we'll see him again."

Mayhap I didn't pity him so much, after all. Or rather I did, but I found I could despise him at the same time.

"There might be more evidence than that," said Margaret. "He never mentioned her in front of me, either. Though once I recognized him, I knew the Liege Lady had to be behind it. But after he ordered his hired thugs to help him kill Rupert, and most of them quit, he had to do more himself. And even before they left, he spent some time riding in the carriage with me. He's got a packet of letters he keeps in his saddlebags. Sometimes, when he thought I was asleep, he'd take one out and look at it, or hold it against his heart without opening it. And if they're from the person I think they're from..."

"Caro." Rupert's head bent till it rested against hers. "Father will be devastated. And if you wanted nothing more to do with me, and court, and my whole wretched family, I couldn't blame you. Do you, Meg? Want to be rid of me, I mean?"

She hesitated, and he added hastily, "Though before you make up your mind, Michael is right about the child. We'll cancel all those projects. Our baby will be born—and loved—just as it is. But...do you still want it to be *our* baby?"

Given all she'd been through, I could see why she wanted to think about it. But after a moment, in which I could count his every heartbeat in Rupert's throat, she dropped her head against his shirt.

"Yes," she said. "I must be mad—and I surely wish your father would hurry up and disown you, because I *hate* the idea of going back to court. But you, I still want. Even after all of this."

"Well, I might be able to hasten that disowning thing," Rupert said. "Will you marry me, Meg? Right now, before we go home?"

My lips parted in a silent whistle. The Liege had threatened to dissolve any marriage, but if Rupert could convince someone to bind them, the laws around marriage were strong enough that—without the consent of both parties to the pledge—'twas hard to undo. Though whether the High Liege would prefer to leave his throne to the son who defied him by marrying a Giftless girl, or the son of the woman who'd plotted to kill his Heir might be a tossup. However...

"I think you're right," said Fisk, beating me to the words by half a breath. "It's easier to present someone with a done deed, and persuade them to get over it, than to persuade them to accept it before it's done. And that being the case... I mean, if Rupert can find someone who'll bind him and Meg, I think we might as well, ah..."

"Oh, for pity's sake," said Kathy. "Of course I'll marry you. Right now, today. *I* wanted to do it when you first proposed. *You* were the one who—"

Fisk, smart man, did the sensible thing and kissed her.

CHAPTER 22

Fisk

After a while, Michael picked up a lantern and went down to check on my prisoner—given the admiration in Kathy's eyes, I meant to take full credit for all the dogs' hard work.

But after a few minutes of listening to their voices, without being able to make out words, Kathy shifted restlessly in my arms.

"We might as well go down. I can tell you're not paying attention anymore."

"Hey," I said, stung. "I'm not the one whose eyes keep drifting toward the stairs."

"How do you know what my eyes are doing, if yours aren't open?"

"Why don't you both go." Rupert sounded amused. "You can get those fellows chained up in the coach before Meg and I come down, so she doesn't have to see them. Unless you want to spit in Noye's face, my dear?"

"No." I could see the shiver that went through Meg's body. "I don't want to see him, ever again."

Trying to murder the Liege Heir might be considered treason—I didn't think the judicars would even have to bend the law very hard—so the only time she was likely to see him would be when she testified at his trial. Though that depended on what evidence lay in those letters she'd mentioned...and whatever confessions Michael could extract from him.

"Come on." Kathy pulled herself from my arms as she spoke. "I'm dying to find out what they're saying."

There was a reason I loved this woman.

But when we went down the stairs, the conversation wasn't worth giving up our cuddle.

"I already admitted I recruited others to aid me," Noye said. "And I knew those smelly trappers would tell the law everything, so you can hardly threaten me with their testimony. You can testify yourself that I wanted to kill the Heir."

"But *why* did you want to kill him?" Judging by the exasperation in Michael's voice, he'd asked this question before.

"I already told you, I hate him," Noye said. "I've hated him for years. I couldn't stand it anymore, so I finally did something about it."

"Seriously? You've got to come up with a better story than that," I told him. "Why would anyone hate Rupert? He's a nice lad. And before you invent some woman, who chose him over you, bear in mind that the judicars are going to want her name. And then they'll go ask her about it. So unless you can think of a girl you actually flirted with, who *did* fancy Rupert..."

Noye, who had opened his mouth to embrace that idea, closed it.

"It wasn't a woman. I acted alone, and I did it because I hated him."

"For no reason at all?" Michael said skeptically. "Hatred enough to kill?"

"There were times in court when I tried to win his favor, his patronage, and he ignored me," Noye said firmly. "He didn't even seem to see me, and I found that an intolerable insult."

I had to admit, this was a better story. When Rupert said he hadn't noticed any attempts to attract his attention, Noye would claim that as confirmation instead of denial. However...

"That's rubbish," said Kathy. "You never paid attention to anyone but the Liege Lady, and everyone who's been in court with you knows it. Including the High Liege."

"Yes, well, he's not a judicar."

"Maybe not," I said. "But he'll make an impressive witness."

"I don't care." Though judging by the stark fear growing in Noye's eyes, this was a lie. "I acted alone, because I hated him. And nothing will induce me to say otherwise."

"Does your fealty mean so much to you?" Michael said gently.

"I owe no fealty to the High Liege," Noye announced. "I hate him, too."

That sounded a bit more sincere...though it made the case against him worse.

"Michael wasn't talking about the High Liege," I said. "He meant your fealty to the Liege Lady. Which reminds me, we'd better take you down to that carriage you've been hauling poor Meg around in, and find those letters she told us about."

I wished Meg had been there then—his face couldn't have shown more shock or anguish at a death blow.

Then he crumpled in on himself, and refused to say more, or even look at us.

So Michael untied him from the pillar and checked my knots on the rope around his wrists. And with Trouble—all right, True—pacing at his heels and Fearless running in wide circles and growling, we left the mill and emerged into the moonlit night.

Unlike mine, Michael's prisoner had escaped. I would have rubbed that in, but he said the reason he'd tied him up so carelessly was because he was in a hurry to save us. And furthermore, that if True hadn't come to help me capture Noye, his man would probably still be there. And we had Noye, so anyway, it hardly mattered.

The carriage was parked in a clearing behind the mill. Before she climbed in to search it for Noye's saddlebags, any concealed weapons, and the key to the shackles, Kathy touched the sprouting scars where the crest had been scraped away.

"I never thought about it," she said, "but before she married the Liege, Carolyn Miller's family crest was an ear of corn, with the leaves spreading out to the sides."

"So what?" said Noye sharply. "Even if it was her carriage once, anyone could have bought it."

The shackle key was in his saddlebags. Remembering Kathy's and Rupert's description of Meg, chained inside this carriage when we attacked it, it gave me considerable satisfaction to lock them on Noye's wrists. While I did so, True and Michael held him at tooth and sword point, respectively.

We took the saddlebags back into the mill, and Rupert and Meg brought down the other lanterns and helped us read those letters; love letters, embarrassingly explicit...and written in what Rupert identified as the Liege Lady's own hand.

"This will kill Father," he said grimly.

"I doubt it. A man's wife can't be doing all this..." I waved a sheet that had made Kathy blush so hard I'd taken it from her. It made me blush too, a little, and left me torn between the hope that it would give her ideas, and the fear that it might raise her expectations too high.

It took me a moment to remember what I'd been saying.

"She can't have been doing all this with another man, without your father seeing some hint of it," I went on. "He may be shocked, he'll certainly be hurt...but he must have suspected."

"But why keep these letters?" Meg asked. "I can see that he loves her, but they're appallingly incriminating. And this last one, where she asks him to 'dispose' of a parcel she's 'come to find too inconvenient.' It's almost enough to hang him, on the strength of that alone! Can he have intended to bring it forward if he got caught, and get himself off the scaffold by incriminating her?"

"No." Michael, Rupert and I all spoke together.

"In the first place," said Rupert, "it won't get him off. In a conspiracy to murder, the man who does the deed is held equally guilty with the man—or woman—who gave the order."

"I know that," said Meg, the law student.

"He kept her letters because he didn't think he'd get caught," I said. "They never do."

Though a man who was willing to kill for love might have risked keeping them anyway.

We'd even found a reply to that letter, which he'd written but waited to send, assuring his "true heart" that he'd properly disposed of "the parcel" she'd entrusted to him. He added that he'd wait a few more weeks before returning to court, but that she had nothing to concern herself with. Along with her original instructions, it was damning.

"But none of that mattered," Michael finished. "Do you know the old root word of 'fealty?' 'Tis the same as 'fidelity.' He'll never betray her, even if he hangs for it."

"And he might not," said Meg. "It convinces us because we lived through his attempts, but Rupert's name is never mentioned. It might not be enough to convince judicars they have sufficient evidence of a hanging crime. That requires a higher standard of proof than a case in which a debt, wrongly settled, can be paid back."

"You may be right," I said. "But it doesn't matter. The only one it has to convince is the High Liege."

And that, it would certainly do.

We waited till dawn to leave the old mill, and despite all the evidence of just how badly love can go wrong, Kathy sat beside me on the carriage bench. She even let me drive, though I suspected she might be better at it than I was.

Michael *was* a better driver, but he and True were in the carriage keeping an eye on Noye. After a half an hour riding on Champion's saddlebow, Meg had switched to riding Tipple, and the other horses trotted behind the coach with Fearless at their heels. When he wasn't whining to join us on the driver's bench, where there was barely room for Kathy and me—not to mention how the carriage horses might react to a big predator perched behind and above them. Though only because they didn't know what a sissy he really was.

I had become somewhat attached to the absurd beast over the last few weeks, but now, with the sun beginning to warm the cool morning air and the world stirring to life, I preferred to have Kathy to myself.

"...but even after we turn Noye over to the sheriff," she was saying, "I don't know how Rupert thinks he's going to convince someone to marry him to Meg. Legally, anyone who's done fealty to the High Liege, even through their own liege, can accept a marriage oath... but there's not a mayor or judicar in the Realm who'd be willing to offend the Liege. And a baron's reaction to this situation would make Fearless look brave."

"Probably." Even as I spoke, Rupert guided Champion nearer to Tipple and reached out to touch Meg's shoulder. If the horses had been the same height, I swear they'd have held hands. "But even if he can't make good on that sweeping promise—and given the determination he's shown so far, I wouldn't bet against him—we're a long way from your father's influence. Kathy...are you sure? Because if you want to back out, now is the time. The Liege is probably ready to throw Michael and me in gaol, we won't see a fract of any reward, and your father has been known to disinherit children if they piss him off sufficiently. And marrying me would just about do it."

"You," said my beloved, "are the most incredible worrywart. The family members I care most about are Michael and Benton, and they won't disown me. We'll figure out the rest of it between us. Are *you* sure?"

"No," I said honestly. "But whatever else went wrong in their lives, my mother and father loved each other till the day he died. And she went right on loving him, after. It doesn't stop with death. That's one of the things that scares me, that kind of grief. Even if it doesn't happen till we're both wrinkled and toothless. But even when we were poor, as long as they were together..."

"I've never been poor," said Kathy. "But I don't think my parents ever loved each other. Oh, they get along fairly well. But they married because Mother's dowry included a river dock my grandfather needed, and her father wanted more fertile farmland. Mother does the woman's work, and Father the men's, but they never seem to work *together*. They sent me off to make the same kind of marriage with Rupert...and I was running from that as hard as I could, even before we...well, we'd met before. But you know what I mean."

She tucked her arm through mine, a casual possession that was almost as heart-stopping as a kiss.

"I can see that," I said. "But even when there's love and partnership, like my parents had, it's not like it is in the plays, when 'A little flame of love sprang up in their hearts, and it never died or wavered, even to the end of their days.'"

She snickered at my recital of one of old Makejoye's gaudier passages, but I went on, "Living without enough money is hard, even with love. And I don't think I could bear it if you stopped loving me."

"So," said my darling, "because you're afraid I'll fall out of love with you, you're trying to convince me not to marry you? And you say your father taught you logic?"

I had to laugh.

My parents did have the partnership Kathy wanted, but it was Michael who'd taught me how to be a partner. And my parents who, despite everything, had taught me love.

"I know love doesn't always work out," Kathy added soberly. "If you want a horrible example, look at poor Noye."

"I grant you, he's poor Noye." The man might hang for his love, after all. "But he loves her as much as it's possible for a man to love a woman. So at least he's had that."

"Yes," said Kathy. "But that's why he's 'poor Noye.' Because he loves her, as you said, as much as a man can. And I don't think she loves him."

"You don't... Didn't you read those letters?"

"That's what makes me think it," Kathy said. "She's made love to him, any number of times and in all sorts of peculiar... Well, they sounded peculiar to me. But that's all there was in her letters, Fisk. Passion, yes. But nothing of tenderness."

I thought back on what I'd read, and this time I managed to think about it with my brain instead of my crotch. Given the content of those letters that wasn't easy, but...

"You're right," I said. "All heat, no heart. I think he knows it, too. That's why he said he had nothing to lose. You're right. Poor Noye."

"And is that how you love me?" Kathy barely waited for my headshake. "'Tis not how I love you, either. So we'll be like your parents, instead of Noye, partners as well as lovers. And that love will make whatever else becomes of us the brighter."

I knew it wouldn't be that simple, because life isn't. Particularly when you don't have much money. But she was right about the rest of it.

"Deal," I said.

And I swear, a little flame of love sprang up in my heart.

If I'd ever doubted that gentle, scholarly Rupert would make a good High Liege, he settled the question when we reached town late that afternoon.

We took our prisoner to the local sheriff, where Rupert announced himself, as himself, and proceeded to lay down the law...almost as if he was already the Liege, who could.

He had returned of his own accord, he told the sheriff, so "that outrageous reward" would not be paid. To anyone.

A moderate reward, for service to the throne in time of need, might be forthcoming *if* he did what Rupert wanted. The first thing he wanted was for Noye to be taken back to Crown City by the sheriff's men. To enable that, Rupert charged Noye with kidnapping, and the attempted murders of the Chosen Heir, the Heir's affianced wife, and the Heir's unborn child.

The sheriff looked at Meg, with her bloodstained dress and wild hair, and his eyes widened. But he hastily summoned a clerk to write up the charges, and quietly sent off several other messengers.

We found out about that when the mayor arrived, just in time to hear Rupert's next demand, which was a bath and a clean dress for Mistress Margaret, so she could be properly clad for her wedding. Which would take place, he said, before sunset. The "or else" was unspoken, but everyone heard it anyway.

The sun sets late in mid-summer, so that left almost three hours before the deadline. The mayor was happy to provide the bath, the dress, and dinner and lodging for the night, as well. But he spent the walk to his house, and the better part of a hastily assembled dinner, explaining all the reasons why he couldn't, possibly, marry the Liege Heir to anyone. His excuses started with the semi-legal quibble that the person who took Rupert's marriage oath should out-rank him, all the way down to his lady's helpful contribution that preparing a proper wedding for the Heir would take weeks, if not months—the dress, the feast, just assembling the musicians...

By the time we'd eaten, the local baron arrived. He'd been to court, and was appalled to discover that "the crazy vagabond" the sheriff was humoring "just in case" really was the Liege Heir. But once he'd heard our story—which wasted another twenty minutes—he cut through all the crap by stating the real problem: "The High Liege will have the balls of anyone who marries his Heir without his consent."

"But I shall be High Liege myself, eventually," said Rupert. "And I promise you, I'll remember this day. Either as the day you won my favor, or the day you lost it. Permanently."

"The current Liege may not be pleased to learn that Master Noye felt free to plot the murder of the Heir on land under your control," Michael added helpfully. "Unless, of course, his victims make it very clear to the Liege that you had nothing to do with it."

"Besides," I said, suddenly inspired, "you can excuse your actions by citing a writ, a Liege writ, given to you by Rupert, that orders you to give all possible aid to the bearer. I grant you, when the Liege gave that writ to Michael and me, he may not have expected us to use it in just this way..."

When I forged it, *I* hadn't expected to use it for this.

"...but you can honestly say that writ commanded you to obey the bearer's orders, in the Liege's name. And Rupert now bears that writ."

Michael opened his mouth to deny this, and then jerked when Kathy kicked him under the table. And Rupert followed up so smoothly, explaining how this took all the responsibility off of them, that my hopes of his making a good ruler grew even higher. Though I'd have to tell him to say he'd bought the thing in a shady tavern, in one of the towns we'd passed through.

In fact, neither the baron or the mayor looked closely at that writ—if they could claim they thought it was real, that let them wiggle out from between the rock of Rupert's orders, and the hard place of the Liege's displeasure. There was a bit of jostling, as they both tried to avoid being the one who administered the marriage. But the baron pulled rank, ordered the mayor to "offer the Liege Heir aid and hospitality," and then fled.

After a few more glasses of wine, we persuaded the mayor that he could use that command to convince Rupert's father that the baron had ordered him to obey Rupert—so it was entirely the baron's fault, and he'd had no choice.

In truth, I didn't think he had much to fear. The worst of the High Liege's wrath was going to fall on Rupert, where it belonged. Whatever was left would splash directly onto us.

So we gathered in the mayor's parlor, with the servants, under his wife's command, whisking dust covers off the furniture and bringing in a big vase of flowers for the side table. And for me, the High Liege's probable wrath was a dim and distant worry because, with the greater problem of Rupert's marriage out of the way, the mayor had agreed to take Kathy's and my oaths without even blinking.

I kept a set of clean clothes in my saddlebags, although my best coat, and even the shirt with a band of lace at cuffs and collar, made me look more like a well-off clerk than a bridegroom.

But the mayor's wife's clothes, which were a fair fit for Meg, would have hung on my girl's slender grace like a sack. So Kathy put on the plain blouse and skirt she'd worn when we attacked the coach, and for the first time in our acquaintance she looked like we... matched.

Maybe it was because of the clothes, but in that moment the thought that she'd soon be my wife became real. My thundering pulse slowed enough that I could hear Rupert and Meg make their oaths to each other, even if I paid them no attention.

Then it was time for Katherine to stand before me, her hands clasped in mine, her heart in her shining eyes.

"I've got the Liege's writ that the bearer speaks for him, so the bearer can consent to the Heir's marriage," the mayor said.

If the writ didn't offer the bearer quite that much power, I wasn't about to correct him.

"But who stands as kinsman to this woman?" the Mayor went on. "To give her family's consent to her joining?"

"I am her brother, and I do," said Michael.

"And is there any legal impediment to your speaking for your family in this matter?" the mayor asked.

My heart skipped a beat, and began to pound sickly. I had thought the mayor was too tipsy to care, but he evidently didn't want to earn Baron Sevenson's wrath any more than he did the High Liege's. If Michael swore there was no impediment, that let him off the hook...but there was an impediment. Michael was unredeemed. His father hadn't just disowned him—he had no legal standing at all. He'd also spent the last two years refusing to lie about it, as a point of principle, and gotten us into no end of trouble.

I saw the sudden panic in Kathy's eyes, and cast wildly for something I could do or say.

"There is no impediment," Michael said firmly. "I speak for my family, as Katherine's kinsman, and I consent to her marriage."

"Oh, very well." The mayor sighed. "I suppose it can't get much worse. Do you, Nonopherian Fisk, plight your future to this woman's, taking her into your home and family as your wife? Do you bind your fortune to hers, as she will to you, to share your lives until death do you part?"

"I do," I said hastily.

Katherine's smile blossomed like the sunrise.

"Do you, Katherine Sevenson, plight your future to this man's, going into his home and family as his wife? Do you bind your fortune to his, as he has to you, to share your lives until death do you part?"

"I do," said Kathy.

That tiny flame of love burst into a conflagration, and consumed me.

CHAPTER 23

Michael

I sat down for breakfast with the mayor and his lady, and none of us were astonished when my companions failed to appear. They did turn up for luncheon—and the sleepy glow in my sister's face, and Fisk's secure smile, made everything right.

When I took up errantry, I swore to myself that I would take my honor as seriously as the knights of old, and never smirch it with greed, deceit, cowardice or lies.

Then I took up with Fisk.

I could never be sorry for that, for Fisk had taught me that lies can sometimes be a force for good, and some truths cause terrible harm. I had learned to see how little in this world was all evil, or all good, but a muddled mix between. This might be less satisfying than "right" and "wrong," but 'twould keep me from ever becoming what Wheatman was. And I knew who I had to thank for it.

After luncheon, the mayor told us that the sheriff had asked Rupert to call on him "at his convenience," and I wanted to see which of Noye's carriage horses might make a suitable mount, so we all went off together.

The sheriff willingly agreed that his deputies would convey Noye to Crown City, and Rupert graciously assured him that he didn't mind that the sheriff wouldn't be able to release the men to do it until next week. The hitch arose when the sheriff said we couldn't take the coach horses. Not that he didn't want to oblige the Heir, but they were branded as the property of a posting inn, to which they had to be returned. In fact, a rider had taken them away this morning.

This was the normal practice—you paid for the horses' return as part of the lease—but it meant we had no horse for Margaret. And after spending so much longer on the road than we'd intended...

"I could demand the baron loan us a horse," Rupert said. "But that's not like asking him to take our oath or arrest a criminal, which he should do anyway. That's the kind of thing that pisses your liege people off in a way they tend to resent. And remember."

"Ah. One of my deputies has a cousin who works for the baron," the sheriff put in. "He says the baron left first thing this morning, to visit his sister. Which will probably be quite a surprise to her."

All things considered, I wasn't surprised at all.

"How much money do we have?" I asked.

"One hundred and eighty-four gold roundels, seven silver, and assorted copper fracts," said Fisk, who had counted it. "But that makes me wonder what Noye was doing for coin. We didn't find much money in his saddlebags..."

The sheriff agreed to let us search the coach again, though he insisted on watching while Fisk tapped on panels and wiggled the upholstery tacks. He found the secret compartment inside a cupboard under the front passenger bench—and it looked as if Master Noye had gone though most of his funding as well. But after the sheriff brought in a clerk to count and record the sum, he was happy to let Rupert take charge of it. He even gave us directions to the home of a townsman whose wife was getting too old to ride, and who might be willing to part with a smooth-gaited mare.

By the time we purchased the neat little bay, the afternoon was almost over. But the sun sets late in summer, and I thought we could travel a reasonable distance before it vanished.

Rupert claimed that Margaret was still too tired from her ordeal to set off today.

"Why do I have to be the weakling?" Margaret complained. "Why can't Kathy be tired? Or one of you men?"

"I'm tired," Fisk said hastily. "Subduing villains takes it right out of me. I'm tired for days afterward. Ask anyone."

"In fact," I said, "it does no such—"

"Ask anyone else," said Fisk.

The upshot was that we set out late next morning, to the mayor's carefully concealed relief. We could have cut at least a day off the ten days it took us to ride back to Crown City, if all four of my companions hadn't developed a sudden penchant for long evening walks. Away from camp, and in different directions.

But they all returned looking ridiculously content— and I think Rupert and Margaret actually spent some of the time in walking and talking. I even obliged my sister and my new brother-in-law by keeping Fearless with me. My heart ached a bit, as Fisk became less my partner and more Kathy's husband with each day that passed. But seeing the two of them so happy reconciled me to this, at least somewhat. And if I lost him as a partner, I had gained him as a brother...which meant he'd never be completely rid of me.

Even with four of the five of us dragging their feet, we reached Crown City on the afternoon of our tenth day of travel.

Despite Champion being tacked out and groomed like a normal horse, several people glanced at him, and then at Rupert—but the Heir's disguise was better than his horse's and no one ventured to speak to him. The nearer we drew to the palace, the stiffer Rupert's spine became, and Margaret's expressive face was wooden.

I couldn't help either of them. The news of their marriage would bring trouble enough. The letters Rupert carried would break lives.

But he was thinking of his wife, as well as his father. As we crossed the street that led to the Merkle's manor he brought Champion to a stop.

"Do you want to go to your parents, Meg? Tell them you're all right, mayhap spend a few days there? I'd understand. 'Tis going to be miserable."

"It is," she said. "And I'll send them a message as soon as I can, and visit them tomorrow. But now, I want to go home."

Rupert's bleak face brightened, and I saw Kathy and Fisk exchange a look I didn't understand. Would I ever find a woman with whom to exchange such looks? I remembered Rosamund fondly, but she'd been married almost a year now, to the man she loved. It suddenly seemed foolish to spend the rest of my life pining over that.

But now 'twas time to put romance aside, and we rode on to the palace. The guards on the wall blew their trumpets—which I'd thought they did only for ceremony—as soon as Rupert was close enough they could be sure 'twas him. As he rode up the drive, servants and courtiers flooded out to see for themselves that 'twas really the Liege Heir, returned. And with "that woman" beside him.

By the time Rupert reached the courtyard, and we pulled our horses to a halt before the steps that led to the great double doors, the High Liege and his Lady had come out onto the portico to greet him, along with assorted courtiers, including Advisor Arnold and Captain Varner. The expression on the Liege's face was an apoplectic blend of relief and fury—and mayhap a deeply buried hint of pride. His scholarly son had completed his difficult quest...even if 'twas a quest of which he disapproved.

The Liege Lady's expression was harder to read; the smile she pasted on her lips might have looked genuine, to anyone who didn't look closely.

Rupert dismounted, then turned to help Margaret down, before leading her up the steps beside him.

The Liege's brows shot up, then lowered in a deep scowl as he gauged the significance of this. The buzz of gossip around us grew to a roar that only abated when Rupert reached his father and everyone strained to listen in.

"Do you have any idea," said the High Liege, "how much this escapade of yours has cost me?"

"It hasn't cost you a fract," said Rupert. "Well, except for the traveling stipend you gave Master Sevenson—

and that wasn't enough, by the way. I need to talk to you, and Master Arnold, I think, about several things. But first, I wish to present my wife, Lady Margaret."

The crowd gasped. The High Liege scowled. The Liege Lady's expression sobered appropriately, and I couldn't tell what was going on behind that lovely mask.

Margaret's spine was even straighter than Rupert's, and if red flags of anger and embarrassment flew in her cheeks her head was regally high. Indeed, she looked so much like an Heir's Lady that the Liege himself took a second look at her.

"That will have to be discussed," he said. "Inside. Just the three of us."

"I think Meg should lie down for a while," said Rupert. "She's carrying my child, and she's had a hard month. But you and I need to talk."

The Liege's expression changed again. "She really was kidnapped? But why would... No, you're right. We should talk privately."

The Liege Lady's expression was impassive, but her eyes slipped aside, toward the gate.

Rupert hugged Margaret and released her, but Kathy darted up the stairs to escort her, acting so clearly as Margaret's lady-in-waiting that even though another buzz of gossip arose, the crowd stepped aside for her.

It seemed to me that someone should do something about the Liege Lady now. I was nerving myself to say so when Rupert caught Advisor Arnold's arm, turning him so his back was to the Liege Lady before he leaned forward and murmured into the man's ear.

This was just as well, for the Advisor's jaw sagged, and only Rupert's grip stopped him from turning to

stare at his liege's wife. Then he straightened, and signaled to one of his clerks.

The matter had clearly been placed in the proper
hands. It could have been enough. It should have been
enough.

On the other hand, I was done with underestimating
that woman.

I left Fisk to escort Kathy and Margaret back to the
cottage, while I jogged up the stairs and approached
Captain Varner.

She came into the stables less than fifteen minutes
later, wearing a dress so ragged I had no idea where
she'd come by it. And she might have fled, or even tried
to fight when Varner's men stepped out of the shadows,
had it not been for the little boy in her arms.

She did try to order them out of the way—she was the
Liege Lady, after all—but Varner wasn't having it, and
he stiffened his men's spines.

She would have fought, I think, when they arrested her, but the child's lower lip had begun to quiver. The adventure his mother had promised him had
turned into a nasty adult quarrel, and he didn't like it.
He shrieked when Captain Varner lifted him from his
mother's arms, but she told him it was all right, that
the nice lieutenant would take him back to his nurse,
and they'd go on a picnic and play in the stream some
other time.

When they carried him out, her eyes followed him...
and found me.

"You! I should have known... I did know, curse it."

They were binding her wrists now, and I was not surprised she'd stopped resisting—her only chance to see her son again was to find some other way out of this snare she'd sprung on herself.

"Know what?" I asked. "I didn't even know for certain you'd try to escape. I just warned Captain Varner that you might."

"And I knew better than to ignore a tip from *Michael Sevenson*," the captain said.

I grimaced, and to my surprise the Liege Lady's mouth quirked wryly. "That was why I went to check you out, you know. I'd heard what you did with Roseman, but I thought it had to be exaggerated. Then you turned up at the levee, on Rupert's heels, so I went to see for myself. You and your partner. And I knew..."

I waited, but whatever her Gift had read on Fisk and me, 'twas evidently too incriminating to say aloud.

"Was that why you set Wheatman after me?" I asked.

"Who's Wheatman?" she said.

'Twas a valiant effort...but in the face of so much evidence against her, no pretense of innocence could last.

I returned to the cottage, which was hot, stuffy, and smelled faintly of dust. Fisk had thrown open all the windows, and Kathy had sent to the palace for a meal, and also a maid who'd been assigned to her from time to time, and whom she liked.

Margaret's own maid, Griswold, arrived soon after I did, along with a small tide of Rupert's servants. She was promptly fired—her first act, Margaret said, as the Heir's Lady, and a most worthwhile one.

Her second was to send a message to her parents. But after that there was little to do besides dine, and wait for the storm to break.

Then the storm broke.

At the end of it, the Liege Lady was removed, under guard, to a small estate where—if she behaved herself—she'd be permitted to live out the rest of her life. And see her son for five days in every two months, since young Liam was not allowed to go with her.

This much was conveyed to us by Mistress...Lady Margaret's new maid, who kept returning to the palace for a better pillow, or a tisane suited to a pregnant woman, and returning more laden with gossip than with pillows and tisanes.

But we didn't need her to tell us Liam had been left behind—we could hear his screams even in the secluded cottage. They went on long enough to make us pity not just the boy, but also his nursery maids. All of us except Margaret were deeply relieved when a desperate message came from Rupert—who'd remembered that she had nieces and nephews—begging her to come and see if she could soothe the hysterical toddler.

Margaret, listening to those shrill cries, went a bit paler. But to her credit, she went without hesitation, and after a bit of time had passed the screaming stopped... renewed...and stopped again.

"He'll cry it out now," said Kathy, hopefully. "He'll cry himself to sleep, probably in Meg's arms, and he'll be fine."

I wasn't so sure of that, particularly when he grew up and came of age as the son of a woman who'd been willing to murder to seize the throne for him.

"However he turns out," said Fisk, "it's his mother's fault, not ours. And Meg and Rupert will look out for him."

That last bit proved true. Another flood of maids soon descended, packed up all Margaret's possessions, and took them off to a suite of rooms adjacent to Rupert's. And also in easy reach of the palace nursery, where the maids said she'd promised to spend the night.

The good part of this was that Liam attached himself to Margaret like a puppy, and even went with her to visit her parents.

This in turn led her father-in-law to grudgingly accept her into his family. He could hardly stand to look at the boy, because of the painful memories he carried, but the Liege also felt guilty about it. Margaret's ability to help the child eased that guilt.

The other good part was that we were left to occupy the abandoned "mistress cottage" in peace, because the High Liege didn't want to see us, either.

Advisor Arnold came to tell us that since we'd "signally failed" to bring Rupert home in a timely fashion, and the Liege had been forced to humiliate himself by publicly revealing the news of Rupert's disappearance—not to mention offering a huge reward—

"Which he didn't have to pay," Fisk pointed out. "Because we brought Rupert home."

—the High Liege had decided he owed us nothing. But Rupert had persuaded him that in exchange for his Heir's life, and that of his daughter-in-law and grandchild, we were owed at least a favor...and one that was of some interest to me.

Fisk was still inclined to sputter about the money, even after Master Arnold had left—more on principle than because he'd expected to be paid.

"You should have known this would happen," I said. "Because you know the difference between the High Liege and a bandit."

"No." Fisk blinked in surprise. "I haven't heard that one."

"Really? Well, mayhap 'tis only used among nobles, grousing about their taxes."

Fisk was staring now. "So what's the difference?"

"'Tis that when a bandit takes your money, you can go to the High Liege and he'll have the bandit arrested. When the High Liege takes your money, the bandit doesn't care."

Fisk and I weren't the only ones to be monetarily disappointed. As news of the Heir's marriage spread, the scholars who'd been working on projects to make his wife's child Gifted swarmed the palace. The possible side effects on the child's mother ranged from a nervous tic, through seizures, to madness and death. Rupert sent them packing.

Benton wrote us a snappish letter about how the scholars had put months of research into those ventures, and deserved some compensation. He seemed to think we should use our influence on Rupert to bring this about. Kathy wrote him back that studying the societal changes that would result from having a Giftless

High Liege would give historians even more to study, write papers and argue about. Benton being a historian, he was content with that.

The Realm's nobility were already beginning to panic over those changes, but no one dared to bring this grievance to the High Liege, who had all but gone into seclusion over the grief of his wife's betrayal. This meant the only one they could complain to, besides each other, was Rupert...so they spent most of their time fruitlessly grumbling to each other.

'Twas only to be expected that my father would turn up, representing the lords and barons of the Derens River Valley. He probably had a mandate to scope out the situation, and try to convince the Liege he was destroying the whole noble class by confirming Margaret's child (if male) as his Heir Apparent. Or if that looked to be unwise, to congratulate the Heir on his marriage.

We assumed this was his mission, because several score of nobles had arrived over the past few weeks with that same purpose. But Father had another reason for coming. Once he'd seen how the land lay, and grudgingly offered his felicitations to Rupert and his new wife, he came down to the mistress' cottage to collect his daughter.

"Why under two moons are you living here, Katherine?" He was scolding before he even entered the parlor, where we'd been upsetting our stomachs with too much tea. Kathy's new maid had warned us of his coming, and we'd been waiting so long for him to turn up that this was our fifth pot.

"I know you made a friend of the Heir's Lady, but living in *this* place...is..." His eyes had found me.

I came to my feet in the respectful, childhood habit, while his gaze struck my face, swept up and down
over the best clothes I owned, and then came back to
search my face once more. He opened his mouth as if
to speak, then closed it again.

"Hello, Father." My own voice came out hoarse, and
he flinched a bit, drawing in on himself. And then he
turned to Kathy as if I wasn't even in the room.

"Send someone to pack your things, Katherine. Since
you failed to attach the Heir, you might as well come
home. We'll see what we can do for you in the neighborhood."

He had come in with a complaint upon his lips, but
his voice then had been paternally exasperated, easy
and familiar. Now 'twas cold, issuing orders and in-
timidation in equal measure. I have never been more
proud of my sister than when she rose to her feet, and
reached out to take Fisk's hand.

"That won't be necessary. I made my marriage oath
to Fisk here, on the same day Rupert wed Meg."

Fisk stood too, and put his arm around Kathy's waist,
mayhap in support, or mayhap to conceal his wobbling
knees behind her skirt.

My father once described Fisk as "a town-bred gut-
terling, with knave written all over him." He evidently
remembered my erstwhile squire, for a wave of astonished fury rose in his face.

"Fisk and I, and Kathy too, have earned the favor of
the Chosen Heir," I cut in before he could speak. "You
might want to consider that, before you do anything...
rash."

Father, in justice, hardly ever acts rashly—but this
moment put that to the test. His angry color, now al-

most purple, didn't fade, but he turned and walked out without another word.

Kathy drew a ragged breath, then another. I knew how she felt; Father had the trick of turning me inside out as well. But her grip on Fisk's hand only grew tighter.

Fisk was almost as pale as his shirt, but he spoke with his usual insouciance.

"Cheer up. It could have been worse. He didn't even send for an executioner."

"He didn't say a word," Kathy said. "He's not going to speak to us, not for a long time. Maybe never."

"I wish we'd be that lucky," said Fisk. "But I doubt it. If he never meant to speak to you again he'd have disowned you, too, and he didn't. So maybe, just maybe, the old bastard is learning."

My reward came just a week later. It seems that when someone who was officially declared unredeemed is pronounced to be redeemed after all, the High Liege himself has to do it—and between getting his marriage dissolved, and tracking down any other plots his wife might have had in play, he was busy.

They had told us to be ready to be summoned at any moment, four days ago. One can't spend that much time doing nothing but wait, so when the footman came to fetch us I was riding Chant about the park, and Fisk was in the cottage kitchen watching Kathy being taught to make bread. She'd been offered a chance to return to her old room in the palace, and bring us along. But she had no desire to take up the threads of her soon-to-be-abandoned life at court, and the secluded cottage suited us well.

I hastily changed into my best clothes—still nothing suited to court—Kathy washed the flour off her hands and brushed it out of her hair, and we all followed the footman to a great hall in the oldest part of the palace. 'Twas paneled in dark wood, with faded tapestries between glassed over arrow slits. Even the summer sunlight pouring through them barely pushed back the gloom, but if the bright joy in my heart had showed as external light, it would have made up for the stingy windows.

A long table had been placed at the far end of the room, with three judicars behind it, just as you'd find in any town square on judgment day—but the law they served was the Liege's law, and his throne had been placed in front of the table. These judicars were here only to bear witness, before the source of the law they served.

A score of nobles had been summoned to witness this as well, but since my father wasn't among them I cared nothing for that. He had ridden out of the palace, Kathy's helpful maid reported, soon after he'd spoken to us—or rather, refused to speak to us. His failure to commute *his* sentence was the only regret I had on this good morning, but I wasn't going to let it blight the day. And I thought Fisk was right; the fact that he hadn't disowned Kathy was a hopeful sign.

Despite our lateness, the High Liege wasn't there when we arrived, though Rupert came in soon after with Margaret on his arm. It might be because her dress was cut differently, but for the first time she looked a bit pregnant, and a bright happiness lurked beneath her serious expression.

I didn't think her joy sprang from the respectful bows of the gentlemen she passed—though that had to be a source of satisfaction. The men of the court had finally figured out that insulting their future Liege's wife was what Fisk called a Bad Idea.

Kathy's maid said the ladies, many of whom had been trying to marry their own daughters off to Rupert, were thawing more slowly. But they too were coming around.

Rupert once more wore the clothing of a wealthy courtier, as he had when we first met him, but his subtle air of authority was new. However, he still greeted us with a wide grin, and in moments we'd all forgotten how he was dressed.

My father would have disagreed with me, but I thought that ability to make others forget his rank was his greatest gift as a ruler—even if 'twas not a Gift—and I doubted he'd ever lose it.

Then the High Liege entered, through a discreet door in the back of the room, and any air of authority Rupert had was eclipsed like a torch by sunlight. As I rose from my bow, along with everyone else, I saw that the Liege's face was more deeply lined than when we first met, and his eyes were tired.

'Twas not only her intended victims who had suffered from Carolyn Miller's plots, and for a moment I couldn't help but regret our part in exposing them. Except that if we hadn't, Rupert and Margaret might now be dead.

In exchange for a few more days added to Liam's visits, the Liege Lady had finally confessed to what she'd done—though with her written order to dispose of "the parcel," which we'd found in Noye's possession, 'twas hardly necessary to establish her guilt. She swore, and mayhap 'twas true, that at first her only purpose had been to keep Margaret from using some potion that might have made her child Gifted, thus "supplanting" Liam as the Heir. The fact that an unmarried woman's child wouldn't be in the succession evidently didn't weigh with her. And in fairness, if Rupert married Meg, even after the child's birth, that might have changed. But the Liege Lady insisted she'd not intended murder, not even when Rupert set off in pursuit of Meg, without money or guards, and vulnerable to all manner of mischance. She hadn't thought of murder, she claimed, until she learned her husband intended to hire *the* Michael Sevenson to find Rupert and bring him home. The Rose conspiracy—which *Fisk* brought down—had so ludicrously overblown my reputation that she had come to test us with her people reading Gift. Whatever she'd seen had convinced her that we would not only bring Rupert back, but find and return Margaret as well. So she sent Wheatman after me, and when Noye reported her assassin's failure at the bridge, she'd been forced to "take that repugnant step, and order Master Noye to... to take care of things."

I was so tired of being *the* Michael Sevenson, I was beginning to take Fisk's jokes about changing my name seriously. I'd not have done it to conceal shame or crime...but fame and respect were a lot more inconvenient.

Now, however, it looked to stand me in good stead. The High Liege took his place before the throne, and began without wasting any time.

"I have lately become aware how easy it is, even for those in power, to make mistakes. I wish to state, for the record—" He glanced at the clerk who was jotting down his words. "—that having read the case against

Master Sevenson, brought to my attention by my son, I believe the judicars who declared him unredeemed were wrong."

I stared at Rupert, who flashed me a smile.

"They were wrong," said the Liege. "But they were acting within the law. However, the basis of our law is that a crime that can be made right, by coin or labor, shall be erased from the law's books once that debt is paid. Right or wrong, Michael Sevenson owed a debt to the law—but in saving the Realm from the civil violence Atherton Roseman sought to bring to it, and then going on to stop disruption in the line of succession, Michael Sevenson has more than paid any debt the law was owed. I therefore, by the power I alone possess, declare him to be redeemed; honorable in the eyes of man, with all rights under my law. If any man's hand be turned against him, he may claim full redress, from his kin, from the law, and from his fellow man. Let it be thus."

"Let it be thus," the crowd answered.

Kathy, weeping, threw her arms around me, but it was Fisk's gaze I met. He didn't embrace me, but his eyes were bright with joyous irony, and his rare, unguarded smile grew wider and wider till it all but took over his face.

There was no time for congratulations, however. That discreet door opened once more, this time admitting two footmen who carried a small, iron-bound lockbox between them. They were supervised by Advisor Arnold, and followed by four guards.

The High Liege himself opened the box, with a key Master Arnold hastily presented, and pulled out a square of rather dirty white cloth. I'd have taken it for a dust rag, if the Liege hadn't held it as if it might bite.

"Come forth, Master Sevenson, and let the outward sign of your status be removed."

I stepped forward, but to my surprise, Rupert went with me. Taking the cloth from his father, he pushed up my sleeve and began rubbing briskly at the broken circles that marked my wrist.

"I've always wanted a chance to use this," he said. "We keep it in the vault, well away from any magica because it's supposed to be able to..."

I already knew what it could do. As the cloth whisked back and forth, the soft glow that had suffused those marks from the day they were set began to fade.

Rupert used his own magic sensing Gift to confirm it was working, holding his hand over the tattoo several times, feeling the presence of magic slowly diminish till he was certain 'twas gone. I could have told him it was, for all trace of magical light had faded, leaving only...

"How can I get rid of the ink?" I asked. In this cause I was prepared to lose some skin, even if it scarred.

"According to our records, the ink should fade away over the next few days," Rupert told me.

The High Liege had stayed to watch this part, evidently curious himself. But finding the process less dramatic than dusting furniture, he now departed. The judicars and most of his flunkies followed him out. The advisor and the guards remained with the box.

"That's another reason we lock it up so tight," Rupert went on. "It's not just magic it removes—or rather it is, but once the magic is drained from a magica item, it falls to dust within a few days. 'Tis almost as if the magic is holding it together, and when 'tis gone..."

He stiffened, evidently just remembering that I had magic in me. But I gave him a reassuring smile, and held out my other wrist for him to work on. I could sense my own magic, slightly roused by the emotion of this day, but secure under its heavy lid. 'Twas not at all impacted by whatever was pulling the magic from the tattoo on my wrist.

His tale did make me wonder, a bit apprehensively, what would become of me if I should ever lose the magic that had become so much a part of me.

There was no answer to that, so I put it aside. The future guards its secrets till the present arrives, and I was content to meet that future as a redeemed man— all debts paid.

But the future arrived sooner than I expected. After that destructive cloth had been locked up and carried away, Rupert asked me to accompany him. He had, he said, a job to offer me.

When he didn't extend this offer to Fisk, my partner bristled indignantly. But Fisk was the one who wanted to get married, after all. It seemed fitting he should pay some price for that, and I may have cast him a rather smug look before I turned and followed Rupert down several halls to a quiet office.

'Twas clearly his, for 'twas crowded with books and a couple of engineering models—and judging by the papers that washed across the desk, he'd been busier than usual these past weeks. But he didn't seem to be in a hurry to proceed, seating himself behind the desk and gesturing for me to take a chair.

"So, what is this task you have for me?" I said. "If it comes with a reward attached, I may ask to be paid in advance."

I smiled, to show this was a jest—mostly. Fisk and Kathy were speaking of trying to buy an abandoned printer's shop we'd come across in Slowbend. But even adding all our purses to what was left of Master Noye's funds...

Rupert looked uncomfortable. "*I* intend to pay you, all I can manage, as soon as Father gives me the next quarter's stipend. But this isn't some 'great risk, therefore great reward' type quest. Though if we succeed, 'twill do the Realm more good than that kind of thing ever could."

"If 'tis not some errand for the throne, then what is it?"

Asked thus, straight on, Rupert seemed disinclined to come to the point. This was unlike him, and I wondered why.

"The thing is, it's come to my attention over the last few weeks—and Father's attention for years now—that there's a problem with the way the Liege's law is enforced."

I could think of a number of problems with the law, but I nodded and waited for him to go on.

"Or maybe I should say, the way 'tis *not* enforced. Because all criminals have to do is cross the border into another fief, and they're virtually un-arrestable. Not without weeks of legal squabbling, which gives them plenty of time to move on. This current system, where every small town sheriff is free to claim he thinks a Liege writ is forged, and refuse to obey it unless 'tis delivered by a troop of Father's guard, is absurd. That's what's given rise to all those bounty hunters, who are almost as big a threat to law and civil order as the criminals they hunt! A crime against the Liege's law is a crime, everywhere in the United Realm. You shouldn't be able to escape justice by hopping from one baron's fief to another."

"Well, given that those barons, and their sheriffs, are responsible for enforcing the law on their own lands, I don't see what you can do about it. Unless the Liege intends to appoint—and pay—every sheriff and deputy in the Realm."

From years of listening to my father's complaints, I knew this would be too expensive even for the Crown's purse—not to mention the barons' reaction to having Liege troops constantly quartered in their lands.

"We're thinking we could give the landholders who go along with the scheme some sort of tax break," Rupert said. "Maybe decrease our share of the minerals tax, or the other tariffs on production. Though that might cause problems in other areas, which we'll have to think about."

"You doubtless will." I was becoming curious about this scheme of his. But I didn't see what these, admittedly challenging, matters of law and justice had to do with me. Although...

"The reason sheriffs are free to claim any writ might be forged is that sometimes, on rare occasions, some daring rogue will forge one. And even more daring rogues might use those writs to do all kinds of wayward things."

Like get married. I saw Rupert suppress a smile.

"We considered that problem," he said primly. "We came to the conclusion that 'tis easy to fake a writ. 'Tis much harder to fake a man."

"I don't understand," I admitted. "You already agreed a troop of guardsmen would—"

"Not a troop." Rupert's voice was sure now, his gaze alight with passion for his work. "We were thinking two to four men, assigned to a given case. With the ability, of course, to requisition any manpower they might need from the local sheriffs—but they'd be in charge. For these men would be a sort of living writ, speaking for the Liege in all matters to do with their assigned task."

I had opened my mouth to protest when he started, but now I closed it, thinking furiously. This was something that, to the best of my knowledge, had never been tried.

"These men...they'd be more like bounty hunters than a military troop, but they would work for, *represent*, the Liege himself?"

"Exactly." Rupert flashed me a grin. "We'll also need to figure out some way to keep people from impersonating them, because they'll wield a lot of power. They'd be able to cross any border in pursuit of a criminal, or even if they only suspect a crime, requisition aid from the local law—mayhap even stay the sentence of a judicar, though we're still thinking about that. So they'll have to be able to identify themselves, instantly, to every sheriff in the Realm. We considered some sort of magica tattoo..."

I grimaced.

"But that can be forged too. 'Twas Meg who suggested we should hire an artist to make a good cameo of each man's face, front and side, that could be pressed into sheets of plaster or wax and sent to every sheriff, along with a good description. A man's face really is hard to forge, and we could redo these cameos every five or six years, to reflect changes in appearance as they age."

"'Tis an interesting puzzle," I said. "And I'm honored you would offer me a post of such great trust. But I never wanted to be a bounty hunter."

"Oh, I don't want you to be one of those men," said

Rupert. My brows drew together in puzzlement, and he added, "I want you to take charge of them."

"You mean... You're mad," I said. "I'm only twenty-one. I've spent the last two years and more *outside* the law."

"Which gives you an understanding of criminals that a sheriff or a judicar can't match," said Rupert. "Such men may have greater age and experience, but they only know how *they* think, not how their prey might reason and react. These new men, these Liege huntsmen of ours, must understand their prey. They must know what 'tis like to live outside the law, as well as within it. How it changes a man to be rich, or to be poor, to be arrogant, or desperate... And as for age, I'm only twenty-four. I'm not saying Father's not going to check on both our work, until we prove ourselves. But if you're looking for a way to help the Realm, Sir Knight...I can't think of a better one."

He was right. This task... 'Twas not a matter of hunting down a criminal or two, but of stopping crime itself, on a greater scale than all the Liege's sheriff's and judicars had previously been able.

'Twould also be a job that pinned me down more firmly than being my brother's steward would have done. The man who commanded these new huntsmen would do great good...but he'd do it in an office such as this, dealing with court politics and law, almost never out in the Realm with his men.

And there's a difference between law and justice. Fisk had taught me that, as well.

'Tis the choices a man makes that define him.

And thus it was that some six weeks later, I stood in the busy street in front of Fisk's and Kathy's shop, bidding them farewell. A farewell that meant I'd see far less of them than I would have, had I taken Rupert up on his offer.

"I still think you're crazy," Fisk said. "You could have done a lot of good in that job...not to mention the money. And the power."

"I don't want power," I said. "And the point of being knight errant is to *help* people, not to hunt them down and arrest them."

I'd spent the better part of the last month in the university town where our last adventure had taken place, helping Fisk and Kathy set up their shop. The cleaning alone had taken the three of us almost a week, followed by carpentry, painting, mucking out the backyard well...

Fearless had proved as incompetent a ratter as he was a watchdog. Poor Fisk was reduced to holding True up to him as a model, for at least, he said, True tried. That problem had been solved by Kathy's rescue of a scarred, half-starved alley cat, who had terrorized Fearless from the moment they met. True took a bit longer to learn, but Peaceable's claws hadn't drawn too much blood before he figured out his proper place in the household. I thought that by the time Peaceable was done, the cat would be ruling Fisk and Kathy as well as the dog. *He'd* have made a fine Chief Huntsman.

"Can't you stay a bit longer?" Kathy asked. "Fisk finally got the press working, but we haven't even printed our first handbills to let folk know that Pressing Business is open."

At least Fisk had scraped together enough money that they could buy paper and ink to print those handbills...but there wasn't much more. The survival or failure of this business was now up to them. As the rest of my life was up to me.

And with Chant saddled and ready, my packs on Tipple's back, and True frisking under the wheels of passing carts as he scouted the fishmonger's wares, I was suddenly eager to get on with it.

"I'll come back whenever I'm nearby," I promised. "And I'll write."

I had already bid Benton farewell—he had classes today, or he'd have been there to see me off. Now I gave Kathy a firm hug. In these months we'd adventured together, she'd become even more dear to me.

Then I found myself facing Fisk, and my throat became so tight I might not have been able to speak, even had I known what to say.

Fisk, of course, is never at a loss for words.

"I won't tell you to stay out of trouble," he said. "Because that would be a waste of breath. But *when* you get in trouble, for our sakes, try to exercise a little common sense. And when that doesn't work... Well, you'll find them tonight, most likely."

So I mounted up, whistled for True to follow, and rode away from my sister and the man who was my brother in truth even more than in law, grieving a bit... but wondering more and more uneasily what was lurking in my saddle bags.

The moment I was clear of town, and the dusty road around me empty, I stopped to rummage through them...for with Fisk, you never knew. 'Twas not a fortune in stolen jewels (which was actually a possibility) or some exotic, poisoned weapon (which was admittedly unlikely). 'Twas something more illegal than the one, and more dangerous than the other. Over a dozen writs and warrants, most bearing a signature that looked very like the High Liege's, and a few more that might actually have been signed by Rupert—though I doubted it. They variously demanded that the bearer be granted whatever funding he might require, the assistance of any troops he needed, and of course, forgiveness in advance for any crimes I might commit "when about the Liege's business."

Possessing even one of them was probably more hazardous than any trouble they might get me out of, and I seriously considered burning them. But they were Fisk's way of trying to keep me safe, and Fisk's saddlebags, which I now carried, had a most cleverly concealed compartment...

I moved them into that compartment, right there on the road, and resolved to keep it *very* secret.

But as I rode on down the lane, gradually gaining on a man who was walking ahead of me, my heart was breaking at the thought of leaving him behind...though it also felt strangely light.

I would miss him. But watching Fisk tinker with the press, strike up relationships with booksellers, and quarrel with Kathy about who would keep the shop's accounts, I had realized that this was the life Fisk was meant for. He was no more suited to knight errantry than I was to be a liege huntsman, so I could hardly demand...

The man who walked in front of me stumbled, over nothing I could see, then regained his balance and trudged on. But I noticed he was walking more slowly than a man starting off on a journey should, and moved stiffly.

So I wasn't surprised when I drew up with him and found, not a man, but a lad mayhap fifteen, with a black eye, a swollen lip, and judging by the way he walked, more bruises under that ragged coat.

He cast me a sullen glance, and kept walking.

"You've run away?" I hardly needed to ask—his situation couldn't have been clearer if Fisk's precious type had stamped Runaway Apprentice across his forehead.

Judging by the bruises, he had reason to run.

"No. I'm on an errand for my master."

He said nothing more as he stamped along, with no document bag, carrying no goods to deliver—not even a bag or basket to carry something back. Fisk would have had a better story ready, even at that age. But mayhap being a bad liar was to the lad's credit.

"You could say instead that you were an under groom, thrown off your perch in a carriage accident," I suggested. "And that being the least injured, you've been sent back to the estate to fetch your mistress, and some sound horses to take your master home."

He looked most struck by this, but 'twas too late to use it on me.

"I told you. You can go back and ask my master, if you care so much. I work for Tom Stirling, at the Red Cock."

This was better. Most towns have a Red Cock, or a Green Cock, or a blue one, and the name Stirling was unusual enough that it didn't sound like an outright lie.

I might not have known it for a lie, had Fisk not taught me to look for the moment a liar's eyes will flick aside.

Fisk would be the first to tell me 'twas none of my business...but he'd have been pulling our pot of healing salve out of the saddlebags as he spoke.

'Tis a man's nature that defines the choices he makes.

"No," I said. "You're a runaway apprentice. That doesn't concern me."

Though if his master was angry enough to come after him, it soon might.

"What does concern me is that you seem to have no place to go. I am a knight errant, in search of adventure and good deeds, and as it chances I have need of a squire..."

The End

ABOUT THE AUTHOR

Hilari Bell

 HILARI BELL writes SF and fantasy for kids and teens. She's an ex-librarian, a job she took to feed her life-long addiction to books, and she lives in Denver with a family that changes shape periodically—currently it's her mother, her adult niece and their dog, Ginger. Her hobbies are board games and camping—particularly camping, because that's the only time she can get in enough reading. Though when it comes to reading, she says, there's no such thing as "enough."

CPSIA information can be obtained at www.ICGtesting.com
Printed in the USA
LVOW08*1733280716

498171LV00006B/39/P